"ARE YOU [...] LUCIEN DEMANDED HARSHLY AS HE FLUNG HIS KNIFE INTO THE EARTH.

Frightened, still quivering from the aftermath of her ordeal at the billabong, Arabella nodded slowly, her heart beating far too hard and fast in her breast, although not solely any longer from the crocodile's attack.

"Damn it, woman!" he grated. "Don't you ever, *ever* walk away from me again like that out here! Do you understand? My God! When I think of what almost happened to you—"

Before Arabella realized what he intended, he had jerked her to him, his hands ensnaring the strands of hair at her temples, inexorably forcing her face up to his, his mouth suddenly crushing down upon hers in a possessive kiss that was like nothing she had ever before known—hot, hard, hungry, unleashing something inside her that was as fierce and wild and primal as the man who set it free.

It was a kiss she was to remember the rest of her life.

Also by Rebecca Brandewyne

Across a Starlit Sea
And Gold Was Ours
Desire in Disguise
Desperado
Forever My Love
Heartland
Love, Cherish Me
No Gentle Love
The Outlaw Hearts
Rainbow's End
Rose of Rapture
Swan Road
Upon a Moon-Dark Moor

Published by
WARNER BOOKS

REBECCA BRANDEWYNE

THE JACARANDA TREE

WARNER BOOKS

A Time Warner Company

WARNER BOOKS EDITION

Copyright © 1995 by Rebecca Brandewyne
All rights reserved.

Cover design by Diane Luger
Cover illustrations by Elaine Duillo
Hand lettering by Carl Dellacroce

Warner Books, Inc.
1271 Avenue of the Americas
New York, NY 10020

W A Time Warner Company
Printed in the United States of America

First Printing: March, 1995

10 9 8 7 6 5 4 3 2 1

For Jerry and Hedy Davis,
good friends, good company.
With affection and appreciation.

The Players

In England:

Colonel Philip Wyndham, a military man
Henriette Wyndham, wife to Colonel Wyndham

Their children:

  Norah
  Gervase
  Christine

Arabella Darracott, ward of Colonel Wyndham

In Australia:

  Lucien Sinclair, a former convict
  Captain Richard Bonniface, a military man
  Black Jack O'Flaherty, a former convict
  Dr. Kendall Munroe, a physician

Contents

Map of the Australian Colonies Circa 1855

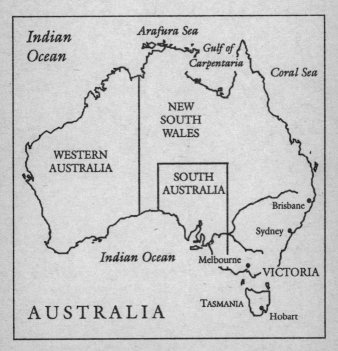

The Jacaranda Tree

The innocence of youth and girlish dreams
Are fled away, and fate lies in her hand.
A wild wind, a storm, and coral rapture's reef
Await to enchant her in a distant land
At the bottom of the world, so far flung,
Along the gold sands of a wilder shore—
There, footsteps hasten at the combers' edge,
And a Demon casts a spell as in days of yore.

Hurry, my love! The bright moon's risen high;
The stars are afloat upon the white-foamed sea,
And the music of the night sings sweetly for those
Twined as one beneath the jacaranda tree.
Pale purple blossoms drift to strew the rich earth,
Where lovers fall, come together, then part—
Not for long, so strong the delicate thread
That wove its magic about each wild heart. . . .

No chains of the past did e'er more surely bind,
No prison walls form so eternal a bower
As that built by a Demon out of petals of love
Wherein he laid her and brought her to flower.
Feverish was the joining; sweet was the sting
Of innocence lost in the moment of a breath—
Gladly lost, surrendered, given up in a dream
Timeless, without end, even in death.

Prologue

Innocence

had been lost in her nightmare, running through a forest

The Fair
and the Fortune

Yorkshire, England, 1845

Although much has been said about the effect of each man's life upon those of others, rarely is that of his death also occasion for such comment. It was not to be supposed, then, that the quiet demise of an elderly, invalid Yorkshire squire should have such far-reaching repercussions as to change the course of lives halfway around the world. Arabella Darracott, unlike the others so affected, was at least forewarned about what was to come; but in later years, she had only a vague recollection of—and little belief at all in—the cryptic mutterings of the wizened old Gypsy woman who had told her fortune in the summer of her ninth year.

The afternoon of this soon-to-be-forgotten event was hot. The cool grey morning mist that earlier had wended through the streets of the popular old seaside resort had long since dissipated beneath the onslaught of the sun's penetrating rays. Although from the North Sea beyond Scarborough's shore, a breeze blew inland, it was salty and sultry, and it did little to mitigate the heat and humidity that clung to the spas and shops, the hotels and railway station, this last of which had recently transformed the once-quiet fishing town into a noisy holiday haven for health seekers and tourists alike.

Beyond the ancient, crumbling Norman castle that towered on a promontory high above the town, the sea gleamed like a mirror in the sunlight, its smooth surface scarcely ruffled by the soughing wind. Waves crested only lightly with foam stirred sluggishly about the long, sodden bathing costumes of tentative waders and bolder swimmers. The once-wild beach was now tamed and cluttered with a profusion of what any right-minded, forward-thinking man of the times would proudly have labeled "Progress": bathing cabins, umbrellas, blankets, towels, picnic baskets, shell hunters, sand-castle builders, and drowsy, sun-basking bodies. Farther on, countless fishing boats, hulls empty of cargo and riding high on the gently lapping water, sails furled, masts and spars looking like a peculiar, spindly, naked woods rising from the sea, bobbed lazily in their mooring slips alongside wooden piers.

Where the shore gave way to the streets, sidewalks, and stores that had through the centuries grown up on the site of the Viking warrior Skarthi's borough, whence the town had taken its name, cacophony reigned amid the hustle and bustle of Scarborough and its fair. The coming-and-going trains at the depot whistled and screeched in discordant counterpoint to the clatter of horses' hooves and carriage wheels on cobblestones, the ring of brass bells on shop doors, and the cries of the street vendors as they hawked their myriad wares. The fragrant scents of hot meat pies and newly baked breads mingled with the tangier aromas of recently slaughtered sheep and freshly caught fish, the sweaty smell of bodies pressed close in the heat, jostling for space amid the crowds that had swarmed to the gracious hotels revitalized by vacationers, to the quaint shops that had seemed to burgeon overnight in response to the tourist trade, to the fashionable spas renowned since the sixteen hundreds for their medicinal waters, and to the fair that would in the next century be immortalized in a soft, melodious folk song that would make Scarborough famous far beyond its modest boundaries.

Arabella had come to the fair that fateful summer's day, in the company of her best friend, Christine Wyndham, and Chrissie's family. Nothing could have been further from Arabella's mind that day than the thought that she would shortly learn her destiny. Indeed, had such a notion been put forth to her, she would have greeted it with no small measure of amusement and skepticism far advanced for her tender years; for, an only child, Arabella was mature for her age, having since birth been the recipient of fond, indulgent, undivided adult attention in an otherwise childless household.

Arabella had often yearned wistfully for brothers and sisters, and her father, Tobias Darracott, squire of Darracott Hall, had equally as often and wistfully longed for a son to carry on the family name, but events that had occurred years earlier had decreed otherwise. At his spendthrift father's death, Tobias, then in his mid-twenties, had found himself heir not only to a much-deteriorated Darracott Hall, his ancestral home, but also to his father's numerous gaming debts. Being possessed of his mother's honest and steadfast nature rather than his father's wastrel character, Tobias had spent the greater portion of his youthful manhood diligently laboring to restore both Darracott Hall and the family fortune, so that he might and eventually did discharge all his late father's obligations and ensure that his mother lived the remainder of her life in security and comfort.

Thus, by the time Tobias had felt he was sufficiently able to provide for a wife and family of his own, in the manner properly befitting a genteel country squire, he had discovered to his dismay that all the young females of his acquaintance who would have suited him as a bride had been claimed by men more handsome and dashing and, more to the point, less tardy in presenting themselves at the wedding altar than he. That there would, as a result, be in all likelihood no son to carry on the Darracott name and to inherit all he had worked so hard to build was a bitter blow. Still, Tobias endured it manfully, resigning himself to both his bachelorhood and dearth of progeny. Thus was his gladness all the greater when, in his middle years, he had unexpectedly found his heart captured by a pair of fine, speaking, sherry-colored eyes, a heavy mass of chestnut hair, and a smile that had utterly transformed the otherwise plain, unremarkable face of Victoria Mayfield.

Since three dismal seasons in London had failed to procure Victoria a husband and the Mayfields had reluctantly but firmly declared her relegated her to a permanent place upon the solitary shelf of spinsterhood, they would have been much surprised to learn that it was not to escape this unhappy fate that had led her to accept Tobias's ardently stammered proposal. Rather, it was that she had seen in the sober, stocky, balding squire, a head shorter than she and nearly twenty years her senior, a keen mind and a kind heart that had equaled her own. Despite the incongruity in both their appearance and age, the marriage of Tobias Darracott and Victoria Mayfield had been a love match, marred only by the fact that after Arabella was born, Victoria, narrow-hipped and never fully recovering following the difficult birth of her daughter, could bear no more children. But for love of Tobias and knowing, despite his efforts to conceal it, how the lack of a son and heir grieved him, Victoria would not desist in trying to provide one. Each subsequent miscarriage had sapped her strength a little more, until she had finally slipped away altogether, and with her the thin scrap of a baby boy she had at last managed to carry nearly to full term.

Another man, in his anguish and disappointment, might have resented the child who lived: a daughter who was a mirror image of her mother, a constant, painful reminder of Victoria's loss and that of the long-hoped-for son who had not survived. But this was not Tobias's way. There was never a day when he did not exult in Arabella's existence, did not think of her as the light of his life since the light that had been Victoria was now forever extinguished. If not for Arabella, Tobias thought, the rest of his days might have been very dark indeed.

As he himself had been and for which he was inordinately grateful, Arabella was a sturdy child. But she had inherited the promise of her mother's height and long, graceful bones, her mother's glorious, thick mass of chestnut hair and startling, sherry-colored eyes, her mother's dazzling smile that made one forget that also like Victoria, Arabella was, in truth, no beauty. She had her mother's straightly chiseled nose that was not in the least retroussé and a generous, vulnerable mouth far too wide for her earnest, heart-shaped countenance. But her winged eyebrows that could knit together in an astonishingly adult frown when she was thwarted or displeased, her sober, steady gaze that was without childish guile or mischief, and her firm little chin that could lift so decisively and set so stubbornly . . . these were Tobias's legacy to her, and they gave her face an arresting character and strength that Victoria's own had lacked.

From both parents had Arabella received her quick, intelligent, insatiable mind, her unwavering dedication to conscience and conviction and common sense, her generous and good-hearted nature that, withal, was tempered by a backbone of steel that was to sustain her through many a trial in her long life. She was neither one to take advantage nor to be taken advantage of. She was not perfect, but her faults were her own—her pride, her spirit, her temper, her willfulness—and they were ever to prove her downfall. There was not a cowardly bone in Arabella's body; in all her life, she was never to learn that, sometimes, it was better to run away than to stand firm and, if necessary, to fight. From the time she was old enough to walk and to talk, she never hesitated to step in where injustice ruled, no matter the sacrifice to herself; and it was only in later years that she began truly to understand that between black and white lay infinite shades of grey.

She hungered for knowledge as others hungered for food. She learned early to read and voraciously consumed not only the classics, but also books on husbandry and agriculture and household management; for all the education and training with which Tobias would have prepared his son to inherit Darracott Hall, he now showered upon Arabella instead. And if ever there were a single moment when he regretted that she and not that thin scrap of a baby boy had been the one to survive, Tobias sternly squelched the hideous thought; and Arabella never knew of it.

Long before she could ride alone, Tobias hoisted her up before him on his big bay gelding to gallop over the broad, rolling acres of Darracott Hall, instilling in her a deep love of land, which was never to leave her. All her life, she would be exhilarated by the feel of the wind against her face, the smell of rich, nurturing earth in her nostrils, the sight of land unfolding endlessly before her—whether it was the desolate, sweeping moors of her native Yorkshire or the wilder shores of the Australian colonies she would someday come to know.

Tobias had known his oldest and closest friend, Philip Wyndham, since boyhood, and Wyndham Grange being the nearest neighbor of Darracott Hall, besides, the two families were frequent visitors. So when Tobias— whose incurable indulgence in rich food and drink had resulted in his not only growing steadily stouter through

the years, but also being troubled by gout—had sadly
proved unable to escort Arabella to the fair, it was only
natural that she should be taken up in the Wyndhams'
own carriage. That was how she came to be standing
before the garish striped pavilion of the Gypsies—which
her father would never have permitted her to enter—
with her friend Christine Wyndham at her side and
Chrissie's whining and wheedling ringing in her ears,
steadily eroding her initial determination to pass by the
tent.

"Gypsies are heathens and thieves, Chrissie—Papa
says so." Arabella's voice was laced with reproof as
she again protested her friend's suggestion that they go
inside the tent. "They don't attend church; and the few
times they dared to camp in the park of Darracott Hall,
they poached birds from the woods and fish from the
stream, and shamelessly strewed the grounds with debris from their feast before our gamekeeper caught them
and drove them away. Papa was most upset afterward,
and he vowed that next time, he would set the law on
them.

"So, do come away, Chrissie! Fortune-telling is
nothing but a fraud, anyway. No one except a prophet
from God can *truly* predict the future, because there's
no such thing as second sight; that's only an old wives'
tale. We'll just be wasting our money to hear a parcel
of lies about traveling to some exotic, foreign land and
marrying a rich, handsome man and living happily ever
after. That's all clever fortune-tellers ever tell anyone,
you know; if they told people the truth—a good deal
of which must naturally be quite unpleasant since life
is a series of ups and downs, Papa always says—no

one would pay to hear them anymore, and then they'd be forced to work for a living, just like all decent, honest folk.''

"Oh, Arabella, you're just like Norah—a proper goose and never any fun at all!" Chrissie complained peevishly, her gracefully arched eyebrows knitted in an unbecoming scowl, her pink, rosebud mouth turned down in a sullen pout. Norah was her older sister and, according to their mother, a paragon of virtue, while Chrissie was spoiled and obstinate and wayward, having been conceived unexpectedly and born late in life to her parents, and, as a result, being doted on by her father. "So what if we don't hear anything but a lot of romantic rubbish? Where's the harm, then? And what if you're wrong? What if we learn something really important about the rest of our lives? Wouldn't that be worth a shilling apiece? Either way, you have to admit that deep down inside, you're just as curious as I am to hear what your future holds in store—and only fancy being able to boast to that spiteful cat Sarah Jane Hartley that we had our fortunes told by a real live Gypsy! She'll be positively pea-green with envy, for you can bet *she'd* never be so brave as to dare to do so! Oh, please, Arabella!''

After that, Arabella was hard put to refuse. Chrissie's reasoning sounded logical, and the idea of recounting the tale later to the disdainful Sarah Jane, the daughter of a wealthy mill owner and who was, indeed, bound to be envious of their escapade, held a certain appeal. Still reluctant, however, to enter the pavilion and hopeful of having the decision taken out of her own hands, Arabella glanced around longingly for Norah Wyndham, who, being several years older than both her younger sister and Arabella, had charge of them today and, not given to whims, could be counted on to put a halt at once to Chrissie's foolishness. But to Arabella's dismay, Norah was still haggling over a bolt of cloth at a weaver's nearby stall; and as there was a familiar, firm note in Norah's voice, the cost of the material did not seem likely to meet with her approval anytime soon. At the realization, Arabella unconsciously heaved a great sigh; and sensing that victory was near at hand, Chrissie tossed her head, causing her thick blond sausage ringlets to dance, and set her chin in a mulish manner much at odds with her delicate, porcelain face.

"Well, wait here for Norah, then, if you're afraid," she taunted Arabella. "But *I'm* going inside to have my fortune told, whether you like it or not!" With that, Chrissie promptly snatched open the tent flap and stamped inside.

The thought of being labeled a coward stung, as was intended; and in the end, it was this that propelled Arabella to follow her friend into the pavilion, where, upon a stool, the old Gypsy woman perched like a bird of prey and waited. In sharp contrast to the brightness of the afternoon, it was dark inside the tent, so it took Arabella's eyes a moment to adjust to the sudden contrast, a moment in which her heart pounded with fear at the thought that perhaps it was no Gypsy at all who lurked within, but a monster or freak such as the barkers had declared could be viewed inside other pavilions and which even Chrissie had not wished to see. When at last Arabella's eyes accustomed themselves to the dim interior, she spied the crone who sat at a small, rickety wooden table upon which two thick, cheap tallows burned, dripping wax onto their tarnished-brass holders. The air was stifling, permeated by smoke and the pungent fragrance of some oriental incense that, combined with the heat, made Arabella feel dizzy and faint. Earlier, at one of the booths, she had eaten more cockles than she ought, and now she was half afraid she was going to be sick. She wished fervently that she had not finally and much against her better judgment given in to Chrissie's cajoling.

Arabella was more than a little frightened by the Gypsy and the eerie atmosphere; for both somehow contrived to make it seem as though the two girls had stepped into another time, another place far distant from the nineteenth century England they had known all their young lives. Even Chrissie, swallowing hard, was taken aback and, half turning, clutched at Arabella's sleeve as though to say they had, after all, made a mistake and should leave at once. But sensing that two coveted shillings were about to slip from her greedy grasp, the Gypsy smiled enigmatically, a snaggled grin that revealed a gleaming gold tooth; and with one yellowed, clawlike hand, she beckoned the two girls forward.

"Come in, come in, an' be welcome, young ladies," she croaked in greeting, like some sinister raven, and bade them be seated at the decrepit table upon which was draped a shabby, fringed silk shawl to hide the worst of the scarred wood.

Before her lay a deck of strange, worn cards that looked none too clean in the shadowy light, as though they had been shuffled by countless hands. Arabella wondered uneasily if she and Chrissie would be exposing themselves to some dreaded disease by touching them; but both girls, being from good homes and well-bred, were too polite to offend the Gypsy by abruptly departing after she had bidden them welcome. They obediently sat, each pushing forward the required shilling. After scooping up the coins, the hag bit down on them hard to make certain they were not counterfeit and dropped them into the pocket of her soiled skirt. Then she instructed Chrissie to pick up the cards and to shuffle them.

Much to her disappointment, Chrissie's fortune proved to be nothing more than the usual rigmarole Arabella had predicted; but as the Gypsy stared down at Arabella's cards, laid in the ancient pattern on the table, it soon became clear that something more than what had gone before was in the offing. Arabella felt another frisson of fear creep up her spine, prickling the fine hairs on her nape; and of a sudden, she did not want to hear her fortune. It was too late. The Gypsy had begun to speak, her fierce black eyes unsettlingly blank in the half-light, as though she had gone blind or become entranced, and her voice was a rasp, a whisper, the rake of talons across stone.

"There be a death in yer future, child, an' a powerful storm o' rain an' wind, an' a sea draggin' ye down ter a coral enchantment, casting ye up upon bleached sands as old as time, a land o' gold an' fire, o' fertile blue mountains an' barren, ghostly trees, o' heaven an' hell. . . . Aye, it be a place o' dreams an' nightmares, on t' other side o' the world, with dangers untold—an' ye be a prisoner there as surely as any poor sod what e'er were clapped inter irons in gaol; fer although ye be innocent o' any crime, 'tis t' devil ye'll pay fer another's own. . . . Aye. Beware o' him, that demon, an' o' t' moonlit twinin' 'neath t' purple-bloomin' tree. . . ."

The beldam stretched out her hands to clutch Arabella's own so tightly that the child winced and longed desperately to break free, to run pell-mell from the tent, so great was her fear of the Gypsy and the mysterious, muttered words. Chrissie's cornflower-blue eyes were like saucers in her pale, scared face; her breathing was rapid and shallow, like that of some small frightened animal cowering in a hidey-hole. She cringed on the edge of her chair as though preparing to bolt at any moment. The thought of being left alone with the Gypsy was horrifying to Arabella. Surely, the harridan was mad! Yes, that was undoubtedly it; she was a crazy woman, escaped from some lunatic asylum. One had only to look at her long, wild, scraggly hair—like that of a witch beneath the dirty kerchief she had knotted about her head, in the fashion of a pirate—and to see the spittle that drooled from her cracked lips to know that it was so.

But just when Arabella thought Chrissie would surely desert her, would abandon her to the Gypsy's ravings, the old woman fell suddenly silent and slack in her chair, releasing her convulsive grip on Arabella's hands and looking dazed and bewildered, as though having awakened from a deep slumber. Arabella and Chrissie did not wait to see or hear any more, but fled from the pavilion, certain they had only narrowly escaped with their lives.

Not until they reached the safety of Norah at the

weaver's booth did the two girls draw up short, panting for breath, their hearts beating fast. They stared at each other, terrified, until Chrissie giggled nervously, gasping:

"Oh . . . Arabella! I've never . . . been so scared . . . in all my life! What a perfectly horrid old bat! And all those strange, terrible things she said to you about your future! What can she possibly have meant? All that talk about a death and dungeons, a demon and a purple-blooming tree . . . Do you suppose you're going to be . . . well, transported and *hanged* by an executioner or something—by mistake, I mean, for a crime you didn't commit?"

"Don't be silly, Chrissie!" Arabella's voice was sharp with anger at Chrissie's words and at herself, for permitting her friend to persuade her to enter the pavilion in the first place. "Of course not! Like as not, that old woman overheard us talking outside the tent and said those dreadful things for meanness, to frighten me, because I told you that Gypsies are heathens and thieves, and that fortune-telling is a fraud. And they are, and it is!" she insisted stoutly, as much to convince herself as Chrissie. The Gypsy's sudden, trancelike state had not appeared feigned; her obscure, gibbered words had seemed to hold an eerie ring of truth that disquieted Arabella even now. "As far as I'm concerned, we just wasted our money!"

"Maybe you're right," Chrissie agreed slowly, but her skepticism was plain. "Even so, I'm glad it was you and not me who got told such an awful fortune." Her voice dropped to an even lower, conspiratorial whisper. "I'm not supposed to know about it, because

Papa did his best to hush up the horrible scandal, but one of my cousins was transported some years back. He murdered his wife, and if it hadn't been for Papa, I daresay he would have hanged for it. But being an officer of some importance in the military, Papa knows a lot of influential men, and so my cousin was sentenced to fourteen years hard labor instead and sent away to a ghastly gaol in a terrible place called Van Diemen's Land. I overheard Papa tell Mama that it was an infernal hellhole, at the bottom of the world. So I'd be scared to death if I were in your shoes right now.''

''Well, I'm not,'' Arabella declared, sternly repressing her doubts and fear, for Chrissie's story had upset her more than she would have liked to admit.

''Yes, but, then, you've always been quite brave, Arabella, and I'm not. So, don't say anything to Norah about what happened today, promise? She'd just feel duty-bound to tell Papa and Mama; and then, like as not, they'd tell your father, and we'd both be punished, for I don't suppose, after all, that having our fortunes told was quite the thing to do—Gypsies having such a bad reputation and all. . . .'' Chrissie's face was flushed now with guilt and contrition.

''Something to which you paid no heed earlier,'' Arabella pointed out uncharitably. Then, seeing that Chrissie intended to argue the issue and being in no mood to hear another barrage of petulant pleas, she added hastily, ''But, oh, all right, then. I promise. There was no real harm done, after all. Frankly, I'd just as soon forget the entire episode!''

With Chrissie being on her best behavior, the remainder of the afternoon passed without incident; and Arabella did indeed, in time, forget all about the fair and the fortune until the day her father died and, following his funeral, she discovered that she must journey to the continent of Australia—a land of penal colonies on the other side of the world.

Book One

A Wilder Shore

Chapter One

Interlude at
The Rocks

Sydney, New South Wales Colony,
Australia, 1855

Beyond two massive, towering crags known as the Heads lay Port Jackson, a sea valley that wended inland past rocky points, washed into a hundred coves and bays, and flowed past small harbor islands to meet the fresh water of the Parramatta River, splitting the town of Sydney in two. This division was not merely physical, but also representative of the invisible barrier that separated the town's haves from its have-nots; for if there were anywhere on earth more English than England itself, it was Australia, whose colonists had done their best over the years to transport not only convicts to its wilder shores, but also a way of life that had been better left behind. The military and the younger sons and daughters of England's landed gentry, dispossessed by their homeland's archaic law of primogeniture, formed the aristocratic class of the Colonies; and to their God and Queen, they had paid due homage with the erection of such grandiose structures as the Town Hall, the Strand Arcade, and several other buildings. The aristocracy had not neglected themselves in the process, but had established manors and town houses, upon whose wrought-iron-lace verandas they devoured English newspapers and fashion magazines that were nearly a year out of date by the time they reached their recipients halfway around the world.

All was not sweetness and soirees in Sydney, however, for over the years, the original and thus the oldest part of the town, at the edge of the harbor of Sydney Cove and known locally as The Rocks, had bred its own equally distinctive class—rising from slums rife with prostitution, alcoholism, crime, and disease. Here, in a place considered the most dangerous for miles in every direction, dismal dwellings and tawdry taverns crowded the narrow, cobblestone streets, and the principal worry in life was not what gown to wear to the governor's ball, but whence one's next meal was to come, if it came at all. Still, the sight of a well-dressed man strolling amid the squalor was not so uncommon as to spark comment; for there were many young bucks and officers of the upper class who often sought the shadier amusements to be found among the lower. Rum, especially, made the world go around in Sydney. Both sexes of both classes drank heavily—a circumstance that the Rum Corps, as the New South Wales Corps had long been nicknamed, had been quick to capitalize on, having at the turn of the century established a virtual monopoly over the rum trade, thereby filling its coffers through both fair means and foul, profiting on first the rum itself and then the dereliction it produced.

At this moment, night spread like the wings of some black carrion crow over The Rocks, but all was not as dead and silent as that bird's prey. The sea rushing in upon the beach whispered ceaselessly, and the salty wind stirred, soughing its way through the twisting, dimly lit streets and even darker alleys littered with refuse that added its own ranker smells to the dankness. Oil lamps glowed at the windows of the grogshops, from whose drab, dirty interiors raucous talk and ribald laughter spilled into the seeping gutters of the night. Inside, ex-convicts and ticket-of-leave men rubbed shoulders with supposed gentlemen and officers equally eager to sample the assorted vices that abounded in The Rocks: drink, gambling, and whores.

For every seven men transported to the Colonies, one woman had been shipped out as well—not for being a member of the oldest profession, which was never a transportable offense, but mostly for petty theft. Still, if she had not been "on the town," as prostitution was known, before leaving England, a female convict inevitably was by the time she arrived in Australia; for while male convicts might eventually redeem themselves through hard work and penance, their female counterparts were denied this opportunity. Such women were considered fair game for any man, it being their lot to suffer the worst kinds of rape and abuse while

aboard a transport ship and then again later at the hands
of their masters and guards.

In the days of transport to New South Wales, those
women deposited on the Sydney docks and not able at
once to arrange, through bribery or connections, for a
ticket-of-leave, or to find a male protector among the
so-called gentlemen and officers who also frequented
the wharves, were shipped off by barge upriver to the
Female Factory in Parramatta. At inns along the way,
kept largely by male ex-convicts, the women were invariably plied with rum, raped, then robbed of their
meager possessions—a practice to which the barge constables turned a blind eye. The Female Factory itself
consisted of a three-story Georgian structure, where the
women's principal work was the spinning and weaving
of the coarse "Parramatta cloth" from which the convicts' winter garments were made. Those women who
had not contrived to bring their bedding from the transport ships must sleep on piles of raw wool infested
with ticks, as the government did not provide either
mattresses or blankets for the females at Parramatta.
Those for whom there was no room at the overcrowded
prison were compelled to lodge with local settlers at a
cost of four shillings per week, a fee that the majority
of the women could only garner by whoring for male
convicts. Since the latter had no money, either, more
than £1,560 was stolen by them each year in Parramatta
to pay the females who serviced them. Once paroled,
a woman with such a history had little choice but to
join the ranks of prostitution if she wished to survive.
Some, harder and crueler than the rest, became notori-
ous "dock women" in Sydney, meeting every incoming

vessel to make seductive advances to its male passengers and crew, to slip them drugs that rendered them unconscious, and then to rob them. Other female ex-convicts not so tough worked the taverns and streets.

This last had proved the hapless fate of one Sally Wheeler, a once-decent young woman who had been a parlor maid in England and who had suffered the great misfortune of being pretty enough to attract her wealthy master's eye. His cold, jealous wife, wishing to be rid of her rival, had falsely accused Sally of theft and arranged for several pieces of jewelry to be found in her possession, a "crime" for which she had been transported to Australia to serve a term of seven years. After her release, Sally, like so many others before her, had migrated to Sydney to wind up in The Rocks. Now, as she hurried along the shadowed cobblestone streets damp and slick from the slops of chamber pots and from the sea air, she drew her threadbare cloak more closely about her thin body and, once or twice, glanced back uneasily over her shoulder.

Now that her hair—shaved off for a minor infraction at the Female Factory—had grown back, she retained a vestige of the good looks that had led to her downfall; and so she seldom lacked for customers, spending most of her nights in a small, sordid room above a sleazy grog-shop, flat on her back, with her ragged skirts rucked up about her thighs, while one man after another took his turn upon her body. Tonight was no exception to the rule, except that she was more exhausted than usual; and so, comforting herself by patting the coins tucked in her pocket, she had actually dared to refuse the last man who had wanted to take her upstairs at the

King's Cross. A real gent, he had been, black-haired and handsome, dressed in a fine, expensively tailored suit of black broadcloth, a black cape lined with red satin, and carrying a silver-knobbed malacca cane. But something about his pale eyes had made Sally's skin crawl; instinctively, she had known he was the kind to beat her, and so she had rejected his overtures, smiling nervously and coughing into her soiled handkerchief to suggest a contagious illness.

In truth, she had not really felt well for the past few days; she feared she was coming down with a cold or, worse, consumption—a hazard of the trade to which she had been reduced. Once, she had chafed at the injustice of it, and fought back. But in the end, the repeated rapes and abuse had taken their toll, leaving her a frail, dispirited shell of the strong, lively women she had once been. Now, she longed only for a cup of hot tea and the warmth of the small fire in the hearth of the tiny, one-room hovel of a flat she shared with two other female ex-convicts in the same straits as she. Another block, and she would be there—home, such as it was. She should have started for it earlier, she thought. The wind had come up to slither like a clammy snake through The Rocks; against its chill, the cloak she clutched to her was little protection. Her breathing was labored as she hastened down the street. Still, Sally did not stop, for she felt certain she was being followed; when she had paused some moments before, it had seemed to her that furtive footsteps had echoed behind her, only to fade into silence when her own had ceased. She had remembered the dark, pale-eyed man at the

King's Cross and grown frightened. The murder of a whore was not uncommon in The Rocks—or elsewhere in the Colonies, for that matter. Still, some months ago, on these same streets, a prostitute had been killed in a particularly shocking and grisly fashion—even for The Rocks. Her throat had been cut from ear to ear, and other unspeakable things had been done with a knife to her body. The memory spurred Sally on; with another swift glance back over her shoulder, she turned down the dark, deserted alley that led to her flat.

A rat skittered across the cobblestones, and from the dustbins in front of doorways, a stray cat searching through the rubbish suddenly howled and leaped with a clatter from the wooden barrels of trash, nearly startling Sally from her skin. She drew up short, her heart pounding, her hand at her throat. Then, spying the cat, she heaved a sigh of relief and gave a nervous laugh that was cut off abruptly by the strong hands that, without warning, grabbed her from behind, slamming her up against a wall. A palm clapped hard to her mouth stifled her scream of terror; the knife that in the moonlight gleamed silvery at her throat ensured her silence as, with a low, threatening snarl, the pale-eyed man she had feared at the King's Cross roughly shoved up her skirts and, expertly freeing himself from his breeches, forced his way into her so savagely that tears streamed down her cheeks. Ruthlessly, he ground her against the wall until his swift release came. Afterward, he coolly buttoned himself up before, at last, he spoke in a hoarse, whispering voice that made Sally shiver.

"You liked that . . . didn't you, my girl? Because

you're a whore, Verity. You've always been a whore, and you'll always be a whore. You know that, don't you?''

The man was mad, utterly insane, Sally thought, petrified, as she stared up into his cold, merciless eyes, sensing instinctively that he was seeing not her, but someone else . . . Verity, he had called her. Still, fearing to anger him, hoping desperately to escape with her life, Sally nodded quickly, mutely, in agreement. The man laughed then, a low, mocking sound that made the fine hairs on her nape stand on end. It was the last thing she heard before the knife struck, slashing open her throat. In a sudden frenzy then, the man stripped her body naked; the blade fell again and again and again until, finally, breathing hard, he was done cutting all the evil from her, leaving her as pure as she had once been before defiling herself with *him*, the hated and feared Other. Upon the man's dark visage was a peculiar expression of sadness and remorse as he stared down at his victim, slowly removing his blood-soaked, red-satin-lined black cape and draping it gently over her mutilated corpse. After searching his pockets, he pressed two copper pennies upon her eyes, so she might pay the ferryman for her passage to the realm of the dead. Then, in a nearby rain barrel, he washed his face and hands and his knife. Picking his malacca cane up from the ground where he had dropped it, he twisted the blade back into the cane, which was cleverly contrived so the handle of the knife formed the knob of the cane.

Without a backward glance, he strolled from the alley

as calmly as though he had not just committed a horrifically brutal rape and murder. The entire episode had lasted less than a quarter of an hour. No one had observed him. No one save his victim ever did—and she never lived to speak of what she had seen.

Chapter Two

The Storm at Sea

Yorkshire, England, 1855

The night before she was to embark upon the first stage of her journey to Australia, Arabella Darracott suddenly awakened in a cold sweat from a deep, laudanum-induced slumber disrupted by a haunting nightmare. Her pounding heart was lodged in her throat. At first, dazed and disoriented, she did not know where she was; for all the furniture in her bedroom—save for the canopy bed in which she now sat bolt upright—was swathed in sheets, in preparation for her imminent departure and expected long absence from Darracott Hall. Panicked, she fumbled with trembling hands in the darkness until she at last managed to light the oil lamp upon her nightstand. The shadowy features of her bedroom now grew discernible, and she heaved a great sigh of relief.

In the lamp's glow, what had appeared to be some dark, sprawling monster slithering from a black abyss to engulf her was revealed as nothing more than her massive pile of baggage, neatly packed and stacked, ready for the menservants to carry it downstairs the next morning to her father's carriage, in which she would travel overland to the port of Kingston-on-Hull, from where she would then set sail for Australia. At the sight of the luggage, Arabella felt the tears of anguish that had come so easily of late, stinging afresh her red-rimmed eyes, and with difficulty, she choked back sobs.

The past few months seemed as unreal to her as the nightmare that had wakened her. Even now, she could hardly believe that her beloved father did not lie sleeping in the master bedroom down the corridor, but was instead dead and buried in the mausoleum upon the grounds of Darracott Hall, where generations of her family had been interred. Tobias Darracott's quiet, unexpected slipping from life had proved a brutal blow to his daughter, leaving her stunned and heartbroken. Over the years, his gout had troubled him so badly that he'd become an invalid. Still, she had not thought he would die. She had scarcely begun to absorb the shock of her father's death when his solicitor had descended upon Darracott Hall to inform her, however kindly, that because she had not yet reached majority, she was now, under the terms of Tobias's last will and testament, the legal ward of his lifelong friend, Colonel Philip Wyndham. She ought to have derived at least some comfort from that, Arabella had thought numbly upon learning the news; for the colonel had always been to her like an uncle, and she had called him that for as

long as she could remember. But although she had kept
in touch with the Wyndhams by letter, she had not seen
them since their departure from England four years ago,
when the colonel had been posted to the continent of
Australia.

There, in April 1851, in the Wellington district of
the colony of New South Wales, a man named Edward
Hammond Hargraves had discovered gold. He had
christened his district after the biblical Ophir; the newspapers had proclaimed it to be "one vast gold field";
and by May of that same year, a thousand diggers had
swarmed the banks of Summerhill Creek and hundreds
of would-be gold miners had clogged the road over the
Blue Mountains. Port Phillip Bay had become a sea of
deserted ships, and other once-thriving ports had been
abandoned almost overnight, as well, growing virtually
uninhabited save for the times when those men who had
struck it rich had returned to run riot in the streets and
grog-shops. If not for the presence of the military, the
reinforcements hurriedly dispatched to Australia, law
and order would have given way to chaos.

The colonel had established the Wyndhams in Sydney, on the southeast coast of New South Wales, and
there they had stayed. It would therefore be necessary,
Tobias's solicitor had explained to Arabella, for her to
close Darracott Hall and to journey to Australia, where
she would remain under the care of her guardian, the
colonel, until she came of age two years hence. Despite
her affection for the Wyndhams and the fact that it had
been hoped by both families since her birth that she
would someday marry the colonel's son and heir, Gervase, Arabella had been devastated by the realization

that having lost her father, she was now to lose her home, as well. Grief-stricken, she had in the end succumbed to an uncharacteristic, hysterical outburst that had resulted in the summoning of the family physician. The good doctor had taken one look at her, dosed her with laudanum, and declared that "a lengthy voyage and bracing sea air would be just the prescription" for his patient's recovery.

At last, her spirit and senses dulled by both sorrow and laudanum, Arabella had ceased to resist the combined and well-intentioned efforts of the solicitor, the physician, and Mrs. Inghram, the housekeeper, who had been at Darracott Hall for forty years and so felt entitled to speak her mind on any and all subjects.

"There, there, child," Mrs. Inghram had crooned one night when, bringing a tray of hot chocolate to Arabella's bedroom, she had discovered her young mistress huddled in the window seat, sobbing her heart out, her face pressed against the cold, rain-streaked panes. Hastily putting her burden down on the dressing table, the housekeeper had settled herself beside her young mistress on the satin cushions, stroking Arabella's long, unbound hair soothingly. "A body'd have ta be deaf an' blind not ta know how much ye loved t' squire, an' his death be a sad thing indeed fer all of us here at t' hall. Still, he'd no like ta see ye carryin' on this a-way, Miss Arabella; fer he was a man who joyed in life summat fierce, an' no matter how ye feel right now, in truth, yer's be just beginnin'. Ye're young—"

"I don't feel young. I feel a hundred years old, and I wish I were dead, too!"

"Aye, well, that be t' lost, frightened child inside o'

ye talkin', Miss Arabella. But life is fer t' livin', an'
t' capable young woman ye've grown inta will face up
ta that sooner or later, I know; fer that's what t' squire
would have wanted ye ta do—an' in yer heart, ye know
it.''

Despite her tearfully uttered protests, deep down,
Arabella *had* known that what Mrs. Inghram told her
was true, that her father would not have wanted her to
mourn his passing, but, rather, to take comfort from
and gladness in the fact that his life had been rich, full,
and happy, and to get on with making her own life the
same. He would have urged her to view the prospective
closing of Darracott Hall and her journey to Australia
not as the loss of all she had ever known and held dear,
but as a wonderful, exciting adventure. He would have
been deeply disappointed that, instead, she had taken
to laudanum and her bed, finding solace in the haze that
clouded her mind and anesthetized her senses. Still,
although in the end, she had done as her father would
have wished, reluctantly swaddling Darracott Hall in
sheets and booking passage on the *Heather Rose*, within
the next few days bound from the port of Kingston-on-
Hull for Australia, Arabella had not been able to shake
off the strange, nebulous sense of impending doom that
had enveloped her at her father's death.

Fearing to be labeled not only hysterical, but actually
mad with grief, she had spoken of her foreboding to no
one. But now, as she thought of it and the nightmare that
had wakened her, she shivered, drawing the bedclothes
more closely about her for warmth; for the fire in the
grate had burned low, and her bedroom was chilly. She
had been lost in her nightmare, running through a forest

of barren, ghostly trees from whose moonlight-dappled branches condemned men, nooses drawn tight about their necks, had hung, twisting haplessly in the wind and reaching out to her menacingly as she had passed by. All the while, an arcane chanting and the pounding of primitive drums had echoed in her ears, goading her to run faster and faster, until she had been gasping for breath and doubled over from the agonizing stitch in her side. Then, suddenly, eerily, silence had descended upon the pale, labyrinthine woods; and when, terrified not by the abrupt hush, but by whatever had engendered it, she had glanced up, it had been to see that at the heart of the stark forest stood a tree like no other, fragrant and fecund with heavy purple blooms. Beneath the tree, amid the fragile petals that had showered and scattered upon the earth, a dark devil on horseback had poised, waiting . . . waiting for her. A scream had torn from her throat at the sight; she had turned to flee. But with a low, mocking laugh, the demon had ridden her down and swept her up into his strong, inescapable arms, the folds of his great cape swirling like a shroud about her.

It had been more than just a nightmare, Arabella thought now, shuddering deeply again as, unbidden from the chasms of her mind, a long-forgotten memory rose to haunt her, and she sat once more within the shadowy, candlelit pavilion at the Scarborough fair, listening to the old Gypsy woman croaking that enigmatic fortune—*Beware o' him, that demon, an' o' t' moonlit twinin' 'neath t' purple-bloomin' tree*. Despite her lack of belief in the second sight, Arabella could not help now but wonder uneasily if the Gypsy had truly possessed some gift of vision, had a decade ago foreseen a glimpse, however swift and misted, of the future of Arabella Darracott. The notion unnerved her, poised, as she was, on the brink of departure for Australia. If not for the fact that the letters written by both Tobias's solicitor and herself to the colonel, detailing her father's death and her imminent arrival in Sydney, had already been dispatched weeks ago, Arabella would almost have been tempted to remain at Darracott Hall. But her bags were packed; her passage was booked. Whatever lay in store for her on the other side of the world, she was bound now to meet it.

Closing her eyes, she burrowed beneath the bed-clothes, as though they might offer some protection from her unknown fate. But although she forced herself to breathe deeply, to empty her mind of her fear and uncertainty, sleep was a long time coming to her again that night.

Standing at the rail of the *Heather Rose*, now months out of the harbor at Kingston-on-Hull, Lieutenant Harry Palliser, attached to the New South Wales Corps and dutifully returning to his post after a leave of absence home to attend his youngest sister's wedding, studied his companion thoughtfully. Arabella Darracott was not what he would consider a beauty. In fact, when he had first spied her standing amid a pile of baggage on the docks at their port of departure, he had thought her unremarkably plain and unprepossessing. She must be a recent widow, he had initially supposed, given her veiled black hat and her mourning clothes, revealed when a sudden gust of wind had set her fashionably cut mantle to billowing about her willowy, hourglass figure—her only saving grace, in his opinion. Still, she was too tall—his chin would just top her head, he had surmised—and wan. Her nose and cheeks, ruddy from the brisk wind, had looked as though bright, garish splotches of rouge were painted upon her face beneath her veil. Her downcast eyes, too, had been red from crying; and her mouth, too generous for her countenance, had trembled vulnerably as she had gazed forlornly first at the departing carriage that had deposited her and her baggage upon the wharf, and then at him. If there were a situation in which Harry felt himself entirely unable to cope, it was one involving a woman's tears. Feeling himself in imminent danger of being compelled to deal with hers, he had hastily passed her by without daring to let his eyes meet hers again. He was a cheerful, caring soul, and widows depressed him. He did not want to be forced to listen to her sobbing into her pillow all night long for the duration of their lengthy voyage, and he had devoutly hoped she was not assigned the cabin next to his.

That hope, however, had proved in vain; Arabella had, in fact, been allotted a cabin next to Harry's own. But if she had wept, she had been so quiet about it that, to his relief, he had not heard her; and when, on the third evening aboard the *Heather Rose*, she had finally emerged from her self-imposed seclusion—born not only of her sadness, but also a bout of seasickness—to join the rest of the passengers at supper in the elegant rosewood salon, he had been compelled to revise his original estimation of her appearance. Her heavy mass of chestnut hair, caught up in a fine black mesh snood, had shone like burnished copper in the lamplight; her thick-lashed amber eyes, set beneath winged eyebrows that cut a startling oblique into her forehead, had gleamed like old Spanish doubloons of fabled sunken treasure, and her milk-white bosom and shoulders rising from the décolletage of her exquisite black mourning gown had glowed with the luster of a flawless pearl. Arabella Darracott had, Harry had recognized in that moment, something more indefinable, more intriguing than beauty—an elusive, arresting quality that would last her whole life long and forever draw men to her. Seated next to her at supper, he had found her totally lacking in coquettish or missish airs, startlingly but refreshingly frank, challengingly keen of mind and wit, a listener who focused all her attention on the speaker, making him feel as though his every word were a pearl of wisdom to be captured and held fast. Harry's military uniform had drawn her interest, providing a conversational gambit whereby he had learned of her father's recent death and that she was traveling to the colony of New South Wales to join her guardian, Colonel Philip Wyndham, who was in charge of the New South Wales Corps and so Harry's commanding officer.

With that in common, he and Arabella had over the passing weeks established such a warm friendship that if not for the fact that she had given him to understand that, while there was as yet no formal betrothal between them, she had expectations of wedding his fellow officer, Lieutenant Gervase Wyndham, Harry would have been sorely tempted to court her. Now, as he gazed at her standing beside him at the rail of the *Heather Rose*, her face lifted to the wind, he could not help but wonder again, frowning, why Gervase had never spoken of her.

"Tell me, Harry," Arabella entreated, as she had so often during the voyage, nudging him from his troubled reverie. "Tell me once more about Australia, about the colony of New South Wales. I want to know everything about this land so far away, which is to be my new home. We shall be arriving there soon, I understand from Captain Beckett, if the wind continues to rise and the barometer to fall."

"Yes, for we're through the Torres Strait now and have rounded Cape York into the Coral Sea. Look over there, in the distance. See the difference in color in that stretch of water beyond the shore?" At her nod, Harry continued. "Beneath that lies a long string of coral reefs that compose what is known as the Great Barrier Reef, which runs all along the entire northeastern coast of New South Wales. It's one of the real perils of these waters; sharks are another. But you needn't worry, Arabella," he insisted as her eyes widened slightly with alarm. "Captain Beckett knows his job. I'm sure he'll steer well clear of the reefs; and aboard the *Heather Rose*, we're quite safe from the largest and deadliest of sharks, even the great whites."

"I should hope so," she declared fervently, not quite certain whether Harry was, in fact, teasing her, which, knowing him fairly well by this time, she would not have put past him. Having two brothers and four sisters, he was prone to such mischief, while she, an only child, was unused to pranks and even less acquainted with the notion that the "best" of them were often inherently frightful. Indeed, a good deal of Harry's attraction for her lay in his, for the most part, brotherly demeanor toward her, giving her a wistful glimpse into what her life might have been like had her own infant brother survived. She was grateful to Harry for befriending her; his cheerful presence had done much to alleviate the worst of her sorrow. "But no doubt, such hazards as the reefs and sharks were among the very reasons why, when America declared her independence from England and refused to accept any more shipments of convicts, it was decided that Australia would serve even more suitably as a gaol," she suggested dryly. "Imagine not only having successfully to escape from prison, but also to make your way off a vast, relatively unexplored island through reef- and shark-infested waters to gain your freedom! A daunting prospect for even the most daring of criminals, I should imagine."

"Indeed," Harry agreed, his blue eyes twinkling, "although there are those who would argue that the idea of settling Australia with convicts was merely England's clever means at establishing the continent as a bastion for trade in the East. Whatever the truth may have been, the fact remains that after the initial expeditions of Tasman, Cook, Bass, and Flinders, the First Fleet set sail for Australia in May of 1787, with eleven ships, including six transports. They landed initially at Botany Bay, a desolate harbor poor in both soil and water, and which they therefore quickly abandoned for the harbor of Port Jackson. There, they hoisted the Union Jack and, at Sydney Cove, founded what was to become Sydney itself. Since that time, the town has grown tremendously; so despite what you may have heard to the contrary, you needn't fear that you are headed toward some small, backwater outpost, Arabella. You will find Sydney at least as amenable and cultured as many English towns, if not more so—although perhaps this would not be the case had it not been for the gold rush, I'll admit. People came to Australia from all over the world then.''

"I know something of that time, for the resulting chaos was why the colonel was posted to New South Wales. Even his predecessor, it seems, had not proved immune to gold fever, unfortunately.'' Arabella's voice held a note of wry amusement.

"Hardly any able-bodied man had—including me, although I'm afraid I was a dismal failure as a prospector,'' Harry admitted sheepishly, with a laugh. "The southern colony of Victoria came into being then, for by the middle of 1852, there were over fifty thousand people at the diggings. At one point, the shipments on the gold escorts from the towns of Ballarat and Bendigo alone averaged more than half a ton of gold a week, and a single vessel bound for London might have ten and a half tons on board! Why, one Aborigine stockman, who wasn't even prospecting, just lazily hacking with his ax at an outcrop not more than fifty miles from Bathurst, chipped off a chunk of quartz that yielded over a thousand ounces of gold! Naturally, being a native, he wasn't allowed to keep it—although his employer, Dr. Kerr, on whose land it was discovered, did give him and his brother a few acres, some sheep, and a couple of horses for the find . . . quite generous, you must agree, and certainly a good deal more than any Aborigine had a right to expect. Another man, who'd never tasted champagne before, after striking it rich purchased a hotel's entire supply and poured it into a horse trough, inviting one and all to drink it dry. Other successful

diggers flaunted their newfound wealth by buying tawdry gowns and gaudy jewelry for their biddies—I mean,
their . . . er . . . women friends—'' Harry corrected
himself hastily, flushing to the roots of his blond hair
at having mentioned doxies in a lady's presence, "and
by using five-pound notes to light their pipes."

"How shocking!" Arabella exclaimed, as she envisioned these excessive, ribald scenes. She could only
associate them with tales of decadence she had heard
about London and Paris, since she had led a relatively
sheltered life and rarely had been exposed to vulgar
behavior. "Such a want of decency and morals cannot
be thought of as anything but low and shameful! I am
surprised and disturbed to learn that the finding of gold
appears to result in a gentleman's loss of all common
sense and good conduct—"

"No, you are too quick and mistaken to tar-and-
feather us gentlemen, Arabella," Harry chided lightly,
grinning at her indignation. "For many of the fortunes,
you see, were won not by respectable men, but, rather,
by blackguards and emancipated convicts from Van
Diemen's Land, particularly. 'Vandemonians,' they
were known as at first, and then simply as 'Demons.'
These criminals, you must understand, had muscles
hardened by years of manual labor, and so they could
sink a shaft twenty feet in the time it took a 'new chum,'
as gentlemen were often scornfully referred to, to dig
three feet of clay. Many of the Demons who crossed
over the Bass Strait from Tasmania, as Van Diemen's
Land is now called, wound up convicted again in Victoria for crimes they committed during the gold rush. But
others, like that Demon Lucien Sinclair, for example, a

murdering, upstart rogue if ever there were one, actually dared to christen themselves the new 'aristocracy,' by God!—pardon my language, Arabella—and used their riches to force their way into the ranks of the Colonies' landed gentry!''

''Indeed? But like the rest, perhaps such effrontery was to be expected from those not to the manner born and so who, one must imagine, knew no better. Still, I suppose that a sense of fairness *does* compel us to admit that if a man has paid for whatever crimes he may have committed in his past, he is entitled to whatever rewards he may, through subsequent initiative and honest hard work, gain for himself.''

''That may be so, but the majority of Australian colonists would argue the issue. And I warn you, Arabella: You shall not win any friends or influence people by voicing that wholly unpopular sentiment in New South Wales. Colonial governors have been recalled to England, and rightly so, for such thinking. Gentlemen do not want to sit down with ex-convicts at their supper tables,'' Harry asserted bluntly, ''nor do they want their wives socializing with them, nor their sisters and daughters marrying them. As a woman of obvious genteel breeding and intelligence, not given, like so many other young women these days, to flights of romantic fantasy engendered by those gothic novels of which my sisters are so inordinately fond, you surely can understand that, Arabella!''

''Yes, of course,'' she conceded, ''for in all honesty, I confess that I certainly should not care to wed a man who had once been incarcerated in gaol for the performance of what one can only assume was some dastardly deed. I meant only, Harry, that a man who has made a mistake but who has suffered the consequences for it and who has since seen the error of his ways should not continue to be punished for his previous lack of conscience and good judgment. That would be as much a miscarriage of justice as an innocent man's being condemned for a crime he did not commit, would you not agree?''

"In theory, yes; in reality, no—because the truth is, regardless of how hard you try, you just can't change the inherent nature of a criminal, Arabella, any more than you can change that of an Aborigine. One's a bad seed from which you'll never reap anything but a rotten harvest, despite all your nurturing; and the other's an ignorant savage, simply incapable of learning even the rudiments of civilization, despite all your teaching. Once you've spent some time in the Colonies, you'll come to understand that. For years, missionaries have been attempting not only to convert the natives of Australia to Christianity, but also to civilize them—without success. Inevitably, one day, the Aborigine reverts to his heathen religion and goes 'walkabout,' that is, he just disappears into the bush, following the 'songlines,' the wild trails of his pagan ancestors. Just as inevitably, an ex-convict like Lucien Sinclair, for example, for all his outward appearance of reformation, will one day commit another crime, another murder. It's merely a matter of time—and that's a fact.''

"Oh, Harry! How I should hate to think that so!" Arabella sighed, more discouraged than she cared to admit by the apparent logic of his statements. "For if it were, it would mean that all good works are essentially worthless, a complete waste of time and effort, that no man can ever really be saved by another, or even by God. It just seems like such a—a hopeless outlook, as though we are, all of us, helpless against fate.'' At the thought, unbidden into her mind came the memory of her fortune told by the old Gypsy woman at the Scarborough fair. Momentarily dwelling on that croaking voice, those clutching hands, and those cryptic words, Arabella shivered. ''I had not thought you such a pessimist, Harry.''

''Not a pessimist, but a realist, I should say—while you, my dear Arabella, are something of a romantic, after all, I am beginning to suspect! But . . . enough of this. You've grown chilly in this rising wind—and unless I miss my guess, the glass is still falling and we're in for a patch of rough weather. I don't like to say so, but those look like storm clouds on the horizon.''

''Yes, they do,'' she concurred, disquieted suddenly as she gazed at the spreading stain that darkened the distant sky—for had the Gypsy not muttered something about a powerful storm of rain and wind, of a sea dragging her, Arabella, down to a coral enchantment? Was it fate or only coincidence that the *Heather Rose* should be upon the Coral Sea, with a storm brewing? She did not know, and she was quite certain she did not want to find out. Beset by an unwelcome premonition, she turned, saying, ''If you'll excuse me, Harry, I think I'll go below to my cabin.'' She would be safe there, Arabella comforted herself, locked inside against the elements, against whatever was to come.

''Good idea, that. Batten down the hatches. I believe I'll do the same after I've had a word with our good

Captain Beckett as to what we may expect—although
I'm sure there's nothing to worry about, Arabella,'' he
said in reassurance, noting the look of anxiety on her
face. "The *Heather Rose* is a stalwart, seagoing vessel.
No doubt she's battled many a squall and won her way
through with flying colors.''

This was, in fact, the case, as Arabella herself learned
from Captain Beckett when, at eight o'clock that evening, after the steward had knocked on her door to
inform her that despite the increasingly inclement
weather, supper would be served in the salon as usual,
she dared once more to venture from her cabin. It had
begun now to rain, a drizzle that was, however, only a
foreshadowing of what was to come, the steward predicted morosely, as he escorted Arabella from her cabin
to the salon; and the rising wind gusted so violently
that, once or twice, he nearly lost his grip on the um-
brella with which he sheltered her until they were once
more inside. The other passengers were already gathered in the salon, listening to Captain Beckett as he
assured them that although a storm was indeed coming,
there was naught to fear. The *Heather Rose* had weathered squalls before and would do so again. Still, Arabella could not shake off her uneasiness; and after the
hurriedly served and eaten meal, rather than lingering
in the salon to chat with Harry and to play a few hands
of whist or loo at the card table as she usually would
have done, she returned once more to her cabin.

Once inside, she locked the door and, after lighting
the oil lamps bolted to the walls, made certain the porthole was secure, even though she longed to open it to
admit the freshening wind; for the cabin was hot and

humid from the oppressive air. Tendrils of hair that had escaped from her chignon tumbled and curled in wild disarray about her face, and perspiration trickled down her neck, bosom, and back, making the fabric of her gown stick to her skin unpleasantly. Struggling with buttons, hooks, and lacings, Arabella gratefully divested herself of her dress, hoops, crinolines, and undergarments. The nightly bucket of water the steward had left in her cabin allowed her to indulge in a welcome sponge bath, after which she drew on her nightgown, then pulled the pins from her hair, brushing and plaiting it into a bedtime braid. Fluffing up the pillows, she climbed into her berth and took up the book she was currently reading. After she had read the same page for the third time in a row, Arabella realized she was not concentrating on the story and was, in fact, having difficulty seeing the words at all because of the pitching of the ship.

She laid the book aside and staggered from the bunk to the porthole, against which—now that the storm had descended in its full fury—rain pelted so hard that beyond the round glass, she could see little in the blackness and had only a terrifying impression of a dark, maddened sea awash with high crests of swirling foam. As the wild wind moaned and shrieked, the straining timbers of the *Heather Rose* groaned and creaked in equally discordant response. To Arabella, it seemed as though the vessel must violently break apart at any moment, no matter what Captain Beckett had said. Had she not, all her life, heard tales of fishing boats that had been caught in storms and had sunk off the coast of Yorkshire? Had she not read stories of sea monsters that, now, as she thought of Harry's deadly great white sharks, did not seem quite so fabulous, so mythological as before? Amid such terrors, the fortune told to her by the old Gypsy woman kept surfacing in Arabella's mind.

She should try to sleep, she told herself dully, although she knew that, even with the laudanum the doctor had prescribed, she would not close her eyes again until the squall had blown over. From above, on deck, she could hear men shouting, their voices ripped from their throats and carried away by the wind; and from below, in the hold, the rumble of the pumps sounded as they worked to keep the ship from being swamped and sinking. Like an untamed, unbridled sea dragon, the vessel itself—its sails struck, its mast bare, its stay raised—rode the angry waves, hurling up with each titanic swell to hang precariously in midair before plunging into the waiting trough, water sweeping over the bow, spilling onto the deck, and raging along the sides.

She should have been stronger. She should have refused to close Darracott Hall, Arabella thought; she should have stayed at home instead of journeying to Australia. If she had, she would be safe. Now, there was no escape for her. Filling her mind were nightmarish visions of the sea bursting violently through her cabin door, smashing through the porthole, pouring into the cabin, sucking her under, drowning her. She longed for Harry Palliser's cheerful face, his comforting presence, but knew it would be madness to leave her cabin. So, chafing at her inactivity, her helplessness to seize command of her own fate, she stayed where she was, returning to her berth to huddle, shivering despite the

THE JACARANDA TREE • 49

stifling atmosphere, beneath the bedclothes, hoping to slip into slumber.

Indeed, she must have dozed, for the next thing Arabella knew, she was flying from her bunk to land with a painful thud against the floor. As she lay there, stunned, disoriented, blood trickling from a gash on her brow, she could feel the ship wildly bucking and shuddering, hear the sickening shattering and splintering of timbers, the gouging and grinding of the hull caught fast upon some unknown object, the roar of the wind and sea, the shouting of men, the screaming of women, the pounding of running feet. In the passageway beyond her cabin, water gushed as though from a broken dam, seeping beneath her door. Powerless against the elements, the *Heather Rose* must have been blown off course, Arabella realized; the vessel must have been driven upon the deadly reefs about which Harry had told her earlier that day. She had not time even to snatch up her wrapper before Harry himself was beating on her door, yelling for her to open it, that Captain Beckett had ordered all the women aboard to be loaded into the lifeboats. As she flung the door wide, a tide of water rushed in, knocking her down, and the vessel heaved and shook savagely again, canting at a dangerous angle.

"Arabella!" Harry lurched toward her, catching her up in his arms and wading back out into the narrow corridor crowded with frantic passengers and black and acrid with billowing smoke from fires started on board by broken oil lamps.

The door at the top of the stairs leading to the deck

had been ripped away by the gale, and now, with a hideous roar, another wave crashed through the opening, tumbling with such ferocity down the steps that Harry and Arabella were slammed against the wall and nearly swept away. Drenched to the bone, shivering with fear and cold in her sodden nightgown, she clung with silent desperation to Harry's neck as he somehow managed to regain his footing and to stumble forward, only to be driven back again by yet another onslaught of the wind and sea. The journey down that dark, water- and smoke-filled passageway and up that short flight of stairs was interminable. This was what it was to die, Arabella thought numbly, vaguely surprised to discover that now that the moment of her death was upon her, she felt no fear, but, rather, a strange calmness and mild curiosity coupled with the certain knowledge that she would presently be reunited with her parents in heaven. But then, miraculously, Harry got through, and together, they stood upon the deck with the rest of those still aboard, clutching the lifelines and buffeted mercilessly by the storm that threatened to wash them from the listing vessel into the turgid sea.

The *Heather Rose* was breaking apart and sinking. There had not been enough lifeboats to begin with; some had been torn from their riven davits and carried away to be dashed to pieces upon the reefs. In the distance, through the blinding rain, Arabella could just discern one small, horrifyingly bobbing craft filled with terrified, screaming women; and—just this moment rendered heartbreakingly useless as it suddenly jerked free from the grim-faced men who had determinedly grasped its ropes—a second, empty lifeboat bounced brutally on the waves. Urgently hauling her across the tilted deck to the rail, Harry cried in her ear, above the howl of the squall, "God be with you, Arabella!" Then, before she realized what he intended, he lifted her up and, with his last ounce of strength, flung her over the side of the drowning ship into the second tiny craft before it could be snatched away entirely by the wind and sea.

She landed painfully in the bottom of the lifeboat, stunned, the wind knocked from her from what had seemed an endless fall but that, in reality, had been no more than half a dozen feet, such was the angle of the *Heather Rose* and the depths to which the doomed vessel had already sunk. But no sooner had Arabella caught her breath than a towering wave hove up over the small craft to smash down upon her, once more forcing the precious air from her lungs. Gasping, coughing, choking, dimly aware that Harry had sacrificed his life so she might have a chance at saving her own, she instinctively wrapped her arms around one of the thwarts, clinging to it desperately to keep from being swept from the lifeboat now wildly jouncing some yards from the *Heather Rose*.

"Harry!" she screamed as lightning exploded across the angry black firmament and she glimpsed his pale, bleak face through the sheets of rain. "Harry!"

It was the last Arabella ever saw of him. At that moment, with a long, terrible groan and a mighty straining and heaving of her broken hull, the *Heather Rose* ripped free at last from the reefs that had held her fast and, rolling slowly to one side, plunged into the great, gaping maw of the frothy sea. Minutes later, the ship and all those left aboard her were gone, and Arabella knew, terrified, that she was utterly alone, adrift upon the raging sea; for even the other lifeboat full of women had vanished. The oars for her own tiny craft were long gone and would have proved useless in any event. It was only a matter of time before she, too, was forever claimed by the sea. Even as the realization seized her in its paralyzing grip, another horrendous wave rose over her. For an eternity, it seemed, it hung there like an executioner's blade, death written upon its grim, forbidding edge, before it descended with the full force of its fury, taking her breath. The last thing Arabella remembered was the cold, dark water closing over her, drenching her, engulfing her, dragging her under, filling her lungs to bursting before a merciful blackness whirled up to envelop her, and she knew nothing more.

Chapter Three

The Demon

New South Wales Colony, Australia, 1856

She had died and gone not to heaven, but to hell, Arabella thought deliriously; for she was burning up, and in the darkness, her dazed, overbright eyes spied the macabre, dancing flames of an inferno, and the devil himself towering over her.

"Somehow, I—I always . . . imagined you'd . . . have horns," she croaked weakly, her lips dry, cracked, and swollen, her throat raw and hoarse. Strange . . . she had thought that when you died, you felt no more pain, but it was not just her mouth and throat that hurt. Her skin was on fire; every ragged breath was agony to her chest; and she ached all over, as though she had been battered and bruised unmercifully. But then, she supposed dully, since she was in hell, she must expect punishment, however brutal, as her due. "And a—a pitchfork."

At that, the devil threw back his dark, handsome head and laughed—wildly, it seemed to her, although the fiendish sound itself was low, mocking, seductive— and the teeth that flashed white against his bronzed flesh were straight, even, lacking the carnivorous, vampirish fangs she had also somehow vaguely expected.

"I'm a demon, all right—in more ways than one— but not that kind, my girl," he drawled, his cool, pale grey eyes still glinting with amusement, as well as concern, as he knelt beside her, "any more than you turned out to be a mermaid washed up onto the beach, so I'm afraid that we are both of us equally disappointed."

"You—you mean ˙ . . . this isn't . . . hell?" In a futile attempt to moisten them, Arabella licked her lips, tasting blood from tiny wounds she had, by speaking, split anew.

"No," the devil said shortly, with another low laugh, before laying his hand upon her feverish brow and frowning, "although I daresay you shan't agree with me once you have recovered enough to argue the issue."

"Recovered?" Her befuddled mind seized on the word, even as she wondered why the touch of his hand should feel so cool against her skin instead of searing her to the bone, as the devil's ought. "Then . . . I'm— I'm not . . . dead, just—just . . . ill?"

"Yes, you've a raging fever still. But at least you've regained consciousness. For a while there, I feared that you would not." He did not add that when he had first discovered her insensate, near-naked body on the wild, desolate shore of the Coral Sea, he had thought that she would almost certainly die. There was no point in alarming her further by telling her how near to death she had lain in the past days since he had found her. Turning aside, he filled a tin pannikin with a dark liquid he poured from a billy kept warm by the fire he had built earlier. Then, his arm lifting and supporting her, he pressed the rim of the cup to her mouth. "Drink," he commanded, in a tone that even in her beclouded mental state, Arabella recognized as belonging to one accustomed to being obeyed; and she was too thirsty and weak to question, to protest his authority over her, as she normally would have done. It was not the tea she had expected that he offered her, but instead a brew bitter and foul—poison, she thought dimly, instinctively frightened; and despite her frailty, she struggled after the first swallow to refuse it. But the arm that gripped her was like an iron band, the hand that held the pannikin to her lips relentless, the masterful voice now hard, impatient. "Drink! It will help to bring the fever down and to clear the congestion in your lungs!" And in the end, reluctantly she did drink, having no choice but to comply with the devil's demand, coughing and choking as the vile liquid ran down her throat.

Afterward, he lowered her back down upon the blankets on which she had lain. Then, after wetting it with water from a canteen, he spread a cool, damp cloth upon her forehead. For a moment, her eyes stared up at him, filled with anxiety and confusion; then, slowly, her lashes fluttered closed. Her irregular breathing grew more rhythmic. She slept.

Slumber, however, did not come so quickly to the

man Arabella had mistaken for the devil. A faint, derisive smile curved his mouth as he recalled her feverish
notion, for he knew there were those who would not
have considered her assumption erroneous. No more
would she, once she learned who and what he was, he
reflected wryly; for despite its hoarseness, her voice,
when she had spoken to him, had been cultured, genteel.
She might not be the mermaid he had fancifully supposed her when he had first spied her lying on the beach,
cast up from the briny sea, her streaming, tangled hair
and almost naked body wrapped with strands of seaweed
and dusted with salt and sand; but although she had
been clothed in little more than the tatters of a thin
nightgown, she was obviously a lady born and bred.
Although he had achieved the outward trappings of a
gentleman, he was not and would never truly be ranked
among her class, not only lacking from birth the requi-
site silver spoon in his mouth, but also having spent
the greater part of his youthful manhood as a convict,
condemned for the heinous crime of murder. That he had
been transported and incarcerated rather than hanged, he
owed to the wealth and influence of the family that,
withal, had spurned him since his birth, saving him
from the gallows only to hush the dreadful scandal of
his disgrace.

As they always did, his glittering, pale grey eyes
hardened and his sensual, sardonic mouth tightened with
bitterness when he thought of that and of Van Diemen's
Land—a paradise, a prison. For a long, hellish decade,
until he had saved enough money to bribe the necessary
officials for a ticket-of-leave, he had labored on that

beautiful island as a slave, a whipping boy for the brutal
guards who had tried but failed to break his proud,
arrogant spirit. He would never forget or forgive that—
nor, he felt certain, would the woman lying on his
blankets, despite his having saved her life. Like the rest
of her aristocratic ilk—save for a hungry, avaricious
few excited by his being forbidden fruit and greedy for
his fortune gleaned from the Ophir district during the
gold rush of 1851—his mermaid would scorn him, mortified that she should owe her life to a Demon, as those
once incarcerated in Port Arthur Prison on Van Diemen's Land were known.

Who was she? he wondered, not for the first time,
as he prepared a fresh poultice for her rattling chest.
He glanced at her restlessly sleeping figure, her bruised
face that, while not beautiful, had an arresting strength
and character. The wreckage and debris strewn along
the shore had told him that she had doubtless come from
a ship driven upon the reefs during the storm the night
before he had discovered her. But other than that, he
knew nothing about her, not even her name. "Mermaid," he called her in his mind; for such she resembled
with her long, flowing hair the red-brown of seaweed,
her wide, luminous eyes the dark gold of wet sand, her
slender, voluptuous body the alabaster of pearls, her
full, round breasts tipped with the pale, dusky rose
of a conch shell's throat. These the Demon had seen,
suffering no gentlemanly qualms about stripping the
remnants of Arabella's sodden nightgown from her; and
although he had afterward clothed her in one of his
woolen blankets, in which he had cut a hole to form a

crude poncho, it had been to warm her against the chill she had taken from the storm and sea, not for modesty's sake. Nor had he hesitated—as he did not now—to raise the poncho over her head, thereby exposing the length of her naked body once more to his lingering, searching gaze. That his thoughts, when he did so, were not wholly of an impersonal, ministering nature did not trouble him. He was a man who had lived for ten years without a woman upon whom to slake his masculine lust, and he had spent the past several months alone in the wild, besides. This woman's body would have tempted a saint; so how much more, then, a devil? The knowledge that while she was helpless and unaware, he had disrobed her and laid his hands upon her, she would neither forget nor forgive, either, the Demon knew. In fact, it was for that most of all that she would undoubtedly despise him, ardently wishing that she had died instead—a stupid, senseless notion to a man such as he, who had fought so hard to survive despite the ignominies he had endured.

Thus, the realization that his mermaid would find death preferable to his tending did not deter him from prying from her chest the old poultice he had applied earlier and his plastering the new one in its place, his hands inadvertently brushing her breasts as he did so. Of their own volition, her nipples puckered and hardened, and she moaned softly, feverishly, tossing fitfully on the blankets, hips instinctively arching a little; so he wondered again whether she had ever had a man or were simply possessed of an untapped sensuality of which it would shame and embarrass her to learn, since decent ladies were taught that while it was a wife's duty to submit to her husband's conjugal desires, only a loose, wanton woman actually enjoyed the act. How well he would teach her otherwise, given the opportunity, the Demon thought as, taking up a jar of healing salve, he began to rub its contents on the worst of her cuts and abrasions. As always, he was aroused by the feel of the woman's body, the little, oblivious, incoherent whimpers she made as his hands roamed over her, the way in which her thighs unwittingly opened, inviting him to explore their downy juncture. But although he was no gentleman, he was not such an unconscionable rogue as to force himself on a woman so delirious and deathly ill. So, reluctantly, when he had finished treating her wounds, he drew the poncho back into place without touching her as he so longed to do.

He added more logs to the fire to ensure that predators did not approach and placed his carbine and revolver within easy reach. Then he stripped to his leather breeches and, to share the warmth of their body heat as he had done each night since finding her, lay down beside the woman in the rough lean-to he had built of branches from the woods along the shore to protect her as best he could from the elements. The shelter was not at all the kind of accommodation to which she was accustomed, he reckoned; still, it would have to serve. Even if she were well enough to travel, they were hundreds of miles distant from Brisbane, the nearest town. As a result, despite whatever softness she had known in the past, the woman would, in the weeks to come, be compelled on their journey south along the coast of

New South Wales to grow used to hardship—just as she would have to grow used to him if she wished him to return her to civilization. Closing his eyes, the Demon slept at last, although the restlessness of his own slumber stemmed from a different kind of fever in the blood.

Chapter Four

Garden of Eden

How long she lay feverish and sick, Arabella did not know. It might have been days, weeks, or even months. She had no awareness of time's passing, only of the Demon's dark, handsome visage as he bent over her; of his voice—low, arrogant, insolent; of his mocking laughter now and then at something she said; and of his hands lifting her, supporting her, holding his cup of revolting devil's brew to her lips, and pressing cool cloths upon her hot brow. Sometimes, she dreamed of lying naked in his arms, of feeling his palms against her breasts and elsewhere upon her burning, aching body, arousing within her peculiar, exciting feelings she had never before known, tempting her to wantonness, to wickedness; and she thought dimly that, no matter what he had told her, he was, in truth, the devil, and she had died and gone to hell. What sins had she committed in her life to be punished so after death? Arabella wondered. But then she dazedly remembered the Scarborough fair, the Gypsy's pavilion she ought not to have entered, and her cryptic fortune muttered by the old woman; and she knew that even then, the mark of Cain had been upon her, that all her life, she had been destined to be condemned for a crime not her own.

Even more than its guardian Demon did the ancient netherworld in which she lay frighten Arabella. Accustomed, as she was, to the boundless sky above the sweeping, nearly treeless Yorkshire moors, she felt stifled by the strange, labyrinthine woods that, by the wavering flames of the inferno, she could see threatened to envelop her—wild, verdant, and fecund, rich with decay and humus. Never before had she beheld their like. Tall, twisted, and tangled, they must be incredibly old, primal, like the atavistic land they encroached upon, shutting out the sky. Although an otherworldly sun might shine here in this perditious place, Arabella was cognizant only of the long twilight shadows, of the night whose stars gleaming through the woods' canopy of intertwined branches formed no familiar patterns, so she knew she was no longer upon Earth. Later, when it was not so hard for her to draw breath, her nostrils were invaded by the woods' heavy, exotic fragrances: the lush perfume of unknown fruits and flowers, the green redolence of alien trees and grasses, the damp scent of stagnant pools and black loam, the salty smell of wet sand and a near sea, and, always, the smoky odor of a constantly blazing fire. Her ears discerned the cries of wild creatures whose voices she did not recognize, mingled with that of the one she did—the Demon who was lord of this paradisiacal hell.

Once, he kissed her in a dream, his carnal mouth hard and hungry upon her soft lips that yielded pliantly to the deliberate, demanding intrusion of his tongue. No man had ever before tasted her mouth; never in her wildest imaginings had Arabella thought that it would be as it was when *he* claimed her lips—hot and savage, a dominant, primeval possession that wakened within her an answering, equally elemental submission. Intuitively, she strained against him, moaning low in her throat, opening her lips for his deepening invasion. Fiercely devouring, his tongue twined and tangled about her own, seeking and finding the moist, dark sweetness within, licking and savoring it as though the taste of her were warm wild honey melting upon his tongue. He tasted of rum and tobacco, masculine tastes that had hitherto been foreign to her tongue and that therefore now both scared and excited her, sending a wild, unexpected thrill through her as, again and again, his tongue stabbed her with its heat. Of their own volition, her arms crept up to wind around his neck, to burrow in his glossy black hair, to draw him down to her. At that, his mouth left hers to slash across her cheek to her temple, the strands of her hair, her ear, before trailing a path of scorching kisses down her throat to her breasts, against which Arabella could feel his own bare, sweating chest, its fine mat of hair tickling her nipples, his heart pounding hard and fast against hers.

Urgently, his hands roamed upon her naked flesh, fingers roughly ensnaring her long, unbound hair, grasp-

ing her buttocks, pulling her hips against his, cupping
her breasts, teasing her nipples into taut twin peaks,
and sending circles of pleasure radiating through her
body. His breath was hot and quick against her skin as
his lips found her breasts, fastened upon one hard, rosebud nipple, sucking deeply, greedily, drawing it into
his mouth, teeth nibbling, tongue laving, taunting. Instinctively, she arched her hips against his, a scalding,
hollow ache that was a different kind of fever seizing
her, burgeoning at the secret heart of her. But despite
her pleading whimpers, her increasingly exigent movements against the hardness of his arousal she could feel
at the vulnerable juncture of her inner thighs, the Demon
did not assuage her fervent longing.

"Oh, God," he groaned against her breasts. "How
you tempt me, mermaid! But I am not yet fallen so low
as the Lucifer you think me."

Then she was alone in her dream, not knowing
whether she was alive or dead, what was real and what
was not, whether he had truly kissed and touched her
or if she had only dreamed its happening.

Then, at last, there came the evening when Arabella
awoke with a clear consciousness, her lashes slowly
fluttering open to reveal wide eyes that, although filled
with confusion, were nevertheless lucid. For a moment,
she did nothing but remain still where she lay, gazing
with a troubled frown at her shadowy surroundings as
she attempted to determine where she was and what had
happened to her. Her head throbbed dully when she
moved it, and her body was stiff and sore, as though
she had been severely beaten, although she did not remember such. Plainly, she was not at Darracott Hall,

but in a place foreign to her, some kind of rough shelter in a woods, a strange, tropical Garden of Eden, revealed to her by the light of a crackling fire at the heart of the small sylvan glade that encompassed her. Silvery moonlight streamed through the interlaced green boughs of the alien, liana-vine-draped trees—gums, mangroves, palms, and jacarandas, she would later learn that some were called—and from one branch, a big, plumed white bird eyed her with interest, emitting an occasional loud squawk, which was the harsh noise that had wakened her. Only the nickering of a pair of horses tethered to a bush at the edge of the clearing, the piercing, forlorn calls of seagulls that winged their way across the patches of starry night sky she could glimpse overhead, and the rhythmic soughing of the nearby sea itself were familiar. As those sounds penetrated her awareness, dark, terrifying memories of the shipwreck suddenly flooded Arabella's mind, and a ragged sob of horror issued from her throat.

"Harry!" she cried, stricken, abruptly sitting bolt upright on the woolen blankets on which she lay, glancing about wildly at what she now knew must surely be Australia. "Harry!"

"It's Lucien, actually," an unknown man said. She gasped in alarm and then screamed softly, for she had not heard his seemingly stealthy approach. Stepping into the dimly lit glade, he tossed a brace of freshly killed, rabbit-sized animals onto the ground by the fire, then propped his carbine up against a nearby rock. "Lucien Sinclair."

It was *he*—the devil of her disturbing, disjointed dreams! Arabella was so stunned by the realization that she could do naught but stare at him, petrified. Never in her life had she seen a man so dark, so demonic, so brutally handsome that he resembled, in truth, the fallen archangel for whom she had in her delirium mistaken him. His was a face bold and beautiful, wild and wicked to behold, his movements like that of a predatory beast, silent, lithe, powerful. The long, shaggy, disheveled hair that hung past his shoulders was blacker than the smoke of the inferno in which she had dazedly envisioned herself, glistening as though frosted by an unholy radiance where the light cast by the flickering fire played across the silky strands. His skin was darker than sweet-flowing honey, bronzed by a sun she had yet to know but would soon learn was as blistering as the man's temper when he was provoked. Thick black brows that swooped like a raven's spread wings across his noble brow framed deep-set eyes as grey as the mist and rain of the sweeping moors she had left so far behind. Beneath his chiseled, aquiline nose, his mouth curved with the carnality and dissolution of the experienced and jaded, setting another shudder of apprehension coursing through her as she gazed at him mutely, still frozen with fear. Tall—standing a couple of inches over six feet—and powerfully built, he was lean and hard-muscled, with massive shoulders and a broad chest that tapered to a firm, flat belly, taut, narrow hips, and thick, corded thighs, all of which bespoke a man well accustomed to manual labor. The rough garments he wore—a stained oilskin coat, flat-brimmed hat, chambray shirt, leather breeches, and scuffed black boots—reinforced her initial opinion that he was no gentleman, and, if not the devil incarnate, he was probably a scoundrel, a rogue.

Had she been able, Arabella, spurred by the memory of her feverish dreams, would have fled from him; but to her despair, she was too weak even to rise yet, much less to run away. Nor, to her vague surprise, did the man make any threatening moves toward her; and after a moment, she realized that she doubtless owed her life to him, that it must have been he who had rescued her from the storm-swept sea and brought her to this clearing. At the thought, some of her fright receded; for why should he have saved her, only to do her harm? Perhaps he was whatever passed for a gamekeeper in Australia; that role would explain his coarse appearance—although not why, upon finding her, he had not straightaway carried her to the manor of his lord and master, or at least summoned help. Arabella decided that she would be wise to keep her own counsel until she learned what had actually befallen her at his hands. She could not believe—did not *want* to believe—that her bizarre dreams had any basis in reality. Nevertheless, a small part of her was forced to acknowledge the fact that this man had perhaps violated her while she had lain helpless and unaware.

Lucien Sinclair. The name sounded oddly familiar to Arabella, although she could not place it, the memory evanescing like mist through her hands when she tried to grasp it.

"You were—you were not aboard the *Heather Rose*?" she inquired, finding her voice at last and thinking that it was just possible that he might have been a

solitary passenger who had kept to his cabin and therefore would not have been introduced to her during her
months-long voyage from England to Australia.

"The *Heather Rose*? Was that the name of your vessel, the one that broke apart on the reefs during the
storm?" At her quick nod of confirmation, Lucien continued, moving slowly so as not to alarm her further as
he hunkered down beside her, for her fear and wariness
of him was plain; and despite the fact that she had not
yet given way to the hysterics he had expected, she
cringed involuntarily as he neared her. "No, fortunately, I was not aboard her. It was, however, I who
discovered you washed up on the beach—the sole survivor of the shipwreck, I presume, since I found no others.
You're a very lucky woman, Miss . . . ?"

"Darracott. Arabella Darracott," she supplied, swift,
hot tears of grief stinging her eyes as, without warning,
she remembered Harry standing on the deck of the sinking ship, his face illuminated by the lightning, and she
realized he must surely be dead, must have drowned
with the doomed vessel.

"I'm sorry. I see that I ought to have broken that sad
news to you more gently," Lucien said as he spied her
tears. "You had family or friends aboard?"

"A—a friend . . . at least, he had become so during
the voyage. He—he gave his life for me. It was he who
rescued me from my cabin and carried me up on deck
after we were driven onto the reefs. There—there
weren't enough lifeboats to begin with, you see, and
the—the last one had just torn away from the sailors
who were trying to hold it steady. But Harry—that was
my friend's name, Harry Palliser—he grabbed me up

and flung me over the side of the ship into the lifeboat before it could be swept away. The *Heather Rose* went under right after that, and then I—I don't know what happened. I remember a huge wave towering over me, smashing down upon me. I guess that it—it must have knocked me unconscious, because everything after that is a blank. I—I don't even know where I am . . . Australia, I suppose, but where? And—and how long have I been here? It seems clear that I've—I've been ill—" Arabella broke off, biting her lower lip anxiously, shocked and horrified as she suddenly realized that what she had taken for her nightgown was, in reality, a crude poncho fashioned from a blanket and that she was stark naked beneath it. Again, memories of her vivid, erotic dreams rose to haunt her. A soft cry of distress emanated from her throat. Her hands tightened convulsively on the makeshift garment, as though it might offer some protection against the man beside her. Dear God, surely, he had not—"We are . . . all—all alone here? It was—it was you who cared for me, who—who . . . undressed me?" she managed to choke out, needing desperately to hear the answer, some reassurance that he had not, in fact, unscrupulously taken advantage of her as she feared.

"Yes." Although the word was terse, Lucien did not mistake her sudden shame or the question in her stricken, bewildered eyes before she lowered them. "Miss Darracott, please know that I am aware of the awkwardness of this situation and of your sense of modesty and your womanly qualms. However, you must understand that when I discovered you on the beach, you were near death, unconscious, and suffering from an extremely bad case of pneumonia. So, at the time, it was necessary to remove the remnants of your sodden nightgown. Although we *are* on the coast of the colony of New South Wales, I'm afraid that the nearest town, Brisbane, is hundreds of miles distant, and you were far too ill to travel, in any event; so, of course, I did and have continued to do for more than a fortnight what I believed was required to save your life."

"Yes, of course," Arabella echoed slowly, dully, after a long moment, daunted to learn how long she had been ill and unconscious. Even if Lucien Sinclair had done nothing more than he claimed, she might have been better off dead. Regardless of her incapacitated condition, once people discovered that she had been alone in this man's company in the middle of nowhere for weeks, her reputation would be totally destroyed. The prospect utterly dismayed her.

Why should she be the only survivor of the wreck of the *Heather Rose*, anyway? she asked herself numbly. She ought to have died with the rest of those aboard— or gone with her father to his grave. Why should God have condemned her to a life of ruination instead? She knew only that, somehow, her fate had been determined by the lay of the ancient cards that long-ago day at the Scarborough fair. Arabella shivered at the thought, for although the Gypsy's words had haunted her of late, she had never until now truly believed in second sight, in powers beyond her ken, in an irrevocable destiny.

"You are cold?" Lucien asked in concern, and pressed his hand to her brow, which, although cool, suddenly felt to her as though it were on fire at the touch of his palm. "Your fever finally broke this morning and has not returned. I expected your chills to dissipate as a result.''

"It—it was nothing . . . a momentary twinge, that's all,'' Arabella lied, wanting him to take his hand away. The feel of it was too familiar for comfort, reminding her that it was not only her brow he had touched while she had lain delirious, even if it had been only to tend her hurts—and even that she did not know for certain, still hesitated to ask.

Had Lucien Sinclair been a gentleman born and bred, she would have known herself inviolate, however disconcerting her situation. That, clearly, he was not, complicated her position. As though sensing her uneasiness, he abruptly removed his hand and, rising, began to stoke the fire. He set a billy full of water on to heat. Then, opening his leather packs that lay to one side, he took from them some clothes, which he handed to her, along with a corked clay jar and a brush.

"The jar contains a healing salve for your cuts and bruises—although even the worst of those are mending." Lucien's voice was carefully noncommittal; still, Arabella could not prevent the tide of color that flooded her cheeks at the thought, once more, that his hands had roamed over her naked body, if only in a ministering capacity. "The garments I found amid the wreckage strewn on the sand; I'm sure they're not what you're accustomed to; still, I have no others but my own to give you. The brush is mine, but you are welcome to it." After that, taking the billy from the fire, he brought it to the shelter, with a cloth and towel. "There's water for washing if you feel able." As he bent to pull one of the blankets from Arabella, she shrank from him apprehensively. "Relax, Miss Darracott," Lucien drawled softly, his lips curving in the sardonic smile she remembered from her dreams. "Should I have any designs on you, I won't hesitate to make them known. I was only going to string the blanket along the front of the lean-to, so you would have a modicum of privacy."

"Oh," she said, feeling suddenly small and ashamed. "I'm—I'm sorry. I don't know what you must think of me! I—I haven't even thanked you for saving my life, for which I am naturally . . . most grateful. I'm afraid you'll have to pardon my churlish manners on the grounds that I'm—I'm . . . not quite myself yet."

"That's understandable. I'm certain the shipwreck was a profound shock to your senses, and then you awakened from a delirium to find yourself alone with a strange man, hundreds of miles from the nearest town. Most women would either have burst into hysterics or fainted by now. I find it not only extraordinary, but also commendable that you have not. Obviously you are a young woman of both intelligence and courage—qualities I admire. You will have need of them in the days to come, I promise you; for I do not think that you will find the journey to Brisbane an easy one."

"Mr. Sinclair, I—I don't want to appear as though I don't . . . trust you; but if there is, as you claim, no other town closer than Brisbane, how did you yourself come to be so far from civilization? Is there not then some estate hereabouts? I mean, from your appearance, I assumed—although perhaps wrongly?—that you were, well . . . a gamekeeper of some sort."

He laughed at that, the low, mocking sound that had haunted her dreams.

"I suppose I should be flattered, since that is doubtless somewhat better in your eyes than the devil you originally thought me." His eyes glittered with amusement in the firelight as she flushed deeply once more. "But, no, Miss Darracott, I am not a gamekeeper, but, rather, an . . . adventurer, an opportunist, let us say. There is a great deal of land to be had in New South Wales, and as I was thinking of acquiring some in this region, it seemed only wise to ensure that I was not buying a pig in a poke, so to speak. Although this part of the colony is, in fact, inhabited, its residents are natives—and not all of them are friendly, for which reason I did not care to take you, a white woman, among them."

"I see. Then I must indeed consider myself fortunate that you happened along," Arabella asserted, only to receive another low laugh for her pains.

"My dear Miss Darracott, I assure you that I am perfectly aware that all genteel ladies are taught that it is their duty to prefer death to dishonor—quite a foolish sentiment, in my opinion, but one, nevertheless, that I am sure you share. So, let me set your mind at ease: Despite the fact that you have been over two weeks alone in the wild and in my company, your virtue is as intact as, from your demeanor, I presume it to have been before I found you on the beach. Further, although I make no promises as to my success, I will certainly endeavor to ensure that upon our return to civilization, your reputation remains equally untarnished by your ordeal."

"Mr. Sinclair! It—it is most improper for you to— to speak to me so," Arabella declared faintly, mortified that he should have put into words what preyed on her mind.

"Yes . . . but aren't you glad I did?" he prodded insolently as he flashed her a wicked grin that told her she was right, that he was no gentleman.

Then, having, on a rope taken from his saddle, hung the blanket to screen the open side of the shelter, he returned to the fire, where he set about skinning the two unfamiliar animals he'd killed earlier. From the small gap between the blanket and one side of the lean-to, Arabella studied him silently for a moment before, wincing at the soreness and stiffness of her body, she slowly drew off the poncho. By the dim light that shone through the breach, she examined the cuts, abrasions, and bruises that covered her. Although they were indeed mending, they were nevertheless ugly and appalling. No wonder she felt as though she had been brutally beaten; the pounding she had suffered from the sea was far worse than what any man might have inflicted upon her. At the sight, she thought that Lucien Sinclair must have spoken truly to her when he had claimed she was yet chaste; for no man could possibly have found her attractive at the moment. Reaching for the cloth and the billy, Arabella sponged herself off as best she was able, realizing as she did so that she stank both of stale sweat and the peculiar, green fragrance of the woods. Uncorking the clay jar, she applied to her body the healing salve it contained, discovering as she did so that the ointment was responsible for the not unpleasant woodsy scent that clung to her. Then she looked over the clothes Lucien Sinclair had given her. They were really only undergarments—a thin white cotton camisole, panta-lets, and a ruffled petticoat, which, although clean, were much mended and so which had come, no doubt, from some poor, unfortunate woman who had traveled in steerage and so would most likely have been one of the first to drown when the hull of the *Heather Rose* had smashed into the reefs and been ripped open wide.

Arabella shivered at the realization, tears filling her eyes again as she thought once more of Harry Palliser and of how, if not for him, she, too, would have died. That she was still alive curiously troubled her, as did her conscience, while with difficulty, she dressed in the dead woman's things. Had her need not been so great, Arabella would have refused the clothes; as it was, she could only hope that the dead woman would understand and forgive her for taking what was not hers. The garments fit fairly well; even so, Arabella felt naked in them. Despite her logical reasoning that Lucien Sinclair had already not only seen, but also touched her body intimately, she felt that she was so immodestly garbed that when he called out to her, she was hesitant to appear before him. But, at last, reluctantly, she drew back the blanket that formed the curtain between them.

"I thought that perhaps you had fallen asleep," Lucien explained at her inquiring glance, "and since you've not had any more nourishment for days than the liquids I managed to force down your throat, it would be best if you got some solid food in your belly so you can begin to regain your strength. Are you hungry?"

"Yes," Arabella replied as, to her surprise, she suddenly recognized that she was, in fact, famished. "It smells good . . . whatever that is you're cooking.'' She indicated the cast-iron pot hanging on a spit over the fire to heat.

"Rat-kangaroo stew."

"*Rat!*" she exclaimed, horrified.

"No, Miss Darracott. Not rat. Rat *kangaroo*. It's a small breed of an animal with which you'll not be familiar, since it's indigenous to Australia. This particular variety is rather like a rabbit, actually—a creature, by the way, that is *not* native to the Colonies, but which, along with deer and various other animals, was brought here over the years by colonists intent on re-creating, so far as was humanly possible, their life in England.'' His voice was dry.

"You . . . sound as though you don't approve of that, Mr. Sinclair."

"I don't." The statement was blunt. "You see, Miss Darracott, I believe that God intended man to live in harmony and grace with nature, not to disrupt and to destroy it; and introducing animals alien to a habitat is an unnatural disturbance that can lead only to chaos."

"Well, that is certainly quite an . . . an original notion, Mr. Sinclair."

"Not at all—since it's shared by many ancient peoples, Australia's Aborigines among them. Despite their so-called ignorance, savagery, and paganism, I have frequently found them to be a good deal more knowledgeable, civilized, and godly than the English gentleman who holds himself up as the sterling example for the rest of the less-favored world to follow."

"Indeed?" Arabella replied faintly, surprised at the contempt plain in his tone for men such as her father and Harry Palliser had been and whom she had been taught all her life to respect.

"You are shocked, Miss Darracott—and no doubt thinking that you have fallen into the hands of some heathenish blackguard, which is not so very far from the truth, I'll admit. Nevertheless, be assured that while justice may be blind, I am not; and it is therefore not my wont to judge as guilty those who are innocent of others' crimes." For a moment, his face seemed frighteningly hard and bitter. Then the look was gone as quickly as it had shadowed his face, and Arabella decided that she must have imagined it. Taking up a wooden bowl, Lucien ladled a portion of the steaming stew into it, then brought it and a spoon to where she sat. "Do at least try to eat," he insisted as she stared down at the bowl, not quite willing to believe that the meat it contained was not, in truth, rat. "Aside from the fact that my stew is really rather tasty, the sooner you recover your health, the sooner we can be on our way to Brisbane, where you may escape from my dastardly clutches." His mouth twitched with cynical amusement at the alarm that showed upon her countenance at his words.

Suddenly aware he was teasing her, Arabella felt the tension drain from her body. No man able to laugh at himself could possibly be quite so bad as he had at first appeared; nor would a man who really had evil designs upon her make light of his own dubious character. Besides, if it were true that they were hundreds of miles distant from any kind of civilization, what choice did she have but to trust him? Perhaps she would be better off dead; but even as the thought crossed her mind, her survival instinct was already asserting itself, struggling to prevail over her sense of maidenly honor and duty.

"I *will* try your stew, Mr. Sinclair"—despite herself, Arabella was unable to repress the wholly unexpected but answering smile that tugged at her own lips—"if only because it would be impolite of me to do anything else."

Throwing back his dark head, Lucien laughed aloud at that.

"Miss Darracott, I begin to fancy that I shall grow to regret the fact that you are, indeed, a lady." From beneath hooded lids, his pale grey eyes gleaming, he glanced at her in a way that made her suddenly all too aware of the thin cotton of the undergarments she wore, of the swell of her breasts above the camisole.

Blushing, she lowered her gaze nervously and applied herself to the stew. Although unfamiliar to her palate, it was, as he had claimed, very good, the meat tender and savory, as were the tubers, berries, and other wild edibles that filled her bowl. There was hard brown bread to eat, too, which she softened by dipping it into the stew, and strong tea to drink. To her embarrassment, Arabella ate ravenously, until her stomach felt as though it would burst; she could not remember when she had last consumed so much food at one sitting. The tightly laced corset she was accustomed to wearing precluded her eating more than a few mouthfuls of a meal before feeling full. But Lucien said only that it was good after her debilitating illness that she had such an appetite and, without being asked, refilled her bowl twice more before she was finally sated.

After supper, while Lucien scoured the dishes with

sand, then washed and packed them away, Arabella tried in vain to work from her long hair the salt, sand, and snarls born of her ordeal.

"I suppose that it will have to be cut off," she said at last, greatly dispirited, because she had been reared to believe that a woman's hair was her crowning glory. If Arabella had any secret vanity at all, it was her thick, heavy mass of chestnut hair, which she felt to be her one redeeming feature. "Have you a pair of scissors, Mr. Sinclair? If not, I can perhaps manage with a sharp knife."

"I've no doubt of that, Miss Darracott, since it would seem you are a capable young woman. However, I find myself curiously reluctant to be a party to the crime that cutting off your hair would surely be. So, let me see if I can help, why don't you?"

Taking the brush from her hand before she could protest, he settled himself behind her, beginning the task she had been unable to complete, his fingers surprisingly sure and gentle as he tugged and separated the tangled strands. That, at first, his hands trembled a little at the chore, Arabella was not aware, conscious only of her own anxious stiffening at his touch; for this was an intimate act that only a man who was a woman's husband or lover would perform for her. But then, again, Arabella reminded herself that she was being foolish, that if Lucien Sinclair had wanted to ravish her, he had certainly already had every chance to do so. There was little she could do at the moment, besides, either to fend him off or to escape from him if he chose to avail himself of that opportunity now. However, he did no more than work patiently on her hair until, at long last, he was finished. For a moment, she was aware of his hands resting lightly upon her shoulders, of his warm breath against her nape. Then, setting aside the brush, he spoke.

"There, it's done. Go to sleep now, Miss Darracott."

There was a raw, hoarse note in Lucien's voice that prompted Arabella to do just as he said. After he had moved away from her, she lay down upon the blankets. But despite her weariness, slumber did not come easily to her. Instead, she watched silently, surreptitiously, as, after feeding and watering the two horses, as well as the plumed white bird—which was apparently tame and which he called "Mate"—Lucien sat down before the fire and began to clean his carbine.

An adventurer and an opportunist, he had proclaimed himself, yet she felt there was more to him than that. He spoke like an educated man; only those of her own class would have detected from his accent that whatever culture and refinement he possessed were acquired and not an inherent part of his background. However rough-and-tumble his appearance, he must have some means, also, Arabella reflected, else he would hardly be in a position to buy land. Perhaps he had been an overseer of some English estate and he had left his lord and master to travel to Australia in the hope of someday owning his own manor in a land where class distinctions had grown increasingly blurred. Harry had remarked upon that new social structure, plainly upset and offended by the thought, it being the duty of the New South Wales Corps, in his opinion, to uphold not only English law, but also English standards.

She wondered what Lucien was thinking as he sat, brooding, in the firelight. For the first time, it occurred to Arabella that perhaps he viewed her as a burden. Plainly, he knew how to live off the land, while she herself was largely ignorant of life beyond Darracott Hall, where there had been a staff of servants to wait upon her hand and foot. Even aboard the *Heather Rose*, she had had Mrs. Beckett, the captain's wife, to chaperon her; one of the young girls from steerage to assist her, when necessary, with her appearance and apparel; and the steward to manage such matters as her nightly bathwater. While she was not a helpless child, neither had she ever before been called upon to care for herself, Arabella realized suddenly. All her life, as the squire's daughter, she had been attended to and sheltered by others. That Lucien Sinclair might find that task, which had been thrust upon him, unwelcome troubled her as she gazed at the deep woods that surrounded her and she thought of trying to survive them on her own.

Abruptly spying Lucien staring at her from where he sat by the fire, Arabella hastily closed her eyes, forcing herself to breathe deeply so he would believe her to be asleep; and presently, she did drift into slumber. Lucien remained awake, thinking about the feel of her soft, silky hair flowing through his hands. It had been more than twenty years since he had brushed a woman's hair, since his mother had died when he was little more than a young boy, leaving him behind, with only the memory of her to sustain him—and a lock of her sweet-scented hair.

Arabella Darracott meant nothing to him, nor he to

her. Yet, for whatever unknown reason, fate had thrown them together. Rising and stripping to his breeches, he lay down beside her, feeling strangely as though she somehow belonged there as, obliviously, she murmured in her sleep and settled unconsciously into the familiar curve of his strong, protective arms.

Chapter Five

Starry Inferno

When Arabella awoke in the morning, she found herself alone again. At first, panicked, she feared that Lucien had left her to fend for herself in the woods, to make her own way back to civilization. But then she spied his horses and packs, and saw that the fire in front of the shelter still burned; and with relief, noting that his carbine was missing, she deduced that he must have gone hunting. As she slowly sat up, she discovered that the dull throb in her head had lessened considerably and that the aches in her body were not so sharp and painful as yesterday. They would grow even better with movement, she knew. So she forced herself to rise, holding on for support to one of the stripped branches that braced the lean-to. She was still weak and faintly dizzy; but after a moment, she felt that she could traverse the short distance to the fire.

Once there, Arabella found that Lucien had set to one side to stay warm a "billy," as she now remembered he had last night called the containers, of water and one of the strong tea. A tin cup was waiting for her, too. Clearly, he had either anticipated her attempt this morning to leave her makeshift bed or else had hoped to entice her from it. As the latter thought struck her, her mouth turned down wryly at the corners. No matter that he had saved her life, he had doubtless, as she had suspected, chafed at the role of nursemaid. He looked to be a man who had lived a hard life and knew little of pampering; nor did he seem the sort to indulge a woman's whims. Well, and what of it? Arabella asked herself, a trifle impatiently. What right did she have to expect any more from a stranger than that? She was lucky he had cared for her; another man might have left her for dead on the beach or, once she had regained consciousness, abandoned her in the woods. Still, she would be wise to do whatever she could to get back on her feet as quickly as possible so as not to be a burden to Lucien. That he did not mean to mollycoddle her further was evidenced, she thought, by the fact that he had left the water and tea. Regardless, she was grateful for both. Pouring herself a cup of the tea, she carried it and the billy of water back to the shelter.

With the cloth and towel she had used the previous evening, Arabella washed as best she was able. Then, with the brush Lucien had given her, she brushed her hair and plaited it into a single long braid that she bound with a strip of ruffle already half torn, by the sea, from the petticoat she wore. As she unwittingly recalled the feel of Lucien's hands upon her hair last night, her cheeks flooded with color and warmth. Curious, that that intimate, husbandly act should somehow prove so unsettling to her, especially when she considered that he had touched her naked body in ways that perhaps had been more than just ministering, if her delirious dreams had any basis in reality. Despite her lack of a mother's guiding hand, Arabella's education was grounded in both life on a farming estate and classic literature; she was not ignorant of what took place sexually between a man and a woman. Since her knowledge, however, did not extend beyond the rudiments, she must rely on Lucien's word that she was still a virgin. Even so, she now believed that he had spoken truly; instinct told her that the harsh, husky note in his voice when he had finished with her hair last night had not belonged to a man recently physically sated, but, rather, to one hungry and aroused. Arabella shivered at the thought, realizing that she must take care to ensure that she did not provoke him beyond his voluntary restraints. She was going to be alone with him for many weeks if Brisbane were, in fact, hundreds of miles away, as he had claimed—and why should he lie, after all? Even if a town lay just over the nearest rise, she had no way of knowing that, as he must be aware.

Shipwrecked, stranded, she was utterly at his mercy. Once the authorities discovered that the *Heather Rose* had sunk, she, like everyone else aboard, would be presumed dead, Arabella realized now—as Lucien, his mind lucid, untouched by fever, would have grasped straightaway. That being the case, he could these past few weeks have done freely, without fear of reprisal, whatever he had liked with her, *to* her; for who would

have been the wiser, especially if he had chosen to
ensure her silence afterward by killing her? He could
still do as much; she would be foolish to think otherwise.
That, instead, he had sent her to bed last night was
surely a mark in his favor, an indication that he was
perhaps not quite such a scoundrel as she had initially
supposed. Still, Arabella decided, it would likely be
best if she made no mention of the Wyndhams—of
Uncle Philip, particularly. As the commander of the
New South Wales Corps, his status was nearly as important as that of the governor himself. Lucien Sinclair
had admitted to being an adventurer and opportunist.
Rape might not be his style, but perhaps holding her
for ransom might—and while Arabella felt certain that
the colonel would, in fact, voluntarily reward Lucien
for returning her safely to civilization, she did not want
Uncle Philip placed in a position where he might con-
ceivably be coerced into doing so. The more prudent
course would be to allow Lucien to believe that she
herself had money, which was, after all, the truth, and
would pay him handsomely for escorting her to Brisbane. From there, she could book passage to Sydney,
although the thought of setting foot aboard another vessel made her shudder.

That resolved, Arabella, feeling much more in command of her awkward situation, was able to greet Lucien, when he finally appeared, with something
approaching equanimity.

"Good morning, Mr. Sinclair. I see that your hunt
proved successful." She indicated the brace of what
she now recognized as rat kangaroos he carried.

"My hunts always do, Miss Darracott." His voice

held a soft, strange, arrogant note that was somehow as unnerving as the intense glance he shot her. "You shall not starve, at least, under my care. I see that you are looking much improved this morning. It seems I am not such a poor physician as I feared I might be." He dropped the dead animals to the ground and, sitting down, began with his knife to skin them.

"Yes—no . . . that is, I am indeed feeling better, thank you—and for leaving the water and the tea, as well. I appreciated both." Arabella paused for a moment, gathering both courage and breath. Then she continued. "Mr. Sinclair, I have . . . been giving considerable thought to the circumstances in which we find ourselves, and it has occurred to me that I must have proved something of a trial to you this past fortnight, perhaps even interrupted your surveying of the land you mentioned you were thinking of acquiring in this area. Further, there is the matter of your escorting me to Brisbane, which, if I have understood you correctly, I gather to be a long, hard journey of several weeks, at least. Since my current predicament is no fault of your own, it therefore seems only fair that you be compensated for your time and trouble, and I am not without the means to do that."

"Indeed, Miss Darracott?" One eyebrow lifted demoniacally, and she saw why, in her feverish dreams, she had mistaken Lucien Sinclair for the devil. The sudden glint in his eyes was both speculative and amused as he appraised her in a way that made her blush deeply. "Pray, do go on. I begin to find this conversation most interesting, I'll admit."

"I meant monetary means, Mr. Sinclair," Arabella

declared hastily, averting her gaze demurely. "Some months ago, my father, a country squire, died, leaving me as the sole heiress to his fortune, and while it is, naturally, being held in trust for me until I come of age, I have no doubt, once I reach civilization safely, that upon learning I survived the storm that sank the *Heather Rose*, my trustees will agree that recompense to my rescuer is very much in order."

"Indeed, Miss Darracott?" Lucien repeated, rather dryly, to her surprise. Then his lips curved in a mocking smile, and he said lightly, "Well, I won't deny that a bit of coin is always welcome. However, you needn't feel that you must bribe me to take you to Brisbane. My investigation of the land hereabouts was concluded, and I was traveling south along the coast, anyway, when I found you."

"Yes, well, that may be. However, I would still feel . . . more comfortable, Mr. Sinclair, if we reached some sort of a business arrangement between us."

"I'm not going to desert you out here in the wild, Miss Darracott, if that is what you fear. But if it will ease your mind, let us say, then, that I will act as your guide to Brisbane, and in return, you will pay me the sum of one hundred pounds. How does that strike you?"

"I—I don't know what the going fee for a guide is in the Colonies," Arabella confessed reluctantly. "So I can only assume that that amount is equitable, especially when I've little or no experience at the kind of trip it would seem from your horses and packs that we must undertake. However, I do not lack for common sense, Mr. Sinclair, and I am quick to learn, also. Therefore, you will not find me slow or unwilling to do my share of whatever needs doing. If you will teach me, I am certainly prepared to butcher and to cook the game you kill; and it cannot be very difficult, after all, to wash pots and pans, and to perform other like mundane chores.''

"Not to one used to such tasks, no, Miss Darracott. Your hands, however, I would venture to guess, are more accustomed to playing the pianoforte or to plying a needle at delicate embroidery, is that not so?''

"Yes, but please do not let that thought deter you from instructing me, Mr. Sinclair,'' Arabella insisted somewhat stiffly. "There is nothing wrong with honest hard work; and I am not so insensible that I cannot recognize how drastically my life has changed for the time being and that, as a result, I must adapt, as well . . . that what served me before doubtless cannot be thought expedient in this situation. Now, that said, perhaps you will be good enough to show me how to skin that second rat kangaroo?''

"Very well. As you wish, then,'' Lucien replied, and although his voice was tinged with amusement at her determination to soldier on in the face of her adversity, it held, too, a note of respect and admiration. There were not many women who would have confronted her current circumstances so intelligently and courageously, despite the recent multiple shocks to her senses, he thought, and without resulting to vapors, hysterics, missish airs, petulant complaints, or high-handedness. He did not mind being saddled with a female, but he was beginning to realize that there were advantages to her being one like Arabella Darracott.

She herself, however, was starting to think that perhaps she had been somewhat hasty with her offer of assistance. Lucien had moved so he was behind her, his arms wrapped around her so he could guide her hands as she worked at skinning the second rat kangaroo. He had done nothing improper; still, she could not help but be aware of his proximity, his masculinity. His whipcord body was strong and hard with muscle; his hands upon hers were sure and steady as he showed her how to grip the knife and to make the first cut. But her own hands trembled when she felt his beard stubble graze her hair, his breath warm against her ear, her cheek; and as a result, the incision was jagged, not at all like his own neat, initial slice in the first rat kangaroo had been. Still, Arabella persevered, forcing herself to concentrate on the task, to ignore her agitation at Lucien's nearness and her squeamish reaction to the skinning process itself. When it was done, he showed her how to scrape the pelt free of flesh and blood, then how to stretch it and, with thong, to lace it to a rough, square frame he fashioned of small branches, which he then placed in the shade so the hide would dry.

"You do not want to leave the skin in the full sun," he explained, "or it will be baked too dry; and while it is possible to cure a pelt over a fire, the heat will make the hide brittle and the smoke will yellow the fur, so it will not fetch so high a price as it would have otherwise. Some cool, airy place is best. And now, Miss Darracott, as you are looking rather pale, I would suggest that you have exerted yourself enough this morning and should return to bed. You have not yet fully recovered your strength, and there is no point in pushing yourself so you suffer a relapse."

Arabella was only too happy to comply with his demand. The combination of being so close to Lucien and the grisly chore of skinning the dead animal had, indeed, proved too much for her. While she had seen cattle, sheep, and pigs butchered at Darracott Hall, she had never actually done the job herself, never fully comprehended until now what it entailed. The thought that she had learned from a man whose hands had touched and handled her as intimately as they had the two rat kangaroos had unsettled her even more than the bloody task itself. Feeling rather sick, she lay down upon the blankets, turning so her back was to Lucien, so he could not see her face. Her mouth was dry, and her pulse raced jerkily. Perhaps her long days of raging fever had deranged her brain, Arabella thought; for she could think of no other explanation for why he should disturb her so, should elicit such strange feelings. His gleaming black hair, unfashionably long, shaggy, and unkempt, had nevertheless felt like silk when it had brushed her skin. His hands, strong and slender but weathered and callused from years of sun and manual labor, had felt like heated iron bands upon her own. His warm breath had seemed to send an electric shock coursing through her entire body. Never had a man affected her so. But then, she had never before been alone with a man for more than a short while, and even then, there had always been other people within earshot. Was it not likely, then, that under the same circumstances as those in which she now found herself, any man would make her feel as Lucien Sinclair did? Somehow, instinct told her that it was not so.

Even if her mind had not been unbalanced by her delirium, she was in a weakened, vulnerable state, Arabella assured herself stoutly, putting from her thoughts the fact that, however rough his appearance, Lucien Sinclair was still undeniably the most handsome man she had ever seen, more attractive than any man had a right to be. Doubtless, there were in his past countless women who had not proved immune to his devilish charm, his earthy appeal. She would be a fool to number herself among them. With innate honesty Arabella had long ago admitted to herself that she was no beauty. If Lucien Sinclair saw anything in her at all to arouse his interest, it was surely only because there was no other woman available to him.

Still, his hand upon her shoulder sent shooting through her a tremor such as she had once felt when she had accidentally struck her hoe against the trunk of a tree while puttering in the gardens at Darracott Hall. He shook her gently.

"Miss Darracott, if you're awake and hungry, there's breakfast now."

"Yes, thank you."

She rose to join him at the fire. He had made stew again, and she ate hungrily, speaking little, as did he. After the meal was finished, she insisted on scouring and washing the pots and pans, which Lucien showed her how to put away in his packs. Then he went to fetch more water from what he called a "billabong," which was a water hole in a dry riverbed.

"Would it not be easier simply to move the camp to the water, Mr. Sinclair?" Arabella inquired, puzzled, now that she thought about it, as to why he had chosen as a campsite a glade without a pond or river.

"Yes, Miss Darracott, it would. Unfortunately, however, this is crocodile country; and while freshwater crocodiles pose relatively little threat, saltwater or estuarine crocodiles are known to attack and to kill humans. They grow to a size of approximately seven meters in length and range widely over this part of the coast, particularly where water is to be found. To be safe, it is therefore best to build one's camp at least fifty meters from any water. As I told you before, you were a very lucky young woman, not only to have survived the wreck of the *Heather Rose*, but also not to have fallen prey to sharks or crocodiles. There are, in addition, in the Colonies several varieties of snakes, including pythons, which choke their victims to death, and others, three-quarters of which are among the most venomous in the world—not to mention spiders, scorpions, ticks, and leeches, as well as predators such as dingoes, which are extremely vicious and cunning wild dogs that run in packs." He motioned toward the blazing fire. "Now, perhaps you understand why I do not permit the fire to burn out, and why I do not suggest that you bathe in either a billabong or the sea, the latter of which, during the summer months, particularly, is a haven for box jellyfish, cone shells, stonefish, and stingrays, all of whose stings are poisonous and some of which can kill even a grown man."

Arabella shuddered as he cataloged these dangerous wild creatures, to none of which she had ever been exposed in England and so could only imagine.

"I . . . hadn't realized," she uttered faintly, aghast. "Mr. Sinclair, are you . . . quite certain, then, that one hundred pounds is a reasonable fee for escorting me to Brisbane? I would have no objection to some additional sum as hazard pay—"

"Thank you, Miss Darracott, for your concern. But, no. I have lived in the Colonies for more than a decade and so am quite familiar with their perils—and, as you can see, I have managed to survive," he observed dryly. Then, carrying a couple of billies and his carbine, he disappeared into the woods, leaving Arabella alone.

Now, however, she found herself unable to lie down and to rest. Instead, she huddled upon the blankets, listening to the strange noises of the woods, the loud chittering and screeching of unknown animals, the soughing of the wind that in her agitated mind metamorphosed into the slithering of some terrible creature through the thick, tangled undergrowth. Lucien's horses, tethered nearby, stamped and snuffled, tails switching away flies and other insects; and Mate—his cockatoo, she had learned the bird was called—preened and ruffled its feathers and squawked as it peered at her from the branch of an unfamiliar tree. A peculiar voice rasped, "Pretty girl," making Arabella nearly start from her skin before she realized that it was the cockatoo, that the bird could talk.

"Oh, Mate, you almost scared me half to death," she murmured, with a small, sheepish laugh. Then, as she had seen Lucien do, she held her hand up coaxingly to the cockatoo. After a moment, with a flutter of its white wings, Mate came to light on her wrist, his sharp talons making her wince. "Pretty bird," she said.

"Pretty girl," Mate reiterated.

"Well, it's kind of you to say so, but I know the

truth——and I suppose I've never looked worse in my life!'' Self-consciously, she brushed from her face strands of hair that had loosened from her braid, then gazed at the fading bruises visible on her bare arms. Lacking a mirror, Arabella could only imagine the state of her face, which she knew from its places tender to her touch was bruised and abraded, too.

Thinking about her appearance, really, for the first time since her ordeal, brought to mind Uncle Philip's son, Gervase, and what impression she might make upon him when they met again. He was several years older than she, which would put him in his early thirties now. She had never known him especially well, and she had been too young for courting when the Wynd-hams had departed from England for Australia. Still, she had always known that both her father and Uncle Philip had hoped that she and Gervase would someday wed. Since, despite her season in London, she had at-tracted no man whom she had felt was more interested in her than in her fortune, she had been glad of the expected match with Gervase. He was the brother of her best friend, Chrissie, so how could she help but come to love him once she knew him better? As in all this time, Gervase had married no one else, it had seemed clear to her that he must be waiting for her to grow up, that he was not averse to taking her as his bride.

But he would believe her dead now; and perhaps when he discovered that she was still alive and had spent many long weeks in the wild, alone with Lucien Sinclair, Gervase would no longer want her, particularly as she was not a woman whose beauty might cause a man to forgive her. The thought was discouraging. No matter what Lucien had said, Arabella feared that it would be difficult to hush up the scandal of what had befallen her, that while her virtue might remain intact, her reputation surely would not—and even if it did, such was her nature that she would feel honor-bound to tell Uncle Philip and Gervase, at least, the truth of her escapade. She wished she knew what Gervase's reaction would be; not for the first time in her life, she wished she were not so very plain, with only her long, heavy mass of chestnut hair and her speaking, sherry-colored eyes to recommend her.

"Pretty girl," the cockatoo croaked again, so Arabella sighed deeply as she abandoned her reverie to pay attention to the bird.

"Oh, Mate, if only that were true!" she whispered, her voice catching on a small, ragged sob of despair as she blinked back tears. She did not want to wind up a permanent fixture on the solitary shelf of spinsterhood, and surely, that now would prove her fate if Gervase refused to marry her.

That she possessed a quality more elusive and intriguing than beauty, Arabella was truly unaware. But Lucien was not. As, from the edge of the clearing, he watched her with the cockatoo, he thought she was indeed like the mermaid he had in his mind first christened her: something rare and captivating, with an unconscious sensuality that was alluring. She had yet to be wakened to passion; he knew that now—and when he thought of her lying with some man who would expect and desire nothing more from her than that she accept her wifely duty in his bed, thereby stifling her inherent wanton nature, Lucien was gripped by a wild, primal urge to fling her down upon the ground and show her what existed beyond the narrow boundaries of her genteel world. That if he did, she would have no recourse against him was a thought that had crossed his mind more than once, especially when he remembered the feel of her naked body beneath his hands, her oblivious, feverish response to him. She would not fight him long; in the end, she would want him; he would make her want him. But then he thought of the deep shame he knew with certainty that she would suffer afterward, and he recognized that no matter what he had become, he could not bring himself to break her proud, gallant spirit in such a terrible fashion. These savage fantasies were born of his hard, unsavory past, of the fact that he was a virile man in his prime and had been too long without a woman. Hell, Arabella Darracott wasn't even his type. Polite, prim, proper, and plain, she was the kind of female who, lest she be tainted by the contact, would twitch her skirts away from him in Sydney's elegant drawing rooms and freeze him with the cut direct. Had they not been caught in the wild together, had he not become aware of what seethed so hotly beneath her cool, calm exterior, he would never have given her a second glance.

He needed to search the beach again, to discover whether any more clothing had washed up on the sand, Lucien thought. The journey to Brisbane would be infinitely longer and more difficult if he had to look at her every day, garbed as she was now. The camisole was a shade too small and so was drawn tight across her full, round breasts, its low, scooped neckline revealing their generous swell, the hollow between them, its thin cotton exposing a hint of the dusky rose nipples beneath. Her waist was so slender that he could span it with his hands. The single petticoat she wore, damp in the muggy atmosphere of the tropical woods, clung to the long, graceful legs that he remembered opening inadvertently for him—and that he had dreamed of ever since, so that when he lay beside Arabella at night, it was all he could do to restrain himself, not to force himself upon her. Then, only the thought of her certain shame and the fact that he would be reduced to such an animal as had been the brutal guards in the Port Arthur Prison on Van Diemen's Land—Tasmania, they called it now— deterred him from reaching for her, from acting upon his violent desire while she lay sleeping. Even so, he knew he was still a predator more dangerous to her than any other about which he had warned her.

A muscle flexed in his taut jaw as he strode to the heart of the clearing, where he set down the billies full of water, and his carbine. Reaching into the pocket of his oilskin coat he withdrew a fistful of peanuts.

"Here." He handed them to Arabella. "Mate likes these."

She had been startled by Lucien's appearance, for she had not heard him approach. He moved like some sleek, powerful wild animal, she thought now, as she had upon first regaining consciousness and spying him—silently, lithely, as though he were one with the land; and he was possessed of a strong animal magnetism, too, as though just below his smooth surface lurked a savagery she could only imagine, for she had never sensed it before in another man. When she tried to envision her father or Uncle Philip in this hellishly exotic setting, Arabella could not, and she thought that perhaps it was just as well that it was a man like Lucien Sinclair, able to survive out here in the wild, who had found her. Most other men would probably have perished. Surely, someone as boyishly charming as Harry Palliser would have. There was nothing boyish about Lucien Sinclair. Even now, as he watched Mate take one of the peanuts from her open hand and, with his tough beak, crack open the shell, Lucien's smile did little to soften the hard, lean planes of his face. Now, by the light of day, she noticed for the first time that his left cheek was marked with a long, jagged white scar. Where had that come from? she wondered.

"What do you say, Mate?" Lucien prodded.

"Thank you," the cockatoo squawked, then, to Arabella's vast delight, gave a sort of little bow before stretching out one clawed foot to pluck another peanut from her hand.

"Why, he does tricks, too!" she exclaimed.

"Yes, a few." After placing on the ground a tin basin into which he had emptied the water from the billies for the horses to drink, Lucien took a currycomb from his packs and, stripping off his hat and oilskin coat, began to groom the two animals. "It takes time and patience to teach a cockatoo, and I've had Mate only a few years. I found him in the wild; he had a broken wing, which I mended, and he's been content to stay with me ever since. Since he's learned to talk, he's been company . . . of a sort."

"You have no family, then, Mr. Sinclair?"

"No."

The answer was so short and forbidding, and Lucien's visage grew so suddenly dark and shuttered, that Arabella knew intuitively that she had touched on a sensitive subject and forbore to ask him any more in that direction. Instead, lifting her thick braid from her perspiring nape and using her hand to wipe away the moisture trickling down her neck, she inquired:

"Is it always so hot and oppressive here in the Colonies in the fall, Mr. Sinclair? I should think you would be stifled by that long cloak." She indicated the oilskin coat he had tossed onto a rock protruding from the moist, grassy earth in the glade.

"It's oilskin, a necessity in the wild, Miss Darracott—and you are confused as to the season here, which I sincerely hope is only the result of your having forgotten that when you voyaged from England to Australia, you passed from the northern into the southern hemisphere, and *not* some ill effect your mind has suffered from your days of high fever."

"Yes, you're right, naturally: I *had* forgotten. How silly of me. Everything is either backwards or upside down here, however the case may be—including me, it would appear. Of course, it must be spring now in the Colonies. That's why the stars are different at night, too . . . why, when I was ill, I thought I had died and gone to hell. I remember looking up at the stars in the sky and thinking that the Big Dipper was gone, and so I could no longer be on Earth, could no longer be alive . . ."

"And that's why you mistook me for the devil?" One black eyebrow quirked upward; a sardonic smile played about the corners of Lucien's lips at the memory.

"Partly . . . yes," Arabella confessed, blushing and lowering her gaze, hoping he would not probe further; how could she tell him about the wicked, wanton dreams of him she had had during her delirium? "And partly because of the fire. Now, of course, I realize that it's a precaution against predators and that you had doubtless banked it higher to force my fever to break. But at the time, it struck me that I lay in an inferno."

" *'Nel mezzo del cammin di nostra vita/ Mi ritrovai per una selva oscura, Che la diritta via era smarrita'?"* he queried in fluent Italian.

" 'In the middle of the journey of our life/I came to myself within a dark wood where the straight way was lost'?" she translated the quote, surprised that he should know it, although she had guessed his education greater than that of most his equals. "Dante's *Inferno*. Yes, it was something like that."

"And have you 'abandoned all hope,' Miss Darracott?" Lucien's pale grey eyes glittered now with amusement and speculation; his voice was mocking—for clearly, he knew, as she did, that line to which he referred in the *Inferno*, as well as another that said: "Without hope we live in desire."

"No, not yet, Mr. Sinclair," she declared, her heart now suddenly pounding too hard and fast in her breast, her hands trembling a little as, Mate having finished his treat and returned to his previous perch in the tree, she brushed the scattered peanut shells from her lap.

"A pity, Miss Darracott," Lucien said lightly.

But the glance he shot her from beneath his hooded lids was such that Arabella had a sudden, wild urge to flee from him into the strangling woods. Only the thought of hideous man-eating crocodiles and poisonous snakes deterred her. If he noticed the pulse jerking erratically at the hollow of her throat, the rapid, shallow rise and fall of her breasts, however, he gave no sign of it as he patted the horses, put away the currycomb, and turned his attention to cleaning and oiling his saddle and boots.

"Leather rots quickly in the tropics if you do not keep the mildew from it," he explained as casually as though the words they had exchanged just moments before had never passed between them. "And you're right: Wearing an oilskin cloak can make the heat and humidity seem sweltering, but it's good protection against the spiky lawyer cane and wait-awhile vines that abound in this region. Where clearing has been done in the woods, farther south, stinging tree has sprung up and is to be avoided, as well." He frowned as he gazed at her delicate bare feet. "Let us hope we can find you some shoes, at least. Tomorrow or the next day, when you are stronger, we'll start south and see what else we may scavenge along the beach from the wreckage of the *Heather Rose*."

After that, the remainder of the day passed smoothly, if slowly. For the most part, Arabella slept off and on, made drowsy by both her weakness and the sultry air. Lucien wakened her at suppertime for a meal of small game birds he had roasted with wild berries and figs. After supper, he brought forth a chessboard from his packs, but she was too tired to play well and underestimated him, besides, so lost the first game miserably. She fared better during their rematch, although he won just the same.

"I have taken advantage of your weariness, I fear," he remarked as he gathered up the pieces and returned them and the chessboard to their leather bag. "We will play again another evening, when you are feeling better."

Arabella was annoyed with herself, for she was capable of more clever play. But she knew that even were she at her best, Lucien would have proved a superior opponent. One could learn much about a person over a chessboard, and now, she thought she would not care to have him for an enemy. His strategy had been both brilliant and ruthless; he had taken her queen without warning, and while she knew that that was the accepted rule among serious players, still, she had grown accustomed to her father's caveat: "Check to the queen, Arabella," he had always said. Tears filled her eyes at this recollection of her father. She would never hear his voice again; she was now truly alone in all the world, without his protection. Yet, strangely, she thought he might be glad that she had been rescued by Lucien Sinclair, would have respected, admired, and even liked him; for Tobias Darracott, being something of one himself, had never, like so many of his class, held a grudge against a self-made man.

The stars that Lucien pointed out to her in the darkness—among them the Southern Cross and the Rainbow Serpent, which, he said, the Aborigines believed to be one of their Dreamtime ancestors who had given birth to the world—shimmered before her eyes and finally vanished altogether as Arabella at last drifted into slumber.

As he had each night since finding her on the beach,

Lucien sat long before the fire, and his thoughts were long thoughts. He had been too many years alone, he recognized. To have Arabella Darracott so unexpectedly thrust upon him had affected him in a way he had not believed possible anymore. He had thought himself dead inside; that with her advent, something had sparked to life inside him was a realization that disturbed him greatly. Such feelings as now beset him had no place in the world he had so toilsomely with sweat and blood clawed out for himself in the Colonies. He would never forget that he had spent ten years of hell in Port Arthur Prison—nor must he be foolish enough to disregard the fact that neither would she, once she learned what he was and of the heinous crime for which he had paid so dearly.

Chapter Six

Walking Matilda

It was, in fact, a few more days before Arabella gained strength enough to travel. Still, once on the road to recovery, she made rapid progress, for she was young, and had since childhood daily taken long rides and walks across the Yorkshire moors; besides, she had been in the best of health before her ordeal. Now, the laborious, unfamiliar tasks she undertook not only quickened her appetite, but also served to take the place of the exercise to which she was accustomed. Between them, she and Lucien soon established a traditional pattern whereby he assumed the role of both provider and protector, and Arabella that of hearth keeper, to which role she would eventually add that of gatherer, as well, once she had learned the lore of survival that Lucien would teach her in the weeks to come.

Both his horses, while neither showy nor high-spirited, were fine, sturdy animals, chosen for their hardiness. Arabella rode mounted before Lucien on one; the other bore the packs. It was, after all, the only practical arrangement, she told herself. Still, his strong arm about her slender waist, his very nearness disturbed her. She was vividly aware of his hard body pressed against her own softer one, of his warm breath against her nape, of the masculine scents of sweat, tobacco, and bay rum that clung to his skin. The smoky fragrance of the cheroots she had seen him smoke once or twice reminded her of the aroma from her father's pipe, a smell that was familiar and safe in a world filled with redolence that was foreign and exotic, from the dank odor of the mangrove swamps thick with grey mud to the sweet perfume of the flowers and vines that tangled amid the tall trees to the salty tang of the Coral Sea, once Lucien had guided the horses from the tropical woods to the beach where the going was far easier.

After a short while, Arabella began to spy pieces of the wreckage that had washed up on the sand, splintered planks from the hull of the *Heather Rose*, a broken cask that might have held water or rum, a shattered crate that had doubtless contained some of the live chickens the ship had carried for its months-long voyage. Her heart ached to see this wrenching evidence of the vessel's tragic fate. Farther on, there lay a small trunk, smashed open by the sea, its sodden contents spilled and strewn upon the shore. Here, Lucien halted the horses, tethering them to a nearby chunk of driftwood, then helping Arabella to dismount. With seemingly no compunction whatsoever, he bent to rifle the sea chest and then to examine the wet garments scattered about, while she stood silently by, feeling like the worst of scavengers.

"Now is not the time for a conscience, Miss Darracott," he said dryly as he observed her inactivity, her expression of reluctance and disapproval. "You are alive and in need, while the poor souls whose possessions these once were lie at the bottom of the sea. Here, see if these will fit you." Emptying them of water, he handed her a pair of what had once been a young boy's leather boots.

"I . . . haven't any stockings," she uttered, demurring.

But those, too, Lucien found in the trunk, which had apparently belonged to a mother and son, Arabella realized sadly, tears stinging her eyes at the thought of the child who had died before he had ever really even had a chance to live. She would have continued to refuse the things Lucien thrust at her determinedly, but his dark, grim face warned her that he would brook no argument; so at last, sitting down upon the sand, she pulled on the stockings and boots, finding that they did fit tolerably well, the boots being only a shade too big for her dainty feet. A plain skirt, a matching, short-sleeved spencer, and a wide-brimmed hat were soaked, but in halfway decent condition. Little else was useable. The few garments they took, Lucien spread across the packs on the packhorse to dry in the sun, along with the boots he secured by means of a short rope to the beast's burdens.

"It is better than nothing, Miss Darracott, you must

agree,'' he insisted as he finished with the lacings. ''Or perhaps you have by now lost not only your sense of practicality, but also that of modesty?''

''Certainly not, Mr. Sinclair,'' she replied firmly, warm color staining her cheeks as his eyes raked her slowly, lingering on the swell of her breasts above her camisole. ''I have lost neither. Only, I cannot help but feel as though I were no better than a common grave robber!''

''Nevertheless, I feel certain you will be forgiven the transgression, since it was both unwilling and a necessity on your part,'' he declared as he assisted her back into the saddle.

She could think of nothing to say to that, so held her tongue, only to receive a low laugh for her pains, which caused her to stiffen her spine with indignation, so she no longer touched his chest. At that, he deliberately tightened his arm around her, easing her back against him.

''I don't want you to fall off, Miss Darracott.'' He spoke with amusement in her ear.

''There is little likelihood of that. I am an excellent horsewoman, Mr. Sinclair.''

''But you're not holding the reins—I am.'' For all his light, mocking tone, there was a note of warning in his voice that Arabella knew she would be wise not to ignore.

Lucien Sinclair had, she suspected, a black temper when provoked, and she did not want to incite him. There was no telling what he might do to her, all alone in the middle of nowhere as they were. With her offer of a guide's fee, she had hoped to put their relationship on a more professional footing, but she was aware that was the palest of whitewashes for the awkward situation in which she had found herself. In addition, while she was indeed much recovered, she had yet to regain her full measure of strength. Although she had never been one to make a choice simply because it was the easiest one to make, Arabella protested no further and allowed her body to rest against Lucien's own.

Overhead, the bright yellow spring sun beat down from an endless, clear blue sky almost devoid of clouds. The heat and humidity were offset along the coast by the breeze that swept in from the foam-crested, sapphire-blue Coral Sea that stretched infinitely to the east; still, for all her hesitation earlier at taking the clothes from the ruined sea chest, Arabella would, in truth, be glad when they had dried. She had always protected her skin from the elements, and the Australian sun was merciless, Lucien had told her. Those men who had proved brave enough over the years to dare to venture into the unknown heart of the continent—the Never Never, the Aborigines called it—where the land was rumored to be the hottest, had never returned. Presumably, they had met their deaths there, from the heat and only God knew what else. Australia was a harsh, unforgiving wilderness, as Arabella was starting to learn, far different from the England she had known all her life, with its cool climes, its grey mist, its inevitable rain, and its vast, sweeping moors abounding with heather and gorse. She so wished that she were home again at Darracott Hall, where she had been safe and secure; she felt as adrift now as though she still clung to the lifeboat that had proved her salvation. But, as she had known from the beginning of her voyage, there was no turning back for her. Whatever was to come, she must meet it head-on—and although Lucien was no knight in shining armor, she had cause to be grateful for him as the days and then the weeks passed. Without him, she knew she would never have survived.

It was he who killed the meat she ate—not only rat kangaroos and game birds, but also hedgehoglike, ant-eating animals called echidnas, fat lizards, and turtles and fish from the sea. From him, she learned how to gather the eggs of such birds as cassowaries and rifle-birds, as well as wild fruits and berries, and edible tubers and roots. He showed her the plants with medicinal properties, such as the gum trees that were prevalent over all the continent, with so many varieties that she could scarcely begin to remember them all. Giant banyans hung with orchids, elkhorns, and other epiphytes flourished in the tropical woods; then, as they moved farther south, acacias, banksias, palms, cabbage trees, and tree ferns with their huge, curled fronds predominated. Kookaburras and flocks of lorikeets and bats filled the trees; the woods rang ceaselessly with raucous noise that could give way, suddenly, to a silence that warned of a predator's approach. Lucien taught Arabella to be still and quiet at those times, until he discovered what danger, if any, might threaten them, and to keep the fire burning to discourage the wild creatures from drawing near. He insisted she learn how to shoot his carbine and the revolver he left with her in case she should need it while he was away hunting. As a further precaution, he showed her how to build the rough shelter and to saddle and to pack the horses, so she could perform those tasks alone if some mishap should befall him. The packs he called his "swag" or "Matilda," and sometimes as he and she traveled along, he sang a melodious folk song about "walking Matilda," which meant to carry a swag, as the Aborigines did when they went walkabout, and which term would before the turn of the century be mistakenly immortalized in a poem as "waltzing Matilda."

At night, they continued their fierce battles over Lucien's chessboard. He won more often than not—although not nearly so easily now that Arabella had fully recovered. When she retired to bed, he sat before the fire, brooding and sometimes smoking a cheroot. At those times, she studied him silently, pondering his thoughts. About his life before she had come into it, she learned nothing; he never spoke of it, and while curious, she was too well-bred to pry. She suspected that his memories of his past were painful, that he had suffered some tragic loss of which he did not care to be reminded. Her imagination, always vivid, conjured a romantic, tortured tale of unrequited love, which stirred in her breast a sense of sorrow for him. Lucien would have laughed at her musings if he had known of them, would have scorned her pity and flung it back into her face; but of this, she remained ignorant, for she could not bring herself to voice aloud her speculations, only to treat him with a kindness she instinctively felt that he had not known in many a long year. That in this, there lay an inherent danger to herself, she did not recognize, did not understand until it was too late.

While Arabella was not Lucien's victim, but, rather, a victim of circumstance, she was nevertheless as dependent upon him for survival as though she were his captive or slave. That this fact was inevitably bound to affect her mentally, she did not know. She knew only that she had never before experienced such a close and intimate relationship with a man as she did now with Lucien Sinclair. She grew accustomed to his dark face, learning to recognize his moods from his expressions; grew accustomed to the way in which his pale eyes watched her, with a peculiar intensity that made her feel strange and faint and feverishly hot, as though she were melting inside, on the verge of relapsing into her illness; grew accustomed to the feel of his strong hands upon her, lifting her into the saddle, holding her against him as they rode along. It was a measure of the familiarity that had developed between them that Arabella was only mildly shocked to discover, when she chanced to awaken one night, that Lucien lay beside her on the blankets, beneath the shelter of the lean-to they had built earlier that day. The curve of his arms about her felt so natural, so oddly comfortable that she realized he must have lain wrapped about her just so for many nights now, perhaps ever since he had found her washed up on the beach. It was, of course, the only practical solution, she told herself. Was he to sleep out in the open, with no protection from the elements, the wild creatures? And to construct two shelters when one would do? If she woke him up and righteously demanded that he find somewhere else to sleep, it was likely that he would only laugh and refuse to budge. Then she would be worse off than when she had been ignorant of his presence beside her. Besides, if he had intended anything untoward, he would surely have acted upon his designs before now.

So, in the end, Arabella did nothing, lying still and quiet in Lucien's embrace, listening to his rhythmic breathing, the steady beat of his heart, until she finally drifted once more into slumber. Her last thoughts before sleep overtook her were that at least she now knew why he always waited until she had gone to bed before he retired, as well as why he was always up before her, and that in the morning, there would be time enough to discuss with him the matter of their sleeping arrangements.

When the grey dawn that promised rain broke on the new day, Arabella found herself somehow strangely unable to broach the subject, after all—a cowardice most unlike her and for which she chastised herself severely, to no avail. Despite all her internal conflict, she still could not rid herself of the notion that it would be ridiculous to object to something that had obviously not only already gone on long enough to become habitual, but also that had done so without any real harm to herself—both facts that she had a dreadful suspicion that Lucien himself would mockingly point out to her. Nor would he hesitate, she felt, to catalog all the practical reasons for his sleeping beside her and that she had already reviewed in her own mind. Besides, what could she do, anyway, if he just point-blank refused to bed down someplace else at night? Leave him? Journey on, alone and on foot, to Brisbane? That thought was as ludicrous as thinking she had any real control over her present situation when, deep down inside, she knew she did not. Never before in her life had Arabella felt so utterly helpless. Frustrated and chagrined, she sought defense in a frosty silence bolstered by a pair of determinedly squared shoulders, coupled with a martial glint in her eye—none of which escaped Lucien's notice as he watched her vigorously brush and rebraid her long hair before she joined him at the fire.

"Got up on the wrong side of the bed this morning, did we, Miss Darracott?" he asked coolly as, together, carrying the billies, they trekked the distance to the billabong they had found for water before pitching camp yesterday evening.

"Actually, it was last night, Mr. Sinclair!" Arabella snapped tartly, the words somehow suddenly just spilling out before she abruptly clamped her jaw shut to cut them off, now perversely angry at herself and cursing her wretched tongue for giving voice, after all, to what she had previously decided would be best left unmentioned.

"So . . . that's it, is it? You awoke last night to find me in your bed."

"Yes, that's it—and you needn't say anything more, because I already know all the reasons for your being there."

"Are you sure?" Even as the provocative, taunting words left his mouth, Lucien knew he should not have spoken them. But if the past several weeks had been difficult for Arabella, they had been no easier for him, either.

"Mr. Sinclair!" Her once-pale white skin—now, despite the limited precautions of which she had been capable under the circumstances, turned the shade of gold dust by the sun, making her luminous eyes stand out like two huge gold coins in her face—flooded with color born of both indignation and humiliation. "You are no gentleman to speak to me thus!"

"So you've said before. But, then, I never claimed I was, did I?"

Unable to think of any satisfactory retort to that, Arabella stalked on to the billabong, so upset that she did not, as Lucien had taught her to, approach the pond cautiously, taking the time to check out her surroundings first. Instead, she knelt at the edge of the stagnant pool and began to dip the billies into the water. With the speed of lightning, what she had so carelessly mistaken for a rotten log floating on the still surface came without warning to life, lunging up from the water at her, massive maw agape, rows of teeth sharp and menacing. She screamed with terror, wildly throwing the billies at the crocodile's mud-encrusted snout as she turned to flee—only to be horrifyingly halted as the creature's powerful jaws abruptly clamped down hard on her petticoat, jerking her back so viciously toward the billabong that she stumbled and fell. Frantically, she clawed at the damp earth, sobbing, screaming, scrabbling for purchase, knowing nothing but that death was imminent.

Such was the tangle of her petticoat that as Lucien ran to the scene, he could not discern how she was caught, whether the crocodile had grabbed hold of her legs and was even now tearing them from her, or merely had a mouthful of billowing cotton. He was afraid to shoot for fear of hitting Arabella because her petticoat was twisted in such a way that he could not see the creature's head, the only sure target, its hide being so tough and thick that a bullet to its body would likely only wound and enrage it. He would have to take the crocodile on hand to hand. At that realization, without hesitation, Lucien dropped his carbine, ripped off his hat and oilskin coat, and, yanking his knife from the sheath at his waist, splashed through the billabong to leap onto the creature's leathery, corrugated back, straddling it, fumbling for its head to try to pry its great maw from Arabella. To his vast relief, at his intervention, the crocodile released her almost immediately, turning its savage attention to him, thrashing, wheeling, tail lashing violently. Recognizing that the creature intended to force him under the water, Lucien inhaled a deep breath of air before he was plunged beneath the surface to fight desperately for survival. He could hardly see in the murky water, could only strike blindly with his blade at the crocodile, while simultaneously clinging to it tightly every time it rolled, knowing that if he let go, it would be on him in moments in its milieu and that he would be finished. His one clear thought was that he must prevail—not only for himself, but also for Arabella.

Shaking so badly that she could not stand, she had by this time managed to haul herself from the pond and lay weakly, in shock, at its weed-grown, mucky edge, knowing only how narrow her escape had been, that it was a miracle that, while her petticoat was torn, she herself was unharmed. As she had watched Lucien and the crocodile both disappear, she had gasped with terror, tears streaming down her face. Now, she thought dimly that he would surely be killed and that it would be her fault, her carelessness that had cost his life. That fear was like a blade to her heart, piercing her to the core, filling her with a pain that was unbearable but that there was no time to analyze more closely now. Through the blur of her tears, she spied his discarded carbine on the ground. With trembling hands, she reached for the weapon, panicking at the realization that her mind was suddenly a blank, that despite all Lucien's lessons, she could not remember how to fire the carbine. But then, somehow, his instructions came to her; staggering to her knees, she moved automatically to carry them out, only to grasp, as Lucien had just moments before with regard to her, that she could not shoot, lest she risk hitting him as the pool's rippling surface suddenly erupted furiously and he and the creature burst from its depths, he slinging his streaming hair wildly from his eyes and gulping air gratefully.

Man and beast were locked in mortal combat, a death embrace as they grappled for supremacy, sending water flying in every direction before they just as abruptly vanished again, leaving Arabella with her heart in her throat. She lost count of how many times this scene was repeated; to her horror, it seemed to go on forever, until she thought that if the crocodile did not kill Lucien, he would surely drown, such was his struggle, his rasps for breath. But then, at last, he and the creature broke through the pond's agitated surface yet again, and he was on top of the crocodile, driving his knife down into the creature's brain, stabbing and twisting the blade, while the crocodile writhed in its mindless death throe, tail whipping slower and slower, until, finally, the brutal creature was dead. Relieved, exhausted, Lucien slid sluggishly from its back. Rolling torpidly, aided by a fierce, vicious shove from him, the crocodile floated away. For a moment after that, he just stood there in the billabong, his whipcord body bent as he coughed up water, strove for air, only dimly aware that it had begun to drizzle, that it was not only the turbid water of the billabong that dripped into his eyes. Then, without warning, his face dark and grim with murderous wrath, he strode determinedly toward Arabella, snatching her so violently to her feet that she lost her grip on the carbine, which slid to the earth, forgotten by them both as dark, primeval emotion suddenly exploded between them and they stared at each other, their adrenaline still pumping wildly.

"Are you all right?" Lucien demanded harshly as he flung his knife into the earth.

Frightened, still quivering from the aftermath of her ordeal, Arabella nodded quickly, mutely, her heart beating far too hard and fast in her breast, although not solely any longer just from the creature's attack. She had never seen Lucien kill before, had never seen him so infuriated; and it seemed to her as though he had metamorphosed into something as atavistic and savage as the crocodile itself, as though whatever feral thing she had sensed coiled inside him had now seized him in its grip. His wet garments clung to him like a second skin, making her all too aware of his lean, hard, muscular body, the power that seemed to emanate from him, like that of some predator preparing to strike. Rain and water streamed from his sodden hair down his cheeks; his pale grey eyes glittered like cold steel in the dull morning light; a muscle throbbed in his set jaw, making the jagged white scar on his left cheek stand out prominently against his bronzed skin. That she was unhurt appeared only to enrage him all the more. With a low growl, he shook her so roughly that she flinched and cried out softly, scared by the perilous, unknown thing that seemed to hover as thick as electric mist in the air.

"Damn it, woman!" he grated. "Don't you ever, *ever* walk away from me again like that out here! Do you understand? My God! When I think of what almost happened to you—" He broke off abruptly, his eyes darkening, his nostrils flaring with both anger and arousal as he took in her disheveled hair, half loosened from its braid, the pulse that fluttered wildly at the delicate hollow of her throat, the heaving of her breasts that swelled and strained against the thin, soaked cotton of her camisole, their dusky rose nipples visible, taut with fear, and something more.

Before Arabella realized what he intended, he jerked her to him, his hands ensnaring the strands of hair at her temples, inexorably forcing her face up to his, his mouth suddenly crushing down upon hers in a possessive kiss that was like nothing she had ever before known—hot, hard, hungry, unleashing something inside her that was as fierce and wild and primal as the man who set it free. Not even in her craziest delirium had she dreamed of Lucien kissing her like this, as though *he* were a fever, ravaging her, draining not only the last ounce of strength, but also the very life and soul from her body and then pouring it back in. Never in her life had a man dared to make free with her so. She was utterly unprepared for the shock of it, for the sudden, deep, insistent penetration of his tongue that brazenly compelled her lips to part and boldly insinuated itself inside, exultantly pillaging the moist, dark sweetness within, leaving no part unexplored, untasted. It was a kiss she was to remember the rest of her life—not only because of the saturnine Demon who took from her so savagely, but also because of her reaction to it. She felt as though she had without warning been swept up by a wild, atavistic wind that ripped her breath from her body, her reason from her mind, shattering her senses as surely as the storm that had shattered the *Heather Rose*, leaving her as weak and helpless as she had felt upon first regaining consciousness in the tropical woods. The earth seemed to drop away from beneath her feet, her knees to buckle; she knew she would have fallen had not Lucien held her so tightly, his hands now moving urgently down her back, deliberately molding her soft body to his own hard one, making her acutely aware of his strength, his masculinity, his desire for her.

Arabella was so stunned by his onslaught, by the hitherto unknown sensations he expertly wakened within her, both frightening and perversely exciting her, that she could summon no resistance, and acquiesced to the demands of his mouth and tongue, his hands that roamed over her as surely as though they had every right to do so. No man had ever affected her like this; and in that prophetic moment, she knew instinctively that here was a man like none she had ever before known, a man who would take what he wanted, seizing life and bending it to his will, as he had seized and now bent her, sending a fiery thrill that was like a lightning bolt shooting through her, setting her aflame. Her lips softened, melted beneath his own, opened, yielded to the forceful intrusion of his probing tongue that twisted and twined with hers until she was oblivious of all but him, was helplessly kissing him back with a fervor to match his. Against his chest, her hands trembled with the instinctive, however unrecognized longing he evoked inside her, crept up of their own accord to wind about his neck, to burrow through his long, shaggy hair as his lips moved on hers, searing across her cheek to her temple, the strands of her hair, her ear, before scorching her throat, the moist valley between her breasts. Roughly, his fingers caught the wide straps of her camisole, pulled them down, baring her delicate shoulders and then her full breasts, swollen and aching with passion, spilling like ripe, burgeoning fruit into his cupped palms that caressed and squeezed and pressed them high, his thumbs rotating across their tips, taunting them into hard, tightly furled buds. His beard stubble grazed her tender skin as he lowered his head, captured one dusky rose nipple between his teeth, drew it into his mouth, sucking hard, greedily, tongue teasing and laving, causing waves of unbearable pleasure to radiate through her body.

She whimpered and moaned again, only dimly aware that the low sound issued from her own throat. She burned as though a high fever raged through her again, as though her delirium were once more upon her. But this was no dream, she abruptly realized as the drizzling rain grew steadily harder, drumming against her up-turned face, her closed eyelids, her breasts that Lucien had bared and claimed so covetously, wakening within her feelings she had until now not known existed, had never imagined. Oh, God, what was he doing to her?

She must be mad or wanton, she thought dazedly, mortified as she struggled to regain her senses. In moments, he would be pressing her down upon the muddy earth, stripping her naked, forcing himself upon her—and to her everlasting shame, she now recognized that she had done nothing to stop him, had allowed him liberties that no man save her husband should have been permitted.

With a soft cry of distress, she began belatedly to strive wildly against him, taking him so by surprise that she managed to wrench free of his imprisoning embrace. She backed away, her eyes wide, dark, and stricken with the emotions he had aroused in her, her mouth vulnerable and tremulous as, with shaking hands, she drew up her camisole to cover her nakedness, acutely conscious of his eyes smoldering like twin embers as they raked her, and that his breath came as harsh and fast as her own.

"Arabella." His voice was low and raw with desire. He took a step toward her, but she held up her hands against him, as though that would ward him off, even though she knew how futile the gesture was.

"Don't . . . please, Lucien . . . just . . . don't." She would have turned and fled, but even as the thought occurred to her, she remembered what had happened before, what had led to his kissing her, and she stood rooted to the soggy ground, fearing the wild creatures of the woods, the man before her, and, most of all, what he had unleashed inside her—the dark, primitive thing that, somehow, she knew would prove, like the wickedness in Pandora's box, unable to be shut back up. "You're hurt!" she exclaimed suddenly in the tense silence that had fallen between them, noticing for the first time the blood that stained his left sleeve, a patch darker than the rest of his wet shirt, and now welling red despite the rain.

"I guess I wasn't quite fast enough during the battle with that crocodile," Lucien said slowly, realizing now how the injury pained him. He had scarcely been aware of it before, when his bloodlust had still been upon him. But now, at the sight of Arabella's distraught face, her pale throat working as she bent to tear a strip from the bottom of her petticoat, already half ripped away by the creature's attack, some of his anger and arousal drained away to be replaced by both pain and the abrupt weariness that follows intense physical exertion coupled with a burst of adrenaline born of fear or exhilaration. He had known both within the past several minutes, during his confrontation with and defeat of the crocodile, and his subsequent feverish assault upon Arabella.

She had wanted him, he thought now as she hesitantly approached and began to bind his wound until it could be treated properly upon their return to the campsite. Even now, he could have her if he chose, he realized as he gazed at her, taking in her long, loosened hair, tangled and streaming in the rain, her soaked undergarments clinging to her, the thin cotton of her camisole molding her generous breasts, outlining plainly her pink nipples, still taut and rigid, if not from passion, then from fear and cold. He remembered the feel and taste of them in his mouth, and it was all he could do not to finish what he had started. Instead, he fetched the billies, his hat and oilskin coat, his carbine and knife, knowing that the scent of the dead crocodile would shortly attract other predators, even those of its own ilk, and that he and Arabella would be wise to be gone from the billa-bong by then—a thought whose belatedness he cursed silently, knowing how he had endangered them both with his lust for her.

Wordlessly, they walked quickly back to the camp-site. The fire had been drenched by the downpour; the only way to build another one now was beneath the shelter itself. From his packs, Lucien withdrew an oil-skin tarp that he secured over the branches that formed the roof of the crude lean-to he and Arabella had fash-ioned last night, while she carried inside from the doused fire the stones that had ringed it. With his knife, she dug another shallow pit into the soft ground; then, with the dead limbs and decaying matter he had foraged from the tangled undergrowth of the tropical woods and so somewhat protected from the rain, Lucien managed to start another blaze, blowing gently on the kindling to fan it to flame as, after the waste of three precious matches, it finally sparked and caught.

Arabella had drawn one of the blankets about her and was using one end of it to dry her sodden hair, studiously avoiding looking at him, glad of the task that gave her something with which to occupy herself. She yearned to change from her wet undergarments into the drier spencer and skirt, but that was impossible with Lucien in the shelter, watching her every movement so in-tensely that she knew instinctively that it would take very little to provoke him into falling upon her again. She shivered at the thought. She dare not turn her back on him; there was no telling what he might do to her. Still, her conscience was such that she could not hold him entirely to blame for what had happened between them. When he had first kissed her, she had done none of the things a lady ought; she had neither protested nor screamed, struggled nor slapped his face. Instead, she had stood there and let him do as he wished with her. Her face burned with shame and embarrassment at the memory, and she could not meet his eyes as he untied her makeshift bandage and rolled up his sleeve to reveal the puncture wounds the crocodile had left upon his arm. She could not repress her gasp of horror at the sight; nor did she hesitate once more to approach him after she had sought cloths, soap, and medicines from his packs. He had saved her life not once, but twice now; no matter what, she could not forget that, and she had learned from Lucien how deadly a wound could be in the tropical woods if not treated promptly and thoroughly, how gangrene could set in, rotting the flesh.

"It—it would perhaps be easier to clean your injuries if you—if you . . . took your shirt off," she suggested, her gaze lowered as, careful to keep the blanket wrapped around her, she set a billy of water on the fire to heat.

"That may be, but I prefer to keep it on, thank you." The dark look on Lucien's face and the grim note in his voice told her that he did not trust himself to restrain whatever it was that had arisen from his struggle with the crocodile and that had found its expression in his passionate assault upon her.

Biting her lower lip, Arabella nodded her understanding, grateful for small favors as, with the hot water from the billy, she wet a cloth and soaped it and began to tend his wounds. To her relief, the punctures were not deep; during his conflict with the crocodile, Lucien had managed to pry the creature's powerful jaws apart before it had got a good hold on his arm. Still, the gouges were bloody and swollen, beginning to bruise, and she knew they must cause him pain. She cleaned them carefully, then doused them with carbolic before applying the healing salve he had used upon her own cuts and abrasions. Then she bound the whole with bandages from his packs. Through the entire process, he said nothing, did not even wince, although she knew that the carbolic at least must have stung agonizingly. When she was finished and he had rolled his shirtsleeve down over the bandages, he spoke at last.

"Arabella, we have to talk."

"We have nothing to say to each other, Mr. Sinclair," she insisted, forcing herself to project a calmness she did not feel and that was negated by the nervous note in her voice, the trembling of her hands as she neatly packed away the soap and medicines, and rolled up the unused bandages. "Except that I sincerely hope that what—that what . . . happened at the billabong will not happen again."

Lucien did not mistake her meaning; he knew she was not referring to the crocodile's attack upon her, but to his own.

"You wanted it as much as I did." His voice was low, harsh. A muscle flexed in his set jaw, betraying his turbulent emotions and how he held himself in check, as though it would not take much to set him off again, to incite his anger, his arousal.

Arabella shuddered at the thought, her heart drumming like the rain that beat its tattoo upon the oilskin tarp he had fastened to the roof of the shelter. Never had she felt as utterly alone with him as she did now, as though there were only they two in all the world and time had somehow frozen, hung suspended, waiting. The lush tropical woods that surrounded them were like the thick, tangled, thorny barrier that had encompassed the castle wherein Briar Rose had pricked her finger on a spindle and lain asleep for a hundred years; and now at this moment, Arabella felt as though she, too, slept, that, presently, she would awaken at Darracott Hall to find that the past several months had been no more than a long, disjointed, disturbing dream, and Lucien Sinclair himself a figment of her imagination.

"Y-y-you're wrong. I want nothing from you but for you to take me safely to Brisbane."

His short bark of laughter made her flinch and flush.

"That's a lie, my girl—and you damned well know it! You wanted me back there—No, don't bother to deny it, for we both know the truth: I could force you down right here and now, with no one but ourselves the wiser as to how it came about, and in the end, you'd want me—I'd make you want me—and don't think the thought hasn't crossed my mind more than once since I found you washed up on the beach, either! Oh, don't look so shocked, Arabella; for you can't tell me that you haven't thought of that yourself, although ladies aren't supposed even to know about such things, much less to dwell on them. Proper or not, you *have* thought about them—and that says something about you, too, doesn't it? Something I find quite interesting, I'll admit!" From beneath hooded lids, his grey eyes glittered intently as he appraised her.

The color that stained Arabella's cheeks deepened, for no matter how she longed to deny his accusation, she knew that Lucien was right, that she *had* thought of these things. Still, that he would put them into words, compelling her to face them, was both shocking and mortifying. She wanted to die. No one in her life had ever before spoken so to her. She did not know what to say, what to do in response. As she had realized before, leaving him to make her own way through the tropical woods, alone and on foot, was not a realistic option.

"Plainly, I am at your mercy, Mr. Sinclair," she observed stiffly, clutching the blanket she had wrapped around her. "Therefore, I can only trust that while you are no gentleman, you will choose to play the part of one."

"Look at me, Arabella. Look at me," he insisted when she stubbornly kept her gaze lowered, refusing to meet his eyes. His hand reached out, caught her chin, tilted her face up to his. "I'm not going to rape you . . . I'm not going to hurt you. Do you understand?" His voice was gentler now; his hand, while firm, was tender against her skin. "I lost my head, and while I won't promise that it won't happen again, I *will* try my best not to let it. Still, I would be foolish—as you are being foolish—to ignore . . . to deny what is happening between us. I want you—badly—and whether you're willing to admit it or not, you want me, too."

Deep down inside, Arabella knew he spoke the truth. She could not forget her horror when she had thought that Lucien might be killed by the crocodile, how bleak and bereft she had felt at the prospect of his loss, his death. What a fool she was indeed! Somehow, despite everything, she had fallen in love with him, she recognized now slowly, stunned. That was why had she had let him kiss her as she had, reveling in the savage feel of his hard mouth claiming her own soft one possessively. She wanted to belong to him. She was sick at heart at the realization, for he was a rogue, a scoundrel; and while she sensed that her father would have liked him, she also knew instinctively that Tobias Darracott would never have approved of him as a husband for her, and that straitlaced Uncle Philip, her guardian, certainly would not. There was no future for her in loving Lucien Sinclair—nor had he spoken of love, only of lust. Somehow, that was the most dispiriting thing of all.

"What you desire is . . . impossible, Lucien—as, surely, you must realize," she said quietly. "We come from two different worlds—"

"And I'm not good enough for yours . . . for *you*, Arabella." The statement was blunt, cynical, bitter. He laughed shortly again, his face now dark, shuttered, so she could not guess his thoughts. "Yes, you're right, of course. I *should* have realized . . . I *did* realize. Still, I dared to hope—Well, that doesn't matter. Suffice to say that I was temporarily mad and have now regained my senses. You needn't worry that I'll lose them again, because I won't."

With that terse declaration, he abruptly stood, shrugged on his oilskin coat, clapped on his hat, and picked up his carbine, ducking beneath the low roof of the shelter to step outside, heedless of the rain that continued to pour.

"Where—where are you going?" Arabella asked, stricken, terrified that he planned now to abandon her.

The expression on his face was so hard, so sardonic that she thought that even if he did not care for her, only wanted her, her rejection had nevertheless wounded him.

"Have no fear, Miss Darracott." The tight smile he flashed her was mocking and did not quite reach his narrowed, steely eyes. "I'm not deserting you—nor, much as the idea tempts me, I confess, will I hold that threat over your head to compel you to surrender yourself to me. We agreed that you would pay me one hundred pounds to escort you to Brisbane—and since I am a man of my word, I will keep my end of our bargain. I am just going hunting, after which I will return to care for the horses, as usual. While I do not insist upon your traveling in this rain, neither do chores cease because of it. You, however, would do well to remain within the protection of the lean-to; no doubt, it is a poor substitute for your world—but to leave it is to enter into mine."

If there were a warning implicit in those last words, he did not enlarge upon it, but loped into the woods, leaving Arabella alone with her thoughts. Naturally, refusing him had been the only sensible course of action, she told herself despairingly; anything else would have been unthinkable. He did not love her.

It was only when she tasted their salt upon her lips that she realized that it was not rain, but tears, that streamed down her cheeks.

Chapter Seven

The Coral
Enchantment

What had he expected—that Arabella would fall into bed with him simply because he wanted her? Lucien asked himself angrily as he strode away from the campsite. God, what a fool he had been! Imagine his thinking even for one moment that she was different from all the other women of her ilk, that she would want a man—an *ex-convict*—like him. Not that she knew the truth about his background, of course, since he had not told her; still, even if he had not spent ten years hard labor at Port Arthur Prison before acquiring his ticket-of-leave, she would have been far beyond his reach. It was senseless to keep dwelling on that long, heavy mass of chestnut hair, those huge sherry-colored eyes, that body that would have tempted a saint. He was a Demon, and Arabella Darracott was not for the likes of him. He ought never to have kissed her, spoken to her as he had of his desire for her. A *gentleman* would have taken her for a moonlight stroll, brought her flowers, quoted love poems softly in her ear—and then seduced her, Lucien thought contemptuously; for he was well acquainted with any number of supposed gentlemen and officers in Sydney and Brisbane, corrupt, unscrupulous men worse than many he had known in prison. Nor was he unfamiliar with the nocturnal habitats of those men, with places like The Rocks in Sydney, or with the vices such hells contained, having sampled them himself on more than one than occasion. But he had never taken advantage of an innocent, of a woman like Arabella. Have her, he would if he could—but not on terms less than honest.

What prompted his feelings toward her, Lucien did not choose to examine more closely. He was a hard man who had lived an even harder life. It had been many long years since he had allowed any of his gentler emotions to escape from the strong wall he had built around his heart. That, somehow, Arabella had succeeded in penetrating that barrier was something he was not yet prepared to admit. The wife he had once loved had betrayed him; for the punishment meted out to her, he had been sentenced to fourteen years in prison and transported to Australia. He had neither forgotten nor forgiven that—nor would he. If she learned of the past that haunted him, how much more then would Arabella spurn him? She was right: There was no hope, no future for whatever lay between them. He would deliver her to Brisbane, collect his £100, and consider himself well rid of her. That he would never forget her so easily as that was a thought Lucien determinedly shoved from his mind.

There was a fresh wariness between her and Lucien now, Arabella knew, although it was very different from what she had felt at the beginning of their relationship. She no longer feared that he would force himself on her, suffered only the smallest qualm that he continued to sleep beside her at night. What unnerved her was the way in which he watched her ceaselessly, intensely, no longer troubling to hide his hunger for her, but devouring her with his eyes. Such was her love for him, her distress at the rift between them, that had he not also been exceedingly cool and polite toward her, she might have relented and given in to him as the days passed and the two of them continued their journey south toward Brisbane.

Although they still encountered patches of tropical woods and swamps, they now journeyed into forests and across savannas that were grassier and more open, overlooked by tree-covered plateaus and hills and sudden volcanic outcrops, and that stretched to mudflats and long reaches of shore upon which the sand dunes were the many colors of a rainbow—from minerals, Lucien informed Arabella when she asked, struck by the wild beauty of the wending beaches that made her think of Moomdagytta, the Aborigines' Rainbow Serpent, about which he had told her and to whose conception, perhaps, long ago, the rainbow beaches had contributed. There was, in the mountains, he said, a place that was the home of Moomdagytta, and so that was holy to the natives. He himself had not seen it, but had heard of it from the Aborigines. He had grown friendly with them over the years, and learned their language and lore. It was with their medicines that he had treated her when she had lain feverish and ill.

How long ago that seemed now to Arabella. Soon, within the next day or two, according to Lucien, they would arrive in Brisbane. She could hardly believe that the end of their travels was at last so near; nor could she rid herself of her despair at the thought of Lucien leaving her life, as he would surely do then. Perhaps she would never see him again. She knew that would be for the best, but her heart still ached at the realization. Why, of all the men in all the world, should he be the one with whom she had fallen in love? she asked herself bitterly, condemning herself for a fool. He was not even a proper person for her to know. Yet, as she slowly removed her spencer and skirt and carefully folded them away, as usual, for the evening, she could not help but remember that, rogue or not, he had saved her life not once, but twice—and had taken nothing from her. Perhaps he did care for her. Perhaps it was only that he was not the kind of man to whom the words she would have him speak came easily—and even if he said them, what would it avail her in the end? Uncle Philip was not in the least likely to give his consent to her wedding such a man as Lucien Sinclair; and as her guardian, the colonel had the legal right to withhold her fortune until she was twenty-five if she married without his approval. Still, if it were her inheritance and not herself that Lucien desired, he would surely, not knowing the terms of her father's will, have taken steps, however unscrupulous, to ensure that she was compromised before they reached Brisbane, so she would be compelled to wed him.

"Miss Darracott, we have company."

As, startled from her reverie by Lucien's low announcement, Arabella glanced up from brushing her hair, she could not repress a gasp as she spied a dozen or more armed men and women emerging from the shadows that engulfed the campsite. How long the natives might have been standing there, watching her, she did not know; for their skin was so black as to have made them one with the night, and what few garments they wore did little to conceal their dark nakedness. Frightened, she instinctively looked to Lucien for protection; but to her surprise, he evinced no concern, greeting the Aborigines in their own language, apparently bidding them welcome and inviting them to be seated around the fire. Then he turned to Arabella.

"There's no need to be alarmed, Miss Darracott. These particular natives are friendly; I've known a couple of them for quite a while. However, I should warn you that as, doubtless, you have never seen a blackamoor, so they are unlikely to have seen a white woman. The women, especially, will be very interested in your hair and clothes, and will probably want to touch you. I would suggest that now is not the time to be standoffish."

From this, Arabella understood with relief that while Lucien believed there to be little danger, he remained on his guard. When she stepped from the shelter, the women did indeed gather around her excitedly, exclaiming and reaching out shyly to stroke her hair and skin and to examine her garments; and she was glad Lucien had thought to forewarn her of this, since she would have been scared by it, otherwise. But the women were smiling, and now, Arabella felt some of her fear dissipate in the wake of their curiosity, warmth, and friendliness. Despite their shocking, primitive appearance, they were not so very different from her, after all, she thought, but like women the world over, with the same interest in clothes, jewelry, households, and children; for some of the Aborigines carried babies in wide slings that permitted the infants to lie nestled against their mother's stomach, hips, or back. A thick savory stew was cooking on the fire, and gesturing to the women, Arabella indicated that they might help her if they wished as she retrieved plates and bowls from Lucien's packs. There were not nearly enough dishes to go around, but it seemed that the Aborigines were not averse to sharing; nor were they slow to produce their own contributions to the meal: dried meat and smoked fish; a mixture of dried fruits, tubers, roots, and nuts that Arabella had watched Lucien himself make on occasion; and a strongly fermented fruit wine.

Somehow in all the confusion, she wound up sitting beside Lucien, sharing his bowl and tin pannikin, an act, it seemed to her, that was fraught with such intimacy and significance that she could hardly eat. As a result, after the initial shock of the potent alcohol upon her palate had passed, Arabella drank far more than she ought to have, her cheeks growing flushed in the firelight, warmth suffusing her entire body, and her head beginning to spin a little. Still, she was afraid that the natives would become upset if she rejected their wine, and so she continued to sip from the cup every time it was refilled by one of the Aboriginal women. All through supper, Lucien kept up a steady stream of pleasant conversation with the men, sometimes translating a remark or two for Arabella's benefit. He sat so close to her that she could feel the heat of his body against her own, was vividly aware of his proximity, of his handsome profile, and, now and then, of how he glanced at her, his eyes openly admiring and filled with that strange, hungry light she had come to recognize so well. Although she suspected that he had a hard head for liquor, she could not help but think that the strong wine was affecting him, too—a thought that made her shiver both with fright and a perverse, perilous excitement that he should lose his head again and kiss her. Deep down inside, if she were honest with herself, Arabella knew she must admit that some treacherous part of her half wanted him to.

"Are you having a good time, Miss Darracott?" he asked her now.

"Yes, actually. Does that surprise you, Mr. Sinclair?"

"A little. Most ladies of your class would not find this an enjoyable experience, but be shocked and offended at the Aborigines' nakedness, for example."

"I . . . do find it . . . primitive and disturbing— however, not nearly so much as I believe I would have before the shipwreck. The heat and humidity of this region are so oppressive that wearing a surplus of clothing must be nearly unendurable. Swathed in a—in a corset and layers of petticoats and undergarments, I think I should never have been able to travel as we have.''

''Then our visitors are most appropriately dressed, are they not?'' Lucien observed, as he gazed at her by his side, wondering if she were aware of the beguiling picture she presented to him, of her own sultriness, as though Australia had somehow left its mark upon her in a way equally as primitive and disturbing as she found the natives' nakedness.

Arabella had not had a chance to rebraid her hair for the evening when the Aborigines had arrived so silently; now, it tumbled about her shoulders and down her back in a wild tangle of curls charmingly disarrayed by the tangy breeze that swept in from the sea. Her sun-gold face and bare arms glowed with rose from the wine and firelight; her eyes were wide and shining like twin gold coins in the soft light cast by the blaze; her ripe-cherry mouth was moist from the wine and slightly parted. Lucien remembered the feel and taste of her lips beneath his own, and his loins tightened sharply with desire at the sight of her. Half drunk, she was oblivious of the fact that one wide strap of her camisole had slipped from her shoulder, leaving it naked and revealing a generous measure of the swell of her breasts he ached to touch and to taste again, no matter how he had tried to tell himself that he felt nothing but contempt for her and her kind. Every time he thought of her passion being smothered by some cold or clumsy husband, of her being sold into marriage with the highest bidder for her hand, something wild and terrible rebelled inside Lucien. She deserved better than that, better than him, too, as she had known, regardless of the fact that her rejection had hurt and angered him. At least he would not stamp out her innate earthiness, force her to suppress her inherent sensuality, to become something she was not and never could be now without slowly dying inside. She had had a taste of freedom seldom granted to women of her ilk; he wondered if she knew how difficult that was going to be for her relinquish upon her return to civilization.

Still, it was none of his concern what happened to Arabella Darracott in the future, Lucien reminded himself stringently. He did not even know why he should give a damn, except that he still wanted her, regardless of how she had professed to scorn him.

The supper was ended; and now, while Arabella and a few of the older women gathered up the plates and bowls, scouring them with sand, then washing them and packing them away, some of the men brought forth instruments they had carried along with their boomerangs and spears: small, crude drums and pipes, mostly. The Aborgines loved to dance, Lucien had told her, and now, it appeared that she was to be treated to that sight as the musicians began to play and the other men and women to move in time to the strange, steady rhythm. After that, the night seemed to Arabella to take on a surreal quality, like the dreams of her delirium. Dimly, she recognized that she had drunk too much wine; her head reeled dizzily as, after the dishes were done, she carefully made her way back to Lucien and sat down beside him to watch the impromptu entertainment. The drums were fashioned from short, hollow logs with animal skins stretched tight across one end; the sound they produced was primal, a tattoo that spoke to something equally atavistic in Arabella, so it seemed that they pounded in her brain, her blood, as the beat grew increasingly harder, more frenzied. The pipes were thin, reedy instruments whose airy, high-pitched tune was like the breath of a wild wind that had blown at time's beginning. The dancing of the natives themselves was like nothing she had ever before witnessed: shocking, unbridled, uninhibited, frankly sexual, making her feel as hot and flushed and dazed as she had felt when her fever had been upon her.

One of the young Aborginal women, beautiful in a foreign, exotic fashion with her long brownish black hair and dark skin, danced before them—but it was obvious that it was Lucien for whom she performed, her arms teasing and beckoning, her full, bare breasts with their dusky nipples swaying, her grass-skirted hips shaking, offering tantalizing glimpses of the naked flesh beneath. His lustful appreciation for her was plain upon his face, and Arabella felt a terrible, unexpected stab of jealousy pierce her being at the sight. Suddenly, she could stand the night no longer. It was horrible; the natives were horrible; *he* was horrible! That he would subject her, a lady born and bred, to these crude, disgusting heathens and their lewd behavior was the height of barbarism and vulgarity! She would not suffer any more of it! Forgetting that she had, until now, enjoyed the Aborigines and the evening despite herself, Arabella staggered to her feet. Holding one hand to her head, which was pounding as hard and furiously as the drums, she stumbled toward the lean-to, cursing Lucien Sinclair and herself, too, for being such a fool as to fall in love with someone so wholly disreputable, indecent, and unsuitable. That he would soon be out of her life was something for which she should thank her lucky stars!

"Arabella? Are you all right? Arabella?"

"Let me go!" she spat, violently jerking away from Lucien, who had followed her, and scrambling into the dark shelter to escape from him, snatching closed the blanket secured to the rope strung across the opening to block the entrance. "Go away, and leave me alone! Do you hear? You are the most—the most . . . *disgusting* man I've ever known, and I don't want anything more to do with you . . . ever! You are hereby discharged from my employment! I'll go the rest of the way to Brisbane by myself and mail you your money once I reach Sydney!" Embarrassed at hearing herself slurring her impetuous words, she flung herself down on the blankets inside, burying her face to muffle the sobs that rose inexplicably in her throat.

But to her mingled despair and sudden, incomprehensible elation, Lucien did not comply with her indignant demand. Instead, he crawled beneath the blanket across the entrance into the lean-to, laughing softly, mockingly, in the blackness as he pulled her now wildly struggling figure into his arms. With her fists, she pummeled his chest until he captured her wrists, with one hand pinioning them behind her back, while with the other, he caught her jaw and forced her mutinous, tear-stained face up to his.

"Why, Miss Darracott, I do believe that you're drunk," he drawled, his voice low, tinged with both an amusement that incensed her and a huskiness that made her breath catch in her throat and her heart begin to hammer erratically in her breast.

"A lady . . . is never . . . drunk." She enunciated each word slowly, carefully, having some dim suspicion that despite her words to the contrary, he was absolutely, infuriatingly right, and wishing fervently to prove him wrong.

"That's a cartload of . . . manure. I've seen plenty of drunken ladies in my day, I assure you, and you are currently definitely to be numbered among them. I thought you were having a good time. So, why'd you run off that way? Hmmm?"

"As if you didn't know!"

"Uh-huh. Jealous, were we?"

"Certainly not!"

"Of course you were. Native or not, she's a very lovely, alluring young woman."

"And I'm not? No, don't answer that! I'm not vain— at least, not very; I know . . . I've always known, ever since childhood . . . that I'm not beautiful."

"I know that's what you think, but you're wrong, Arabella. You *are* beautiful . . . beautiful, bright, beguiling, bewitching . . . A man would have to be a fool not to see it—and I'm no fool, my girl, I promise you. That's why I've wanted you so badly; why, despite everything, I want you still. . . ."

His hand still cupped her face; his mouth was just inches from hers in the darkness, his breath warm against her skin. He still held her arms imprisoned behind her back, so she was arched against him, the sensitive tips of her breasts just brushing his chest. Now, at his words—which filled her with wonder and gladness—and at the raw desire in his low, hoarse voice, an electrifying shiver ran through her, and her pink nipples grew taut against him. The rough chambray of his shirt rubbing the thin cotton of her camisole against them was an exquisite sensation, sending ripples of delight spiraling through her body. Outside the shelter, the drums of the Aborigines continued to pound exotically, a rhythm as hard and fast as that of her heartbeat; the pipes soared and dipped and echoed, teasing, taunting, enticing, like the dancers themselves, whose sensual movements had branded themselves on her memory. When Arabella thought of them, liquid heat suffused her body, made her blood burn as though it were molten. Lucien was going to kiss her, she knew; what was more, she wanted him to.

Her eyes fluttered shut, her lashes casting crescent smudges against her cheeks; her mouth parted for Lucien's own as it inexorably closed over hers, roughly, rapaciously, as though he were a man starving and would swallow her, devour her. His lips nibbled and sucked hers; slowly, lingeringly, his tongue traced the outline of her mouth before plunging deep inside to plunder the dark, moist secrets within. The taste of her was sweeter than nectar upon his tongue as he probed and explored and savored, his tongue wreathing hers until she whimpered and moaned against him, gasping for breath as he slanted his lips fervidly across her cheek to her temple, her hair, setting her atremble, aflame with the fierce, wild sensations he aroused in her, that left her as dazed as the heady wine had, her senses scattered to the four winds. Her will and her mind seemed to melt away; if she had once known wrong from right, she did no longer, knew only Lucien and desire.

"I'm no good for you, my girl," he muttered thickly in her ear, "and in your heart, you know it. So tell me that you don't want me, Arabella. Tell me now . . . because if you don't, I'm going to take you right here and now on this hard ground, and make you mine, I swear it! There won't be any holding back for me then—or any turning back for you. So consider this fair warning. Speak now, or forever hold your peace, as the saying goes. Tell me that you don't want this, that you don't want me. . . ."

"But I do, Lucien. I *do* want you." Was that really her own voice, Arabella wondered dizzily, so soft, so slurred, so breathless? He had insisted she was drunk, and surely, she must be to have said such a thing. Or perhaps she was mad. But somehow, she did not care, could not bring herself to call the words back. "I love you. God help me, but I do. Take me. Make love to me. Please. . . ."

At that, with a rasp, a groan, a whispering of her name, Lucien claimed her mouth once more with his own, kissing her again and again, as though he could not get enough of her. His lips were hard and demanding against hers, his tongue soft and insistent. His teeth grazed the tender flesh of her lower lip, and she tasted blood upon it. A wild thrill of pleasure and pain such as she had never before experienced shot through her, inciting and exciting her, filling her with violent longing as he lowered her down upon the blankets, his weight covering her so she could feel the hard evidence of his desire pressed against her thighs. At that, she shook with both fright and anticipation, wanting desperately to speak of her ignorance and uncertainty, the gnawing feeling that she would not please him and her fear that, when the time came, he would hurt her; for she had heard that there was always pain for a woman the first time.

But it was too late. Raining searing kisses on her mouth, her throat, the swell of her breasts, he was already slowly unfastening the buttons of her camisole one by one, then pushing the garment's edges aside to reveal her burgeoning breasts taut with passion. Moaning, he cupped them with his palms, squeezing and kneading them, pressing them high for his lips as he bent his head and his tongue rasped across first one rosy nipple and then the other, circling and teasing it before he drew it into his mouth and sucked it so hard that it was flushed, rigid, and distended when he at last released it. He nipped it gently then with his teeth, laving it with his tongue before seeking and capturing her other nipple to taunt it as exquisitely as he had the first. Ripples of rapturous delight radiated through her at his kisses, his caresses. Without her even realizing she did so, Arabella reached up to wrap her arms about his neck, her fingers twisting and twining in his long, shaggy black hair as, with small, oblivious whimpers, she urged him on, instinctively yearning for more.

Dimly, she realized that no matter how she had tried to fight her feelings, to deny them, she had spoken truly when she had told him that she wanted this, wanted him. Perhaps she had wanted him from the very beginning, when, in her delirium, she had dreamed of his making love to her like this. Now, she would know in reality what she had before only imagined and longed for; she would learn firsthand those secrets and mysteries about which she had hitherto only read in her father's library, in books he had surely not intended her to peruse. Now, she would discover those things about which other young women had whispered behind their fans and palms, and giggled slyly, eyes wide with disbelief or narrow with knowing—as Lucien's were when he lifted his head to look at her, to kiss her lips again possessively, his tongue opening them so they yielded pliantly for his thrusting invasion.

Such were the feelings he evoked inside her that she was hardly aware of his hands easing her camisole from her shoulders, then slipping her petticoat from her hips and casting it aside. His mouth trailed hotly down her throat, found the sensitive place where her nape joined her shoulder. Gently, he bit her there, the bite turning into a kiss that was like an electric shock coursing through her entire body as he dipped his tongue into the delicate hollow. Then he lowered his lips to lick away slowly, tantalizingly, the sweat that trickled down the valley between her breasts as he stroked and fondled them again before kissing her belly, the curve of her hip as, despite her soft cry of sudden protest, he deliberately tugged away her pantalets so she lay naked beneath him.

Despite the darkness of the shelter illuminated only dimly by the moonlight and firelight that filtered through its closely woven branches, Arabella attempted to cover herself. She had not thought that Lucien would want her completely naked and was shocked and shamed by the realization; for she had been led to believe that not even her husband would see her thus, that he would do no more than lift her nightgown to exercise his conjugal rights.

"Shhhhh," Lucien murmured against her mouth, kissing her reassuringly as he caught her hands again and, with one of his own, pinned them over her head so she could not conceal herself from him. "This is how I want you, how I've wanted you since that day I found you on the beach, how I've imagined you in my mind: naked and opened for me . . . like this, Arabella. . . ." Inexorably, his free hand glided down her hip, her leg, to insinuate itself between her thighs, compelling them to part, although she struggled a little against him, suddenly afraid. "Shhhhh," he repeated, kissing her again, calming her maidenly fear as one corded leg spread her wide. "I'm not going to hurt you, but to give you pleasure, so it will be easier for you, this first time, when I take you."

She shivered at his words, for they meant that there was indeed some pain, however slight—and that he did not intend to take her only once, but more than that, countless times, perhaps, in countless ways. . . . Erotic images filled her mind, turned into reality as his hand found her, cupping her mound, touching her where no man ever had, eliciting a small, ragged gasp from her lips at the intimate caress. She could not escape; he held her down, gently but firmly as, at first, he just rested his palm against her, continuing to kiss her deeply, his tongue tangling with her own, muting her paradoxical whimpers of both demurring and longing. Then, lightly, he began to rub his hand against her, his fingers stroking the narrow channel that cleaved her nether lips, his thumb flicking the small key to her delight until he felt the tender folds of her burgeon, trembling and melting beneath his onslaught, the secret heart of her unfurling like a bud bursting into flower. Her low moans bespoke a different kind of distress as she strained helplessly against him, seized at the very core of her being by a burning, hollow ache that cried out for fulfillment. His mouth scorched her throat, her breasts, fastened greedily upon one nipple as, slowly, deliberately, in a sensuously torturous encroachment so intimate that Arabella wanted to die, Lucien slipped a finger deep inside her, only to withdraw it, not yet assuaging her increasingly frantic need, spreading quicksilver heat as, to his satisfaction, he found her hot and wet for him. He delved into her again then, a second finger joining the first, stretching and widening her as, at last, he began the rhythmic movement that would bring her to her peak, his lips sliding down her belly to her womanhood, his tongue finding the hard little nub of her desire, licking and laving as he thrust his fingers into her again and again, honing her craving for him to a keen edge.

Oh, God, it was indecent . . . what he was doing to her, Arabella thought dazedly, stunned and chagrined that she should revel in it, that she should be like a mad thing beneath him, sobbing aloud with pleasure, arching her hips against him uncontrollably as he tongued her, plunged his fingers into her harder and harder, faster and faster, filling her with blind sensation, exigent need for something she did not yet understand, but felt she must know or die. She was only nebulously aware of the primal drums that continued to throb outside, as she throbbed inside, her hands free now, snarling wildly in Lucien's hair, clutching him to her desperately as the crescendo came without warning, exploding inside her in waves of unbearable intensity that left her dizzy, weak, and breathless.

Slowly withdrawing his fingers, Lucien kissed her belly, her breasts, her mouth again, then settled back on his knees, beginning to unbutton his shirt. His eyes gleamed dark with passion and triumph as they raked her, taking in with hunger and safisfaction her disheveled hair that tumbled and curled wildly about her, her eyes sensuously half closed, her tremulous lips bruised and swollen from his hard kisses, the pulse that beat jerkily at the hollow of her throat, her body slack and glistening with sweat, her full, heaving breasts with their flushed, taut nipples, the moist, downy juncture of her wide-open thighs. He tossed aside his shirt; his hands fell to his belt buckle and unfastened it.

"You liked that . . . didn't you, my girl? You liked it very much indeed."

"Yes," Arabella breathed helplessly, shocked and shamed by her unbridled response to him, of how wanton and carnal she must appear, sprawled and naked before him, waiting, even so—burning, aching, despite her momentary easement—for him to take her fully. "Yes . . ."

"You're ready for me now—and I'm ready for you, Arabella; I'm aching to possess you, to thrust myself deep inside you. You see how I desire you, my sweet?" Naked now, Lucien knelt over her in the darkness, his saturnine features making him appear like some half man, half beast of age-old legend, his lithe body lean and powerful with muscle, his bold sex hard and heavy with arousal, making her shudder both with fear and anticipation at the thought that he would soon be a part of her. "Come. Touch me. Taste me. . . ."

His strong arms slipped beneath her back, arching her, lifting her up, so they were knee to knee, to meet his mouth that took her own savagely once more, his tongue shooting deep, one hand ensnaring her hair to hold her still as he kissed her, the other grasping her hand, wrapping it around his thick shaft. He taught her the motion, and as Arabella continued it on her own, he groaned with pleasure, his lips branding her cheek, her temple. He buried his face in her hair, against her throat, inhaling deeply the sweet fragrances of sunlight, eucalyptus, and musk that clung to her. He had never before had a woman as passionate as she, had never in a million years thought to find her like, and he told her as much, his voice low and husky in her ear, his breath warm against her heated skin. Other things he said, too, things that both shocked and tantalized her, made her blood sing as he dipped his head to her breasts to suck her nipples again, while his hand sought the mellifluous, engorged folds of her womanhood that now, wakened by him to ecstasy, quivered and yielded to him of their own eager, needy accord. Honey melted between her thighs as he slid his fingers once more deep into the dark well of her carmine softness, his thumb circling and rubbing the hidden heart of her moist, tender cleft, fanning anew the flames of her smoldering desire for him.

More than the potent wine she had drunk earlier, Lucien intoxicated her. The dark hair that matted his chest was like silk against her flesh, her lips that she pressed ardently to his throat, his chest, licking away the earthy sweat that sheened his bronzed skin, tasting the salt of it. She relished the feel of him, the planes and angles of his powerful, muscular body, his flesh as smooth as ivory in places, as hard as horn in others, where, although she could not make them out in the darkness, she could tell that old scars she had not known he bore puckered his flesh. She wondered where he had got them, but he would not tell her, stilling with his mouth her questions, his tongue parting her lips, mimicking the sweetly agonizing movements of his fingers that continued to tease and to torment her, to plunge into her as she discovered him as he had her, touching him everywhere she could reach.

"Kiss me, Arabella. Take me in your mouth," he urged hoarsely, gently pushing her head down a little so she would understand exactly what he meant, what he wanted.

Hesitant but afraid of angering or disappointing him, she slowly lowered her head to his maleness, kissed its glistening tip beaded with moisture, opened her lips to it. Her tongue darted forth to imitate in manner the taunting caresses with which he had earlier propelled her to her own release, flicking and laving, before, at last, she took him in her mouth as he had commanded, sucking him as he had sucked her breasts, swirling her tongue about him as he had done with her nipples, instinctively sensing that she was driving him to the brink of madness, as he had driven her, and feeling power and pleasure that, for all her ignorance and uncertainty, she should prove capable of that.

"Oh, God, Arabella," Lucien groaned, his breath quick and harsh as he pushed his fingers deep inside her again, his strokes increasing in speed and intensity, so her own desire mounted rapidly to match his. "My sweet, beautiful innocent, you don't know . . . what you're doing to me, how damned . . . good that feels. Oh, God. I can't take . . . much more. I can't—"

Roughly wrapping his hands in her hair, he jerked her head away, swiftly pressing her down upon the blankets, and poising himself above her. Because he had possessed the necessary skill and patience to prepare her fully, Arabella was hot and slick and open for him, scarcely even felt the brief moment of pain as he drove down into her, piercing her cleanly with a single hard, deep thrust that caused her to buck wildly against him, unwittingly aiding his entry that took her breath away, leaving her gasping and trembling against him. She had not known that it would be like this, so absolute an invasion, demanding an equally consummate surrender that both frightened and exhilarated her. She was his now, belonged to him in a way that she never would another man. As though Lucien sensed her thoughts, he spoke softly, fiercely.

"You're mine now, Arabella . . . all mine . . . forever mine. Because after tonight, no matter what, I'll never let you go, do you hear? I swear it!"

For a long moment after that, he lay still atop her, kissing her deeply as he accustomed her to the feel of him inside her, filling her to overflowing, stretching and molding her to accept him, throbbing within her as he fought to restrain himself, to hold back just a little while longer so he could bring her again to climax. Then, at last, he began to move in and out of her in a rhythm as old as time, as primitive as the drumbeats that had finally died away in the night but that he heard still in his mind, in his blood, as he plunged into her, his hands grasping her buttocks, pulling her tight against him, lifting her to meet each bold, deliberate thrust in such a way that his body kneaded her mound, the pulsing font of her, raising her passion to a feverish pitch. From the soaked blankets wafted the musky scent of their mating, sharp and sweet, spurring them on, flogging them to frantic want and need. Arabella's head thrashed from side to side as she enfolded him, clasped him wantonly, her fingernails furrowing his broad back as Lucien surged into her again and again, harder and faster, until she rushed headlong with him down a wild, storm-swept shore to be snatched up and born aloft, carried to the stars. There, the Rainbow Serpent twisted and twined, swallowed her with its great, gaping maw to take her to a dark, pulsating place that was time's beginning, the Dreamtime whence a thousand songlines spiraled endlessly into an infinite void, filling it with light and color so dazzling to behold that she gasped and cried out in wonder, in awe at the power and beauty of it. Lucien's head was buried against her shoulder; his breath was harsh, hot against her skin. From someplace far beyond the shelter, it seemed, she felt his fingers tighten on her painfully, his nails digging into her skin, heightening the intensity of the explosion that burst within her. Then he cried out as a long, frenzied shudder racked the length of his body and he spilled himself inside her.

Beneath him, Arabella lay exhilarated and exhausted, weak and faint from what had happened between them, her body limp, even though her heart still beat too quickly in her breast, as did Lucien's own, pounding against hers until, slowly withdrawing, he rolled a little to one side of her, raising himself on his elbow to study her in the darkness, the quiet afterglow of their lovemaking. She looked just as he had always imagined, naked and gleaming with sweat, her eyes drowsy with passion and satiation, her mouth soft and slack. Pulling her into his embrace, he cradled her head against his chest, holding her close, kissing and stroking her gently as reality gradually returned.

He half expected her to weep, but her mind was still too clouded by both the wine and their lovemaking for the full import of what she had done to strike her. Even if it were not, it did not matter anyway, he thought. As he had warned her at the start, there was no turning back for her now. Ex-convict or not, he had had her. She was his now, a woman like none other he had ever known, his to mold and to shape as he willed, to do with as he wished, to take however and whenever he pleased, to teach the things she would never have learned in another man's arms—and in the end, she would be glad that it was so, that she had surrendered not only her virginity, but also her heart to him. Deep down inside, if he were honest with himself, Lucien knew that he had always intended that she somehow should. That he had perhaps taken advantage of her vulnerable state, that she would hate both him and herself for it in the morning, he no longer cared. She would get over it in time; passion was headier than any wine, more addictive than any drug—and he had wakened her fully to hers, would continue to arouse and to sate her until she was so strongly bound to him that the bond was irrevocable, eternal. He would lose her to no man, as he had lost Verity, his wife.

"Arabella, you have made me very happy," he uttered in the silence.

"Have I, Lucien? Have I, truly?" She glanced up at him shyly, blushing as she thought of all they had done together, things she had never dreamed of in her wildest imaginings, the exquisite emotions he had evoked in her. He had called her beautiful . . . and said she would belong to him forever. For that, she had dared to leave her world and to enter into his, unable to continue to deny that, rogue or not, some dark, wild, earthy thing inside herself wanted him, regardless of the cost. But as she lay in his embrace, Arabella knew in her heart that, no matter what, there was no place else on earth she would rather be. "I was afraid, at first, that I would not please you."

"Believe me, you pleased me, my sweet—more than any other woman I have ever known. And now, I should like very much for you to do it again." Rolling her over, weighing her down, his naked body slid determinedly to cover hers again; his mouth swooped to capture her own, his tongue delving deep between her lips. "Open your legs for me, Arabella," he demanded softly, his hand fondling her breasts, gliding down her belly.

Trembling with rising passion once more at his kisses, his caresses, she did as he told her, her breath catching in her throat as she felt the hot, now-familiar rush of moisture between her thighs. He felt it, too, when he touched her, a quick, light stroke that was but a prelude to what was to come, as she had this night learned. Satisfaction curved his mouth.

"Yes, my love . . . that is what I want from you . . . and this . . . and this . . ."

Arabella did not know then where she ended and Lucien began; they were as one, no space between, lips and tongue and hands unstill until, kneeling, he drew her onto his corded thighs and thrust himself deep inside her, arching her back, his mouth upon her swollen breasts, his hands at her slender hips, helping her to find the rhythm as she rode him. Her long chestnut hair was like strands of silk riband enwinding them, a love knot binding them together forever as her sweet, low cry of surrender pierced the night, followed swiftly by his own.

From above, loosened by the soughing wind from their fecund boughs, a scattering of fragile, fragrant petals drifted through the interwoven branches of the lean-to to lie, unheeded, upon the earth, where the lovers slept and dreamed and, waking, twined again upon the exotic purple blooms.

Book Two

Chains of the
Past

Chapter Eight

The Purple-Bloomin' Tree

New South Wales Colony, Australia, 1856

When Arabella awoke the following morning, it was to the slow realization that her head ached horribly, that Lucien lay beside her on the blankets, and that they were both stark naked.

She did not become aware of this all at once. At first, she was cognizant only of the warm, buttery morning sunlight spilling through the branches of the lean-to's roof, melting upon her closed eyelids, and of wondering vaguely why Lucien had not yet wakened her for breakfast. When she stirred and stretched, she realized that her head pounded as though it contained a pump from the *Heather Rose* and that pump were going at full speed, that her mouth tasted as dry as the hide of one of the animals Lucien had killed and skinned over the

159

passing weeks, and that her stomach churned as though she were about to be violently ill. When her lashes slowly fluttered open, she felt blinded by the sun, and her surroundings seemed to spin about crazily. Feeling faint at the sight, she quickly shut her eyes again, thinking only that if she lay very still, she might not be sick. After a long, queasy minute, however, the sun's brightness and thus the morning's lateness penetrated her mind, and a nebulous sense of anxiety assailed her at the realization that Lucien should not have permitted her to sleep so long. Something must have happened to him! At that frightening thought, her eyes flew open wide, and she endeavored to rise, moaning weakly at how her head swam as she lifted it from the blankets. But she could not get up; a heavy weight was pressing her down.

Carefully turning her throbbing head, Arabella saw that the weight was Lucien himself, who lay with one of his legs riding intimately between her own, his arm encircling her body, his palm cupping her breast. For an instant, she thought dazedly that she was not truly awake or aware, that she was delirious and dreaming again. Then, suddenly, the events of last night came rushing back to her . . . the Aborigines, the potent wine, the beating drums, the sensual dancing, the surreal atmosphere, the wanton lovemaking—A soft, low cry of distress and disbelief emanated from her throat. She had lain with Lucien Sinclair—willingly!—had given herself to him in a wild, passionate moment of drunkenness and desire. . . . Dear God, what had she done? she asked herself. She had been reared to restrain her emotions, not to give them unbridled rein, to allow them to run away with her. Now, she was fallen from grace, the teachings of a lifetime made dust in the wind by a single, fleeting night of vulnerability and need. Yet her love for Lucien, the thought that he would surely marry her now would have soothed Arabella's conscience, dispelled her panic had she not abruptly, pierced to the heart, spied upon his naked bronzed back the scars she had only felt last night in the darkness of the shelter. Now, as she stared at them, shocked, paralyzed, she recognized that they were the result of his having been flogged—not once, but many times; and upon his shoulder was the most horrifying thing of all: a deep, dark brand that marked him as a murderer.

Dear God, she thought again feverishly, so stunned, so stricken that her brain initially refused to absorb the impact of the violent blow: She had loved and lain with a convicted criminal—a *murderer*!—had surrendered her maidenhead to him!

Now, as though her memory had been triggered by this dark, terrifying realization, Harry Palliser's impassioned words to her aboard the *Heather Rose* flooded her mind: *That Demon Lucien Sinclair . . . a murdering, upstart rouge . . . an ex-convict . . . will one day commit another crime, another murder . . .*

That Demon Lucien Sinclair. Over and over, those words rang in Arabella's brain as she now grasped why, when Lucien had first spoken it, his name had seemed familiar to her.

I'm a demon, all right—in more ways than one. . . . Lucien's low voice in her ear when she had first regained consciousness after the shipwreck. In that moment, he had told her himself what he was; she just had not understood until now, had never once even thought to consider that he might be an ex-convict, although she knew that Australia was, first and foremost, a land of penal colonies. In her mind, convicts were brutal, bestial men, appallingly coarse and dull-witted, lacking even the appearance of civilized behavior, the rudiments of education—none of which was true at all of Lucien. A mere ruffian, she had thought him, never once guessing the terrible truth, not even suspecting when he had not wanted to take off his shirt to let her tend his wounds from the crocodile attack, because then she would have seen the scars, the brand . . .

She had to get away, to escape from him before he awoke! There was no telling what he might do to her, alone out here, as they were, and so near to Brisbane now. He had already committed one murder; and while he perhaps would not kill her, he had—not knowing the terms of her father's will—undoubtedly taken advantage of her vulnerable state last night to seduce her so that, compromised, she would be compelled to wed him, thereby enabling him to get his hands on her fortune! Naturally, a willing victim must be infinitely preferable to an unwilling one, especially when she must still be gotten to the altar after the deflowering. But now, Arabella had no doubt that if she had not surrendered to Lucien, he would have raped her and found some means of ensuring—at least in the presence of the necessary minister or magistrate—her silence as to how she had been coerced into marriage.

She was terribly conscious of his hand upon her breast, of the sexual demands he would surely make upon her again when he awoke to find her lying naked in his embrace and that now at whose memory she was deeply sickened and ashamed. She could not believe the things they had done together, things that must surely, given Lucien's carnal, criminal nature, be lewd and perverse, she thought now, waves of nausea sweeping through her. Worse still was the memory of how she had reveled and gloried in those things, had so eagerly opened herself to him, done whatever he had demanded of her—and been glad to do it. What a gullible, besotted fool she had been! Arabella realized now as the full import of what she had done struck her pitilessly, and she recoiled in fright and revulsion at the thought of the consequences of her actions. If last night should ever become common knowledge, she would become an object of scandal and disgrace; the doors to her world would irrevocably slam shut in her face. Decent ladies would shun her, and no gentleman would marry her—although there would doubtless be many who would make her offers of another kind. Gervase . . . Gervase, if ever he learned of last night, would think her as vilely vulgar and degraded as the cheapest prostitute, a convict's whore, and would rightly spurn her. Despite being her guardian, stern Uncle Philip would perhaps refuse to countenance her presence in his household and would send her packing to a convent, or worse.

She must tell no one what had befallen her, Arabella determined, the wheels of her mind churning furiously. Somehow, she would travel on alone and afoot the rest of the short distance to Brisbane; and there, she would put about some false tale of having followed the coast southward by herself. It seemed unlikely that the authorities would know precisely where the *Heather Rose* had sunk, and even if they did, they had no way of proving that she had not subsequently drifted for miles in the lifeboat before she had been cast upon the shore. Yes, that story would serve to protect her; it *must*! Furtively, so as not to waken him, she eased herself from Lucien's strong arms, terrified when he murmured and stirred in his sleep. But to her vast relief, he did not rouse; and at last, she was able to gather her clothes and to slip from the lean-to.

Gratefully, as Arabella tugged on her garments and leather boots, she observed that the Aborigines had vanished. Only Mate witnessed her emergence from the shelter, and fearing that he would otherwise set up a squawk—he had learned now to say "Hello, Arabella"—she shushed him with a handful of peanuts, which he cracked open busily as, in one of the blankets she had taken from the lean-to, she wrapped up one each of Lucien's canteens and billies, as well as a cup, a bowl, and a spoon, along with some tea and food. Then, picking up her bundle, she turned to go—only to draw up short, gasping with horror at the sight before her: the spreading jacaranda tree that overhung the lean-to, its branches dripping purple blooms.

Beware o' him, that demon, an' o' t' moonlit twinin' 'neath t' purple-bloomin' tree . . . The words of the old Gypsy woman echoed in Arabella's ears. She had not noticed the tree last evening, or perhaps it had burst into blossom overnight; she knew only that she must escape from Lucien before it was too late.

Clutching her burden to her chest, she began to run.

Chapter Nine

Sydney

What Lucien had informed Arabella would be a journey of another day or two to Brisbane took her longer, of course, on foot, particularly as she was compelled to conceal herself every time she heard some sound that was out of the ordinary, because she did not know if he was stalking her. She lived in fear that, being so knowledgeable about the wild, he would track her, catch her, and forcibly restrain her—or worse. But it was not only for that reason that she skulked through the woods along the shore, but also because she was afraid of the wild creatures, especially the crocodiles; for she was not certain whether she still trespassed upon their territory.

Still, Arabella had, from Lucien, learned much about surviving in the wild, and now, she put her knowledge to good use, keeping herself alive. She had no way to hunt game—and she cursed herself for not taking

Lucien's revolver at least, with which she might have shot small animals at close range and which would, in any event, have provided her with some means of protecting herself. But other foods were plentiful: cabbage palms, sea almonds, pandanus, and fruits, including coconuts, plums, and figs, as well as nuts. For that, she was most grateful, for she did not think she could have brought herself to eat the green ants and moths, the grubs and foot-long ooli worms that Lucien had told her the natives frequently consumed and that he himself had dined upon on occasion. At night, not daring to risk a fire lest Lucien should spy the smoke, she climbed some likely tree and settled herself uncomfortably in its branches, although she only dozed off and on, seldom sleeping well.

Then, finally, there came the day when Arabella reached her destination. At first, she mistakenly thought that she had chanced upon some Aboriginal village, for Brisbane was an unsightly, ungraceful town, consisting of nothing more than wooden *umpees* and rutted dirt streets. It had originally been a convict settlement; and although now a busy port inhabited by immigrants who had arrived by means of government-assisted passages, it had yet to boast any substantial buildings. Gazing incredulously at the crude, backward town, Arabella, stricken, could not believe she had traveled so far for so little. Only the sight of men in the uniform of the New South Wales Corps reassured her that she must indeed have reached Brisbane—or at least a place where she could expect to receive aid. Moaning, sobbing with relief, she staggered toward the cluster of ugly, primitive huts.

A short while later, she was ensconced in one of the structures, pouring out the wild, emotional tale she had concocted of half-truths, half-lies to account for her awkward situation. Listening, Captain Richard Bonniface was jolted from his usual downcast state, born of the conditions under which he must labor, by learning that she was none other than the presumed-dead ward of Colonel Philip Wyndham, commander of the New South Wales Corps; and hearing that, the captain took charge immediately. Until other, more suitable arrangements could be made for her, Arabella was given the temporary use of his *umpee* and was soon sinking with deep gratitude into a bathtub full of steaming-hot water. With the coarse soap provided, she scrubbed herself vigorously, as though she could not only wash away the weeks of accumulated sweat and grime, but also the stain of Lucien's possession. Now, whenever she thought of this last, it seemed to her as though it, too, must be one of her delirious dreams, that it could not truly have happened, have been real—even though, deep down inside, she knew, dismayed, the awful truth. For the first time in her life, she was acutely aware of her body in a sexual way, of her full, round breasts, of the soft, downy juncture between her inner thighs that still retained a vestige of soreness to remind her of the feel of Lucien deep inside her. Somehow, Arabella had vaguely expected to find her body changed, some visible mark left by him upon it, like the brand upon his shoulder, but there was nothing other than a few faint bruises from the strength of his hands. She was glad of that, glad that no one, looking at her, should suspect her terrible shame and, worse, that it was to an ex-convict that she had—willingly—surrendered her virtue. Her belated fear now, as she stared at herself, was that Lucien might have left her with child.

Despite the warmth of the bathwater, Arabella grew cold at the thought, for she did not know what she would do in that event, what would become of her. She shuddered as she remembered the stories she had heard about women who had found themselves in such circumstances, women so desperate to rid themselves of the indisputable evidence of their disgrace that they would risk anything, even death, in an attempt to expel the unwanted fetus from the womb. Every other day, it had seemed, the London newspapers to which her father had subscribed had reported that some poor, destitute woman, cast off by her lover, had been found dead in the city's meaner streets, the victim of some filthy butcher masquerading as a doctor or midwife. Socially ostracized, Arabella might be; but at least once she reached her majority, she would not be penniless, she reassured herself, drawing meager comfort from the thought, unable to repress the violent shiver that ran through her again at the prospect of the potentially bleak future that loomed before her.

Hurriedly, she finished rinsing her hair, then stepped from the tub to dry herself off briskly with the towels that had been provided her. Captain Bonniface had canvassed the town's female residents, and when word of Arabella's miraculous survival and current plight had become known, the women had responded by producing from their own chests an assortment of clothing for her. After donning both chemise and pantalets, she struggled to pull tight the lacings of the whalebone corset that had been among the garments, gasping for breath as it cinched in her waist and cut off her air. So long had she been free from wearing the constraining piece of apparel that Arabella could not now view it as other than a torturous device. Longing to remove it, she stood panting from her exertions, faint from lack of breath, the stays digging painfully into her flesh. Next came stockings, hoops, crinolines, a gown that was only slightly too big, and a pair of morocco slippers that pinched her feet dreadfully. By the time she was through, she was sweating as though she had not just bathed and was so hot in and confined by the layers of raiment that she felt she might faint. Only with the greatest of difficulty did she restrain herself from ripping everything off and replacing it with the simple clothes to which she had by now grown accustomed.

That the freedom of those modest, elementary garments was but the first to be stripped from her, Arabella quickly learned when, next, Captain Bonniface, not being one to shirk his duty, duly secured for her a chaperon from among the ranks of the female populace. Miss Bodkins was a fortyish spinster who had come with her brother as a missionary to Australia, to bring the word of God to the Aborigines. That she had only partially succeeded at this task was the cross she bore with a martyr's glad suffering—just as she bore Arabella's presence in the Bodkinses' hut, wherein there was little enough room for two people, much less three. Despite all her protests that she had grown used to sleeping on the hard ground, for the next several days that Arabella was compelled to lodge with the missionaries, Miss Bodkins insisted upon giving up her own narrow, lumpy bed to Arabella and sleeping on the floor beside her, declaring fervently that Arabella's need for a proper night's rest was by far the greater. Nor would Miss Bodkins leave Arabella to board alone the packet that regularly plied mail and supplies between Sydney and Brisbane; even on the final leg of her interminable journey, Arabella was not spared Miss Bodkins's unwelcome presence. Instead, she was forced to share a tiny cabin with the missionary, to listen to her constant complaints about burdens she must willingly endure for the Lord's sake, and to pray with her morning and night, both to give thanks for Arabella's miraculous survival and to beseech God for the fortitude necessary to carry on in the face not only of Australia's native paganism, but also the continent's lack of creature comforts.

Once, when even Arabella's good-hearted nature could take no more and she lost her temper and spoke sharply to Miss Bodkins, the missionary plaintively accepted the rebuke as her due, declaring in long-suffering tones that she had heedlessly rattled on, without thought or care for Arabella's shattered nerves born of her dreadful ordeal. So Arabella was left feeling guilty and reproached, as she suspected that Miss Bodkins had secretly intended; and conceived within Arabella was the deep, gnawing anxiety that, having lost her virtue to Lucien, she was now destined to wind up like the missionary: as a peevish, pathetic, prune-faced spinster who, by taking on the trials and tribulations of others, made of herself something equally and unbearably as unpleasant. It was no wonder, Arabella thought, dejected, that Miss Bodkins's brother had been such a sad, nervous little man, meekly agreeing with his formidable sister at every turn. Arabella did not want to become a tiresome burden to anyone; and such was her despair at the prospect that if not for the presence of Captain Bonniface, who had considered it his duty personally to escort her to Sydney and Uncle Philip, she was afraid she might have been tempted to fling herself overboard, to let the sea claim her as it had failed to do following the wreck of the *Heather Rose* upon the Great Barrier Reef.

Before the end of the voyage, Captain Bonniface— Richard, as she soon came to call him—she counted as her friend; for if not so cheerful and unreserved as Harry Palliser, he was nevertheless equally as earnest, considerate of her feelings, and dedicated to his career. It was he with whom she spent most of her time aboard the packet that, having ferried its cargo to Brisbane, now returned to Sydney. Often, he stood with her at the rail, as Harry had done aboard the *Heather Rose*, entertaining her with tales of his adventures in Australia; and if he harbored suspicions that the story she had told him of her own escapade was not entirely truthful, Richard was too well-bred even to insinuate that a lady might also be a liar. He knew both the colonel and Gervase, and was slightly acquainted with the rest of the Wyndham family, having had occasion to dine at their house once or twice; and as Harry also had done, Richard took pains to assure Arabella that, unlike the shockingly crude town of Brisbane, she would not find Sydney lacking in either culture or amenities.

This she soon discovered for herself as, after sailing through the massive Heads of Port Jackson, the packet meandered its way inland to Sydney Cove to drop anchor in the sparkling blue harbor. Along the way, Richard pointed out some of the local sights to her—including a much-celebrated lookout point that was whimsically known as Mrs. Macquarie's Chair.

"Elizabeth Macquarie was the wife of Governor Lachlan Macquarie, who was directly responsible for much of the building up of Sydney," Richard explained to Arabella as they waited for the mooring lines to be secured and the gangway to be put into place. "He had a grand, farseeing vision for this town that, unfortunately, the Imperial Office in London did not share, refusing to allocate him either the necessary funds or the men with the expertise to make his dream come true. Nevertheless undaunted, he hired an ex-convict named Frances Greenway, who had been an architect before being transported and incarcerated in prison, to design many of the elegant edifices you will see—Hyde Park Barracks, Parliament House, the State Library, and Sydney Hospital, among them—and paid for them with the profits from the rum trade. Not to be outdone, Mrs. Macquarie commissioned her chair, which is carved entirely out of the rock upon the promontory at the tip of the Domain, the governor's private park. There, she would often sit and survey the harbor. When you are invited to Government House, as, being Colonel Wyndham's ward, you surely shall be, you must ask to visit the chair, Arabella. The view is quite lovely and a favorite spot of female guests, some of whom have done watercolors there of the landscape."

"I shall. It sounds beautiful," Arabella replied as, from the deck of the packet, she gazed at the town.

"Already, I can see, thankfully, that Sydney is far more civilized than Brisbane."

Indeed, this was the case; for from gentle green hills and long tawny beaches nestled at the foot of the towering Blue Mountains that hove up majestically behind, Sydney rose in all its magnificent Victorian splendor. To the right, the close-packed dwellings and grog-shops of The Rocks crowded along narrow, twisting cobblestone streets and alleys joined in places by steep flights of steps that climbed the hills; and warehouses built by convict labor clustered along the wooden wharves that reached like long fingers into the harbor. To the left were the imposing Government House, the home of the governor, and sprawling, flower-filled parks that along Macquarie Street bordered the heart of the town that stretched inward from the Circular Quay, where the dockside noises were familiar and comforting to one long accustomed to those of Scarborough. In a strange way, Arabella felt as though she had come home. Richard quickly hailed a passing hansom cab so they need not linger on the piers, assisted the two women inside, and gave directions to the driver.

"Colonel Wyndham's estate lies along the southern shore of Port Jackson, not far from the South Head, as do those of many others you will come to know socially," he informed Arabella as they rode along, the vehicle's wheels clattering over the cobblestones. "However, the Wyndhams also maintain a town house in Sydney, naturally, where I shall take you, as I'm sure you are longing to be reunited with them."

"Yes, of course," Arabella said slowly, realizing of

a sudden that she was no longer as certain of this as she had been before the wreck of the *Heather Rose*.

Now that, at long last, this moment was upon her, she was filled with misgivings as she thought of Lucien Sinclair and of that night of mad, drunken passion they had shared between them. To her vast relief, he had not left her with child. But it was not likely, she believed, that Uncle Philip's interrogation about her weeks following the shipwreck would be so innocuous as Richard's had proved; and although her innate honesty insisted she should make a clean breast of the matter, Arabella instinctively cringed at the notion, recalling her fear that if he learned the truth, the colonel would not have her in his house. That to compel her into a convent, or worse, he might also cut off her funds so she could not return to Darracott Hall was something she did not even want to consider. Now that she had had time to regain her senses, she felt as though she had committed a crime as terrible as Lucien's own. But while the enormity of what she had done filled her with anxiety, she was even more frightened of being found out and made to suffer the consequences. When she had merely thought Lucien beneath her socially, she had, she recognized now, been willing not only to become his wife, but also to endure such small slights as might have come her way in a land where the boundaries of class were already eroding. But as brave as Arabella was, even she was not prepared to be labeled a convict's whore and cast off by her surrogate family and her friends alike—especially for the sake of a loveless marriage to a man who had, in her mind, unquestionably compromised her for the sole purpose of getting his grasping hands on her inheritance.

Not once had Lucien spoken of loving her, only of wanting her. Somehow, that realization wounded her worst of all, no matter how often she sternly reminded herself that he was a brutal murderer, a hardened ex-convict, a sly seducer, a greedy fortune hunter, and heaven only knew what else. He had no morals, no scruples whatsoever. She must put him from her heart and mind, and pray to God that she never saw him again, that he never learned her whereabouts in Sydney, else he would surely seek her out and threaten her with exposure if she did not comply with whatever demands he made of her. Arabella's imagination ran wild at the thought, wreaking such havoc upon her that she was hardly aware of the drive through Sydney, of the buildings and parks that Richard pointed out to her as the hansom cab wended its way through the town's traffic, finally coming to a stop before a lovely, multistoried town house of grey stone, with elaborate, wrought-iron-lace colonnades on the first and second stories. White wooden jalousies hung at the doors and the narrow casement windows. The grounds were enclosed by a fence composed of short stone pillars and wrought-iron spikes, and planted with flower beds and ornamental trees—one of which, Arabella observed to her dismay, was a jacaranda. From the front gates, a stone path led to a short flight of wide steps ending at the stout wooden front door with its polished-brass knocker.

"Ah . . . here we are," Richard announced, handing the two women down from the vehicle, then paying the driver. "As you can plainly see, this is a far cry from my humble *umpee*—for which you are no doubt inordinately grateful, Arabella—and after your travails, how glad you must be to have arrived home at last!"

"Yes . . . yes." She nodded, self-consciously smoothing her wrinkled skirts and tucking back into place stray wisps of hair loosened from her chignon, suddenly all too aware of her too-large gown, her too-small shoes, and her skin turned to gold by the sun. "I only wish I looked more presentable. When I think of all my lost baggage—"

"As John Wesley observed, cleanliness is, indeed, next to godliness, my dear Arabella," Miss Bodkins quoted briskly. "The rest is all vanity and so need not be considered. If not the height of fashion, your appearance is clean and neat; and charity compels us to give thanks for that and for your miraculous survival, as well."

Given that Miss Bodkins was even plainer than Arabella had always considered her own self to be, and garbed in a drab gown of unrelieved black bombazine, which the missionary thought quite suited to her life's work, Arabella could take small solace from her companion's words. She was even more disheartened—after Richard had knocked upon the door and it had been opened by a footman to admit them—to be greeted by the sight of a breathtakingly beautiful young woman floating down the angled staircase inside the entry hall, her blond ringlets artfully arrayed, and she herself modishly attired in a black mourning gown that nevertheless somehow contrived to appear as the airiest of confections. She seemed like nothing so much as a fairy princess from some children's tale.

At first, Arabella did not recognize her. But then, halfway down the steps, the dainty young woman paused, her big blue eyes widening at the sight of those standing upon the threshold, her pink-rosebud mouth forming an oh of shock and disbelief, one delicate white hand going to her slender throat. Then, with a glad, astonished cry of "Arabella! Oh, Arabella! Is it really you?" she came flying down the stairs to envelop Arabella in a heartfelt embrace whose fragrance was that of lilies and roses.

"Chrissie, oh, Chrissie . . . yes, yes, it's I!" With difficulty, Arabella managed to get the words past the huge lump in her throat and the sudden flood of tears she could not halt as she clung tightly to her best friend, Christine Wyndham. All her trials since the death of her father and her departure from Darracott Hall abruptly overwhelmed her in that joyful moment of reunion. Then, finally, Richard's polite clearing of his throat to remind her that there were witnesses to this emotional scene recalled Arabella to the present and her manners; and tremulously dashing away her tears, she turned to make the necessary introductions. "Chrissie, you will remember Captain Richard Bonniface, of course; he has dined here at Wyndham House on occasion. And this is Miss Bodkins. She is a missionary in Brisbane and has been kind enough to serve as my chaperon these past weeks."

Taking a lacy, embroidered white handkerchief from the sash at her waist, Chrissie dabbed gracefully at her tearful eyes as she extended her hand first to Miss Bodkins and then, more lingeringly, to Richard. Her thick, golden lashes fluttered like the wings of a butterfly as she gazed up at him, with an unconsciously calculated coyness, a dimple peeping in her rosy cheek.

"Captain, how nice to see you again—and under such happy circumstances; for it is you whom I presume we must thank for restoring our dear Arabella to us, is it not? Oh, let us not stand here another moment longer! Come into the drawing room, do!" Tugging excitedly on Arabella's hand, Chrissie led the way, throwing open the double doors to the drawing room. The footman had already apprised both a stunned and disbelieving Mrs. Henriette Wyndham, Chrissie's mother, and an equally astounded but calmer Norah Wyndham, Chrissie's older sister, of Arabella's entirely unanticipated arrival. "Mama, look who is here! Our own dear Arabella, miraculously returned to us from a watery grave. Thank heavens, we may be rid now of these dreadful black mourning gowns and show our faces socially once more!"

Whether it was this last, wholly irreverent remark or the sight of Arabella herself that agitated Henriette the most, no one knew; regardless, the effect was such that Aunt Hennie, as Arabella had always affectionately called Mrs. Wyndham, promptly swooned on the sofa. For the next several minutes, chaos reigned as Norah directed Chrissie to ring for the servants, and they were subsequently sent to fetch both water and hartshorn to revive Aunt Hennie, as well as for refreshments for the guests. Norah herself, after rising, swiftly kissing Arabella on both cheeks, and bidding her welcome, turned her attention to Aunt Hennie, plumping up the cushions on the sofa and arranging her mother's unconscious form more comfortably, while Miss Bodkins, not to be outdone, produced her own vinaigrette and proceeded to wave it vigorously under Aunt Hennie's nose.

"Oh, dear, the poor woman. The shock of seeing Miss Darracott was simply too much for her, I fear," Miss Bodkins intoned in the voice of a tragedienne, "and she was overcome. One can readily see that Mrs. Wyndham's constitution is, even at best, not robust. But, there, that is not to be wondered at, after all; so many a fragile English flower wilts out here in these godforsaken Colonies, such is the unbearable heat— although, of course, that has been a burden I have borne gladly to bring the word of God to the unenlightened Aborigines, who are so sadly ignorant of our Lord Jesus Christ. We must pray that no damage has been done to your mother's heart, Miss Wyndham."

"You must not fret yourself on that account, Miss Bodkins," Norah answered firmly. "Mama is prone to these fainting spells. There, you see? She is already coming around. Yes, do sit up, Mama dear; you are not imagining things: Arabella is, indeed, alive and well. Captain Bonniface—you do remember him, don't you, Mama . . . that nice officer Papa has asked to dine with us once or twice?—has brought her safely home to us. Richard, if you wouldn't mind terribly, I think that a small glass of sherry—"

"No, brandy, Richard—just for medicinal purposes, you know," Aunt Hennie uttered weakly as the captain strode to a nearby table, upon which reposed a number of crystal decanters and glasses. "Oh, I still can hardly believe it! Arabella . . . Arabella . . . my dear Victoria's child . . . alive—when they told us that you were dead, that you had drowned when the *Heather Rose* sank. One would suppose that the authorities would make some effort to get these things right and not cause people unnecessary grief—and I shall certainly tell the colonel so!" Aunt Hennie's lower lip quivered with petulant indignation at what she had been made to suffer for the past several weeks. Then, recovering after a few sips of the brandy Richard had poured and handed her, she said to Arabella, "Come, dear child. Sit beside me, and let me look at you. My goodness! You're as dark as a nut-brown maid! And that gown . . . those shoes . . ."

"Of course, all of Arabella's baggage must have been lost with the ship, Mama," Norah pointed out logically.

"Yes, I'm afraid that is indeed so, Aunt Hennie," Arabella confirmed. "I've naught save what you see me in—and would not have even that were it not for the kindness of Miss Bodkins and some of the other women in Brisbane, from where she and Richard escorted me to Sydney."

Arabella then went on to recount the tale of half-truths, half-lies that she had told the captain, of drifting for miles in the lifeboat, subsisting on its meager store of supplies, before finally washing up on the beach to journey on afoot to Brisbane, surviving on bananas and other fruits she had discovered along the way. At the story's end, Aunt Hennie was aghast and Norah filled with respect and admiration for Arabella's bravery and good sense. Chrissie was agog with excitement and envy that Arabella should have had such an adventure and been so romantically "rescued" by Richard—"for even if he is a rather stolid fellow, he *does* cut a very dashing figure in his uniform!" she confided in Arabella's ear.

Shortly thereafter, Colonel Wyndham himself, summoned home by the urgent message that the report of his ward's untimely demise had, thankfully, proved false, appeared, whereupon Arabella was forced to relate her tale yet again. This, however, she did in such a flushed and faltering manner under Uncle Philip's severe eye that, at last, Norah broke in, saying:

"Oh, Papa, can't you see that poor Arabella is exhausted? Indeed, I don't know how she is still on her feet after all she has been through!"

With that, Norah, Aunt Hennie, and Chrissie whisked Arabella away upstairs to show her to her bedchamber. Both Richard and Miss Bodkins had by then taken their leave, there being, fortunately, a mission in Sydney at which the latter intended to lodge before her departure back to Brisbane. With calm, obviously familiar authority, Norah ordered a bath to be prepared for Arabella straightaway, after which Arabella flung herself down appreciatively upon the canopied, mosquito-net-draped featherbed in her room and, for the first time since leaving Darracott Hall, slept the moment her head touched the pillow.

When she finally awoke, it was to discover that she had slumbered for nearly two days, in a complete mental and physical collapse following her lengthy ordeal. In that time, she would presently learn, Aunt Hennie, upset that anyone should sleep so long, had insisted on sending for the physician, Dr. Kendall Munroe. But after his examination of Arabella, he had declared that she was suffering from no more than strain and exhaustion, and had advised allowing her to rest without interruption.

Now, as her lashes slowly fluttered open, Arabella did not, at first, know where she was. She was conscious only of the wondrous fact that she lay in a real bed, in a real house. The room's casement windows were open, and along with sunlight, a gentle wind streamed inside, stirring the gossamer mosquito netting that swathed the canopy bed. Of course, she was in Sydney, at Wyndham House, she remembered after a moment. She rose to find that on the washstand hung fresh cloths and towels, and that there was water in a pitcher for pouring into the porcelain basin. On the dresser lay a silver-backed brush with matching comb and mirror, as well as a round, silver-topped crystal container of hairpins, and flacons of perfume; and in the armoire hung gowns and slippers that, while not new, were at least au courant and that appeared as though they would fit Arabella. She guessed correctly that they had come from Norah, who was much the same size as she.

Startled from her reverie by a timid knock upon the door, Arabella opened the portal to admit a young woman whose dress marked her as a servant of the household.

"Oh, miss, thank 'eavens ye're awake at last!" the young woman greeted her. "Missus Wyndham's been ever so worried. I'm Tilly, an' I'm ta serve as yer maid if ye'll 'ave me. 'Twas me job in London . . . afore I was transported fer theft. So I know 'bout gowns an' 'air an' such—an' I'll not steal so much as tuppence from ye, miss, I swear! I don't want ta go back ta t' Factory. I never would o' stole ta begin with if it weren't fer me little brother . . . 'e was so sick an' all—an' then it didn't matter anyways, 'cause 'e died after I was arrested . . . I'll work 'ard fer ye, miss, I promise. Oh, please say yes, miss! Else, Missus Wyndham might not 'ave a place fer me 'ere, an' I'm afeared ta wind up in The Rocks! 'Tis a most wretched an' dangerous part o' town, an' I've learned me lesson! Truly, I 'ave!''

"I'm sure you have, Tilly." Arabella spoke reassuringly as she at last managed to comprehend the gist of this breathless barrage; for although she was shocked to learn that Aunt Hennie had hired an ex-convict, she was not unmoved by Tilly's obvious fright, her tearful eyes, and her sincerity. "So if you would be good enough to lay out that green gown, we shall see what may be done toward improving my appearance."

"Oh, miss, ye've a 'eart o' gold, ye do! Thank ye, thank ye! Ye won't regret this, I swear it!" Tilly cried, abruptly flinging herself to her knees before Arabella and sobbing pitifully with manifest relief and gratitude. "I'm . . . sorry, miss . . . sorry," she choked out. "But ye don't know . . . ye can't dream what 'tis like fer women convicts 'ere, t' 'ell they must suffer—beggin' yer pardon, miss. I'll—I'll get t' green gown straightaway, miss."

Her hands trembling as she brushed away her tears, Tilly hurried to the open wardrobe as Arabella, her brow knitted in a puzzled, concerned frown, gazed thoughtfully at the young woman, unable to understand her apprehension. During the trip by packet from Brisbane to Sydney, when Arabella, remembering the scars upon

Lucien's back and the brand upon his shoulder, had inquired about the life of a convict, Richard had assured her that only the most incorrigible prisoners were flogged and branded. The remainder of the convicts, he had insisted, were treated far better than any criminal deserved, many being lodged with settlers instead of in the prisons and many more being awarded their tickets-of-leave, which permitted them to be placed on parole for the duration of their sentence and to hire themselves out to households, farms, merchants, and so forth, thereby earning a wage; so that in effect, they escaped punishment for the crimes they had committed. Yet it would seem from Tilly's words and behavior, Arabella now reflected soberly, that perhaps not all the convicts were treated so humanely as Richard would have had her believe. Disturbed by the thought, she later broached the matter to Norah, asking her opinion.

"Arabella, you must understand that with a few rare exceptions, such as Sydney, which owes its progress principally to Governor Macquarie's foresight, the Colonies are still relatively primitive, in many cases lacking even the necessary amenities one would expect of a civilized society. Nor has funding to improve either towns or prisons been especially forthcoming from the Imperial Office. Nevertheless, I feel quite certain that the idea that the convicts are cruelly treated is merely an annoying rumor put about by the prisoners themselves; for they are ever complaining about their lot— as though they should be rewarded rather than punished for their dreadful crimes! No, Richard has the right of it: Many are not only what I would call mollycoddled, but also far better off than decent settlers. Why, the

Female Factory at Parramatta, for instance, where Tilly was incarcerated, is a lovely, three-story Georgian building that was specifically constructed to replace a crowded loft where female convicts were previously gaoled—and it is certainly vastly superior to the wooden *umpees* with which many poor townspeople in Brisbane and elsewhere must make do. The convicts are both fed and clothed by the prisons; and because there is a dire shortage of labor in the Colonies, many of those transported are seldom required to serve their full terms, but given tickets-of-leave instead. Those convicts, such as forgers and embezzlers, who generally have some modicum of manners, education, and training, are naturally preferred over violent murderers, common highwaymen, and thieves, and, so, invariably find employment among the gentry. One wishes, of course, for proper, respectable servants; but unfortunately, they are simply not to be had. However, I thought that since Tilly had once worked as a lady's maid, she would suit better than most in that capacity. But if I have erred—''

"No, no," Arabella interjected hastily, not wanting either to offend Norah or to cause Tilly to lose her place. "I'm certain she'll be just fine. I was . . . merely curious, that's all. While I understand that crimes must be punished, surely if that punishment is not meted out justly and humanely, we must count ourselves little better than the criminals themselves."

"Yes, I quite agree." Norah's voice held a firm note of conviction. "One should not stoop to their level. However, let us not forget, Arabella, that methods that may appear harsh or even cruel to you and me are oftentimes necessary to impose discipline and to retain order. Why, even in the military, a man may be flogged for disobedience. Are you advocating that a convict should receive more lenient treatment than what an officer and a gentleman of our own class must endure?''

"No, no . . . of course not," Arabella said slowly, troubled, as she attempted to sort out her confused thoughts and emotions; for as she recalled the crosshatching of scars upon Lucien's back, she could not help but think that no one, whether an officer or a convict, should be forced to suffer such a horrible beating, no matter the infraction.

"Well, I am certainly very glad to hear it!" Norah declared fervently. "For, I warn you, Arabella: Papa does not hold at all with the radical, reprehensible views of the Colonies' Emancipists, who would see the lowest, meanest convict given equal status with the governor himself! We are Exclusives, as is most everyone connected with the New South Wales Corps. I sincerely hope that you will remember that, Arabella, as well as the fact that all you say and do here in Sydney will reflect upon Papa and his position as the commander of the corps."

"Yes, yes . . . of course." Inwardly, Arabella shuddered at the realization, for she had not previously thought to consider this; and now as she did so, she became more determined than ever to conceal the truth of her journey following the wreck of the *Heather Rose*, her willing seduction at the hands of a convict, a murderer. Of course, she should have recognized that if ever the facts became known, the scandal would affect not only her, but also the Wyndhams. Selfishly, she had worried only about her own disgrace.

Now, although she quailed at the thought of Uncle Philip's wrath descending upon her, even worse was the notion of hurting Aunt Hennie, Norah, and Chrissie, who had welcomed her so kindly, with such open, loving arms—and Gervase . . . what an object of scorn and ridicule he would be if it were discovered that the woman his family had hoped he would marry had instead given herself to Lucien Sinclair! Even so, how could she wed Gervase now? It was not within Arabella to—with a lie that would surely be exposed on their wedding night—deceive him or any other man into marrying her. Perhaps because she had fallen in love with Lucien, she should spend the rest of her life as a spinster, denied a husband and children, for, like the convicts, she deserved punishment for her crime.

More than once during the next several days, Arabella was tempted to blurt out the whole of her tale at least to Uncle Philip. But to her mingled relief and dismay, he was too busy with the affairs of the New South Wales Corps to pay her any more heed than he did his own family—although he did call her into his study one evening, not for a more piercing scrutiny of the story she had told upon her arrival at Wyndham House, but, rather, to explain to her various legal matters concerning her father's will and the disposition of his estate and the trust fund that had been established for her. During their discussion, Uncle Philip also gave her what would henceforth constitute her monthly allowance.

"Naturally, there will be additional disbursements,

for items such as the replacing of your wardrobe, Arabella, which I shall not expect to be covered by your pin money, but will myself take care of with the amount stipulated in Tobias's will for your living expenses—which amount is quite generous, I might add," the colonel asserted. "So, while I sincerely hope I need not anticipate foolishly lavish and wholly frivolous expenditures on your part, neither should you feel constrained to stint on what is necessary for a young woman of your station, Arabella. You should go on much as you did at Darracott Hall—with, however, the understanding that we do quite a bit more socializing here in Sydney than to what you were accustomed at home. Henriette and Norah will know what is required, and since you have always been a sensible young woman, I know that you will trust to their judgment."

"Yes, of course, Uncle Philip." Recognizing that the interview was at an end, Arabella rose from her chair, the envelope containing her allowance clasped in her hand. But as she was leaving the study, the colonel spoke again.

"Arabella, I want you to know how deeply I was saddened by Tobias's death. He was my best friend, and I shall miss him. Further, while I realize that no one can take his place in your heart, I do hope that you will be happy with us here in Sydney." The colonel's voice was gruff with an emotion she had not expected and that touched her deeply, as did his words.

Tears filled her eyes; here was a glimpse of the kind, indulgent father that usually only Chrissie was able to coax from behind the colonel's stern-officer facade.

"Thank you, Uncle Philip," Arabella said quietly.

Then she hurried from the study, not wanting, with her tears, to distress him—and more concerned now than ever lest her relationship with Lucien bring the taint of scandal upon the Wyndhams.

As had become her custom in the early evenings, she sought the beautiful gardens at the back of the town house, which, at twilight, were refreshingly cool after the heat of the day. At the gardens' heart was a stone fountain that gurgled soothingly and in whose deep, wide basin large goldfish swam and water lilies floated serenely. Nearby sat a stone bench surrounded by white trellises of bougainvillea, hibiscus, and morning glory vines; roses and other, more exotic blooms filled the flower beds, their lush fragrances perfuming the evening air; and in one corner, a jacaranda tree spread its weeping branches. Arabella was at once strangely drawn to and guiltily repelled by the ornamental tree. It was, she thought, a living symbol of her sin. Every time she saw it, she was reminded of lying naked in Lucien's strong embrace, of the heated passion and intimacy they had shared, of her bittersweet love for him, the taste of it now as ashes in her mouth. Still, like a moth to a flame, she came of an evening to sit beneath the tree, to gather in her hands the purple blooms that strewed the stone bench, and to press them to her face, inhaling their sweet scent, feeling the fragile petals as smooth against her skin as Lucien himself had felt.

She was mad, she told herself time and again—mad and wanton and foolish to think of him, to dream of him. He could bring her nothing but heartache and ruin. Yet, so strongly did she sense his presence at the tree that she could not seem to keep away; and now, of a sudden, her heart leaped to her throat when she spied him standing there in truth—no dream, but real. She drew up short on the narrow cobblestone path that wended through the gardens, a soft, low cry emanating from her throat at the sight of him. He turned at the sound and stepped from the shadows. Only then did she realize that it was not Lucien who stood beneath the tree at all, but a tall, dark, handsome man in the uniform of the New South Wales Corps and who must surely be Gervase. Since her arrival, he, a lieutenant in the corps, had been away on duty, so she had not yet seen him. Now, observing her, he walked toward her slowly, his hands outstretched to her, his eyes gleaming as blue as a pale-washed summer sky, his sensual mouth curved in a smile of greeting as he spoke.

"Arabella . . . my dear Arabella, you've grown up at long last!"

Chapter Ten

Interlude at
The Rocks

Ever since Verity had betrayed him with the despised and feared Other, he had hunted the night—the ultimate predator seeking the ultimate prey. Only men and rats killed their own kind, he had heard it said, and wondered vaguely if that was true. It did not matter. He was no mere man, but a prince of the darkness, a god, all-powerful, holding within his hands the very life of another human being, snuffing it out as easily he would have the flame of a candle. They were all Veritys, his victims, every last one of them—cheap, faithless whores to the bone, promising, teasing, lying, deceiving. . . . The only way to save them, to make them pure again was to cut their treacherous black hearts from their breasts. He did it both to punish them and for their own good, their own salvation, always making sure that, afterward, they could pay the ferryman to carry them to the realm of the dead, so they would not wander, lost, for all eternity. They all bore her face, her name: *Verity* . . .

The word seemed to whisper on the wind as he moved swiftly, silently, down the narrow, cobblestone streets and alleys that wended through The Rocks, up the short, steep flights of stone steps that climbed the inclines of the gentle green hills that had once been so pristinely beautiful, but that now, since the advent of the white colonists, were filthy and ugly—a perfect hunting ground for a creature of the night, such as he. He was a raven, a carrion crow winging his way through the shadows, his black cape swirling like a shroud about his tall, dark, handsome figure as he stalked his prey. His pale eyes shone in the moonlight that streamed from the firmament, the lamplight that spilled from the windows of the deteriorated dwellings, the tawdry taverns that lined the serpentine streets.

No one paid him any heed—and if they glanced his way, his gaze sent them hurriedly scuttling off like cockroaches fleeing sudden light. His eyes were chilling, as cold and steely as twin gun barrels, blazing with a devilish flame. His booted footsteps rang softly on the cobblestones, echoed on the soughing wind, only to fade into unnerving silence as he sensed his quarry pause ahead to glance back fearfully over her shoulder before her own light footsteps sounded again, faster, skimming the streets, the alleys, the steps.

Yes, run, Verity, run, he thought with grim satisfaction at how she fled like a frightened rabbit before him.

You shall not escape from me, even so. My hunts are always successful. Always, Verity. Remember that. . . .

His nostrils flared; his mouth curved in a sardonic smile. He could smell her fear, taste it sweet upon his tongue, hear the sound of her gasps for breath, of her frantically beating heart as she ran on, feel the stitch in her side that made her draw up short again, doubling her over. A hot rush of blood flooded his loins, then surged through his entire body. Power . . . pure and primal and so strong that he almost expected to see it burst from his fingertips, an explosion of blue fire such as was commanded by those privy to the darkest of mysteries and magics. But he knew the darkest secret, the darkest necromancy of all: death—the scent of it, the taste of it, the sound of it, the feel of it as he called it forth. In his hands, death reigned, its scepter his malacca cane, its silver knob twisted free to reveal its gleaming blade. The cane clattered to the cobblestones—a warning, did she but hear it. But he knew she would not; her own heartbeat, pounding as hard and fast as the palms of an Aborigine upon the taut hide of a primitive drum, would drown out all other sounds.

Listen, Verity, listen! Hear the sound of power. . . .

He grabbed her from behind, flung her up against one wall of the dark alley in which he had captured her, brutally clamping one strong hand over her mouth to stifle her screams of terror. Her eyes were wide and glazed; the pulse at the hollow of her throat beat erratically where he pressed the point of his knife threateningly to keep her still and silent as he freed himself from his breeches. His engorged maleness throbbed in his hand before he roughly shoved up her skirts and viciously pushed his way inside her, impaling her again and again, grinding her buttocks against the wall, spurred on by her utter helplessness against him, her stricken, pleading eyes, by her quick, fearful breaths and desperately muted cries of pain as he drove into her ruthlessly. When, shortly, he was done, he at last spoke.

"You liked that . . . didn't you, my girl? Because you're a whore, Verity. You've always been a whore, and you'll always be a whore. You know that, don't you?" Taking her terrified nod for granted, he went on softly, hoarsely, hardly even aware of her any longer as he stared at her blindly, seeing another before him. "But it doesn't matter now, for at long last, I've found someone to take your place, my love. Her name is Arabella. Arabella . . . Arabella . . ." he whispered again and again as the blade descended and the blood spilled forth in crimson rivers.

"Her name was Rose O'Doul, sir—but most folks called her Rum Rosie. She was a convict, of course, transported seven years ago for the usual petty theft. She hadn't been on the town long; she was only released from the Factory . . . let's see . . . er . . . three months ago," the constable said after glancing at the sheaf of papers he held in one hand. "Normally, I wouldn't have dragged you out for the death of a mere prostitute, sir, but . . . well, the doc there"—he motioned toward Dr. Kendall Munroe, who was bent over, examining the corpse—"has got some notion in his head that we've got a crazed convict on the loose, murdering whores."

"That is my belief, yes," the physician announced as he glanced up gravely at the other three men, who, besides the constable, included Colonel Philip Wyndham and Captain Richard Bonniface, the latter of whom had recently been transferred back from Brisbane to Sydney as a reward for his assisting Arabella and escorting her to Wyndham House. "I won't be sure until I can examine the body more closely; nevertheless, I'm fairly certain the unfortunate Miss O'Doul was killed with the same sharp instrument—some kind of stiletto, I'm guessing—that was used to murder poor Sally Wheeler and at least three other victims over the past four or five years. Also, there are the pennies on the victim's eyes and the cape draped over her corpse, which would seem to confirm my theory; for it's extremely unlikely that more than one murderer would have hit on those particular touches—unless, of course, we've got some kind of gang at work, raping and killing doxies."

"Really, Kendall!" the colonel groused disbelievingly. "These cheap-street creatures are found dead—murdered—all the time—"

"Yes . . . beaten to death, strangled, even stabbed—but not like this, Colonel, not carved up like a Christmas goose, for God's sake!" The doctor's face and tone were grim. "I'm telling you that I've never seen anything like this in my entire medical career—nor heard of a murderer behaving as though his crime were one of these novels serialized in the magazines, with a new installment due periodically, lest his audience lose interest. No, this is the work of a madman, a convict undoubtedly—since I cannot envision that any officer or gentleman would stoop to this, not even if he were an insane escapee from Bedlam or just plain drunk at the time!"

"It perhaps would not be amiss, sir, to go through our records to see if any convict transported to the Colonies and paroled or pardoned within the last five to seven years was guilty of this kind of crime in England," Richard suggested respectfully.

"Murderers are generally hanged, Captain," the colonel observed dryly.

"Yessir. Still, there have been exceptions, sir. Lucien Sinclair, for instance, is a prime example of what connections, influence, and wealth may achieve in reducing a man's sentence—for he is rumored to have been transported for murdering his wife, is he not?"

"Yes, I believe so. . . ." the colonel admitted slowly, reluctantly, his face still betraying his skepticism at the whole idea, although, inwardly, he felt cold with apprehension, cold enough that, at last, he conceded, "Well, perhaps you are right, Captain: Perhaps there are indeed more convicts than I thought who, despite their having committed a murder, somehow managed to escape the gallows and to be transported to the Colonies. Institute a search of our records, then. Constable, make arrangements for the woman's body to be taken to Rum Hospital," the colonel instructed, referring to Sydney Hospital, so nicknamed for the trade whose profits had funded its construction. "Kendall, you'll let me know the results of your examination?"

"Naturally, Colonel. However, I cannot promise any

information more specific than what I've already given you. Unfortunately, there is only so much that modern medicine and science can tell us about a body—especially in a case of extreme mutilation such as this''— as he glanced once more at the corpse, the physician shook his head, dismayed by the incredible violence that had been done to the dead woman—''although I feel certain that, someday, we will be able virtually to reconstruct a murder, based on findings gathered from the victim's body.''

"Aw, go on with you, Doc!" A wide grin split the constable's broad, cheery face at this ludicrous notion. "Next, you'll be telling us that victims will actually come back to life, sit up, and talk!"

"In a manner of speaking, I believe that they will," the doctor insisted stubbornly, seriously. That idea, however, to his annoyance, only provoked all three of the other men to snorts of laughter.

"May I have this dance, miss?" the constable, emboldened by the mirth, inquired of the corpse as it was loaded onto a stretcher by two other constables who had now appeared on the scene. When there was no response, he turned back to the others, asking, "Do you suppose it was something I said? She seemed a little stiff to me!"

Scowling amid the resultant chortles and muttering sourly under his breath about gallows humor, Dr. Munroe snapped shut his black bag and took his departure to accompany the wagon carrying the body to Sydney Hospital. The constable, whose shift was at an end, hurried to the nearest grog-shop, where he could be certain of several free mugs of rum in exchange for the titillating story he had to relate. The colonel and Richard headed back to the headquarters of the New South Wales Corps, so that moments later, all that remained in the alley to speak of the grisly murder done there last night was the dark stain on the cobblestones.

Chapter Eleven

Unexpected Tryst

The shock and rage and, most of all, desire that Lucien felt upon seeing Arabella again were such that it was all he could do to restrain himself from striding across the ballroom floor and violently dragging her away with him in front of all the guests gathered at Coral Reef, the Howland estate on the southern shore of Port Jackson. When he realized she was on the arm of Gervase Wyndham, Lucien actually longed to commit murder.

Arabella! How she had haunted him! As faithless as his dead wife, Verity . . . he knew that now, and still, he wanted her, had dreamed of her endlessly, unable to put her from his mind. She loved him, she had whispered fervently beneath the jacaranda tree. Obviously, though, that love had not proved strong enough the following morning to prevail when she saw the terrible scars, the dark brand he bore. A contemptuous smile curved Lucien's lips at the thought that he should have been fool enough to expect anything else from her, that he should have dared to hope that she would be different from the rest of her ilk.

Seeing her now, he knew she was one of them. The golden glow born of Australia's blazing sun had by this time nearly faded from Arabella's flawless skin, the tiniest trace that remained imparting the luster of a pearl to her rose-kissed face, her swanlike throat, and the generous swell of her breasts revealed by the décolletage of her exquisite ball gown of amber silk. Her chestnut hair was swept up in an artful array of tumbled curls threaded with silk ribands and tiny flowers; two long ringlets were draped enticingly over one bare shoulder against which he remembered pressing his lips feverishly. A fan, reticule, and morocco slippers completed her ensemble.

Indeed, she was not beautiful, not in the way that Christine Wyndham and some of the other women present at the ball were; still, there was an arresting, alluring quality about Arabella, a sensuousness of which, Lucien recognized, she was still as yet unaware. Whether she liked it or not, he had left his mark upon her, he thought with grim satisfaction. She would not easily forget how she had lain naked beneath him, her long, unbound hair damp and disheveled, her flesh dewy with the sweat born of their lovemaking, her thighs opened for him as he had taken her. He inhaled sharply at the memory; his loins tightened with desire. She was his, damn it! He wanted to shout that to her, to the world. Instead, he stood rooted to the floor, feeling as though the unexpected sight of her had impacted him like a hard punch to his midsection. A muscle flexed dangerously in his taut, set jaw; his hand clenched so convulsively around the glass of rum punch he held that he was vaguely surprised the crystal did not shatter; he expected to see shards cutting and bloodying his palm—as Arabella, with her desertion, had carved up his heart and soul.

He had arrived late at the ball, had almost not come at all. Only the fact that Eugenia Howland was one of the grand old societal matriarchs of New South Wales, secure in her rank and position as a leading hostess and malicious enough to invite both the Exclusives and the Emancipists to her soirees, had persuaded him to attend. Lucien took cynical amusement in seeing the Exclusives gathered at one end of the ballroom, the Emancipists at the other, while elderly Eugenia perched on her thronelike chair in between, her eyes glinting with spiteful enjoyment at the wicked brew she had deliberately stirred. That the two groups should now and then cross paths was unavoidable: They met at the long tables covered with white linen cloths and laden with an array of food and drink; at the green-baize card tables set up, in the drawing room, for those too jaded for dancing, and where whist, loo, and euchre made all men equals; in the smoky billiard room, where the clink of rum-filled glasses mingled ceaselessly with the clack of the billiard balls; and on the wide veranda upon which the French doors that lined one wall of the ballroom opened to give way to the gardens. Such meetings ran the gamut from the cold ignoring of one another to heated arguments that were generally of a political nature and that, sometimes, if the opponents were drunk enough, degenerated to fisticuffs, providing both Eugenia and her guests with titillating excitement. That Arabella had not yet spied him was due to the fact that she was knee-deep amid a circle of Exclusives—something else that made Lucien's face darken with wrath.

Why it should matter, why *she* should matter, he did not know, did not care to examine more closely. Her running away from him had spoken to him more eloquently, more hurtfully, than words telling him what she had thought when she had awakened to discover herself lying in the arms of an ex-convict. He had attempted to follow her that day she had left him, cursing the sea that had obliterated her footprints in the sand, but he had lost her. Somehow, while he had been backtracking along the coast, trying to find her, she had reached Brisbane; he knew that, for once in Sydney, he had heard through the grapevine about the miraculous survival of Colonel Philip Wyndham's ward, how she had been "rescued" and escorted to her guardian by Captain Richard Bonniface. Lucien's lip had curled sardonically at this last piece of news; for from it, he had understood that Arabella had concealed the knowledge of the weeks she had spent with him in the wild, of the night she had lain naked in his embrace and surrendered herself to him.

Having learned her whereabouts, he had been strongly tempted to seek her out, would have done so had he not known with certainty that he would be refused admittance to Wyndham House, the door slammed shut in his face. Besides, what excuse could he have given for wishing to see her when she had yet to be formally presented to New South Wales society and, so far as the world knew, had no acquaintance with him whatsoever? His calling on her at that point would, in light of her having been missing for so many weeks after the shipwreck, have exposed her to a great deal of unwelcome, unsavory speculation and gossip. Plainly, Arabella had wanted nothing to do with him, Lucien had told himself angrily, sternly resolving to forget her.

But despite everything, he had not forgotten, *could* not forget her. Watching her now, he knew that she had somehow seeped into his blood, like a drug, that he would never be free of her as long as they both lived. When he saw her slip away unobtrusively at last from those who surrounded her and make her way from the ballroom to the gardens, he set down his glass and determinedly followed her.

She was suffocating, Arabella thought wildly, being smothered to death by the crowd that pressed around her—curious, inquisitive, fawning, judgmental. Her head was splitting from the heat, the noise, the questions. She wanted nothing so much as to return home to the Wyndhams' estate, Blue Trees, and lie down in her bedchamber. Since that was not possible, her only choice was to escape into the gardens. Excusing herself, ostensibly to visit the powder room, she found her way to the veranda instead and within moments was outside, hurrying down the wide steps and along the narrow cobblestone paths that twisted through the gardens rich with the heady fragrances of a profusion of flowers in bloom. The silvery light of the full moon that shone like a pearl against the black-velvet night sky and the yellow glow of the hurricane lamps alight on slender wrought-iron poles here and there illuminated her path as she wound deeper into the darkness, farther away from the house, to a spot where someone's happening upon her was unlikely.

Finally, in a secluded arbor with a stone bench, Arabella sat down, heaving a sigh of relief. Tonight marked her formal debut into the society of New South Wales. Before now, Aunt Hennie and Norah had insisted she remain sequestered to give what talk there had arisen a chance to die down and to allow her skin time to lose the tan that only women of the lower classes exhibited. Accustomed, as she was, to being out of doors, the fact that she had been unable to leave either the town house or, once they had moved to Blue Trees for the summer, the manor house, except for evening strolls in the gardens, had proved very frustrating to Arabella. She had come more and more to feel like some kind of caged animal, a virtual prisoner; more than once, she had wondered if that was how Lucien had felt in gaol. Remembering how he had seemed like an animal himself, as though he were one with the land, she had thought that confinement must have been torture for him, perhaps even worse than the floggings, the branding he had endured. Her heart had ached at the notion, although, resolutely, she had attempted to harden herself against him.

Gervasc had both helped and hindered that process— helped because it was flattering to have such a handsome man pay court to her, and hindered because she could not forget the fact that she was no longer chaste, no longer worthy of the honor of becoming his wife. More than ever, that thought had preyed upon her mind as she had gradually come to realize that he fully intended to fulfill both his family's and her own father's long-held wish that she and Gervase marry. What was she to do? Arabella had asked herself time and again. And time and again, she had found no answer. She was now quite certain that Uncle Philip, being such a staunch Exclusive, would indeed turn her out of the house if ever he learned she had lain with Lucien Sinclair. Yet it was not right to deceive Gervase into thinking that his suit would receive a favorable response, when, if she were honest with herself, she knew in her heart that she could never wed him now—or any man. The enormity of the mistake she had made was crushing; she would undo it if she could. But she could not; nor could she see any way around it. She was inevitably doomed to spinsterhood, to the sort of life that Norah and Miss Bodkins had mapped out for themselves.

Still, she had at this moment managed to escape from everything for just a little while. She had not until this evening realized what an unsocial person she had become, used to having only her father for companionship for so many years at Darracott Hall, only Harry on the months-long voyage from England to Australia, and then only Lucien for weeks in the wild. She had grown unaccustomed to being amid throngs of people. Even living with the Wyndhams in their town house had proved something of a strain, although that had lessened with their retiring to their larger manor house for the summer, where there was more room, a greater chance to slip away.

Now, for the first time all evening, Arabella felt the tension drain from her body. The cool breeze that swept in from the sea was welcome after the sultriness of the crowded ballroom, as was the quiet of the gardens, into which only muted talk, laughter, and music floated from the ballroom's French doors that stood open to the veranda. Above, the full moon hung low in the sky, its shower of silvery beams filtering through the swaying branches of the trees, and the stars that were its companions glittered like diamonds strewn across black satin. The sweet, distinctive scent of gum trees filled the air, mingling with the perfume of the flowers. Leaves rustled amid the plaintive calling of the night birds and the drowsy murmur of the cicadas, and from the distance came the whisper of the sea as it washed in upon the beach.

Closing her eyes, Arabella could imagine she were in the wild again, that the boughs above her head were those of the rough shelter she and Lucien had built when they had halted for the night. Life had been so simple then. She had not needed a chaperon just to take a walk. There had been no subjects she was forbidden to discuss. It had not mattered if she had forgotten to wear her hat. Of a sudden, she had a crazy impulse to strip off her ball gown, the hoops and layers of crinolines, the hated corset, to dance in the moonlight, as the Aborigines had danced, half naked, primordial, unbound by any rules— so different from Eugenia Howland's soiree, with its sedate waltzcs and polonaises, its lively but strictly patterned quadrilles and reels. It came to Arabella then that despite all the hardships she had suffered, she had been strangely happy with Lucien, happy in a way she had not been before or since. For the first and only time in her life, she realized now, she had been free.

She had belonged to no one save Lucien, to whom she had chosen willingly to give herself. Now, she saw with cruel clarity that she had returned to a world wherein a woman was a prisoner as surely as though she were incarcerated in gaol, shackled by chains, the chattel of men, legally bound first to her father and then to her husband or to some other male guardian, with no rights, no power of her own to wield in any matter that counted. She could not vote, and, consequently, had no voice in the laws that governed her. It was a rare woman who owned property, and once married, it became her husband's; so she must be inevitably dependent upon whatever some man chose to bestow upon her. She could be bartered away by her father or guardian, bought by and sold to the man who would best endow her family with power and wealth or spare them the agony of scandal and disgrace. A woman could be beaten, locked away in a madhouse, or raped by her husband, and no one would lift a finger in her defense; for it was the lot of a woman to belong to her husband as surely as his house, his carriage, and velvet smoking jacket did. Above all, she must never, ever lose her reputation—for it was, truly, her only possession.

Arabella shivered at the thought. She should go back inside, she told herself—for even to linger too long in the beautiful gardens was to invite gossip and censure, and a woman must take care to guard her virtue and good name. She had already lost the former; to lose the latter might prove far more devastating. As she lingered in the moonlight, she understood that she was already too late, that her absence had already been noticed, that Gervase had come in search of her. But then the man who had entered the arbor stepped from the shadows, so the moonlight and the hurricane lamps illuminated his dark visage, and her breath caught in her throat.

"Lucien!" Arabella breathed, utterly stricken. She could not believe that it was he who stood there, that he was real and not some figment of her imagination. It was both a dream and a nightmare come true, and as is so often the case in the latter, she could not seem to make her legs obey her brain, which pressed her urgently to flee. The scene appeared suddenly as though it were a vignette, blurred at the edges, adding to her sense of disorientation. One hand flew to her throat. "Lucien!"

"You were expecting Gervase." It was a statement, not a question—and a recognition that angered him, making the scar on his face seem to stand out even more prominently. "Were you promised to him all along, Arabella? Are you really so fickle, so faithless as that?" His voice was low, harsh with emotion; a muscle throbbed in his cheek.

"No, no . . . of course not. It was always hoped by our families that we would someday wed, but there was never any formal understanding between us." She was so stunned to see him that she hardly knew what she said to him, was conscious only of her heart, beating far too hard and fast in her breast, and of him—tall, dark, menacing, and all too real.

She had never seen him look so well, so attractive, so dangerous, like some sleek predator. Gone was the coarse woodsman; in his place stood a man clearly at ease in the finest drawing rooms. His exquisitely tailored black silk tailcoat clung to his broad shoulders and muscular arms that she now knew owed their development to the hard labor of prison. How many years had he spent there? she wondered dimly, as though it mattered. The frothy lace jabot of his crisp white cambric shirt spilled down his massive chest that tapered to a belly firm and flat beneath his expensive grey-and-black paisley waistcoat, from which hung a sterling silver watch chain adorned with a single fob and seal. His black silk pantaloons hugged his thick, corded thighs and calves in a way that reminded her all too vividly of the feel of his legs entangled with her own. At the memory, Arabella trembled so violently that she felt that her knees would buckle beneath her. She had not expected to feel like this upon seeing him again. In fact, she had never expected to see him again at all, and so had not prepared herself for that. It had never occurred to her that Lucien might move in the same social circles as she in Sydney, that whatever his background, he had climbed so high. The realization frightened her. What might he do with the truth of what had befallen her after the shipwreck? Only now, when it was too late, did she wonder, like any other woman who had foolishly given herself to a man, if he would tell. Would he? She could not bring herself to ask, as though if only she remained silent, she could somehow blot out the stain of that night as though it had never happened. Still, the thought of it was uppermost in her mind.

Belatedly, Arabella attempted to gather her wits.

"I—I must go back inside." She spoke softly, nervously, hoping she could slip past him into the darkness, run toward what she now perceived as the safety of the ballroom.

But without warning, Lucien's powerful hands shot out, seizing and yanking her to him roughly, making her gasp and shudder—although, to her deep shame, not solely with apprehension. His face was dark, unreadable in the diffuse light as he stared down at her, his gaze lingering hungrily on her tremulous mouth, the pulse that fluttered wildly at the hollow of her throat.

"Did you really think I would let you escape from me so easily as that, my sweet?" His pale grey eyes glittered intently; a faint, derisive smile curved his lips as he felt her quiver against him, as helpless as a moth beating its wings against a flame. "What is mine, I keep, Arabella—and like it or not, that includes you. Did you honestly believe otherwise?"

"You deceitful scoundrel! Take your hands off me!" she demanded, her fear that he would make a scene in the gardens, that she would be discovered alone with him, giving her strength and courage. "I am not yours! You took unforgivable advantage of me when I was in a—a vulnerable state—and you know it! You seduced me, Lucien!"

"Maybe. But let us not forget that you were more than willing to be seduced, my girl!"

Arabella blanched as though he had struck her, for deep inside, she knew that he had spoken no less than the truth—a truth that she did not want to face. Her eyes fell before his; she turned her head away; her white throat worked with emotion.

"That was before I—before I—"

"Before you learned that I was an ex-convict? A murderer?"

Somehow, despite all the evidence to the contrary

and what her own eyes had witnessed, Arabella had not in her heart really believed he was guilty of that crime; she had not *wanted* to believe it. But now, hearing him put it so baldly into words, she knew it must be the truth. How she had managed to deny it, she did not know, but his last word hit her as hard as a devastating blow, so that for a moment, she could not breathe. In that instant, she was at once conscious of nothing and of a thousand details: Lucien's fingers gripping her arms so tightly that she knew she would have bruises upon them, his breath warm against her skin, the scents of tobacco and bay rum that clung to him, the rustling branches of the gum trees that never lost their fragrant leaves, the droning of the cicadas, the sighing of the sea as it swept in upon the shore, the distant howl of a dingo baying at the moon. *Murderer.* The word rang like a merciless bell in her mind, a death toll. She felt faint and sick.

"You might at least have given me a chance to explain, Arabella. You owed me that much, I think."

"No," she protested, not wanting to believe that he might be right. "No, whatever I owed, I paid—dearly. Now, I only want to get on with my life, to be free of you, Lucien. There's nothing for you to say, to explain. You killed someone, committed a murder, and somehow, you managed to escape the gallows. In all the time we were together, you never chose to tell me that—"

"You wouldn't have stayed if I had, would you? You'd have been terrified, and the first chance you had, you'd have run away and died out there in the wild! I kept you alive, Arabella. Doesn't that tell you anything?"

"Only that you . . . needed a woman . . . wanted me—or, more likely, my inheritance."

"Your inheritance? My God! Do you think I give a damn about that?" Lucien grated, giving her a little shake that caused her to flinch. "I struck it rich in the goldfields of Ophir, my sweet. I'd hardly be welcome here tonight if I had not, believe me! But money buys most everything in this world . . . even admittance to polite circles for an ex-convict, if you've enough—and I do."

"But not love, Lucien . . . it doesn't buy that," she said quietly.

"No, that's a gift, freely given—as you gave it to me. Do you now say that what we shared meant nothing to you, Arabella? I don't believe that . . . I *won't* believe that! I wakened you to passion; I gave you pleasure and joy such as you would never have known in the arms of another man. I won't let you throw that away!" On his face was an expression of fierce determination that she had learned to recognize and that now scared her.

"What—what do you intend to do?" she asked, her voice barely a whisper.

"I want to marry you." The words shocked him almost as much as they did her. He had not meant to say them; yet now that he had spoken them, Lucien realized that he had no desire to call them back, that he did, in truth, want her as his wife—wanted her at Sinclair House and at his manor house that had no name and, most of all, wanted her in his bed again.

"No . . ." Arabella shook her head, horrified and yet perversely tantalized by the idea. Before she had learned what he was, she had wanted nothing more than what he now offered. Now, how could she wed him? "No, I—I can't marry you—"

"Can't . . . or won't?" Lucien's low voice was hard, sarcastic; his pride was stung, had felt the deep prick of her rejection too many times to accept it now. He was intensely aware of the feel of her in his arms, as she had been that night in the lean-to and as he had longed for her to be ever since, no matter how often he had tried to tell himself otherwise. "You were alone with me for weeks in the wild; you lay with me, my girl! If ever the scandal of that became known, I think you would be glad enough to wed me then, would you not?"

"Oh, I should have known that you would hold that threat over my head! I *did* know it! For that is the kind of man you are, isn't it, Lucien? A common, contemptible criminal—" Arabella's voice broke on a ragged sob. After a long moment, bitterly, she dashed away her tears, struggling to compose herself. "What a fool I was ever to trust you, to—to care for you! But you shall not find me so gullible now, I warn you! If you dare to voice them, I shall call your accusations lies . . . yes, *lies*, do you hear? I shall say you are a base coward who has chosen this means to strike at my guardian—for all of Sydney knows what a zealous Exclusive he is, while you must surely count yourself among the ranks of the Emancipists. It will be your word against mine, Lucien—and who will believe *you*, a convicted murderer, over the ward of Colonel Wyndham?" The cruel words Arabella uttered had seemed to come pouring out of their own volition, as though she were powerless to halt their flow, her fear making her as pitiless as she now believed him to be. "Now, let me go—else I shall scream—"

"I don't think so." Lucien cut her off abruptly, furious and wanting to hurt her as badly as she had hurt him. He had never until now thought to marry again; that he had expected her to scorn him still did not lessen the bitter blow of her refusal, especially when he remembered her standing with Gervase Wyndham—who was everything that he was not.

Hate and jealousy roiled within him. His eyes narrowed, darkened; a low, animalistic snarl erupted from his throat. Before Arabella realized what he intended, Lucien crushed her to him and ground his mouth down on hers hard—a savage, punishing kiss that took her breath and shattered her senses, leaving her feeling as though the earth had suddenly dropped from beneath her feet, sending her tumbling into an endless black void. Her head spun dizzily at the sensation; her stomach heaved in a way that made her fear she would swoon. Desperately, she tried to wrench free of him. But effortlessly, with the merest flex of his steely, corded arms, he tightened his grip upon her so she could not escape, tangled his hands in her hair to hold her still. She was acutely aware of how the hard, whipcord length of him rippled with muscle against her, painfully reminded of lying beneath him, of the feel of him driving in and out of her, taking her to the glorious heights of rapture and back. Now, despite herself, he wakened within her again that same primal instinct that had responded to him before, that leaped like a hungry tongue of flame through her body as he kissed her, his sinuous, beguiling tongue tracing the outline of her lips before roughly compelling them to part for his invasion. Deep, his tongue plunged into her mouth, searching out its innermost secret places, ravaging them until, moaning low in her throat, she unconsciously melted against him, her lips softening and yielding as she began to kiss him back, her tongue twining with his.

Lucien's mouth grew gentler then, although no less devouring as he tasted her, savored her, thinking how frantic he had been when he had awakened to find her gone from him, how mad, how wounded, and, most of all, how bereft. He did not want her to matter to him; but the hell of it was that she *did* matter. Somehow, she had got into his heart and soul, however much he longed to deny that. He wanted her, and no matter what she had said, she was his.

He molded her soft body to his hard one, his hands tense, fingers splayed, gliding slowly down her back, rubbing, kneading, lingering on sensitive places along her spine before he grasped her hips, drawing her thighs against his, so she could feel the evidence of his arousal. Her soft gasp as his maleness brushed against her intimately was a sound that inflamed him. Feverishly, he sucked and nibbled her lips, thrust his tongue in and out of her mouth, teasing, taunting, before he licked her throat and pressed his lips to her bare shoulder that had so tormented him earlier. Gently, he bit her there, then covered her breasts with kisses, reveling in the feel of the soft mounds that swelled against his cupped palms, nipples pebbled, the incoherent whimpers that issued from her throat. He could have her right here and now, Lucien thought, before, slowly, he realized that tears were trickling down her cheeks, that he could taste them, salty and bittersweet, upon his tongue.

"Arabella . . .?" His breathing harsh, labored, he drew back a little so he could see her face, his thumbs tracing the tracks of her tears, brushing the crystal beads away.

"I'm—I'm so confused," she confessed softly, biting her lower lip to hold back the sobs that rose to her throat at the recognition that even now, despite everything, he somehow had the power to arouse her, to reclaim the heart she had tried to take back from his keeping. Her breath came quickly, shallowly; her head swam as she strove to order her befuddled senses. She would surely have been missed by now. Even as the thought occurred to her, the sound of Gervase's slightly angry, impatient voice penetrated her consciousness.

"Arabella! Arabella, where are you?"

"I've—I've got to go." Panicked at the thought of Gervase coming upon them together in the gardens, she twisted wildly from Lucien's grasp, praying that he would not constrain her, that he would keep silent about what had passed between them in the wild. "Please, Lucien. You—you must let me go." Her face was pale and imploring in the moonlight, her mouth tremulous, bruised and swollen from his kisses.

There was nothing now of the woman who earlier had threatened him so boldly despite her tenuous position. How easy it would be to hold her here, to permit Gervase to find them together. For a long, taut moment, Lucien was almost tempted. But now was neither the time nor the place, he at last understood. Arabella's eyes were wide and dark with apprehension. Her survival instinct was strong, he knew; backed into a corner, she would fight, would perhaps resort to the lies she had so rashly told him that she would use against him in such an event—and she had been right, unfortunately: Who would believe him, an ex-convict, over her, the colonel's ward?

"Be warned, my girl: By no means have you seen the end of this!" he muttered fiercely, unwillingly stepping aside to let her pass as, gathering her skirts, she ran from the arbor, leaving him alone in the darkness.

Chapter Twelve

The Carriage Ride

Gervase's footsteps echoed ominously on the cobblestone paths of the gardens as Arabella hastened toward the lights that glowed all along the veranda. Nervously, her hands fussed with her hair and ball gown as she made her way toward him, for she had no mirror to check her appearance and could only hope that Lucien had not disarranged it too badly. Her heart was pounding; in her mouth, she could taste her own fear acid upon her tongue, mingling with the taste of Lucien himself, and that filled her with guilt and shame as she thought of how, ignoring every moral teaching she professed to believe, she had kissed him, had responded to him with the passion he had wakened inside her that night she had lain in his embrace and let him do with her as he willed.

Perhaps those days of high fever and delirium had

indeed deranged her brain, had left her mad, or perhaps she was, in truth, a wanton—no better than the dockside prostitute who had recently been found murdered in The Rocks and whose sad tale Tilly, frightened, had whispered to Arabella afterward, viewing her mistress as a savior who had undoubtedly spared her a like fate. The grisly murder had surely been the work of a madman, a lunatic convict, Arabella had thought, and she had shivered, remembering the brand upon Lucien's shoulder. Yet all fear had fled in the face of his desire for her. Now, unconsciously, she scrubbed hard at her mouth, as though, with her hand, she could remove the stain of his kisses.

"Arabella?" Gervase's voice echoed again. "Ah, there you are! Where have you been? You disappeared more than a quarter of an hour ago. People were beginning to remark upon your absence; and I'm sure I don't need to tell you, my dear, that under the circumstances, you would be wise to guard your behavior—not that I'm casting any aspersions upon it myself, you understand. But . . . well, you must know how people talk, Arabella."

"Yes, yes, I *do* know. I'm—I'm sorry, Gervase. It was just so—so hot and noisy inside, and I'm afraid I've got a dreadful migraine. I thought perhaps some fresh air and quiet . . . but it has not served, after all. Would you—would you mind very much taking me home?" She spoke in a rush, aware she was babbling, but unable to stop, praying he would put her flustered state down to the headache she had, in reality, begun to suffer.

"No, of course not. Poor Arabella. I suppose that it

really has all been too much for you. Mama ought to have had better sense and introduced you more gradually into society. But, then, Eugenia Howland's invitations are practically a royal decree here in New South Wales. Come. Let me take you back inside, where we can make your excuses. Then I'll drive you home in my carriage.''

It seemed from his solicitous tone that Gervase noticed nothing amiss. Gratefully, Arabella nodded her head and allowed him to lead her into the ballroom, where they said their farewells to Eugenia Howland, as well as to the rest of the Wyndhams, who had arrived separately from the two of them, and so need not depart with them. Following that, Gervase ordered his carriage brought around to the front of the manor house and assisted Arabella inside, making certain she was comfortably settled upon the squabs before rapping his cane against the box to signal his driver to get under way. The crack of the driver's whip resounded, and with a lurch, the vehicle rolled forward into the night, wheels crunching upon the crushed seashells that formed the wending drive of Coral Reef.

Resting against the cushions, her eyes closed, Arabella was nevertheless uncomfortably aware of Gervase beside her, his arm draped casually over her shoulder. Since her arrival in Sydney, he had been so kind to her, so caring, that he made her feel guilty and disloyal, as though she had betrayed him with Lucien. Clearly, Gervase expected to marry her, and thus far, she had done nothing to let him know that his proposal would not be accepted. Even now, when she could feel his hands at her temples, massaging her aching head, an

intimate caress, she was not bold enough to speak—
because what explanation could she give to him for
her refusal to entertain his suit? He was handsome and
charming, a lieutenant in the New South Wales Corps,
heir to his father's estates, and had given her no cause
for dislike. What could she say to him? That she wasn't
ready for marriage? She was almost twenty years old—
by many people's reckoning, already passed over, a
spinster. He would not believe any excuse for demurring—nor would the truth serve her. So she kept still,
moaning a little at the pleasurable sensations he aroused
in her as he rubbed her temples and stroked her hair,
his shoulder now pillowing her head.

Arabella was unused to strong spirits—her experience with the Aborigines' potent wine had taught her
that—and she realized, now, that she should not have
drunk so much rum punch at the soiree. But the drink
had tasted deceptively mild, and every time she had
emptied her glass, it had been refilled. She was also
unused to such a long, tiring evening. Between Gervase's ministrations, the punch, and the lateness of the
hour, she was so drowsy that she half dozed on the
carriage seat, her usual polite but determined defenses
against him lowered.

"Feeling better?" he asked, his voice low in her ear.

"Yes . . . much," she murmured.

The broadcloth of his evening jacket was smooth
against her skin; his deft hands were soothing; the rhythmic turning of the carriage wheels was lulling. He
smelled faintly of rum punch, tobacco, and sandalwood,
exotic fragrances that conjured in her mind images of

the tropical woods along the northeastern coast of New South Wales, and of the time she had spent there with Lucien.

Lucien. Inevitably, it seemed, he intruded upon her thoughts, even though she had tried so hard to drive him from them. It was *his* breath she felt against her skin, *his* strong arm she felt about her—not that of Gervase—as though the two men had somehow become confused or fused in her mind, although their personalities were nothing at all alike. Lucien was like a storm— dark, wild, savage—while Gervase was just the opposite—bright, conventional, civilized. There could be no comparison between the two men. Only a madwoman would not prefer Gervase—and indeed, Arabella thought she must be such, for as she felt his lips tentatively brush her hair, soft, gentle, caressing, she was not stirred, but apprehensive that he sought to press his suit more strongly.

"Arabella . . . Arabella . . ." He spoke quietly against her hair. "We are so seldom alone together that I've had little chance to speak of what has been on my mind these past several weeks. But you must know how I've come to feel about you. Ever since that day I saw you in the gardens at Wyndham House, I've known that I was right to respect the wishes of our families that we marry and to wait for you to grow up. Now, you are a woman . . . a woman to be put upon a pedestal, admired and worshiped, like a perfect statue of the purest, most pristine marble, so precious, to be only carefully touched . . . very carefully. . . . I *do* want to wed you."

His words were flattery, surely, yet Arabella was

conscious suddenly of a chill, as though a goose had just walked over her grave. Marble was cold and dead, while she was warm and alive. The images Gervase evoked in her mind made her shiver; instinctively, she knew there was nothing in them of the impetuosity, the fierceness, or the passion she had known with Lucien. She remembered standing in the mud by the billabong, with the rain pouring down on her, and Lucien kissing her, hard and hungrily. She realized she could not envision that scene with Gervase in it, and for some unknown reason, that thought filled her with uneasiness. But she brushed the feeling aside, telling herself that it did not matter, that she could not wed Gervase anyway, not now.

"I . . . like you, too, Gervase. But I—I need more time. I've really only known you a few months, after all, and—"

"Dear Arabella. You'll have a lifetime to come to know me better. But I shall not press you just yet. I know that you've had a harrowing experience and that tonight was a sore trial to you, too. It is only that I have already waited so long that I've grown impatient to have our future settled, and I know that Father, especially, wishes it, as well. As you saw this evening, the New South Wales Corps constitutes much of society here, so a wife can only be counted an asset to a man's military career—and of course, a man always longs for heirs to carry on his family's name and to inherit all he has worked so hard to achieve. As a woman, you must yearn for a husband and children, Arabella."

"Yes, I do. Still, it was clear to me tonight that I have in many ways led a sheltered, solitary life, that I will have to learn to adjust to new ways here. With Papa being so ill, we did not entertain much at Darracott Hall, you know.''

"Yet I think that you would make a success of whatever you set out to accomplish. You are much like Norah in that respect. She is a sensible woman, not given to flightiness, like Mama and Chrissie. You do well to emulate her, for although she is not beautiful, Norah has many other admirable traits a wise woman would choose to cultivate.''

The implication was that neither was she, Arabella, beautiful. There was nothing for her to say to that, because she knew she was not. That Lucien had thought her so, had called her so, she must put from her mind. Lucien had surely lied to her, saying only what he had known she had wanted to hear. Gervase, at least, was honest, a gentleman—although that balm was surprisingly small comfort to her battered heart.

"However," he continued, "I should not like to think you intend to follow Norah's example and never marry."

Gervase's mouth was very near to hers as he spoke, and Arabella became aware of the fact that he was going to kiss her. A strange curiosity came upon her at the realization. At least she could discover whether Lucien alone had the power to make her feel as he had. So she made no attempt to turn her head away as Gervase's lips claimed hers. The pressure of his mouth was firm, although not unduly so, and he tasted of the rum punch that had been served at Eugenia Howland's soiree. He kissed her unhurriedly, without hunger, as though his foray were a tentative exploration to test her response, almost as though he were conducting some kind of scientific experiment, Arabella reflected dully, feeling vaguely affronted by the notion. After a long moment, he delicately thrust his tongue into her mouth, seeking and discovering its soft, sensitive places. This, too, was a leisurely incursion, and she thought of his likening her to a marble statue, and she sensed instinctively that this was precisely how he would make love to her, what he had meant by his words that she must be "touched carefully." It came to her then that he was the kind of man who, as her husband, would never dream of stripping her naked, as Lucien had. Rather, Gervase would do no more than lift her nightgown to claim his conjugal rights—and that for the primary aim of begetting an heir, as she had been reared to expect of the marriage bed. Her own duty was to lie still and submissive while her husband took his carnal pleasure, she had always heard; it was a distasteful act that no woman enjoyed, except possibly, perhaps, those low creatures who did it in exchange for a man's money.

Yet if she were honest with herself, Arabella knew she must admit that she *had* enjoyed it when she had lain in Lucien's arms—and that he had taken as great a delight in giving her pleasure as he had in receiving it, as though it were the most natural thing in the world that she should know joy in his embrace. Even now at the memory of their lying naked and sweating together, she could feel her breasts swell, aching to be touched, her nipples tauten with desire, and the sweet rush of honeyed moisture between her thighs. She moaned low in her throat. Of their own volition, her arms crept up around Gervase's neck; her fingers tunneled through his hair. She touched the tip of her tongue to his, tracing, twining. But whereas Lucien would have fallen upon her blindly, passionately, at her response, Gervase instead stiffened abruptly and, without warning, drew away from her coolly, his mouth tight with anger and suspicion.

"Where did you learn that, Arabella?" he inquired, his tone deceptively soft but icy, his pale blue eyes as hard-edged as a cloudless Australian sky in which the sun burned mercilessly.

For a moment, she could only gape at him, startled by his sudden transformation from a perfectly pleasant and charming suitor to a rigid and formidable military officer seemingly bent on a ruthless interrogation. She had thought to please him by kissing him back; instead, she had shocked and offended him, she saw. It was true, then: Only a wanton or a whore enjoyed a man's lovemaking. Stricken, she cast down her eyes, shame flooding her being.

"Arabella, I asked you a question: Where did you learn that?"

"No-no-nowhere, Gervase," she lied, her voice barely a whisper. She was nervous, sick with fright; she realized that she had made a mistake, that she had displayed a knowledge she ought to have lacked. "I— I was merely following your lead, that's all. I'm—I'm sorry if it—if it was wrong." Yet even as she spoke, she grasped dimly that although she had just kissed him, which was hardly cause for chastisement, Gervase was making her feel more soiled and despoiled at this moment than Lucien, to whom she had surrendered her virtue, ever had.

Still, to her relief, Gervase relaxed at her admission.
"My dear . . . of course, you are an innocent and
so could know no better. But your kissing a man in that
fashion could lead to . . . misperceptions about your
character, Arabella. You might be thought fast and common and more experienced in these matters than a lady
ought to be. Naturally, no man would be pleased to
think that those traits belonged to a woman he wished
to take to wife."

"No, of course not," Arabella replied woodenly,
now more certain than ever that she could never wed
Gervase, that he would be horrified and enraged to learn
that she had lain with Lucien Sinclair. Any gentleman
would.

She was glad that they had reached Blue Trees at
last. Once inside the manor house, pleading her headache, she made good her escape from Gervase and,
after retiring to her bedchamber, cried herself to sleep,
feeling as though some vital spark that had once been
stirred to flame inside her had now been cruelly extinguished.

Chapter Thirteen

Chrissie

Ever afterward, for so many reasons, Arabella was to think of that night of the soiree at Coral Reef as the turning point of her life; for perhaps even without what had gone before, it would have proved pivotal. That following morning, Chrissie was all agog, bursting with the tale of how, on the way home from the Howland estate, the Wyndhams' carriage had been set upon by a gang of convicts bent on robbing them. Such attacks were not at all uncommon in the Colonies. Many prisoners, whether paroled or pardoned, were not willing to turn over a new leaf, but preferred to continue their lives of crime, banding together in dangerous gangs, the better to ensure their survival and to thwart the authorities. Most often, such men took to the high toby, robbing the coaches of the gentry and of prosperous merchants and farmers, or to smuggling. Sometimes, they raided outlying farms, pillaging and burning the countryside.

"Oh, you should have seen them, Arabella!" Chrissie declared excitedly, referring to the highwaymen, as she spread her toast generously with marmalade. "They had black hoods over their faces, of course . . . like executioners! And I was so scared! I thought they were going to shoot us all. But they wanted only our jewelry and money. Naturally, Papa would have resisted. But Richard"—Richard had accompanied Chrissie to the ball—"said that putting up a fight would only make matters worse—which I thought was *very* poor-spirited of him, I must say. Just think of his insisting that I meekly hand over Grandmama's pearls to those ruffians! Why, if he had just consented to lend me his pistol, I should have shot those scoundrels myself! But of course, he would not—for all the good his refusal to defy them did. They clubbed him over the head anyway—and I daresay they should have treated Papa the same were it not for Black Jack."

"Black" Jack O'Flaherty was, as Arabella knew, the Wyndhams' groom and coachman. The Irishman had been transported seven years ago for highway robbery, and because of his ability with horses, he had, once granted his ticket-of-leave, been hired by the Wyndhams. He was handsome in a coarse, devil-may-care fashion and so charming that one would have thought he had not only kissed, but also consumed the Blarney Stone. Arabella had found him far too smooth for her liking; she suspected that for all his outward appearance of reformation, he was still a rogue and probably still involved in some type of criminal activity on the side.

Chrissie, however, although she chided him for his insolence, was prone to blushing and dimpling at his flattery.
More than once, she had remarked to Arabella that it
was really too bad that Black Jack was not only a groom
and coachman, but also an ex-convict—"because he's
ever so much more exciting than boring old Richard!"
she would declare, her impudent shrug of dismissal
accompanied by a tiny moue of exasperation that the
captain should, since his transfer to Sydney, have
proved such a persistent but uninspired caller.

Chrissie had always had a penchant for danger and
excitement, Arabella thought at such moments, remembering that it had been Chrissie who had forged first
and headlong into the Gypsy's pavilion that day of the
Scarborough fair. More than once, Arabella had subtly
suggested to Richard that a bit of dash, spontaneity,
poetry, and a few moonlit, stolen kisses would go a
good deal further toward winning Chrissie's wayward
heart than all his stilted stories of military life and the
sedate strolls he escorted her on among the gardens.
But Arabella's hints along those lines had gone ignored,
and she had not pressed, feeling that Richard had been
somewhat embarrassed at her attempt to intervene in
his personal life. It was clear to her that he was smitten
with Chrissie; it was equally clear to her that Chrissie
mistook his kindness for dullness, his perseverance for
plodding. Now, Arabella felt a prickle of uneasiness as
she realized, as Chrissie continued to chatter on animat-
edly, that in the encounter last night, Richard had come
off looking cowardly and foolish, while Black Jack had
assumed gallant, heroic proportions in Chrissie's mind.

Daring to draw his pistol in the face of the threat the blackguards had offered, he had succeeded in driving them away with several loud shots.

"Only think, Arabella! Why, if not for Black Jack's bravery, I might have been carried off and ravished!" Chrissie's tone suggested a certain titillation at the prospect—as though she dreamily envisioned Black Jack riding to her rescue and making love to her himself afterward.

"Christine!" Norah, who had joined them at the table, chided sharply. "As a lady, it is not seemly that you would even think of such a thing, let alone mention it! How fortunate that Papa has already left for the corps headquarters this morning and that Mama was feeling too indisposed to join us for breakfast, else you would surely be punished for your unruly tongue!"

Chrissie's response to this quite accurate observation was childishly to stick out the tongue in question at Norah.

"You're just jealous because no man in the gang would have bothered to carry *you* off, Norah!" she retorted crossly. "You're worse than a missionary about what's proper and what's not, and never any fun at all. Why, if you'd been kidnapped, I daresay that those convicts would have paid *us* to take you back, they'd have been so relieved to be rid of your company! I swear . . . if you don't sweeten your disposition, you're never going to get a man, because no man worth his salt wants to be managed by an overbearing busybody for the rest of his days—and that's the plain, unvarnished truth of the matter!"

Norah went very still, white-faced, and thin-lipped at that, as though she had received a stunning slap. Then, after a moment, she spoke quietly.

"I don't suppose it has ever occurred to you, Chrissie, that with Mama's health not being robust and with Papa being so busy with the affairs of the military, the responsibility for running our household has, more and more through the years, naturally fallen upon my shoulders, whether I wished for that burden or not. However, I do not complain; for just as Arabella tended to her father, I conceive it my loving duty to take care of Mama and Papa—and even you, Chrissie. I know that you are not deliberately wicked. Nevertheless, I fear that your selfishness and lack of sensibility, to say nothing of your wildness and foolish romanticism, shall prove your undoing one day. You would do well to put these silly flights of fancy from your head and to give serious thought to settling down with someone like Richard, who cares for you more deeply than you realize, I think, and who will be a sober, steadying influence upon you. Now, if you'll excuse me, I must get on with my work."

Rising, Norah vacated the morning room, leaving behind an awkward, uncomfortable silence and a Chrissie who at least had the good grace to look shamefaced.

"I suppose I should feel sorry for her," Chrissie said at last. "I know that things haven't been easy for her. But . . . oh, Arabella! Don't you ever think that there simply *must* be more to life than just getting married and having babies—or winding up like Norah? I mean . . . it all seems so . . . so *tame* and boring! Only think how your life will be when you wed Gervase: the same routine of housekeeping and meal-planning day in and day out, the same parties attended by the same people every other evening, the same man making the same husbandly demands of you at night—and none of it hardly any fun at all for *you*! Why, a woman might as well be a . . . a porcelain doll, without thoughts or feelings. Sometimes, I feel as though I shall go mad, thinking about it! I feel like one of those poor birds in those gilded cages the vendors sell in the marketplace, and I long to fly free at least once in my life. . . . Oh, how lucky you are, Arabella, to have had at least that chance, no matter how terrifying your experience following the shipwreck!''

"Yes, I—I suppose so," Arabella agreed slowly. "I confess that it has been . . . difficult in many respects to return to a civilized society, much harder than I had realized that it would be—and yes, there has been a certain loss of freedom that I deeply regret."

"Then you *do* understand! I knew that you would. But Norah never will. She wants me to marry Richard."

"Is that truly such a dreadful prospect, Chrissie? He is a kind and good man, and he *does* love you."

"Yes, I know . . . but to go from my father's house to my husband's house, without having ever experienced *life*, Arabella! I just don't believe that I'm ready for that. I keep hoping that fate will intervene, as it did for you, and that something wild and wonderful will happen to change the course of my life. Otherwise, I very much fear that I shall wind up like Mama. She's not really ill, you know—at least, not in the way that everyone supposes. She drinks. It's how she escapes, I have always thought. It's become worse since we came to the Colonies, where everything revolves around the

rum trade. . . . Oh, good heavens, Arabella! Look at
the time!'' Chrissie cried abruptly as she glanced at the
ornate ormolu clock ticking upon the mantel over the
fireplace. ''We're to be at the dressmaker's shop this
morning. I was so upset over the quarrel with Norah
that I nearly forgot. Come. We must hurry if we're not
to be late.''

Together, they hastened from the morning room; and
presently, after a flurry of activity that included Chrissie's changing her gown twice, they sat ensconced in
the Wyndhams' carriage, its wheels rumbling over the
road into Sydney. Chrissie spent most of the trip chatting
with her maid, Peg, and Tilly, going over the shopping
lists with which they had been entrusted by Aunt Hennie, Norah, and the cook. All that was required of Arabella was an occasional interjectory remark, for which
she was thankful. The argument in the morning room,
while unpleasant, had nevertheless been enlightening in
a number of respects; and she welcomed the opportunity
to reflect upon it while it was still fresh in her mind.
Now, she saw clearly that the weeks with Lucien after
the shipwreck had altered her more than just physically,
that she had indeed, as Chrissie had declared, tasted
freedom in a way that was denied to most women of
her status in life. Whatever else it had been, life with
Lucien *had* been exciting, filled with the kinds of experi-
ences for which Chrissie obviously hungered. Perhaps
even Norah wished for them but had subverted her desires for her duty. As she herself must, Arabella reminded herself sternly. She would not wed Lucien; she
could not wed Gervase. She must live out, in New South

Wales, the remaining year before reaching her majority as circumspectly as possible so as not to bring disgrace upon the Wyndhams. Then she could return home to England, to Darracott Hall, where she would live quietly, a spinster, yes, but not one like Norah or Miss Bodkins. Arabella had always loved the land. She would give her whole heart to that, to continuing what her father had built, she decided now, thinking that the answers to her questions had been so simple that she did not know why they had not occurred to her before. It might not be the future for which she had once hoped, but it was far better than the one she had feared.

As for Gervase . . . he himself had given her a clue as to how best to answer him when he spoke again of marriage. Likening herself to Norah, Arabella need say only that she, too, had decided never to wed but to devote herself instead to her father's memory and to his dream of Darracott Hall. Gervase would be hurt and angry; still, he would get over that in time and would need never know the pain and insult of learning how she had betrayed him with Lucien. Lucien himself, Arabella intended to finish with today. In an envelope in her reticule, she carried his guide's fee of £100, which she had garnered from her pin money. Earlier, she had spoken to Tilly, who adored her in much the same manner as a faithful puppy might. Sworn to secrecy about her errand, Tilly had agreed to deliver the envelope to Sinclair House, while Arabella and Chrissie were at the dressmaker's shop. There, Arabella would undertake the final fittings to complete her new wardrobe, some of which, like the ball gown she had worn last night, had already been finished and delivered to Blue Trees.

All her decisions made, Arabella felt a sense of inner peace she had not known since before her father had died. She had made a mistake, falling in love with Lucien and lying with him, but she would atone for that by never marrying. She could endure one year here, and then she would go home, where she would live on her memories, her adventures ended. So she thought until that evening, when Tilly came to her room.

"Miss Arabella . . .?" the maid said tentatively after knocking, cracking open the door, and poking her head inside.

"Yes, Tilly. Come in, come in. You're not disturbing me, if that is what you fear." Arabella laid aside the book she was reading. "What is it?"

"Well, there weren't no chance ta tell ye earlier, miss, but . . . t' message ye 'ad me deliver today? T' Sinclair 'ouse."

"Yes?"

"I know that ye didn't expect one, but there were a reply, miss." Reaching into the pocket of her apron, Tilly drew forth an ivory vellum envelope.

"A reply!" Arabella cried softly, leaping from her bed, her heart beginning to race. "Let me see it!" Her hands trembling, she snatched the missive from Tilly and, breaking the seal, tore open the envelope. She was so stunned that she read twice the bold black words scrawled therein:

You think that your payment of my fee has ended the matter between us. But you're wrong, my girl.

It seemed that Arabella saw Lucien everywhere after that. It was as though, like a dingo, he stalked her, now and then nipping at her heels to remind her that he had her scent and was hard on her trail. She lived in a state of constant agitation and turmoil. To think that she had foolishly unleashed this devil, this Demon upon herself! She could not believe that he wanted her still—and yet what else *could* he want save her? Her inheritance, she had once thought. But now, after a seemingly endless string of parties, routs, and soirees, she knew that he had spoken truly that night in the gardens at Coral Reef, that he had, in fact, made a fortune in the goldfields of Ophir. As he had said, it bought his entrance into many a household into which he would not otherwise have been permitted to step foot.

Even the whispered rumors that were circulating about him, that he had murdered his wife back in England and now perhaps was murdering young women on the town in The Rocks, appeared only to enhance his notoriety, his undeniable mystique, his intriguing menace. Although he had been questioned by the New South Wales Corps regarding the murders, Lucien had not been arrested, there being only suspicion and no hard evidence against him. The Emancipists, naturally, held that he was innocent and that the unsavory gossip was an attempt by the Exclusives to blacken his name and character because he had managed to climb so high following his release from gaol. The Exclusives, of course, believed him guilty. Yet even among their ranks, it was claimed that he was too smart and, more important, too rich now ever to be brought to trial for his crimes. They further pointed to the fact that, clearly, he was not without influential connections, else he would not have escaped the gallows in England.

Lucien himself never commented on the matter, and few were brave enough to remark upon it to his face: He was known to be a marksman capable of shooting the pip out of a playing card at fifty yards. She was perhaps, Arabella thought, the only person in the entire continent of Australia to whom he had ever spoken of the crime for which he had been transported; of the rest of the killings, he made no mention, and for a long time, she did not ask him about them, too afraid of the answer. For he *would* answer *her*, she sensed instinctively.

He was obsessed with her.

It was as though whatever madness had possessed her that night under the jacaranda tree had also seized him with a vengeance. She was not safe alone at any function she attended. Like the proverbial hawk, Lucien watched her every move ceaselessly. If she slipped away or somehow found herself unaccompanied, he materialized at her side to press his seduction of her, to insist that she marry him.

"Sooner or later, you *will* be my wife, Arabella," he would declare harshly, "so why do you not save us both a lot of grief and give in to me now? This refusal of yours to wed me is not only infuriating, but also foolish. You're already mine—and I greatly dislike seeing you on Gervase's arm everywhere I go. God knows that having surrendered yourself to me, you're too damned decent to marry him or any other man. So it's me or no one, my girl!"

"Then no one it shall be, Lucien! Now, release me. Please."

She had learned that it did no good to fight him. He would hold her for as long as he wished, kissing her with a savagery and an urgency that was almost frightening, his hands roaming over her body however they willed, as though she did, in truth, belong to him and he had every right to do with her as he pleased. A score of times he might have taken her, for no matter how hard she struggled against the feelings he evoked inside her, her will and mind seemed to melt away at his touch, leaving her weak and faint in his embrace, her body aching for fulfillment. How Lucien restrained his own self, Arabella did not know, although she feared that it was only a matter of time before his determined self-control snapped and he did something wild and volatile. She knew she was playing with a fire whose flames were already burning dangerously high. Still, she felt herself powerless to halt its onslaught. Lucien would not cease his pursuit of her, and she dared tell no one of their relationship in order to end it.

So preoccupied was she with her own dilemma that Arabella was unaware of the other intrigues that seethed beneath the calm surface of the Wyndham household, until the morning when she awoke to discover the entire estate in an uproar. In the dead of the night, Chrissie had packed a bag and run away with Black Jack O'Flaherty.

"I blame myself," Arabella said quietly to those gathered in the drawing room as she slowly folded up the note Chrissie had left behind. "I—I should have realized from . . . certain things she told me and the way she looked at him and spoke to him that something like this was in the offing. But I just never dreamed that she would—would take such a drastic step as this."

"No, of course, you wouldn't, Arabella," Norah concurred, not unkindly, as she alternately clenched and unclenched her handkerchief in her only outward sign of anxiety and grief. "No more would I or any other decent lady of our class. The very idea of any genteel, well-bred woman stooping so low as to consort with a common convict . . . well, it is simply not done; it is not even to be thought of. That Chrissie could behave so shockingly, so shamelessly, so selfishly, with no heed as to the scandal and disgrace that she has loosed upon us all—" Norah broke off abruptly, her mouth tight with anger, disapproval, and hurt.

In the tense silence that fell upon the drawing room, broken only by the sound of Aunt Hennie's pitiful weeping, Arabella's heart pounded so hard and loud in her breast that she thought that the others could surely hear it. Terrible guilt ate at her—not only because she had been so wrapped up in her own problems that she had missed any inkling of Chrissie's purpose and failed to prevent it, but also because she knew she was no better than Chrissie. Worse, perhaps—because at least Chrissie had not sought to deceive her family by keeping her relationship with Black Jack O'Flaherty clandestine, but, rather, had boldly eloped with him and honestly admitted to that fact. Arabella felt dreadful, like a coward, a criminal. In that instant, she had a wild urge to leap from her chair, to blurt out her own secret culpability with regard to Lucien. She bit her lower lip so hard that she drew blood in an effort to hold back the hot words of shame and remorse that rose in her throat.

"I've ordered the carriage brought around front, Father," Gervase announced as he joined them in the drawing room, pulling on his black leather riding gloves. "They've some hours head start; still, they were traveling in the dark. It is possible that they have not yet got so far that we cannot overtake them if we drive hard and fast. If Black Jack has not yet compromised her, we can bring Chrissie home and have any marriage ceremony they might have undergone annulled. Chrissie is under age, after all, and cannot legally wed without your consent, Father. It may be that we can hush up the whole affair, with no one the wiser."

"No . . . depend upon it: Black Jack will have her in her bed by now to prevent just that, Gervase." The colonel spoke slowly, shaking his head, like a man who had received a stunning physical blow. "He always was a shrewd, sly bastard, and I've no doubt that he believes that if we're presented with a fait accompli, we'll have no choice but to swallow it, lest we choke on it. I'm quite certain he thinks to extort not only Chrissie's dowry from me, but also a town house in Sydney and a handsome living allowance for the two of them, as well. However, he shall soon learn that I am made of sterner stuff than that! No . . . send the carriage back to the stables, Gervase. Chrissie has made her bed, and now, she must lie in it. From this moment on, she is no longer my daughter! I will not hear her name mentioned in this house again! Is that clear?"

With those severe, unrelenting words, the colonel stood, abruptly striding to the table where the family

Bible reposed. Opening the book to its record page, he picked up a quill and, after dipping it into the inkwell, coldly, firmly, began to cross Chrissie's name and birth date from the page, the furious scratching of his pen seeming to drown out even Aunt Hennie's sobs of protest and despair. Frozen where she sat, Arabella could only watch mutely, horrified, shaken to her very bones by his callous words, his brutal gesture. Chrissie had been Uncle Philip's favorite child; yet now, it was as though she no longer existed for him, had never been a part of the Wyndham family at all. How much more coldly, then, would he deal with her, Arabella, should he ever learn of her relationship with Lucien? She could expect no mercy whatsoever. Thank God she had never told anyone what had passed during those weeks following the shipwreck and her journey to Brisbane! Nor, she noted, was Gervase's visage any less hard and austere than his father's; plainly, his condemnation of Chrissie was equally ruthless and absolute. Had Arabella harbored even a glimmer of thought about wedding him, it would have been utterly extinguished in that moment. Even Norah was stony-faced—although Arabella thought she saw a spark of sorrow and regret in Norah's eyes. Only Aunt Hennie was grief-stricken and distraught. At last, Arabella rose.

"Come, Aunt Hennie," she urged softly. "This has all been too much for you, I fear. Let me take you upstairs and put you back to bed."

Clutching at Arabella's hand, Aunt Hennie nodded gratefully, tears streaming down her withered cheeks, her face so pale and drawn that she seemed to have aged twenty years in as many minutes. Wordlessly, then,

Arabella led the older woman from the drawing room, trying not to wince as she heard the dusting of sand upon aged yellow paper, drying the ink, before, with a thunderous thump, Uncle Philip slammed shut the Bible, irrevocably sealing foolish Chrissie's wretched fate.

Upstairs in Aunt Hennie's bedchamber, Arabella helped her to undress and get into a nightgown. Then, after settling the older woman in bed, she poured her a snifter of brandy from the crystal decanters arrayed on a sterling silver tray on the dresser.

"Leave the bottle there, Arabella." Aunt Hennie motioned toward her nightstand as, her eyes closed, her hands trembling as she raised the glass to her lips, she drank a long draught of the mellow liquor, sighing deeply after she had swallowed it.

"Of course, Aunt Hennie," Arabella said gently after a minute.

"Always such a dear child," Aunt Hennie mumbled tremulously, her tears starting afresh, trickling down her cheeks—but Arabella did not know if the older woman was referring to her or to Chrissie, although she suspected the latter. "Such a dear, dear child . . ."

Not wanting to intrude further upon Aunt Hennie's grief, and feeling, too, as though, as little as it was, she had done all she could at the moment, Arabella tiptoed from the room, closing the door softly behind her.

She never saw Aunt Hennie sober again—not then nor in the long weeks that followed, when, one terrible, shocking morning not long after an extremely subdued, solemn Christmas and New Year, Chrissie's poor, brutally butchered body was discovered in The Rocks.

Book Three

So Eternal a Bower

Chapter Fourteen

Under the Blue Gum

Blue Trees, New South Wales Colony, Australia, 1857

" 'E sold 'er, miss. When 'e found out 'e weren't going ta get so much as tuppence from 'er father, Black Jack took poor Miss Chrissie inta T' Rocks, an' 'e sold 'er inta whoredom, that's what 'e did!'' Tilly's low voice was filled with shock and horror as she related her sordid tale to Arabella. " 'E got drunk all t' time an' beat 'er up regular-like, till she were too afraid ta defy 'im anymore, miss, an' 'e kept 'er locked up in t' awful flat where they lived, so's she couldn't run away or send fer 'elp. An' all t' while, 'e sold 'er ta them men what wanted 'er, miss. But then a few nights ago, Black Jack were set upon in some dark alley, an' some'ow afterward, Miss Chrissie escaped an' fled. But T' Rocks ain't no place fer a woman alone; an' that's when it 'appened, miss. That's when t' filthy butcher got 'er, raped 'er, an' carved 'er up like all them other poor young biddies.''

"How? *How* do you know all this, Tilly?" Arabella asked slowly, her white face stricken and disbelieving. "There's been no word sent here to Blue Trees that Chrissie is dead."

"Nor will there be, miss. But there's them what know what's what in T' Rocks, ye mark me words. An' now that Black Jack's disappeared, they ain't afeered ta tell what they knows. What's more, t' constable what found 'er body notified t' colonel straightaway, an t' colonel went inta T' Rocks, along with that nice Cap'n Bonni-face, ta identify t' body. Constable MacGregor said as 'ow 'e'd ne'er seen anything like it in 'is life, miss. The cap'n got so ill when 'e saw poor Miss Chrissie's body all mutilated up thataway that 'e were like ta pass out, an' 'e stood there vomiting up 'is insides, poor man. But t' colonel . . . t' colonel, miss, 'e said just as cold as ye please that Miss Chrissie weren't no daugh-ter o' 'is—an' when Doc Munroe asked what 'e should do with t' body once t' autopsy were finished, t' colonel told 'im ta bury Miss Chrissie in a pauper's grave!''

"No . . . oh, no, Tilly!" Arabella cried, sickened and appalled. "That—that can't possibly be true! I— I just can't believe that Uncle Philip would be so cruel!"

"Well, 'tis t' God's 'onest truth, miss—I swear it! I 'ad it from Joe, one o' t' footmen, who 'ad it from Constable MacGregor 'imself at t' Cock's Crow—that be a grog-shop, miss, in T' Rocks. An' this morning afore breakfast, t' colonel 'imself called all us servants inta 'is study an' said as 'ow 'e felt certain some of us at least 'ad already 'eard t' news 'bout Miss Chrissie's murder an' that if we breathed a word o' it ta any o' t' family, we'd be turned off without a reference or, worse, 'ave our tickets-o'-leave revoked an' wind up back in gaol! But I just *'ad* ta tell ye, miss, even so. I couldn't 'ave lived with meself otherwise, knowing 'ow worried an' grieved ye've been 'bout poor Miss Chrissie, 'er being yer best friend an' all. Oh, miss! I'm so sorry fer yer loss, so sorry 'bout Miss Chrissie. 'Tis 'ard ta believe she's dead, I know. She were so young an' alive.''

"Yes . . . it—it doesn't seem real, more like a—like a nightmare—not that I'm doubting your word, Tilly. It's just that—just that . . . oh, Tilly! I think I'd like to be alone now, please."

"Of course, miss. I understand. An' if there's anything ye need, miss . . ."

"I'll ring for you. Thank you, Tilly."

Bobbing a respectful curtsy, the maid exited the bedchamber, softly closing the door behind her and leaving Arabella alone. For a long moment, she just sat there, so stunned and incredulous that her brain initially refused to absorb the impact of the horrible blow she had received. This just couldn't be happening, she thought dully; it just couldn't be real; it just couldn't be true that Chrissie had been forced into such a hideous life at the end and now was dead. For as long as she could remember, Chrissie had always been there—beautiful, headstrong, petulant, but always her best friend, loving and beloved, as dear as a sister to her.

"Oh, Chrissie, why did you do it?" Arabella whispered, tears stinging her eyes at last. "Why did you ever run away with Black Jack O'Flaherty?" But in her heart, she knew the answer: Chrissie had wanted to be more than just a porcelain doll. She had reached out to a man whom she had thought would offer her freedom— and instead, he had put her in a cage far worse than any she would otherwise have ever known. How could something like this have happened? Arabella wondered, angrily dashing away her tears that, now that they had started, would not stop flowing. How could a man get away with seducing a woman, beating her, imprisoning her, and selling her as a whore? How could a man get away with raping and murdering a woman? It was not right. There were laws; surely, there were laws. . . . But then she thought of Lucien's scarred back and his branded shoulder, and of Tilly's terror of the Factory and The Rocks, and of Uncle Philip denying his daughter's very existence, blotting her name from the family Bible, and condemning her to a ghastly life and a grave in a potter's field; and Arabella realized that perhaps justice under the law was only for the rich, aristocratic gentlemen Lucien had sneered at that day in the tropical woods.

Lucien. If the terrible rumors about him were to be believed, then it was *he* who had raped and murdered Chrissie! Yet despite the evidence upon his body her own eyes had seen and the words he had spoken to her about his past, every fiber of Arabella's being cried out against his being guilty of this crime, at least. It was irrational, insane that she should think him innocent. But the heart, she had learned, as Chrissie had, was a foolish, fragile thing that did not know wrong from right. Arabella wept violently for that, as well, and when, at long last, she was all cried out, she rang for Tilly.

"Tilly," Arabella began once the maid had returned, "is there someone among the male servants whom you can trust to keep his mouth shut, someone who would take you to Mr. Sinclair's estate to deliver a message, no questions asked?"

"There be Declan, miss, Declan O'Neill, 'im what took Black Jack's place. 'Im an' me . . . we've kind o' been seeing each other, courting, ye know. 'E ne'er liked Black Jack, so if this be something ta do with poor Miss Chrissie, I'm sure 'e'd 'elp."

"Good. Then I want you to take this note to Mr. Sinclair." Arabella dusted away the last of the sand she had used to dry the ink on the letter she'd written, then sealed the missive in an envelope. "You're to give it only to him, Tilly, no one else—and be sure to wait for his reply. Do you understand?"

"Yes, miss."

"And, Tilly, thank you again. I won't forget all you've done for me, I promise."

He rode a big black horse like the one in her dream, the nightmare that had wakened her on the eve of her departure for Australia; and for a strange moment, when she spied him galloping toward her, Arabella thought she *was* dreaming, for he seemed to shimmer like a mirage in the waves of heat that rose from the sweeping blue-and-green land. Not for the first time, she had the most peculiar feeling that, presently, she would awaken to find herself in her own bed in Darracott Hall, to learn that, like Briar Rose, she had slept a hundred years, ill and feverish, lost in the Aborigines' Dreamtime, in an endless, dreadful delirium, while the world had moved on and passed her by. In slow motion, he seemed to come toward her, his stallion's powerful muscles quivering, bunching, legs churning, thundering over the earth baked hard by the sun—a demon animal, ridden by a Demon rider. But then he was drawing up short, pulling the beast alongside her own mare, and Arabella knew that she was awake, that he was real, too vibrant ever to have been just a figment of her imagination.

"You look like hell," Lucien observed softly as his gaze took in her pale face, her eyes red-rimmed from hours of weeping, the dark circles like crescent smudges beneath them. "And yet, somehow, you are still beautiful to me. I think that perhaps I am mad. Of all the women in the world, I do not know why it should be you who has got into my blood, like a drug, a fever. But it is so. Have you decided at last to marry me, Arabella?"

"No."

If, with that answer, she hurt him, she did not know; for he swiftly hooded his eyes against her, so she could not guess his thoughts. A sardonic smile touched his lips.

"For so sensible a woman, you are behaving quite foolishly, you know, as I've told you before. For I *will* have you, my girl—one way or another. Do not deceive yourself into thinking I will not. But we will leave that for some other day. My curiosity is piqued: If not to wed me, then why did you send for me?"

"Because I need help—and I—I did not know where else to turn."

He went so still and silent at that, that for a moment, Arabella was half afraid he did not mean even to answer her, but, instead, to ride off without another word, leaving her alone and desperate. But then, to her relief, he spoke.

"I'll say this for you, Arabella: You have a great deal of presumption—refusing to wed me and then expecting favors from me, anyway. However, unlike you, *I* am at least willing to hear you out before rejecting you. So why don't I help you dismount, and we can walk a piece together, while you tell me what it is you want."

She thought that perhaps he mocked her. Yet his voice was strangely kind, and when he lifted her down from the saddle, his hands were surprisingly gentle around her waist. He tethered the horses to a gum tree. Then, taking her hand in his own, he led her slowly across the wild grasses that covered the rolling, lightly wooded terrain, halting now and then as, nervous and needing to do something with her hands, she bent to pick a wildflower, until she had a bouquet, damp and wilted in the heat. Curiously, Lucien did not press her to speak, but seemed content to wander with her in companionable silence, while she plucked anxiously at the blossoms, pulling off the petals of some, dropping others, until, finally, she sat down beneath one of the blue gums from which the Wyndham estate had taken its name, strewing the flowers in her lap and picking at the pale, peeling bark of the tree. Lucien sprawled beside her on the ground, his hands clasped behind his head as he studied her, a half-smile curving his mobile mouth. Yet she could have sworn that in his pale grey eyes, there was tenderness and concern for her, and that gave her courage at last to speak.

"It's . . . about Chrissie . . . Christine Wyndham . . . that I need your help."

"Yes, I thought that perhaps it might be," he said, his dark visage abruptly sober now. "Please believe me when I say that I was very sorry to learn of her death, Arabella. I know she was your friend. For that, I, too, valued her."

"She was murdered, Lucien—*murdered*!—and I'm not even supposed to know that she's dead! After she eloped with Black Jack O'Flaherty—that was our groom—Uncle Philip was so enraged that he—he struck her name from the family Bible and forbade all of us to speak of her again. I kept—I kept hoping that I would hear from her—a letter, even a note—but nothing ever came, and I didn't know where she was to write to her, to find out if she was well. At the time, I thought that perhaps Uncle Philip had confiscated any correspondence Chrissie might have sent to me. Now, I know that Black Jack kept her a—a *prisoner*, and that she couldn't write to me. I feel horrible, Lucien, as though I failed her when she desperately needed me. She was like a sister to me. The worst thing of all is that Uncle Philip told Dr. Munroe that after he was done with the—the autopsy, he could bury her in a pauper's grave!"

"Shhhhh. Hush, sweetheart," Lucien murmured as, sitting up, he gathered Arabella into his arms, stroking her hair soothingly as she broke into violent sobs against his chest. "Hush. I know that it hurts, but you'll only make yourself ill with this. Shhhhh. Tell me how I can help. What is it that you want me to do?''

"I—I don't want Chrissie buried in a—in a potter's field, Lucien! I—I want you to claim her body and see that she's—that she's buried decently. I'd do it myself, but Uncle Philip . . . he has control of my trust fund, you see, and if he could—could cut off his own daughter in such a terrible fashion, he certainly would not hesitate to do the same to me. Of course, I—I don't expect you to bear the cost of the funeral; I'll pay you for that.''

"Good God! Do you think I care about that? The money's not important. But have you thought at all, Arabella, how . . . very awkward it will be for me to request that Chrissie's body be turned over to me for burial? For you cannot tell me that you have not heard the rumors that are circulating about me, and that I have been brought in twice now, as well, for questioning by the authorities with regard to these killings. Do you truly believe me innocent of Chrissie's murder—or is all this just some elaborate scheme you have devised with the hope of somehow compelling me into a confession?''

"No . . . I mean, I don't know . . . I don't know what to believe, Lucien. For whatever reason, you—you *must* have killed your—your wife, I think, else you would not have been found guilty and transported for that crime, sentenced to fourteen years hard labor. But as for the rest . . . I—I suppose I—I simply don't want to believe that you are capable of that. Are—are you, Lucien? Did you—did you murder Chrissie and those other pitiful women?''

"What is it that you hope to gain by that question,

Arabella? You must know that if I did, I would hardly admit it—especially to the ward of the commander of the Rum Corps! And if I tell you honestly—because it *is* true—that I have never killed any woman, including my poor wife, will there not, even so, remain some niggling doubt in your heart and mind? Damn it, Arabella!'' he grated harshly, a muscle throbbing in his set jaw. ''I'll say this for you: You've never lacked for courage! There are men not bold enough to dare what you have today. But by God, if I were what you suspect, you would be taking a terrible chance by coming here alone this afternoon to meet me, by asking me these questions, would you not?''

''I am scarcely alone, Lucien, as you must be aware. Declan, the Wyndhams' groom, is with me.'' She nodded toward the young Irishman, who waited quietly at a respectful distance for her to conclude her rendezvous.

''Don't be a fool, my sweet!'' Lucien hissed, obviously angry now, his gaze narrowed. ''From here, I could shoot him right between the eyes before he ever even knew what struck him—and then you'd be utterly at my mercy! This is a dangerous game you have embarked upon, Arabella. Tell me: Am I the only suspect on your list—or do you have others whom you have dared to question in this manner?'' He gave her a small, rough shake that made her cringe and gasp with fright, her eyes widen. ''Answer me, damn you!''

''No . . . no, I've said naught to anyone else.''

''Well, thank God for that! Now, listen to me, my girl, and listen well: You are playing with something here that you don't in the least understand . . . something that is quite likely to get you killed if you persist—

and that, I will not permit! I will make the arrangements for Chrissie to have a proper burial, since that is your desire. But in return, you must promise me that you will go home to Blue Trees and put this entire affair from your head, is that clear?"

"No. You must know that I can't promise that, that I *won't* promise that, Lucien! Chrissie didn't deserve what was done to her; none of those poor women did! And from the things that Til—that I've heard, I just can't believe that justice will be done in this matter. No one in New South Wales seems to care about the murder of a—a woman on the town, and that is what Chrissie— what Chrissie was in the end. Instead of being outraged at her fate, Uncle Philip is doing his best to hush up the scandal! So if I don't speak for Chrissie, no one will. I want you to—to take me into The Rocks, Lucien. I want to see for myself what it is like there, and where she died. I need to understand how something like this could happen, how it could go unpunished. And if you won't take me, if you won't help me, I'll keep on until I find someone who will, I swear!" she threatened, shaking and breathing hard from the force of her emotions, her fear at the dark scowl upon his face.

"Yes, you're just stubborn enough to do that, despite my cautions against meddling in what you do not comprehend. Very well, my girl. Since you won't let me into your world, I'll drag you down into mine. But be sure . . . be *very* sure that this is what you want, Arabella, because I warn you: You will get far more than you are bargaining for, and there will no turning back for you afterward. Do you understand?"

"You speak in riddles, Lucien. But if, by that, you

think that you can scare me off, you are mistaken. This much and more I owe Chrissie, for all she was to me—and it is a debt I *will* pay, regardless of the cost!''

"Regardless of the cost," he echoed softly. "That was your phrase, Arabella. Remember it, for you will have much cause to, I think."

But even his words and their inherent warning would not deter her. After that, then, there were only the arrangements to make as to how they would meet in Sydney, so Lucien could escort Arabella to The Rocks. Perhaps because Declan was watching discreetly, Lucien did not kiss her before they parted, merely assisted her back onto her mare, in his eyes as he did so a strange, triumphant light that unnerved her and left her wondering if she had not, after all, made a hideous mistake in trusting him. But she had spoken truly when she had told him that she had no one else to whom to turn for help. Even Richard, she had felt, although he had loved Chrissie and was grief-stricken at her murder, would hesitate to flout the orders of the colonel, his commanding officer. Richard was firmly devoted to his military career; he would do his duty, regardless of his own personal feelings in the matter. And Gervase had turned his back on Chrissie as surely as Uncle Philip had. No, there was no one save Lucien. Still, the enigmatic smile he gave her as, releasing the bridle, he stepped back from her mare sent a tiny, cold shiver of fear up Arabella's spine, despite the heat of the summer sun that blazed in the clear blue sky. As she rode away, she could feel his eyes upon her intensely, and his words earlier that day rang in her mind:

I think that perhaps I am mad, he had said upon seeing her.

Had she not wondered as much about her own self? That perhaps they were drowning together in a sea of insanity was a terrifying thought that Arabella did not even want to contemplate.

Chapter Fifteen

Interlude at
The Rocks

It had been easy enough for Arabella to persuade Uncle Philip to allow her to return to Sydney for a few days. Although not officially in mourning for Chrissie, the Wyndhams had curtailed their social life until the scandal of her murder should die down, giving out the story that Aunt Hennie was seriously ill, when she was, in reality, simply drunk on brandy and rum most of the time. That despite all of Uncle Philip's efforts to keep the news from her, Aunt Hennie had learned of her younger daughter's death, anyway, Arabella had no doubt. The many times when Arabella checked on her, she observed that Aunt Hennie's eyes were red-rimmed from weeping, and once, she had spied the older woman shoving under her pillow a miniature, gilt-framed portrait of Chrissie.

The entire family's denial of Chrissie's life and death

angered and grieved Arabella. At least when her father had died, she had, seeing his body and arranging for his funeral, experienced some sense of finality, of closure. But because she had been refused that confirmation of death with Chrissie, it was difficult even now for her to believe that Chrissie was truly gone. Sometimes, Arabella felt as though Chrissie had only just journeyed somewhere for a visit and would be returning home at any time. She found herself listening for Chrissie's light step on the staircase, the tinkle of Chrissie's bright laughter, the trill of music Chrissie's delicate hands had brought forth from the pianoforte. Arabella thought that regardless of how horribly he had hardened his heart against his youngest daughter, Uncle Philip must feel the same; for when apprised of Arabella's desire to spend a few days at the town house in Sydney, he agreed that, of course, she should go.

"I suppose that Blue Trees can't be much fun for you these days, Arabella," Uncle Philip said when she approached him one evening in his study, "with Henriette too sick to entertain or to go about socially these days and Gervase so involved with the corps and his own business affairs. Norah doesn't mind, naturally; she's used to it, being a spinster, and she has the household management to occupy her, after all. But no doubt it's very quiet and dull for a bright young woman like you, Arabella, especially after all the soirees and so forth, eh? Well, by all means, stay as long as you like in Sydney. You'll probably see a good deal more of Gervase there, in any event, which should please you both. I know he frets that he's not had as much time lately to spend with you as he'd like. But I told him that you were an understanding sort and that the wife of a military man—which both I and Gervase hope you'll agree to become soon—must learn to accustom herself to his long absences, anyway. The corps always comes first, don't you know?''

"Yes, of course, Uncle Philip—and—and . . . thank you. I know that a change of scenery will do me good. The governor's wife has invited me to visit Government House, which I really must do, naturally. Besides, I'd like to see the Domain and Mrs. Macquarie's Chair. I thought I might paint a landscape or a seascape there, so I need to replace my box of watercolors, too, which sank with the *Heather Rose*. I can do that in Sydney, I assume.''

"Yes, I'm sure that there are several shops that will have whatever you require. And since I frequently make use of the town house myself when I work late at the corps headquarters, it's always fully staffed, and there can be no impropriety attached to your staying there with neither Henriette nor Norah in attendance. You'll take that maid of yours—what's her name? Tilly?— with you, I presume.''

"Yes, Uncle Philip.''

"Then Declan can drive you both into town tomorrow.''

Thanking her guardian again, Arabella, with a deep sigh of relief, made her escape from the study. Once outside in the hallway, she leaned against the wall, trembling violently from the force of her emotions. She had never in her life hated or felt contemptuous toward anybody. Yet such were her feelings now for Uncle Philip that it had been all she could to restrain herself from physically attacking him. She had wanted to grab him and to shake him ruthlessly, to scream at him that Chrissie had been his daughter and that she had deserved better than to be disowned and condemned to a pauper's grave. Arabella had yearned to demand why the colonel wasn't doing everything in his power to discover who had murdered Chrissie and to bring the evil culprit to justice. But of course, Arabella had grimly held her tongue. Now, in addition to her anger, she experienced a sense of both elation and guilt that she should have gulled Uncle Philip so easily and thoroughly. She felt like a spider, weaving an ever more tangled web of dishonesty that was utterly foreign to her nature. She was ashamed of her deceit, but she was also practical enough to realize that the truth would not have served her nearly so well in view of her guardian's stringent sense of propriety.

Upstairs, not knowing how long she would need to remain in Sydney to ferret out Chrissie's murderer, Arabella packed one of her new trunks, including among its contents one of the mourning gowns Norah had worn when she had thought that Arabella was dead. Along with the dress, she also took one of Norah's black, veiled hats. Both would serve not only to honor Chrissie in death, Arabella thought, but also to conceal her own identity when Lucien escorted her to The Rocks. That her plan was rash and that she might be placing herself in jeopardy and certainly at Lucien's total mercy were considerations that Arabella determinedly thrust from her mind. If she dwelled on them, reason might prevail over emotion, and she might lose her resolve to carry out her scheme. That, she was determined not to do.

Had not Lucien kept silent about the weeks they had spent together in the tropical woods, she might have suffered the same cruel fate as Chrissie, cast off to fend for herself in a world that was more unkind to its women than Arabella, so sheltered and beloved by her father, had ever before realized. Now, everything inside her that was moral and decent cried out against that cruel world. It was a voice that she could not, *would* not ignore.

"Here is the list, Tilly," Arabella announced as she stepped down from the Wyndhams' carriage. "Since I do not know how long I'll be, don't hurry to finish all the shopping; take as much time as you need. I had the cook prepare a picnic basket for you, as well. I thought that perhaps you and Declan might like to have an alfresco luncheon in Hyde Park."

"Ye're e'er so kind, miss. We *will* enjoy that. Oh, miss, ye will take care, won't ye?" Tilly's young, plain but caring face was anxious as she glanced at the vehicle waiting nearby for Arabella. "I know 'ow ye loved poor Miss Chrissie. But she's dead, an' nowt will e'er bring 'er back; an' I just know she wouldn't want ye ta put yer own self in danger fer 'er now that she's gone, miss. Ye can't know—ye just *can't*—what a 'orrible place The Rocks be! An' Mr. Sinclair! Well, miss, ye must know that 'e murdered 'is wife—an' p'rhaps Miss Chrissie an' them other poor women, too. I just don't like ta see ye going off with 'im this way. I'm afeered fer ye—an' that's t' God's 'onest truth, miss!"

"I'll be all right, Tilly . . . really, I will. That little

pistol your Declan gave me is in my reticule. Be assured that I know how to use it, as well. Although it's been some time since I fired a gun, I know how to shoot one, and while I am hardly an expert, I can scarcely miss at close range, can I?"

"No, I don't suppose so." But both the maid's face and her tone revealed her skepticism and worry that even a pistol would be useless against the Demon Lucien Sinclair.

"Go on with you, now," Arabella insisted, trying to hide her own nervousness. "I really must have those watercolors if I'm to paint any sort of a picture at Mrs. Macquarie's Chair to show Uncle Philip later. I'll meet you in the park just as soon as I can."

"Yes, miss."

Once the maid had gone, Arabella made her way to where Lucien waited with his carriage, its calash top up, both to guard against the sun and to help conceal her from any passersby who might be curious as to her identity. As further protection against her being recognized, Arabella wore the black, veiled hat she had taken from Norah's closet, as well as the mourning gown. She felt fairly confident that no one would know that it was she who accompanied Lucien; besides, if any speculation arose, she also had Tilly and Declan to provide her with an alibi. Under the circumstances, it was the best that Arabella could hope to achieve.

"I take it that since you are here, you have actually decided to go through with this madness of visiting The Rocks," Lucien greeted her when she approached.

"Yes, I have. Did you think I would not?"

"No . . . I counted on it, my girl." Before she could

ponder that peculiar, enigmatic statement, he handed her up into the carriage seat, saying, "In you go, then." Then he climbed in beside her and, gathering the reins, clucked to the horses, a pair of plain brown geldings. "This vehicle and horses are rented; I thought it safer that way," he explained as they wended their way through the traffic, "as my own carriage and my matched greys are well known in Sydney."

"And in The Rocks, as well?"

"I have been there upon occasion, yes—but only to gamble, Arabella. Strange as it may seem, I've had no interest in any other woman but you since that night I had you. Nor, as I told you the other day, am I in the habit of stalking, raping, and murdering doxies."

"You—you ought not to speak so to me, Lucien. I—I don't want to be reminded of that—of that night . . . and gentlemen don't refer in a lady's presence to those—to those women."

"I thought we had months ago agreed that I am no gentleman . . . and so, like it or not, my sweet, I shall speak to you however I damned well please. Unlike your precious *gentlemen*, I have never believed in sparing a woman's sensibilities. That kind of false gentility inevitably leads to ignorance and repression, which generally manifest themselves in frigidity, drunkenness, waywardness, or a tiresome morality—coupled, at least in your case, with a hellishly dangerous curiosity. Women were not meant to be put, like porcelain figurines, upon pedestals, my sweet."

"Nor we were intended to be used as doormats!"

"No . . . but, then, I didn't say that you were, did I? There are many things I would like to do to you,

Arabella—but I assure you that wiping my feet on you is not one of them!''

Both his implications and the lingering, appraising glance he gave her brought a telltale blush to her cheeks. He was determined, it seemed, to remind her of that night she had spent in his arms.

"I don't wish to continue this discussion," she said stiffly, only to receive a soft, low laugh for her pains. "It obviously pleases you to mock me."

"No . . . only to tear down that wall of righteousness you are determined to hide behind. I know, you see, that where I am concerned, it is only a facade. My dear Arabella, were you never taught that there is no point in closing the barn door after the horse has escaped? You should count yourself fortunate that I am not quite the rogue you think me, else the fate of those poor women over there might have been your own.''

They had by this time reached the Circular Quay, and now, Lucien drew the carriage to a halt at a place that, while out of the way, still provided Arabella with an unobstructed view of the long wooden wharves that stretched into the harbor. A ship moored at one of the piers was just now discharging its passengers and crew; and as she watched, sluttishly dressed women calling vulgarities ran forward to accost the men.

"Those are what are referred to as dock women," Lucien elucidated. "Many of them were at one time, of course, convicts at the Female Factories, such as those at Parramatta, Brisbane, and elsewhere. In the days when New South Wales still accepted deliveries from the transport ships and not just transfers from other prisons, you would also have seen here the female convicts being herded out onto the wharves, where gentlemen and the officers of the Rum Corps would have been lined up to take their pick of the lot—preying upon the youngest and the prettiest, naturally. There would have been more disreputable men, as well, promising tickets-of-leave in exchange for the prisoners' money and belongings—to say nothing of the whoremongers and pickpockets and other assorted, sordid parasites of humanity. Those male passengers and crew foolish enough to take up the offers of the dock women will awaken tomorrow morning to find themselves lying in a gutter somewhere, their wallets and jewelry stripped from them. What's more, if they are lucky, they will not have contracted some foul disease.''

"But . . . if such practices as this are common knowledge, why do the authorities not take steps to put a halt to them?'' Arabella's face was both stricken and puzzled.

"My dear innocent''—Lucien's voice was tinged with both sarcasm and amusement—"are you honestly unaware that everyone from your 'Uncle Philip'—as you call him—on down through the Rum Corps' officers and the constables to the lowest, meanest churls in the alleys and gutters of The Rocks is getting his share of the booty, one way or another? Greed is the reason such practices and such places as The Rocks exist, Arabella. Greed and prejudice, lust and addiction, ambition and corruption. If ever we come into power, we Emancipists will try to stop it, to pass laws that ensure that all are treated fairly, that convicts have the same rights as the aristocracy. That is why the Exclusives call us the 'Slumocracy' and despise seeing an ex-convict like me rise above his origins and background. I am a threat to them, you see . . . a very great threat indeed. Now, have you seen enough, or shall I drive on?''

"Drive on, if you will.''

He took her into The Rocks then; and Arabella knew that for as long as she lived, she would never forget what she saw there, things of which she had never dreamed, because her life had been so sheltered. She had never before been exposed to the misery of the human refuse that littered the twisting cobblestone streets, alleys and filthy gutters of The Rocks. She had not known that there were places where people lived packed together like rats in a cage and who behaved just as viciously. She saw whoremongers and prostitutes, rum-runners and drunks, gamblers and derelicts. The children were the worst of all . . . orphaned, most likely, Lucien told her, as well as beaten and crippled, homeless, many without hope, others already sly and hardened far beyond their years. Girls who looked no more than twelve or thirteen openly sold themselves on the streets.

More than once, Lucien's whip snaked out to drive off beggars who approached the carriage, "because many of them are not beggars at all, but cutthroats and thieves, Arabella,'' he explained when she cringed and protested. "Trust me. They would knife us to death for what is in my pockets and your reticule—and were you, out of pity, to throw money to them, we would undoubtedly be set upon in moments by a frenzied mob.''

She stared at the rows of cheap, dirty, run-down flats and thought with horror that it was certainly in just such a dwelling that Chrissie had been held prisoner by Black Jack O'Flaherty, had been beaten and forced to whore for him. In such a place as this, it was no wonder that Black Jack had been able to get away with what he had done to Chrissie. The narrow alley where she had died, had been brutally raped and butchered, was strewn with garbage, running with offal, crawling with rats. Unable any longer to hold back the gorge that rose in her throat, Arabella abruptly raised her veil and vomited over the side of the carriage until there was nothing left to come up. Faint and shaking afterward, she was embarrassed to have been sick before a man, before Lucien. But as he cradled her in his arms and tenderly, with his handkerchief, wiped her sweating face and her mouth, she remembered how he had cared for her in the tropical woods and knew that he had seen her in far worse circumstances. Reaching into his jacket, he withdrew a silver flask of rum that he unstoppered and held to her lips, compelling her to drink. Afterward, she lay limply against the seat of the carriage, her eyes closed.

"I've seen enough . . . more than enough. Take me home, Lucien . . . please," she whispered.

With a soft command and slapping the reins against the backs of the horses, he quickly maneuvered the carriage through the wending cobblestone streets, out of The Rocks and into Sydney's business and fashionable districts.

"Chrissie *did* have a decent Christian burial, Arabella. I promised you that, and I kept my word. I claimed her body from Dr. Munroe when he had finished with it, and I saw to it that she was buried on the grounds of my estate."

"Thank you so much for that, Lucien. It was . . . kind of you."

"My . . . kindness, as you call it, has a price. So, don't thank me yet, Arabella—for I think that you may not wish to, after all, when this day is done. You see, the price for my good deed is one that I very much fear that you shall not enjoy paying." His tone, as he spoke, was grim; and when, startled by his words, she opened her eyes, it was to see that his face was dark with some unreadable emotion.

"Why? What—what do you mean? Where are you going? You have passed by Hyde Park, where I am to meet Tilly!" Suddenly alarmed, Arabella sat up straight on the carriage seat, her voice rising anxiously. "What do you think that you are doing, Lucien?"

"I supposed it to be quite obvious: I am kidnapping you, my girl."

If he had slapped her face, she could not have been more stunned.

"You—you can't be serious!"

"I assure you that I was never more serious in my life." He paused for a moment, allowing her to absorb the impact of that statement. Then he continued. "You must admit, Arabella, that I have been more than patient with you. To protect your reputation, I have remained silent about all those weeks you spent alone with me following the shipwreck, as well as the fact that you lay with me. I have permitted you to amuse yourself at all the parties, routs, and soirees to which *I* should have escorted you instead of your hanging on the arm of Gervase Wyndham—who doesn't even deserve to be called a man, much less an officer and a gentleman! I had hoped that, eventually, you would come both to your senses and to me of your own accord. But as it began to appear that that was not likely to happen, and as you are placing yourself in a great deal of danger by your stubborn insistence, despite my advice, on meddling in the matter of Chrissie's murder, besides, you have left me with no other choice but to claim you as mine, Arabella. For you *are* mine—and as I've told you before, what is mine, I keep.''

"What are you saying? What do you mean to do with me?'' she asked, aghast, not quite able to believe that this was actually happening to her.

Lucien's eyes glinted with possessiveness and desire as they raked her slowly. A mocking smile touched his mouth.

"Don't be tiresome, my sweet,'' he drawled softly. "You know perfectly well what I intend to do with you.''

Shame flooded her being at his words; hot color stained her cheeks. Her heart began to thud so hard and loud in her breast that she thought he must surely hear it. The pulse at the delicate hollow of her throat fluttered wildly, and she clutched the reticule she held in her lap, feeling, with a start, Declan's pistol inside. The wheels of her brain churned as furiously as those of the carriage that was now swiftly bearing her from Sydney—to a destination where there would surely be no help for her, no way to escape from Lucien.

"You cannot possibly hope to succeed at abducting me, at holding me as your—as your mistress, Lucien.'' Arabella forced herself to speak calmly as she began, with trembling fingers, to try to untie the strings of her reticule.

"Mistress? I had hoped that you knew me better than to think that I would ever settle for that, Arabella—or would demean you with such a proposition. No, I mean, as I have told you all along, to marry you. Before this day is done, you will be my wife and the chase will be ended. I warned you—did I not?—that my hunts were always successful, that since you would not let me enter yours, I would drag you down into my own world, that you would be getting more than you bargained for when you refused to listen to me, and that there would be no turning back for you afterward. And did you not say that you *would* pay your debt to Chrissie, regardless of the cost? *Regardless of the cost*," he repeated slowly, with emphasis. "Do you remember those words, my girl? I warned you not to forget them. Well, this is the cost: marriage to me!"

"You *are* mad! You cannot force me to the altar, Lucien!"

"Oh, no? Arabella, when will you realize that I am utterly ruthless in attaining my desires? You *will* wed me, and you will not tell the magistrate that I have coerced you to the altar, or I will ruin the Wyndhams both socially and financially. I have in my pocket, you see, thousands of pounds worth of IOUs belonging to Gervase, gambling debts that I have methodically bought up one by one ever since I realized that you were the colonel's ward and that Gervase intended to marry you. If you do not do exactly as I tell you, my sweet, I will call those markers. The total sum due is so staggering that Gervase—who has relied on his expected inheritance to play on credit—cannot possibly pay it. The colonel will therefore be compelled to cover the notes—at such a cost to himself that it will be extremely difficult, if not impossible, for him to recover financially from the expense. As a result, the Wyndhams will be ruined socially, as well, since one of the prerequisites for membership among the aristocracy is a great deal of wealth, or at least the expectation of it. Bankruptcy, following hard on the heels of Chrissie's elopement, whoredom, and murder, will create such a disgraceful scandal that the Wyndhams will not be able to hush it all up and so will find themselves outcasts, pariahs.''

At this last, there was such a note of grim satisfaction in Lucien's voice that Arabella could not fail to heed it.

"Why should you want to destroy the Wyndhams?" she inquired, her brow knitted with puzzlement as she at last succeeded in unknotting the strings of her reticule and reaching inside.

"I have my reasons. However, there is no need for you to know more about them at this particular moment than that they are excellent ones. So do not assume that I am bluffing you, Arabella, because I am not. If you do not wed me, I *will* do precisely what I have threatened."

"No, you will not—because I won't let you, Lucien." She drew forth the gun in her bag and pointed the barrel at him, trying hard not to allow her hand to shake. "Aunt Hennie and Norah, at least, don't deserve that. Stop the carriage. Stop it at once, or I'll shoot you!"

After glancing casually at the small, silver-barreled pistol she gripped so tightly, Lucien obediently pulled the horses to a halt along the open road. To her dismay, Arabella realized that she had been so agitated that she had failed to notice in what direction they had traveled from town. She had no idea where she was, except that they had left Sydney behind, and that she was all alone with Lucien, who could, she knew, easily overpower her if he somehow managed to get hold of the gun.

"Show me the IOUs!" she demanded with more confidence than she actually felt. "Do it carefully, Lucien. Don't make any sudden moves. Although you taught me how to shoot, I'm not familiar with this pistol, and so for all I know, it may have a light trigger."

"Indeed? And where, may I ask, did you get it?" Slowly, reaching into the pocket of his jacket, he drew out a thick sheaf of markers upon which Arabella could plainly see Gervase's name scrawled in bold black ink. As Lucien had said, Gervase owed thousands of pounds.

"Declan, the Wyndhams' groom, lent it to me, just in case. Now, put all those notes into my reticule"— with her free hand, she thrust her bag at Lucien—"and then get down out of the carriage. Do it, Lucien! Don't make me shoot you!"

To Arabella's horror, instead of doing as she had ordered, Lucien calmly stuffed the IOUs back into his jacket pocket, then leaned back against the carriage seat.

"No . . . I'm afraid that you'll just have to shoot me, my girl—if you can.. But I don't think that you can. You said once that you loved me, Arabella, and I believe that you still do. It's not easy to take a person's life. I know. No. Don't look at me like that. I told you that I didn't murder my wife. Or Chrissie. It was a man in prison whom I killed, because if I hadn't, he would have killed me. But it's even harder to kill someone you love, someone who's a part of you, as I am, Arabella. Here. I'll help you do it." One by one, he slowly unfastened the buttons on his fine white cambric shirt, then drew its edges aside to reveal his broad expanse of heavily muscled chest dusted with a fine mat of black hair, the chest she remembered lying against so intimately. "Now, all you have to do is to place the barrel against my heart, cock the hammer, and squeeze the trigger. Then I'll be dead, and you can take the markers, push me out of the carriage, and drive on back to Sydney, with no one the wiser as to how I met my demise. As I'm an ex-convict, an Emancipist, I don't think that the authorities will bother to investigate my murder too closely, if at all."

"Damn you, Lucien!" Arabella cursed softly as, after a long moment, he reached out and gingerly took the gun from her grasp. Hot tears of fury and frustration and defeat stung her eyes. "Damn you to hell!"

"Believe me when I say that I have already been there, my sweet." He tucked the pistol into his jacket pocket. Then, after untying its long streamers, he removed her hat and, with one hand under her chin, deliberately tilted her tear-stained face up to his own sober one. "Understand this, Arabella: Although that is a part of it, it is not just because I want you that I insist upon our marriage, whether you are willing or not. You will doubtless not believe it at this moment, but your becoming my wife is for your own protection, as well. I know that you are frightened . . . no, do not attempt to deny it. Your face is easy for me to read. But you needn't fear. I'm not like Black Jack O'Flaherty. Despite the parallels, I won't mistreat you, as he did Chrissie. I'll be good to you, I swear it! And in time, you will come to realize that wedding me was all for the best, after all.''

''How can I believe you?''

''How can you not?'' he asked huskily before his mouth descended upon her own, taking it hungrily, with certainty—when, recognizing desperately the futility of it, she made no attempt to struggle against him—irrevocably sealing her fate.

Chapter Sixteen

The Bridal Bower

For the rest of her life, the next several hours always remained clouded in Arabella's mind. She seemed to see the images, the memories as though through a glass darkly, never clearly but blurred at the edges and long with shadows, as the day itself soon grew at twilight. Sensing her fear and fury, Lucien spoke to her reassuringly as he guided the horses over the open road. But although she knew that her silence angered him, Arabella mutinously refused to respond; and at last, he gave up the attempt at conversation, lapsing into an equally frosty silence. She had hoped that in the face of her unwillingness to marry him, he would come to his senses and give up this mad plan. But when she glanced at him, his jaw was thrust forward, set with determination, and a muscle flexed in his taut cheek; she knew that he would not relent. Lucien intended to wed her, and she saw no means of avoiding becoming his wife. She could hardly leap from the moving carriage, and even if she somehow *did* manage to run away from him, he would still have those devastating IOUs. She should have shot him when she had had the chance! Arabella told herself with hot despair. How could she have been so stupid, such a coward as not to have pulled the trigger? It had been her one opportunity to escape, and like a fool, she had thrown it away. Perhaps in doing so, she had even signed her own death warrant. After all, she had only Lucien's word that he was not guilty of murder—and did not all criminals profess their innocence? What if he were, in truth, driving her not to some magistrate's house, but out somewhere to rape and to kill her?

Arabella's vivid imagination ran wild, although common sense told her that when they had been alone in the tropical woods, he had had every opportunity to do whatever he had liked to her, and instead of harming her, Lucien had saved her life. Why would he have done that, only to murder her now—unless, of course, he really were mad? At that thought, fright gnawed anew at her insides. Surreptitiously, from beneath the fringe of her thick, sooty lashes, she studied him beside her on the carriage seat. He was handsome, aggressive, powerful, arrogant, and insolent, exuding both animal magnetism and menace. He did not, however, look insane—but, then, she had not, until she had seen the scars on his back, the brand on his shoulder, suspected him of being a convict, either. Obviously, she was no real judge of a man's character and could not rely on her own instincts in the matter, she thought, disheartened.

Dusk fell, and a silvery moon rose over the rustling gum trees, turning their pale, gnarled branches into ghostly arms that seemed to reach out to Arabella threateningly when the carriage passed by, reminding her somehow of the dream, the nightmare that had wakened her the night before she had departed England for Australia. The boughs creaked eerily in the wind, their fragrant leaves soughing. Despite herself, Arabella shrank back against the carriage seat, closer to Lucien. It was not uncommon for the limbs of gum trees to break without warning from their trunks and to come crashing down upon passersby, which was why the gum trees were sometimes referred to as "widow-makers." She did not wish to be struck by a falling branch, although she thought dully that perhaps even that dismal fate was better than that to which Lucien was taking her.

Ahead now, she could see a house, and as he turned the carriage onto the drive, she guessed that the dwelling must belong to the magistrate he had mentioned earlier. If Lucien had spoken truly—and, surely, there was no longer any reason to doubt him—she would in just a short while be his wife. He would, under the laws that she had come to understand offered so little protection for any woman, own her as surely as though she were a slave. Of their own volition, her hands clenched into fists at the realization; her nails dug so hard into her palms that she winced from the pain.

"Lucien . . . please," she whispered imploringly. "It's still not too late to turn back from this madness. Give me the IOUs and let me go. Please."

"No, Arabella." He shook his head resolutely as he

drew the carriage, wheels crunching upon the pebbles, to a halt before the house and set the brake. "That I will not do. I should have liked for things to be different between us; but if this is the only way I can get you, then it will have to serve. Remember, now: Not a word to the magistrate about why you have agreed to wed me, else the Wyndhams will suffer for it. Do you understand?"

Mutely, she nodded her head, with fright and reluctance permitting him to assist her from the carriage and then to lead her toward the house. Once inside, she saw clearly that this was not just some scheme that Lucien had dreamed up on the spur of the moment. Rather, his plans had been carefully laid; for he had a license, and the magistrate was expecting them, and the magistrate's wife and her sister were there to serve as witnesses to the wedding ceremony that was nothing at all as Arabella had imagined in her girlish daydreams of years gone by. She and Lucien stood together in the magistrate's parlor; the rite itself was plain and brief, without the nuptial mass. In just moments, Lucien was sliding a heavy gold band onto her finger, then kissing her possessively to seal the vows they had spoken—his own voice sure and steady, hers faint and tremulous. She could not believe that it was not all happening in a dream, that it was actually real. Through it all, like an ominous litany, an old saying kept running through her head: *Married in black, you'll wish yourself back.* She felt desperately sick at the unbidden thought that perhaps this was the same magistrate who had performed the ill-fated wedding rite for Chrissie and Black Jack O'Flaherty, that perhaps they, too, had stood here in this same parlor, Chrissie excited, full of hopes and dreams, Black Jack plotting even then how much money he could get for her from Uncle Philip—then, later, enraged to learn that not a single tuppence would be forthcoming.

Even when the ceremony was ended, Arabella found it difficult to grasp the fact that she and Lucien were truly married. She was appalled by the entire hole-in-the-corner affair. She felt somehow degraded, as though she had been the victim of a crime—or had committed one herself and now were a prisoner for it. But, of course, it was Gervase's sin for which she had paid; and as she remembered the words of the old Gypsy woman that day of the Scarborough fair, Arabella shivered. The gold ring upon her finger was like a shackle, she thought numbly as she stared down at it. Her hand trembled as she signed her name upon the wedding certificate, beneath Lucien's own bold black scrawl. Then he paid the magistrate—a sum that included a substantial bribe, she felt certain, since she was not of an age legally to marry without her guardian's consent. Even so, considering how coldly he had washed his hands of Chrissie, his own daughter, Arabella had not the slightest hope that Uncle Philip would take steps to annul her own marriage. She doubted that even Gervase would protest.

She wondered—almost idly now that she was Lucien's wife—how long Tilly and Declan had waited for her at Hyde Park, had searched for her before sending a message to Uncle Philip, whether Blue Trees were even now in an uproar at her disappearance. Initially, of course, they would correctly presume her to have been abducted by Lucien, but they would not know that marriage rather than rape and ransom had been his intention. They would—surely—be furious and frantic at what they would believe had befallen her. And because Lucien, for whatever unknown reasons, hated the Wyndhams and wished to see them destroyed, he might not inform them straightaway what he had done with her.

Outside, Lucien handed Arabella wordlessly into the carriage, then climbed in beside her. His pale grey eyes gleamed with triumph and satisfaction as he gazed down at her before, with a low growl, he dragged her into his arms and kissed her fiercely, his hands moving on her in a way that made her fully understand that she was truly and utterly his now, that he was free to take her however and whenever he pleased. He could force her down on the carriage seat and ruck up her skirts at this very moment, and she would be helpless to prevent it. She shuddered at the thought and tried halfheartedly to wrest herself from his steely embrace. But this he would not permit, deliberately tightening his arms around her and compelling her lips to part as he boldly thrust his tongue into her mouth, ferreting out its innermost secret places, touching, tasting, savoring until, despite herself, Arabella gasped and moaned, melting against his hard, lean body.

That he should, even now, possess this strange power to make her feel as though all her bones were liquefying, turning to quicksilver inside her, deeply humiliated her. Still, her body was as treacherously responsive to him as though it had a will all its own. As though she were dying of thirst, her lips soaked up his feverishly, opening, drinking, as he swallowed her breath, wreathed her tongue again and again with his own. His hands ensnared her chestnut hair, impatiently yanking the pins from her chignon, freeing the heavy mass, so it tumbled down in a long, wild tangle of curls about her. Then his fingers were at her slender throat, swiftly and deftly unbuttoning the collar of her black gown, parting the edges of her bodice to reveal the swell of her generous breasts, pushed high by her corset. His mouth scorched her tender skin as he pressed hot kisses to her throat, his hand dipping beneath her undergarments to cup one burgeoning breast, thumb rotating slowly across its quickly stiffening peak. He groaned against the valley between the full, ripe mounds, his breath searing her flesh.

"God . . . it's all I can do not to take you right here and now upon this carriage seat!" he muttered thickly, echoing her own earlier thought.

"No, please, Lucien! Don't!" she entreated softly as she struggled to regain her senses.

"You don't have to be afraid." With obvious difficulty, he tore himself away from her, his breath harsh and labored. "It's our wedding night—and a bride deserves better than to be tumbled in a carriage, as though she were some cheap doxy. I've a place ready and waiting for us. I but wanted a taste of what you have for too long sought to deny me, Arabella—what I will soon have this night. No, do not cover yourself against me," he ordered as, discomfited by the way in which his eyes, glittering in the moonlight, strayed over her, she began, with shaking fingers, to fasten the buttons of her gown. When she dared to continue at her task, his hands shot out rapidly and forcefully, imprisoning hers. "Let us get one thing straight between us right from the start, my girl," he insisted, his voice deceptively low and silky—but with an underlying note of determination. "You will find me an extremely caring and generous husband . . . provided that you recognize that I will be master of my own house and of you. I expect to be obeyed, just as you pledged a short time ago to do. Do you understand?"

"Y-y-yes, Lucien."

"Good. Then we shall deal very well together."

Releasing her wrists, he kissed her again, lingeringly and thoroughly, his tongue shooting deep between her lips, his hands once more tangling in her hair before, at last, with reluctance, he drew away. Gathering the reins and clucking to the horses, he guided the carriage on down the dirt road gleaming like a winding riband of silver in the moonlight that shone through the trees. Arabella was acutely aware of him beside her on the carriage seat, of his strong, corded thigh pressed intimately against her leg, of the desire that darkened his eyes and the smile of satisfaction that curved his mouth when he glanced at her. That she should be filled not only with fear, but also with anticipation at the prospect of his making love to her unnerved and shamed her. Silently, she cursed both her traitorous heart and body that made such a mockery of her will and mind. She should feel nothing for Lucien but hate and contempt. That, if she were honest with herself, she must admit that she felt neither of those emotions toward him was a bewildering, devastating recognition. What a fool she was that despite everything, she should still love him. Yet, she knew that, inexplicably, it was indeed so.

Her heart pounded uncontrollably at his nearness. She
had a wild urge to reach up and to brush away the long,
glossy strands of his black hair that fell across his dark
face in the wind. She thought of him kissing her, touching her, slowly undressing her, and making love to her;
and she could not prevent the sudden, hot, sweet rush
of moisture between her thighs at the images her mind
conjured. Her cheeks flooded with color that she hoped
Lucien did not notice in the darkness, even though she
sensed instinctively that he was somehow deeply and
intimately aware of everything concerning her. There
were any number of women he might have had. Yet he
had chosen her. She did not know why, knew only that
her life had never been the same since she had awakened
from her delirium following the shipwreck to see him
standing over her, the devil, the Demon of whom the
old Gypsy woman at the Scarborough fair had warned
her to beware. Arabella shivered at the memory.

"Are you cold?" Lucien inquired solicitously, rein-
forcing her sense that he was conscious of her every
thought, her every emotion, her every sensation. It was
as though she could hide nothing from him, so attuned
was he to her. Any small hope that she might still
have harbored of escaping from him vanished at the
realization.

"No, it was . . . just a momentarily chill, that's all."

"I'm not a monster, Arabella. I'm not going to hurt
you."

"You forced me to marry you—"

"Only because I could get you no other way. But let
us not argue the issue. In time, when you have come
to know me better, you will discover that I have always

spoken truly to you—after all, why should I not? As I've told you before, you're mine, my sweet. You have been mine since that night beneath the jacaranda tree, as, tonight, you shall learn." Turning the carriage off the road onto another serpentine drive, he finally drew the vehicle to a halt before a small, snug cabin.

"Where are we? What is this place?" she asked, curious.

"It's the house I originally built for myself once I was a free man. It sits on the grounds of what is now my estate. I wanted to be alone with you for a few days, to allow you some time to accustom yourself to me again, and to our marriage, before you were compelled to deal with my household and servants, as well as with the inevitable gossip that will ensue once news of our elopement spreads. I thought that perhaps things would be easier for you that way."

"Thank you for that much, at least," Arabella said as he handed her down from the carriage. "I confess that I did not expect to be shown such—such kindness and consideration."

"You are my wife, Arabella." Lucien spoke those words with a good deal of relish. "How often must I reassure you that I am not Black Jack O'Flaherty, that I do not intend to mistreat you as he did Chrissie? Did I ever once harm you all those weeks we were alone together before, when I had every opportunity to do so—and without repercussions, I might add?"

"No," she admitted sheepishly, after a moment.

"Then why should you harbor even the slightest fear that I would do so now? Come." Without warning, Lucien swept her up into his powerful arms and, after opening the front door, carried her over the threshold into the cabin.

It was dark inside, and so Arabella's first impression of the house was its fragrance. It was so sweet and exotic that had she not known where she was, she would have believed she was back in the tropical woods with him again. He set her down in what she presumed was the middle of the room, whispering, "Close your eyes," seductively in her ear.

"Why?" She was startled to hear how equally low and husky her own voice was.

"Because I asked you to. Humor me. Are they closed?"

"Yes."

She stood there in the darkness, her eyes closed, and as she breathed in the lush redolences that surrounded her, her heart beat fast with a wild, crazy excitement. She could hear Lucien moving about the cabin, and from the sudden glow against her eyelids, she realized he must be lighting the oil lamps. Then, without warning, she felt his hands gathering her long, unbound hair, sliding the mass over her shoulder to bare her nape. His warm breath brushed her skin just seconds before he pressed his mouth to her nape, sending such a tremor through her that her nipples hardened of their own accord and her knees weakened as though the earth had suddenly dropped from beneath her feet. His palms glided sensuously down her shoulders to cup her swelling breasts, slowly circling their stiff peaks, so the fabric of her gown stimulated them even further, making her gasp. His mouth found her throat; his hands slipped to her waist.

"Now, open your eyes," he commanded softly.

Her lashes fluttered open; her eyes widened; her lips formed an oh of astonishment and delight. She had never before seen anything like the room in which she now stood. It was something out of a fairy tale, a secret, magical garden. Flowers were everywhere; buckets and buckets of them sat on the long mantel over the fireplace, on the stone hearth where a small fire burned, on the wooden dining table, on the nightstands that flanked the canopy bed, on the puncheon floor, filling every single corner of the house. Bougainvillea, hibiscus, and morning glory vines twined their ways up the rough wooden posts of the mosquito-net-draped bed; branches of jacaranda and eucalyptus interwove the slats that formed the canopy. The clean white lacy linen sheets that adorned the bed were strewn with dusky pink rose petals. In a large, hammered-copper bathtub near the hearth, water lilies floated. Where blossoms and boughs did not hold sway, oil lamps and candles flickered, casting shadows that danced like fairies on the walls. Along the counter of the kitchen nook to one side of the simple room, ice-laden platters and bowls held an assortment of meats and cheeses, fruits and vegetables, breads and chocolates. A bottle of champagne reposed in an ice-filled bucket; crystal goblets sparkled amid an array of trailing lilac blooms. Tears stung Arabella's eyes as she recognized what thought and care had gone into the preparation of this bower for her wedding night.

Wonderingly, she turned in Lucien's arms to look up at him, not quite believing that he had done all this for her. His face was oddly gentle in the diffuse light, and before he hooded his gaze against her, she surprised in his eyes that peculiar, eager, searching light she had glimpsed once or twice before. It came to her then that although he had never told her that he loved her, he must surely care for her in his own fashion. His whipcord body was taut, expectant, even quivering a little against hers, like that of an excited horse before a race, she realized slowly, marveling, as though he had wished desperately to please her and now were anxiously awaiting her response.

"It's lovely, Lucien," she breathed, indicating her surroundings. "The most beautiful thing I've ever seen. Nobody's ever done anything quite so special for me before."

"I am glad of that," he murmured before he took her mouth, his tongue slowly tracing the outline of her lips before insinuating itself inside, searching out her moist, inner recesses, thrusting in and out of her mouth, sliding over her lips, teasing her tongue.

The kiss was lingering, insidiously arousing, and Arabella could not seem to resist it, clinging to him and kissing him back with rising passion as his mouth grew harder, more insistent. His hands, previously entwined in her hair to hold her still for him, now moved gently over her face, down her throat to her breasts, where he began to unbutton her bodice, eliciting a small gasp from her as his lips slanted across hers to her cheek, her temple, the strands of her hair. Trembling as she realized that her gown was slipping from her shoulders to her waist, she caught his wrists, shaking her head in mute appeal, her eyes half shuttered, unable to go on meeting his own.

"Arabella." He pressed light kisses upon her brow, her eyelids, the corners of her mouth. "Arabella, don't fight me. Please. You're mine, my wife, and I *will* have you. But I would rather not spoil this night by forcing you to submit to me." His voice was low and as soft as velvet, but she did not mistake the iron note of determination it contained. He would do what he had so quietly threatened. He had the right, now; he was her husband.

Her husband. She glanced down at the gold band on her left hand, tangible proof that they were indeed wed, that this was not a dream. Of course, he intended to consummate their marriage, whether she were willing or not. Aside from the fact that he wanted her, his possession of her would prevent an annulment, she realized, remembering Uncle Philip's certainty that Black Jack had wasted no time in deflowering Chrissie for precisely that same reason. If an underage bride were no longer chaste, her guardian was not very likely to protest that she had wed without his permission, but, rather, belatedly to consent to the match.

"It is nothing that we have not done together before, Arabella." Lucien's voice recalled her to the present, making her blush at the memories he evoked of how he had made love to her that night under the jacaranda tree.

He was right, after all, and there was no point in fighting him. Slowly, she let her hands slip from his wrists, demurring no further as he divested her of her dress, hoops, and crinolines, her shoes and stockings. Her corset proved a more difficult obstacle, and at last, impatiently, with a powerful jerk of his strong hands,

Lucien ripped the lacings apart, breaking them. Despite herself, Arabella heaved a sigh of relief.

"I never have become used to wearing it again," she explained as he tossed the offending garment aside. "Sometimes, I can hardly breathe in it from the combination of its constriction and the heat."

"Then don't wear it anymore. *I* certainly won't complain if you don't; in fact, I would prefer that you didn't. Besides, your waist is so slender that you don't need a corset anyway, my sweet." He demonstrated the truth of his words by spanning, with his hands, her willowy waist before his palms glided upward to cup her breasts, their taut nipples straining against the sheer lawn of her chemise. His thumbs circled the peaks sensuously, sending waves of pleasure radiating through her, while he kissed her again deeply. Then, his voice ragged, he drew away, saying, "I have to go unhitch the horses from the carriage and make sure they're fed, watered, and put away in the byre. I thought that perhaps while I'm doing that, you'd like to bathe. There's no stove here, so I'll set a kettle on the fire to heat. You'll find everything you need on that dresser or in its drawers. The night is not yet late; we have plenty of time, and before I am through, you will want this as much as I do, I swear."

With that vow, Lucien left her alone—and feeling slightly dazed—in the cabin. Her breasts were swollen and aching; she felt molten at her core. Aware of her arousal—as Arabella suspected he must be—he was truly wicked to tease and torment her in this fashion. She did not know how she would bear it if he continued along these lines. Surely, he would drive her half mad with desire. That was his intention, she realized, as she determinedly stifled a moan of passion and despair. She had responded to him, *would* respond to him, because she could not seem to help herself, was powerless against him. No matter what Lucien was or had done, she wanted him just as much as he wanted her.

Moving to the dresser, Arabella saw that, here, too, was evidence that he had thought of everything. A silver-backed mirror, brush, and comb reposed on the top, along with tortoiseshell hair combs and pins, perfumes, a basket of soaps, and a stack of fresh linen towels and washcloths. Inside the drawers, she found peignoirs and wrappers, chemises and camisoles, pantalets and stockings, all clearly new, undoubtedly made especially for her. She had rarely seen such beautiful lawn, cotton, and silk, such fine work, such detailed embroidery and lace. Slowly gathering up her hair, she secured it atop her head, with one of the combs. Then she took the bath essentials and placed them on a low stool by the bathtub. By now, the kettle had heated over the fire, and she poured the steaming-hot water into the tepid liquid that filled the bathtub halfway. After removing her remaining undergarments, she stepped into the bathtub.

Unstoppering a flacon of perfume, Arabella tipped a few drops of the fragrant liquid into the bathwater. Its sweet scent permeated her senses as, taking up a washcloth and a bar of soap, she began to lave herself, enveloped in an aura of decadence and sensuality as she gazed at the water lilies floating in the bathtub. It was as though she bathed in some paradisiacal pool, encompassed by flowers, the flickering flames of the oil lamps and candles like stars in the darkness. Before she had finished soaking, Lucien returned; and she saw that he, too, had washed, probably under a pump outside. Trickles of water still streamed down his dark face from his tousled mane of black hair, reminding her of how he had looked that day at the billabong, with the rain pelting down upon him. He had taken off his jacket and waistcoat, and unbuttoned his shirt to reveal his broad chest matted with fine, damp black hair. He was barefoot, too. After a long minute in which he leaned against the doorjamb, watching her, he prowled inside like some predatory animal, tossing his bundle of clothes and boots into one corner. Vividly conscious of his gaze, of her nakedness, Arabella pressed her hands to her chest, the washcloth clasped between them, her forearms concealing her breasts.

Did she know how she looked to him? Lucien wondered. A few long curls had tumbled from the thick mass of hair she had twisted up with a comb, and now trailed provocatively over her bare shoulders, the ends of the tendrils dripping water. Rivulets seeped down her creamy skin that glowed with the luminescence of a pearl in the soft light. The swell of her breasts gleamed above the water's surface, and the fragile petals of a water lily caressed her flesh, as, presently, he himself would. She was Eve in the Garden of Eden, tempting him, her wide eyes the color of golden apples. She had never seemed more beautiful to him than she did at that moment, her thick, sooty lashes sweeping down demurely, her slender white throat working, her long, graceful hands trembling a little, the washcloth she held to her chest rising and falling with each quick, shallow breath she took. His own breath caught in his throat at the sight; his loins tightened sharply with desire. Picking up one of the linen towels from the dresser, Lucien padded toward her.

"Come," he demanded softly, holding out one hand to her.

After a long moment fraught with significance, Arabella slowly rose and stepped from the bathtub. Her body quivered as he began to dry her off, drawing the towel with excruciating prolongation across her naked skin as he kissed her mouth just as lingeringly, caressing her throat, her breasts, rubbing the material over her nipples until they puckered and hardened, like cherries ripe to bursting. His lips swept down her throat to envelop first one stiff peak and then the other, sucking and laving, his tongue rough, tormenting. Delight pooled at their centers, rippled through Arabella's body, and she moaned as his mouth traveled lower still, down her belly. Kneeling, Lucien dried her feet, his hands moving upward along her legs and her inner thighs that were damp with her own musky moisture. An ache had erupted at the very heart of her that burned for assuagement. Still, Lucien did not yet touch her there, but toweled her buttocks, his dark head bent, his lips trailing kisses along the tops and insides of her thighs, sending a shiver through her, causing her knees to weaken and incoherent little whimpers of pleading to emanate from her throat.

At that, without warning, his hands found her at last. His thumbs slid slowly up the hot, delicate seam of her, parting the glistening, honeyed folds of her womanhood. He pressed his mouth to her burgeoning mound;

his tongue darted forth to flick the tightly furled bud of her—a quick, light stroke that was torture to her, made her inhale sharply and sway faintly upon her feet. Her fingers burrowed through the silky black mane of his hair, tightening and twisting convulsively as his tongue lapped at her, taunted her. Just when Arabella thought she could bear no more, would go crazy from the agonizing hollowness that cried out to be filled, he slid two fingers deep inside her. A ragged gasp caught in her throat. Then her breath came fast and harsh as he began to thrust his fingers in and out of her, tonguing her all the while. Were it not for his other hand, now gripping her buttocks, pressing her to him, she knew she would have fallen. Within moments, tremors like those he had evoked in her that night under the jacaranda tree seized her, heightening to an unendurable intensity before she climaxed violently, shuddering long and hard against his mouth.

After a minute, Lucien rose, kissing her belly and breasts as he did so, then found her her lips. His tongue cleaved her mouth, twined with her own. His hands tugged the comb from her hair; she felt the heavy mass fall, cascading about her in wild disarray. He pressed his lips to the sensitive place upon her shoulder and then, moving behind her, to her nape, his fingers spreading her tresses so they lay like a velvet mantle about her.

"Look, Arabella," he muttered hoarsely in her ear. "Look . . . and tell me that you don't belong to me . . . that you don't want me. . . ."

As her lashes fluttered open, Arabella saw that he and she were together before the dresser, its big, dark, silvery mirror reflecting their images as she stood naked in Lucien's arms. She hardly recognized herself. Surely, that smokily seductive woman was not she. Her long, unbound hair was damp and disheveled, framing a piquant face flushed and dewy from his lovemaking. Beneath the ebony fringe of her lashes, her eyes shone the dark gold of old sherry and were drugged, drowsy with passion. Her cherry-red mouth was slack, swollen, and bruised from his kisses, moist and parted even now, as though aware that what had gone before had been but a prelude to what was still to come. The graceful arch of her throat was bared, her head resting languidly against his shoulder. Like evening mist, her skin gleamed in the diffuse light; shadows cast by the flickering oil lamps and candles danced across her full and heavy breasts, their crests the dusky pink of the rose petals scattered upon the bed. The fleecy curls between her thighs were moist. She looked as wanton as she felt, Arabella thought dimly, stunned at the realization. She would have turned away from her disturbing reflection, but Lucien, having slipped off his shirt, now tightened his embrace around her, his dark bronzed flesh in sharp contrast to her own pale ivory skin.

"Look," he demanded thickly again, refusing to release her.

Slowly, he drew the pad of his thumb along the curve of her lower lip, tugging gently, before his fingers traced the arch of her throat, slid down to squeeze her breast possessively, to tease its tip until it sprang to life again, growing flushed and taut. Arabella did not want to watch, but somehow, she could not seem to tear her eyes from the erotic images in the mirror. His teeth caught her earlobe, biting gently, sending a wild thrill coursing through her as his palm swept lower still, down her belly to cup her mound. His eyes glittered with triumph and satisfaction to find her still hot and wet when he stroked her, plunged his fingers deep into the well of her carmine softness.

"No other man is ever going to see you like this, to touch you like this, Arabella," he murmured, his hand emphasizing his words, making her burn and melt once more, fire and ice, so she yearned desperately for the explosion that she now knew would bring satiation. This time, he did not fulfill her craving, but left her trembling and aching instead as he deliberately withdrew his fingers.

"No . . ." To her shame, she was unable to prevent the small cry of dismay and longing from escaping her lips. "No . . . please . . ."

"Please what, Arabella?" he asked throatily, kissing her shoulder, his words letting her know what he wished to hear her say.

"Please . . . I—I . . . do want you, Lucien." Had that really been her own voice, speaking those words? she wondered in some dark, dreamlike corner of her mind. Somehow, it seemed to Arabella as though she had become two women, one who still looked into the mirror, watching as the other was abruptly swept up in Lucien's arms and carried to the canopy bed.

Amid the rose petals, he laid her down upon the soft white linen sheets, kissing her, caressing her for a moment before he pulled away, his tall, handsome figure towering over her as he stared down at her, his eyes dark with desire. His hands were at his belt, unbuckling it; and then he was stepping from his breeches and undergarment, tossing them aside. Naked, he came to her, his weight settling upon the feather mattress. He was like some saturnine half-man, half-beast kneeling over her, his bold shaft hard and heavy with passion.

"Open your legs for me, Arabella."

In a daze, she did as he had so softly but urgently commanded, as though she no longer had any mind or will of her own. Even the shame and embarrassment she felt at being so vulnerably exposed to him was nothing compared to the burning desire, the aching need building inside her. His hands caught the backs of her knees, pushing her legs higher, spreading them even wider apart. His sex pressed against hers, rubbing the heated, mellifluous folds of her that quivered and opened to him of their own eager accord. Again and again, he stroked the tiny nub that was the key to her pleasure, his maleness sliding over her until she writhed and bucked beneath him, frantic for release. He thrust into her then, hard and swift and deep, taking her breath, making her gasp and then cry aloud. Her nails dug into his broad back as she clung to him, took him inside her, arching her hips to meet his own as he carried her with him on a tide of violent sensation, increasingly faster and harder as he plunged in and out of her. She was like the wild sea, rushing inland, catching upon coral reefs for a fleeting eternity, poised, uplifted, before exploding, shattering against rocks and driftwood, then washing up gently upon rainbow sands. As she lay beneath him, she could feel Lucien's face buried against her shoulder, his breath hot against her skin as, with a groan, he spilled himself inside her. Then he collapsed atop her, his weight pressing her down, a weight that, now, was intimately familiar and—yes, Arabella could no longer deny it—deeply beloved.

He was a part of her. Even now, their hearts beat as one; his mouth moved on hers, so they breathed as one. Only after a long moment did he raise himself on his elbows and, still kissing and caressing her, slowly withdraw. Rolling to one side of her, he pulled her into his strong embrace, cradling her head against his chest. He was warm, and she was drowsy and languid, content to lie in his arms.

"I am indeed mad—or truly wanton." Her voice was soft; her hand traced tiny circles in the fine, silken hair upon his chest.

"No, you are but an earthy, passionate woman, my sweet."

"It is not right that I should feel . . . such pleasure at these things you do to me, Lucien. They are shameful, indecent—"

"No, they are not. Nothing is wrong when done between lovers if it is what they both want—and that is a truth that all women should be taught. If they were, there would be far fewer cold, empty beds in the world and fewer unfaithful men. But that is something you need never fear, Arabella. You are all I have ever wished for in a woman; I have no desire or need for any other, nor will I ever, I swear." He paused for a moment, then asked lightly, "Are you hungry?" smiling at her rosy blush. "For food, I mean . . . although for the other, too, I have an appetite not so quickly sated, as you will learn. But I think that perhaps you have not eaten all day. Am I right?" •

"Yes."

Rising, Lucien strode naked across the room, obviously not in the least self-conscious about his nudity as he filled a plate from the platters and bowls arrayed upon the counter of the kitchen nook. Covertly, from beneath the fringe of her lashes, Arabella studied him, marveling at the hard, lean planes and angles of his dark body, the powerful muscles that bunched and rippled in his back, arms, and legs as he moved. He was, in truth, like some animal, she thought, and she had responded to him on that primitive level. But clearly, he had been deeply pleased rather than shocked and offended by that unbridled response, quite unlike Gervase's reaction when she had kissed him back. How strange that it should have been Gervase, a gentleman, who had made her feel base and humiliated. Gervase had not wanted, had not expected passion from her, only her dutiful submission to him.

Now, as Arabella remembered Lucien's words to her earlier, she thought that if she had married Gervase, he would surely have proved an unfaithful husband to her, would have kept her on his mental pedestal and sought his pleasure elsewhere, with women such as those she had seen at The Rocks, no doubt. How many nights would she have been left to lie alone, untouched, unloved, in her cold, empty bed, withering away like a flower deprived of nourishing sun and rain? she wondered, shivering at what she now perceived as her narrow escape. She thought of Uncle Philip and Aunt Hennie, of their separate bedrooms and poor Aunt Hennie lying drunk in her bed; and for the first time, Arabella suspected that perhaps Uncle Philip had reasons other than working late to remain in town overnight, that perhaps he himself upon occasion frequented The Rocks and its whores.

Abruptly, Arabella sat up in bed, drawing the top sheet, folded down neatly at the foot of the bed, up around her for modesty's sake and plumping up the numerous fluffy pillows behind her. The sweet, heady perfume of the rose petals that she and Lucien had crushed beneath them permeated the sheets, mingling with the musky scent of their lovemaking. Yet the shame that she had felt earlier had lessened. Even the sight of Lucien's scars and brand did not fill her with horror, as they had before. She just could not believe that some-one who would expend so much thought and care in preparing her bridal bower and who had made love to her with such infinite patience and tenderness was guilty of rape and murder.

"Lucien . . . do those . . . women we saw today at The Rocks . . . enjoy what they—what they do?" she inquired hesitantly but unable to stifle her curiosity and knowing, by this time, that she could discuss anything with him, that nothing would shock him or cause him to censure her for her unladylike thoughts.

"Some do, perhaps. But truthfully, my sweet, most of those poor women are not what you would call wan-ton, but, rather, are driven by unfortunate circumstances into a life that is degrading and hellish at best. There is a great deal of difference, you see, between what we have shared between us and what is done between men and women for money, or even for mere sexual gratifi-cation," he told her as he rejoined her on the bed, setting the laden plate down, then opening the bottle of champagne he carried, pouring the pale alcohol into the crystal glasses that had previously reposed among the boughs of lilacs.

"In—in what way?"

"In any number of ways. You saw The Rocks and how the dock women live. In the time that I have spent with you tonight, a dock woman would probably have lain with two or three different men—perhaps even at the same time. And this would have taken place not in a bower such as I have made of my one-room cabin, but in the cramped quarters above some sordid grog-shop, upon some filthy, lice-infested pallet that probably lacked even a single sheet or blanket. The men might have been drunk, dirty, or diseased. They would per-haps have been abusive, beating or otherwise hurting the woman; certainly, they would not have cared whether she were willing or ready to be taken."

"Ready? I—I don't understand what you mean—"

"The kissing, the touching, and all the rest, Arabella . . . that is what arouses a woman, makes her ache for a man inside her, makes her open to him, as you did for me—and will again," he declared, with a possessive, knowing glance that made her flush as she remembered how she had wanted him and realized how, even now, his very nearness stirred her. "But imagine if, instead, I simply held you down and brutally forced my way into you or, worse, slapped you beforehand. What defense would you have against me? At best, you would know no pleasure in the act. At worst, you would be physically injured—and if that happened often enough, you would learn to lie still and silent and submissive beneath me, as women are taught to do and as most other men would have expected of a wife.''

"You did not.''

"No, but, then, I am not most men.'' He paused for a moment, then continued. "My parents were very happy together, very much in love; and when I grew old enough to understand such things, I realized that a great deal of that stemmed from the fact that my mother had dared to rebel against all she had been taught. Although from a rich, genteel family, she eloped with my father, a working man, a groom, who had little to offer her other than himself. Of course, her family cut her off without a cent for making such a misalliance, but she never regretted it. I remember my parents kissing and touching often, holding hands, my father stroking my mother's hair—she had beautiful hair, like yours, Arabella. Sometimes at night, I would hear them both cry out with joy; and years later, I knew why.

"I thought to find the same happiness in my own marriage. But my first wife, Verity, was very young, ignorant, and afraid. She was deeply shocked by my ardor; and after the first few times, it became clear that there would never be any pleasure in the act for either of us. I couldn't bring myself to force her, to listen to her weeping; so after that, I just left her alone.'' Lost in his memories, Lucien fell silent again. Then, after a moment, collecting himself, he said lightly, "I thought that you were hungry, my girl. Yet you've hardly eaten a bite—and the strawberries are from my own vines, the grapes from my own vineyards.''

He fed her then, explaining how everything except

the chocolates on the plate had come from his own estate, the meats from the cattle, sheep, and chickens he raised; the cheese, butter, and other dairy products from his own outbuildings; the vegetables and fruits from his own gardens and orchards. Even the champagne had come from his own winery, the sugar, into which they dipped the strawberries and grapes, from his own cane fields, the breads from his own fields of grain. He relied on no one for anything, but was totally self-sufficient. Arabella suspected that this carefully developed independence, too, derived from his past, about which she longed to hear more.

But although he himself had opened the door to his background a crack, she was wise enough not to batter her way forcefully inside. She sensed that although he desired her, Lucien's commitment to her had not come easily. He had spent many years alone, and had built around himself many guarded walls that would take time to overcome. If he were, in fact, as he had claimed, innocent of his wife's murder, then he had been wrongly imprisoned, had had fourteen years of his life cruelly stolen from him. That was reason enough for bitterness and mistrust and the other, harsher aspects of his character that had led him to kidnap her, Arabella, to coerce her into marriage, to compel her to respond to him. Yet if he had taken much from her, he had also given much in return. So when he reached for her again, she did not protest, but went willingly into his arms.

He made love to her until the candles guttered in their sockets, the fire died in the hearth, and dawn broke on the horizon. There was nothing he had not done, had not taught her. She had never dreamed that such exquisite sensations, pleasure so intense that it was almost painful, such closeness to another human being was possible. When, at last, it was done, she lay in his embrace, her heart filled to overflowing. She had never stopped loving him, she realized as she drifted toward slumber. Right or wrong, he held her heart in his keeping—now and for always.

"I love you, Lucien," she whispered. Then, wordlessly, not trusting herself to speak further, she raised her head and pressed her mouth gently to the dark brand upon his shoulder, so he would understand all she felt inside for him, no matter what.

"Oh, Arabella . . . Arabella . . ." His voice was low and smoky with emotion as he suddenly tightened his arms about her, as though he would never let her go. "I have been searching all my life for you. I *do* love you, you know."

Then he buried his head against her shoulder; and she held him close in the early grey dawn light, still and silent, her heart aching for him as she felt his tears, damp upon her skin.

Chapter Seventeen

Memories

They stayed for three days in the cabin, going nowhere, seeing no one. Servants arrived now and then to leave picnic baskets of food and drink upon the porch. But other than that, it was as though time had stopped and Arabella and Lucien were all alone in the world. She had never known such happiness as she did then, could not believe that she had ever feared him, that she had ever doubted his innocence. She did not know how or why he had been convicted and imprisoned, but she now felt certain that it had been wrongly done.

"Will you tell me about the scars, the brand?" she asked once as they lay naked together in the quiet afterglow of their lovemaking. "Richard—Captain Bonniface—and Norah both told me that the convicts are well treated, that many receive their tickets-of-leave straightaway and so seldom serve any time at all for their crimes, that only the most incorrigible of the prisoners are flogged and branded. But now, having seen The Rocks and knowing you, I think that that must not be so . . . that Tilly, my maid, had good reason for her fear when she first came to me . . . that you were cruelly punished, hurt without just cause—'' Arabella broke off abruptly when a dark, unreadable expression came upon Lucien's face at her words, as though he had emotionally withdrawn from her, closed himself to her.

The notion wounded her, for she did not want to acknowledge that although he had said he loved her, there were still barriers between them, places inside of him that she had yet to reach through the walls he had erected around his heart and soul. He would, she had come to realize, always be moody and brooding. The scars he bore from his past were not just physical, and the ones she could not see were far worse than those that crisscrossed his back, and perhaps would never completely heal, regardless of the solace she offered. Still, she felt she had to try, and now, her heart sank when he did not answer, but rolled away from her instead. Sitting up in bed, he ran his hands raggedly through his long, shaggy hair. Then, reaching for his gold case of cheroots lying upon the nightstand, he lit one of the thin black cigars, pulling on it deeply while he poured himself a glass of rum from the decanter that also sat there. He downed the fiery liquor in one swallow and began to speak, his voice flat, expressionless, and his words somehow all the more horrifying for that.

''We were crammed like slaves into the holds of the transport ships, so many of us that there was scarcely room to breathe, much less to find a modicum of privacy or comfort. Fights broke out over the bunks and hammocks, because if you didn't get one, you slept upon the hard floor. There was never enough of the rotten food, nor the brackish water. When the hatches were battened down, there was no fresh air and no light, because oil lamps and candles were forbidden, lest we start fires on board with them. Disease was rampant among us; wounds caused by our irons festered in the heat. Maggots feasted upon decaying flesh; there was hardly ever any proper medicine.

"To those of us who reached it alive, Van Diemen's Land seemed a paradise. It is, truly, one of the most beautiful places on earth, I think. That it should have been home to such ugliness as Port Arthur, the prison where I was incarcerated, is undoubtedly one of the greatest ironies, the greatest sacrileges of all time. It was a hell, a highly efficient police state, divided into nine districts and with seven levels of punishment. Port Arthur, Macquarie Harbor, and Norfolk Island were the worst places a convict could serve time. There, the cat-o'-nine-tails were unusually cruel. At Port Arthur, the knout was fashioned of the toughest whipcord, inordinately thick, and the cord itself was first soaked in salt water and then baked in the sun, so it was like wire, and had eighty-one knots to cut the flesh.

"Although Charles O'Hara Booth, who ran Port Arthur for part of the time that I was there, preferred solitary confinement to the lash, when he did hand down a sentence of corporal punishment, it was often for a hundred lashes. Attempts at escape—and I made more than one—were invariably so punished. Afterward, unless it were mealtime or night, you were sent back to work, your back like raw meat and blood in your shoes. You were not permitted to go to the hospital until the following morning—not that it did any good to go there, anyway, since all you'd ever get was your back washed by the doctor's mate and some rancid hog grease smeared on your wounds. Then, afterward, like as not, because you couldn't pull your weight on the chain gang or in the coal mine that day, you'd be flogged again for neglect of work.''

If he heard Arabella's gasp of shock and horror or were aware of the tears that had begun to seep slowly down her cheeks, Lucien gave no sign, staring off into space, lost, she knew, in some dark hell in his own mind, where his memories festered like the gangrenous flesh crawling with maggots, about which he had spoken earlier.

"The solitary cells were seven feet by four feet," he continued in that same monotonous voice, "and pitch-dark, with only an old rug to lie upon—and nights are cold on Van Diemen's Land. If you went in wet, after having tried to wade across Eaglehawk Neck, the isthmus that is the only way to leave Van Diemen's Land by land, you damned near froze to death, because you didn't get any dry clothes, either. Strings of sentries, dogs, and searchlights guarded the Neck; the cockle shells cut your feet; and the lookouts made a habit of throwing offal and blood—which they got from the slaughterhouse at Forestier's Peninsula a few miles away—off the beaches to attract sharks, so that if the guards and dogs didn't get you, the sharks would. There were boxes like dog kennels, too, in which a man could be chained, with a pile of stones in front of him, which he must spend his day breaking. And if his irons were not heavy enough to suit his crimes, he got the 'log on his toes,' a weighty balk of timber that was attached to his ankle chains and that he must drag along as he walked.

"Perhaps worst of all was to be sentenced to the coal mines at Norfolk Bay, where you spent hours at hard labor, expected to hew thirty trolleys full of coal a day in dark, confined shafts that threatened to cave in at any moment and that, because the deepest were a hundred feet beneath the sea, ran constantly with salt water, burning the wounds caused by your shackles—although at least the salt kept your flesh from putrefying.

"Branding wasn't all that common, but the jailers were some of the lowest, most sadistic bastards on earth; and if they hated you and got drunk enough on rum or wine, they picked you out to torment even more severely than usual. One night, four of them came for me. One of them, Constable Hogg—Wart, we called him—had a knife, and I saw that they meant to kill me—or worse. We fought . . . that's how I got this"—he indicated the thin scar upon his cheek—"and somehow during the struggle, I got hold of the blade and stabbed Wart to death. Afterward, the other three held me down and branded me. I figure that, afraid of being reprimanded for their own part in the incident, they must have pitched Wart's corpse to the sharks later, because there were never any charges brought against me; there wasn't even an inquiry."

Lucien fell silent after that, inhaling long and deeply

of his cheroot before he ground it out methodically in a brass ashtray. Pouring another glass of rum, he drank that, too, in one long draught. Then, at last, he turned to Arabella.

"Now, you know," he said quietly, almost absently brushing the tears from her cheeks, his thumb tracing the outline of her mouth, tugging at her lower lip. "After I got my ticket-of-leave, the gold rush ensued, and I broke parole to head for the Ophir district. For the first time then, I had reason to be grateful for all those years of hard, grueling labor." He held out his bare arms, flexing them so the powerful muscles bunched and rippled sinuously beneath his bronzed skin. "In hours, I could sink a shaft that it would have taken a new chum days to dig. I struck it rich . . . bribed the officials to forget that I still had four years of parole left to serve . . . bought this land, and built this cabin.

"I thought that it would be enough—until that morning I found you washed up on the beach, Arabella. Fate had dealt you a rough hand . . . and just like me, you fought so damned hard to survive—I wanted you from that first moment I laid eyes on you, neither a convict woman, used by hundreds of men, nor a genteel, schoolroom miss to shrink at my very touch. No . . . there was passion and fire in you, my girl, coupled with your bright, inquisitive mind, your practical, realistic nature, your kind, romantic heart. Another man would have stifled your spirit, smothered some vital spark inside you. I couldn't let that happen. You were meant for me, Arabella. I knew it then—and you know it now, don't you?"

"Yes . . . yes," she breathed as he moved with sudden urgency to cover her pale body with his own dark one, his strong hands capturing her delicate ones, pressing them down on either side of her head, inescapably trapping her.

His mouth closed over hers hungrily, his tongue parting her lips as she opened herself to him, took him deep inside her, as though she could enfold him, cocoon him, protect him from the world and further hurt. Eagerly, she arched her hips to meet each fierce, hard thrust, sensing instinctively how losing himself inside her held his terrible, painful memories at bay, if only for a little while. He was like a high, wild wind, sweeping her up and bearing her aloft. They reached their peak swiftly and together, crying out, then shuddering into a silence broken only by the violent drumming of hearts that beat as one. Slowly, smiling down at her, Lucien kissed her, then released her hands and eased himself from her, propping himself up on one elbow, his fingers trailing idly over her breasts, her belly, her thighs, twining in soft, damp curls. After a long while, he sighed and spoke.

"Much as I would like to, we cannot stay here forever, my love. I've an estate to run. Come," he insisted, reluctantly rising and holding out his hand to her. "However much I regret it, it's time to go."

"Oh, Lucien, must we . . . truly?"

"Don't you think you've had more than enough?" Both his glance and his grin were wicked, causing her to blush. "Besides, unlike most husbands and wives, I don't intend for us to have separate bedchambers. My room at the big house will do nicely for us both."

"Indeed? What will people say to that, I wonder?"

"Publicly, they will be scandalized, of course; and since we eloped, there will probably be speculation about our having a seventh-month child, as well. Privately, however, they will be envious of our good fortune."

A child. Arabella had given no thought to that. Unconsciously, her hand moved to her flat belly as she imagined a babe of Lucien's making growing there.

"Yes, after these past three days, a child is certainly a strong possibility, my sweet," he declared gently, reading her mind, his face tender as he gazed down at her.

"And would that . . . please you?" she asked, a trifle shyly.

"Yes, it would. It would please me very much."

Arabella was silent for a moment, thinking of caps and cradles. Then, getting to her knees and recalling herself from her reverie, she ventured another question:

"People say that your estate has no name, Lucien. Is that so?"

"It was—for a time. But I have since given it a name. For reasons that you alone will understand quite well, I call it Jacaranda."

Both touched and pleased, Arabella stretched up, wrapped her arms around his neck, and kissed him fervently. Then, flushing with embarrassment at her own boldness, she tried to draw away. But he held her tight, and she knew from the expression upon his face that he was not at all displeased by her forwardness.

"And will you show it to me yourself . . . the house and grounds, I mean?" she asked quickly to conceal her fluster. "I should like that . . . that is, if you won't be too busy."

A half-rueful, half-mocking smile curved Lucien's mouth.

"How swiftly you have learned to use your charms upon me, Arabella, and how prettily you have learned to beg for what you want. But there are still some things I have to teach you, and regardless, I will always be your master."

"Will you, Lucien?" she jested lightly, then gasped, her eyes widening as, without warning, gripping her buttocks, he lifted her powerfully from the bed and brought her down upon him, impaling her with his hard, eager manhood that had stirred anew at her abandoned kiss and her teasing. Swinging her around, he pressed her back against the thick, sturdy bedpost, holding her motionless there, his sex throbbing deep inside her.

"What do you think?" he taunted in response to her question, his voice low and husky. "I will always be stronger than you—you wouldn't respect me if I weren't—and now, you see where all your begging and teasing will lead."

Slowly, watching her all the while, he began to plunge in and out of her, grinding himself against her, making her intensely, frantically, aware of his strength as he effortlessly supported her, conscious of his power to arouse her body. His chest brushed her breasts, stimulating her nipples, as each bold, barbarous thrust rubbed torturously against the rigid little bud that was the key to her delight. He moved against her until she was desperate, burning, aching for release, clinging to him, her legs wrapped around his waist in an attempt to draw him even closer, deeper into her. Dimly, Arabella could hear herself moaning, pleading with him, hoarsely urging him on as, at last, his body quickened feverishly against hers, driving into her fiercely, frenziedly, bringing them both rapidly to climax.

Afterward, she was so breathless and trembling that if Lucien had not held her, she would have fallen to the floor. Finally, gently laying her on the bed, he withdrew, kissing her mouth, her breasts, his palm cupping her still-pulsing mound.

"Get bathed. Get dressed," he demanded softly, "before all I have worked so hard to build falls to rack and ruin about me—or we are both dead of exhaustion! Ten years in prison have left me practically insatiable, but even I have limits, my girl—and I cannot help but think that despite all the care I have taken to ease the chafing, you are more sore and swollen than I would wish."

"I am . . . just a little," Arabella confessed reluctantly; for he *had* been careful, taking the time to arouse her, to ensure that she was ready for him, and more than once rubbing her with a soothing balm to make his penetration, his possession of her easier. Yet, despite her occasional twinges of soreness, she had wanted him as much as he had her. "But I don't mind."

"Perhaps not. But I do. I don't want to hurt you and must take you less often and more gently these next few days, until you grow less tender, more accustomed to my being inside you." After pulling on his breeches, he set the kettle on the fire to heat for her bath, then unrolled a bundle that had been left on the porch earlier by whatever unseen servant had also brought their breakfast. "There are fresh clothes for you here, and under the circumstances, I don't think that Chrissie would object to your laying aside your mourning."

She went very still at that. It was, she realized, the first time in days that she had thought about Chrissie; and as she looked at Lucien and the bridal bower he had created for her, Arabella recognized that it must have been something very much like her own experience that Chrissie had been expecting when she had run away with Black Jack O'Flaherty.

"I feel so—so *guilty* of a sudden, Lucien." Tears stung Arabella's eyes as she slowly stood and walked to the bathtub. "To be so happy . . . when she lies cold in her grave."

"She was your friend, Arabella. She would not grudge your finding what I think she must have sought. Believe me when I say that she would be glad that one of you, at least, escaped from that unhappy house of the Wyndhams."

"How do you know that it was unhappy?"

"Trust me. I know. It is with an iron fist that the colonel commands the Rum Corps. One does not suppose that he runs his household any less gently. Mrs. Wyndham exhibits the same symptoms as the wives of many officers and gentlemen in New South Wales— the signs associated with the habitual imbibing of too much liquor. Norah is a repressed, dictatorial old maid; and to pay for his profligate ways, Gervase supplements his income by smuggling rum and, I suspect, among things not quite so pleasant, by heading a gang of ex-convicts who have taken to the high toby.''

"My God, Lucien!" Arabella breathed, stricken. "Surely, you—you must be mistaken! About Gervase, I mean. And if what you say *is* true, then how could you—how could you possibly know such things?''

"My dear, although—since nothing marks a man more certainly as an ex-convict and prevents his rise in society—I have worked hard to rid my language of prison cant, I can, when I so choose, still speak it with the worst of them. Nor have I thought it prudent to disassociate myself from all my former cohorts. So I know a great deal in New South Wales to which others are not privy. It is unfortunate, and I very much regret it, that I was away in Melbourne when Chrissie made her bid for freedom. Had I known she had decamped with the Wyndhams' groom, I could perhaps have taken steps at least to prevent her eventual death. I am truly sorry that I was not in time to spare her that. I have tried to make amends for my failure and to you by claiming her body and giving her a decent burial. You will want to visit her grave, I know. Meanwhile, please don't, out of guilt, throw away this happiness we have found together, Arabella. It will change nothing, except to make us both miserable.''

"Yes, you're right, of course," she replied after a moment.

Lifting the kettle from the fire, Arabella began to fill the bathtub that Lucien had emptied yesterday, while, from outside, he carried in a bucket of water to cool it to bathing temperature. Soon, she was ready to leave the cabin, although the thought of doing so tugged at her heart, filling her with regret. It had been paradise here as in the tropical woods. Still, something of both places lingered within her as she reached for Lucien's hand. The rented carriage and horses had been returned by the servants to the livery stable, and he had, Lucien explained as they strolled along, thought she would prefer to walk to the big house, so she would have an opportunity to see something of the grounds. She felt gay and carefree at his side, partly because she was happy and partly because Lucien had destroyed her corset and failed to provide her with another. He had also got rid of her hoops and crinolines. Her pale green gown of sprig muslin was simplicity itself; her petticoats were soft, unlike the scratchy crinoline. Arabella felt almost as unfettered as she had in the tropical woods.

"If I did not know better, I would think you a child, my sweet." Lucien's lips curved in an indulgent smile as he glanced at her.

One hand flew to her hair at his words. She had left the thick, heavy mass hanging down, as he had insisted, merely pulling it back with two of the tortoiseshell combs. She was barefoot, too, carrying her slippers and stockings. She had so regretted leaving the cabin that she had allowed Lucien to dress her as he had wished. Now, it belatedly occurred to her that she hardly looked the part of mistress of his estate, prepared to meet his staff of servants. But Lucien, when she voiced her concerns to him, simply laughed.

"Do you honestly believe that I give a damn what

anybody thinks?'' he drawled insolently, his eyes glittering. ''The only person you have to please is me, my girl—and I love you just the way you are.''

Forever after, Arabella remembered those words and how, at that exact moment, the big house at Jacaranda came into sight, more beautiful than she would ever have thought possible, beckoning her home.

Chapter Eighteen

Jacaranda

Nestled amid a grove of banksias, acacias, and gum trees, Jacaranda was a lovely house, two stories high, built of whitewashed brick, with a black slate roof and towering chimneys. Wide wooden verandas painted a deep forest green, with tall, slender white columns covered with morning glory vines and ivy, encompassed both the first and second stories, and morning glory vines and ivy interwove the slats of the white balustrade on the upper balcony, too. Wooden jalousies painted to match the verandas hung at the French doors that from every room in the house opened onto the shady porches, so the cooling breezes that swept in from the sea could dissipate the heat of Australia's long, hot summers. Here and there were white wooden trellises laden with bougainvillea and hibiscus that rose from green planter boxes to climb the walls. A circular drive of crushed white seashells that gleamed against the sweeping green lawn led to the house. At the rear, set among the gardens with their serpentine white brick paths, were a large, graceful gazebo with lacy wood trim and an equally big, charming aviary, where Mate, Lucien's cockatoo, lodged with a number of other native birds.

"Hello, Arabella," Mate squawked upon seeing her.

"Hello, Mate, you pretty bird," she replied delightedly, pressing her face and hands against the screen of the aviary momentarily before Lucien pulled her on toward the house.

The house was just as beautiful inside as it was outside; its spacious rooms had high ceilings, whitewashed plaster walls, and, in stark but lovely contrast, dark, hardwood floors covered with Aubusson carpets. An opulent staircase leading to the second floor dominated the center of the huge entrance hall, which was flanked by the drawing room to the right and the dining room to the left. The furniture was sparse but exquisite, so the entire effect was one of capacious, harmonious elegance and grace that Arabella found utterly pleasing. Clearly, Lucien had excellent taste. As she ventured inside, she turned to him, her eyes shining.

"Oh, Lucien, it's . . . it's everything I could have wished."

"I'm glad you find it so, my love."

Drawing her forward, he presented her to the servants who were lined up in the hall, waiting to greet her. To her great surprise and gratitude, Tilly and Declan numbered among them. Lucien had rightly suspected that following Arabella's disappearance, the colonel would turn both the maid and groom off without a reference once he learned that they had permitted Arabella to go off alone with Lucien; and so Lucien had made arrangements to hire them at Jacaranda, positions they had been quick and eager to accept upon learning that their new employer had married Arabella.

"I thought that it would make things easier for you to have a familiar face or two about the place," Lucien explained to Arabella, "and as you seemed quite attached to Tilly . . ."

"Yes, I am," she confirmed as she turned from hugging the tearful maid. "I'm—I'm so overwhelmed by your kindness, Lucien. I don't know how to thank you."

"I'll show you . . . tonight," he whispered.

He had only to look at her, and she trembled, went weak in her knees, melted inside. It was as though he possessed some rough magic, had cast some bedeviling spell upon her, she thought—a notion that only grew stronger as the days passed and her new life at Jacaranda settled into a pattern. She loved the estate. It was much like Darracott Hall; and now that she was out from under the aegis of Aunt Hennie and Norah, Arabella resumed the managerial role that she had once held in her father's house, so there was much to occupy her time. She was aided in her task by the servants. Although, as usual, they were all ex-convicts, they were a great deal more respectful and harder working than those at Wyndham House and Blue Trees had been; for, good help being so difficult to acquire in the Colonies, it was not at all uncommon for the mistress of a household to be cursed to her face by her servants and otherwise treated poorly. Lucien, however, tolerated no disrespect whatsoever. He did not, as so many other masters did, resort to the lash or other equally cruel punishments permitted by law; but he had once stripped to his breeches and personally, with his bare fists, thrashed a belligerent coachman. That Lucien was himself an ex-convict, scarred and branded, and that he also paid the highest wages for miles around were two other reasons his servants behaved so well.

He himself worked hardest of all at Jacaranda, rising at six o'clock each morning and sometimes not retiring until the small hours. When he was not going over the account books with Arabella or helping her with some other household chore, he was busy with the estate itself, in its pastures, vineyards, and fields, making certain that all he had struggled so hard to achieve did not slip from his grasp. Of those who served him, he asked naught that he would not or could not have done himself; of the rest of the world, he asked nothing, having learned from his years in prison to rely only on himself. His book-learning had come from his mother; the rest of his education he had received from the school of hard knocks, and he never forgot what he had been taught. He was what society most hated and feared: a self-made man—and proud of it. The more she came to understand him, the more Arabella realized how complex Lucien was. If arrogance, insolence, and a hot, black temper were his faults, they were compensated for in equal measure by his intelligence, compassion, and sense of humor. He knew how to play as well as to work.

There were mornings when he woke her and teased her ruthlessly, tickling her until she screamed with laughter and pleaded for mercy, after which he would make love to her, with a swift savagery that brought her quickly and violently to her peak. There were afternoons when he tossed aside her apron to whisk her away in his carriage for a picnic luncheon beneath the gum trees or to Sydney for some other amusement or to the cabin they had shared at the start of their marriage. There, at this last, he would take her so slowly and deliberately that she was begging, desperate, half mad for release by the time he gave it to her. There were nights when the two of them sat and talked, and Lucien revealed to Arabella more of his thoughts and emotions than he had ever told anyone else; and his trust in her touched her deeply.

Sometimes, when she looked at him, her heart ached with all the love it held for him. She would trace the scar upon his dark face, those on his back, the brand on his shoulder; and in the white, puckered slashes and crescents, she would see a beauty she had not seen before, a tangible testimony to his will to survive. That he did love her, she could not doubt; it was in his gleaming eyes when he glanced at her. And his fierce possessiveness that was at once frightening and exciting sent a wild thrill coursing through her. Sometimes, the realization of how much she loved him, how happy she was, scared her. She felt as though her life were too good to be true, that it would be snatched from her at any moment, as it had been once before, when the storm had descended upon the *Heather Rose*.

Lucien, however, only laughed at her fear.

"My God! Do you really think I'd let anything happen to you, to *us*? That day will never come, my girl!

Now, take off that delightful but thoroughly maddening gown before I rip it from you!"

Still, Arabella's foreboding lingered.

This was due in part to the fact that when—a few days after their move from the cabin to the big house—Lucien had finally deigned actually to call on Uncle Philip, he had somehow managed to persuade her guardian to release her inheritance. She could think only that he had threatened Uncle Philip with Gervase's IOUs, which Lucien had locked up in the safe in his study—"insurance," he had called the markers grimly when Arabella had dared to question him about them.

"But I did as you asked, Lucien," she had protested, confused and anxious. "You got what you wanted. I married you. There's no need for you to ruin the Wyndhams now. Please. Give the notes back to Gervase."

"Like hell I will!" he had snarled in reply, on his face such a forbidding expression that Arabella had actually taken a step back from him, all her previous fears about him returning. Seeing her eyes widen with alarm, Lucien had spoken more gently. "There's no need for you to be afraid, Arabella. I would never hurt you. You must know that. Please believe me when I tell you that I have good reasons for my actions."

"All right, Lucien," she had said after a moment, not wanting to think she could not trust him, that his protestations of love for her were all lies.

Afterward, Arabella would perhaps have been more inclined to suspicion had she not seen all about her tangible evidence of Lucien's riches and if not for the fact that, following its transfer to him, he turned her entire fortune over to her, opening an account in her name at the bank in Sydney and depositing her funds therein.

"I want you to understand that it is *your* money, my sweet, to do with as you please. I have no need of it, and I'll not have people claiming that I married you to get my hands on your inheritance. Under the circumstances, there will be gossip enough as it is without adding fuel to the fire," he declared dryly; for indeed, although most of the aristocracy were still at their estates for the summer and had yet to return to their town houses in Sydney, rumors had already started to spread about her and Lucien. He continued, "However, as I have knowledge about business in the Colonies, while your own experience has been limited to that of Darracott Hall, I will, if you would like for me to do so, be glad to advise you with regard to financial opportunities you may wish to consider. There are, as well, some investments made by both your father and the colonel over the years that you would be wise to continue. Other holdings ought, however, to be sold and the resulting funds invested elsewhere."

"Have I enough money to buy a house in town?" Arabella asked thoughtfully.

A frown darkened Lucien's face at that; one eyebrow lifted questioningly.

"For what purpose, may I ask, my girl? I already own a town house in Sydney, as well you know. Are you still upset over Gervase's IOUs? Do you have some desire to leave me? For if you do, I warn you: I will not permit that."

"No . . . no, it's nothing like that. How could you think so? I want to found a—a home for convict women, to help them in some fashion, so they don't wind up on the streets, in places like The Rocks. I thought that perhaps if the women were given the training necessary to help them find employment . . ." Her voice trailed away at Lucien's smile, which was at once sardonic and sympathetic.

"My dear Arabella, you cannot save the world," he declared lightly.

"Perhaps not. But I can at least try to change it, which is something that, as an Emancipist, you ought to understand." She paused for a moment, gathering courage for what she would say next. Then she continued. "And maybe . . . maybe if the women come, I can learn something about Chrissie, about her murder."

"Arabella, I thought that we agreed that you would leave that to me." Lucien's grave face gave evidence of both his anger and his concern.

"I know we did, but I want to help in some way. Every day, I visit her grave, and I—I just can't believe that she's gone, that no one's done anything about her death."

"That's not so. I am making inquiries. However these things take time, and it has not helped that Black Jack was stabbed to death in a grog-shop brawl a few days after Chrissie's murder. Nevertheless, I'm afraid that I must once more insist that you do not meddle in this matter. On that condition, I will consent to your house for convict women and will set about to look for a suitable piece of property. But I must have your word, Arabella, that you will let me handle uncovering the truth about Chrissie's murder in my own way, in my own time."

"Very well," she said at last. "I give you my word."

They were standing on the balcony outside the master bedroom. In the black firmament, the moon glowed silvery, its beams filtering through the branches of the trees, dappling the ground. The stars glittered like a titanic Catherine wheel frozen in the midst of its spinning. The soughing breeze was damp with the sea and the river, its fragrance mingling with the perfume of the gum trees, and with the morning glory vines that twined through the slats of the balustrade. From below wafted the scents of the bougainvillea and hibiscus that climbed the trellises, of the roses and other flowers that filled the gardens, and of the rich earth itself. The stillness of the night was broken only by the chirping of the night birds and frogs, of locusts and crickets, and the howl of a dingo in the distance. It was a peaceful scene, yet suddenly, Arabella shivered.

"What is it, my love? Are you cold?" From behind her, Lucien drew her into his embrace, his hands rubbing her arms to warm her.

"No . . . it's just that . . . some days after our marriage, I began to feel as though someone were . . . well, *watching* me, Lucien."

"Watching you?" Lucien's voice was sharp; his hands were rough as he turned her to face him. "You said nothing of this before, Arabella! Why have you not told me?"

"Because at first I thought that it was only my imagination, and I felt as though I would be foolish to make an issue out of nothing . . . mere fancies. But although I have attempted to banish them from my mind, the feelings have persisted. Just now . . . I had that strange sensation of eyes fastened upon me, as though someone were out there, watching us, Lucien, watching *me!*''

"Go inside to our bedchamber!'' he commanded softly. "Draw the drapes; lock the doors behind you, and don't open them for anyone but me! Do you understand?''

"Yes, but—''

"No questions, Arabella. Just do as I tell you.''

Lucien waited until she was safely inside their room and he heard her locking the French doors and saw her pulling the sheer curtains closed across them. Then he moved stealthily from the balcony. Inside the bedchamber, Arabella watched his shadow flit across the French doors, then disappear. He was gone—but into what danger, she did not know. Could it be that her mind was *not* playing tricks on her, that there was really someone out there? But who—and why? She remembered, suddenly, Lucien saying that by poking into Chrissie's murder, she was involving herself in something she did not understand, something dangerous; and for the first time, Arabella thought that perhaps he had spoken truly and not merely to try to deter her from venturing into The Rocks. Her heart leaped with fear for Lucien. What if, lurking out there, was one of the gangs of escaped prisoners or ex-convicts who terrorized the countryside? As strong and smart as he was Lucien was still only one man.

Although, by the ornate ormolu clock that sat ticking upon the mantel over the fireplace, no more than thirty minutes had passed, Arabella felt as though hours had gone by. Like some restless, caged animal, she paced the floor, worried for Lucien. More than once, she moved to the French doors, tempted to unlock them, to go outside, and to look for him. Only the thought of his wrath should he discover that she had disobeyed his order prevented her. Drawing back one drape a little, she peered out into the darkness but could see nothing. Nor, when she pressed her ear to the glass, could she hear anything. She thought perhaps that was a good sign. Surely, if Lucien were in trouble, the sounds of a struggle would reach her ears; he would not be taken without a fight.

Then, at last, to her relief, he returned. He prowled so quietly along the balcony that Arabella did not hear him, and grew frightened when a tall shadow loomed up suddenly before the French doors. Then Lucien rapped peremptorily upon one door, telling her to open up; and with relief, she let him in.

"Did you see anyone?" she asked.

He shook his head. "No, but I think that you were right and that there was somebody out there. There've been some minor troubles on the estate—a few head of cattle and sheep rustled, some fields trampled, some equipment damaged. Mind you, these things aren't unusual. Every farmer suffers such mishaps; small farms, especially, are prey to the gangs of escapees and ex-convicts who roam the countryside. Still, I believe that it would be wise to post extra guards to patrol the estate. Meanwhile, I don't want you riding out alone, Arabella. I'll not risk you. I couldn't bear to lose you."

His mouth captured hers hungrily as he swept her up into his arms and carried her to their bed, laying her down, his hands moving over her feverishly, reassuring her of the depth of his love for her as he took her to paradise and back again.

A few days later, the outbuildings were torched. Jacaranda was an estate of several thousand acres, and despite the extra sentries that Lucien had posted, there just were not enough men to cover the land. In the middle of the night, the household was roused by the violent ringing of the bell that usually summoned the hands to supper. One of the guards had spotted the flames and sounded the alarm. Lucien's face was grim as he hurriedly yanked on his clothes and boots. Fire was especially dreaded in the Colonies. It could sweep through fields and pastures, through savannas and woodlands, destroying everything in its path, leaving the land unfit for man or beast. Kangaroos, wallabies, koala bears, cattle, sheep . . . all fled for their lives before the blazes that nature sometimes ignited with lightning and that, just as often, men started with matches. Controlled burning could be good for the land, Arabella knew, but a wildfire was something else entirely.

Once outside, Lucien took control of the situation, issuing commands right and left, effectively bringing order to the chaos that reigned as men and women ran toward the burning outbuildings. Hasty and uncoordinated efforts already under way to contain the fire were quickly organized; a bucket brigade was formed to haul water from the river and a trench dug around the outbuildings to keep the flames from spreading. Arabella gave her own commands, which were as swiftly obeyed.

Several of the women she sent back to the house to fetch medicines and bandages for any burns, cuts, or scrapes. The rest of the women she told to prepare food and drink for the firefighters.

Acrid, billowing smoke and flying cinders filled the air, making it difficult to see and to breathe. But eventually, toward dawn, the fire was extinguished. As the charred timber of the outbuildings sizzled and smoldered, Lucien and Arabella took stock of their situation.

"Well, it could have been worse," he observed as he surveyed the damage. "At least no one was seriously hurt—thank heavens—and we lost only a few of the outbuildings entirely. We can repair the rest. I've sent one of the men into Sydney to make a report—not that I expect that to do much good."

"Then you believe that the fire was deliberately set," Arabella said.

"Oh, yes. I don't think there's much doubt about that, really. The smell of oil was unmistakable, and we found a couple of empty oil containers, besides."

"But . . . who would want to do such a thing—and why?"

"I have my suspicions. But of course, without any proof, there's little I can do, except to keep a closer watch on things in the future. Come, Arabella. You're practically dead on your feet, and you're covered with soot, as well."

"So are you," she uttered with a tired smile, only too happy to lean on Lucien, her arm around his waist as he led her back to the house.

Her muscles ached from hefting the heavy buckets

of water passed along the brigade, and there were blis-
ters on her palms that she knew would be sore for the
next several days. She ought to have worn work gloves,
she thought belatedly, but when she had spied the
flames, she had thought only that they must not spread
to the stables and house; and she had fought like a
madwoman to save her home. Only now did she realize
how she must appear, her nightgown and wrapper
streaked with black from the smoke and ashes, her hair
tumbled wildly about her. Naked to the waist, sweating
and grimy, his skin singed in places where he had got
too close to the blaze, Lucien looked no better.

She ordered a bath, which they shared, soaping and
washing each other, then tending each other's wounds.
After breakfast, exhausted, they went back to bed and
slept past noon, awakening to make love before they
reluctantly rose and turned their attention to the estate.
It took a few days for the rubble to cool; then it was
quickly cleared away, and the task of rebuilding began.
Richard rode out to the house to inspect the damage,
after which he remained closeted with Lucien in the
study for some time. But what they discussed, Lucien
would not say, merely handing Arabella the letters that
Richard had been kind enough to bring to the estate.

In the morning room, she sat down with a sterling
silver envelope opener to look at the mail. To her disappointment, there was nothing from the Wyndhams, although she had told herself that it was unrealistic to
expect even a note. Uncle Philip had made it plain that
he had washed his hands of her, as surely as he had
Chrissie, and it was not to be expected that his family
would go against his wishes. Still, he had been her

father's lifelong friend, and Arabella could not help but be disheartened by the rift that had formed because of her marriage to Lucien. There were, however, several invitations to various parties, routs, and soirees, including one at Howland House in Sydney a few weeks from now. At least she was not to be socially ostracized by everyone, Arabella thought, with a sense of relief—and trust Eugenia Howland to be among those who had extended invitations. No doubt she had asked the Wyndhams to her soiree, as well, hoping to stir up trouble.

This was, indeed, the case, Arabella discovered when, on the appointed evening, after she and Lucien had alighted from their carriage before Howland House and after they had made their way through the receiving line, she spied the Wyndhams across the ballroom floor. Aunt Hennie was conspicuously absent, and that worried Arabella; but when she started across the room to speak to Norah and ask about Aunt Hennie, Lucien prevented her.

"Trust me, my love. Norah will give you the cut direct, and I won't have my wife publicly insulted and humiliated. By all means, send a private note inquiring about Mrs. Wyndham's health if you must—not that I believe that you'll receive any reply. But don't approach the Wyndhams in public, especially here. Eugenia Howland would doubtless love nothing better than to see Gervase and me at each other's throat—and since dueling is illegal, I would rather not be compelled to issue a challenge resulting in pistols at dawn. I've worked too hard to see everything I've built thrown away."

"Of course you have! I'm sorry, Lucien. I wasn't

thinking clearly. Except for Gervase, I never really had any serious beaux. Naturally, as my husband, you would feel yourself honor-bound to come to my defense. Since I have never before thought of myself as the kind of woman men would fight over, I confess that I find a certain pleasure in that. Is that terribly wicked of me?"

"No—although you *are* surely wicked for not thinking of me as a 'serious beau'!"

"But you weren't, Lucien. In fact, you weren't a proper beau at all!"

"Wasn't I?" His eyes raked her slowly, meaningfully, causing her to flush. "Hmmm. Well, perhaps you have a point. Let us see if I can remedy that. Come." He held out his hand to her. "Will you dance, Mrs. Sinclair?"

That she was utterly happy, the epitome of the blushing bride, Arabella thought that no one could possibly doubt. However rude it might have been, Lucien deliberately pitched away her dance program, possessively claiming every dance for himself, glowering threateningly at any other man who dared to approach her. He waltzed expertly, holding her more closely than was proper had he not been her husband, and smiling down at her, making it clear to all that there was no other woman in the room for him, save her. Of course, people gossiped about them. More than once, Arabella was aware that all eyes were upon them; and she saw more than one woman's fan raised to hide her face as she whispered to her friends. There were those, of course, principally the Exclusives, who ignored Arabella, so she knew they considered her disgraced and ruined. But the ranks of the Emancipists, for the most part, welcomed her, except for a few obviously jealous, spiteful women; and it came to Arabella then that although he was an ex-convict, Lucien had, in his own circle, been considered a highly eligible bachelor, an extremely desirable catch. Yet he had chosen her—and called her beautiful. A lump rose to her throat at the thought; tears stung her eyes. With difficulty, she blinked the crystal droplets away. Why had she ever fought so hard agains* him, doubted that she loved him? There was nowhere in the world that she would rather be than in his arms. She knew that now.

They moved together as though they had been made for each other, Arabella thought dreamily, through a haze of rum punch and a rainbow of colors that spun and shimmered beneath the blaze of hundreds of candles melting in the crystal chandeliers of the ballroom, casting their glow upon strings of dangling prisms that bent and reflected the light. Lost in reverie, she did not protest when, without warning, Lucien skillfully guiaed her out through the ballroom's open French doors that led to the veranda beyond. Only when she felt the night air, cool and touched with autumn, against her skin was she startled back to reality to take notice of her surroundings and to realize that she and Lucien had left the bright lights of the ballroom behind.

On the edge of her consciousness, Arabella perceived that, here and there, couples seeking escape or a breath of fresh air circumspectly strolled within plain view of the ballroom; and at the east end of the veranda, a group of men puffing cigars had gathered, talking and laughing amid drifting clouds of smoke. Somehow, all this seemed far removed from her, and she paid it scarcely any attention. As though entranced, she and Lucien continued to waltz along the moonlit veranda toward its darker, deserted west end. Moments later, the last strains of the music died away, and Lucien was kissing her passionately, until she was breathless and demurring, insisting that somebody might see them.

"So what if they do? It's not as though I don't have the right," he muttered huskily.

"Yes, but . . . *still*, Lucien! What would people think . . . what would they say?"

"That we're very much in love—which is no less than the truth."

"I know, but . . . I think I could use a glass of rum punch."

He quirked one eyebrow.

"I'm sure you must be quite thirsty," he drawled, grinning. "You know, if I didn't know that we'd be going home together later, my sweet, I don't believe that I'd permit myself to be put off in this manner. In fact, I may still drag you out into the gardens and ravish you in some secluded arbor."

"Lucien!"

"Well, I might. Think about that while I'm gone, my girl!" His eyes glittered with desire and devilry as they appraised her; then, turning on his booted heel, he slipped back inside to fetch her the glass of rum punch she had requested.

Arabella was glad of the relative darkness, for she knew that her cheeks were flaming at his impudence. Surely, he would *not* do such a thing! But the fierce pounding of her heart told her that deep down inside, she suspected that he might, and she was both shocked and terrifyingly excited by the idea. Her very first impression of him had been right: He was a demon and a rogue—and always would be. Waiting on the veranda, listening to the music that wafted into the night, and plucking idly at the hibiscus that twined along the balustrade, she broke a bloom from its stem and tucked it behind her ear. Then she lifted her face to the gentle wind, thinking how much she had always loved the feel of it against her skin, of it streaming through her hair as she galloped on horseback across the land. She could remember from the time she was small her father lifting her up before him on his big bay. It was no longer the broad, sweeping acres of Darracott Hall she rode across, but those of Jacaranda, with Lucien at her side. Still, somehow, the feeling was the same.

Since their move back to Sinclair House in town, Arabella had missed the estate, missed riding out with Lucien in the mornings. Accustomed to life at Darracott Hall, she loved the country. Except for the burning of the outbuildings and a few other minor incidents, it had been peaceful there, away from Sydney and its gossip. She had, she realized now, enjoyed having Lucien all to herself, had not missed the parties, routs, and soirees, so completely had he filled her hours, her life. The only good thing about returning to town was that Lucien had found a piece of property for her house for convict women. He was taking her to look at it the next day. She was very excited at the prospect, especially since tonight some of the wives of his Emancipist colleagues, upon learning of the project, had agreed to help her with it. She was particularly grateful for the assistance of Faith Langston and Theresa Durrell, both of whom were from the upper classes, and so who would excel at teaching elocution. Arabella had not forgotten what Lucien had told her about prison cant being the primary obstacle in preventing ex-convicts from getting ahead socially. Nothing marked a man more surely as an ex-convict than his opening his mouth and referring to soup as "smiggings," bad bread as "scrubbing brushes." Lucien himself had "napped fourteen penn'orth," as he had once put it, meaning he had drawn a sentence of fourteen years' exile. Her amusement at hearing him speak in the dialect had been tempered by the realization that he had spent too many years among the prisoners. Seeing her discomfort, he had grinned at her and, flinging her down upon their bed, had pretended to be an escaped convict, bent on ravishing her. There had been just enough truth in the game for Arabella to be both frightened and exhilarated by it.

Now, as she remembered, a half-smile curved her lips; and as she felt Lucien's hands slide along her bare shoulders, she turned to face him.

"Gervase!" she cried softly.

"You thought I was Lucien." It was a statement, not a question. Without waiting for her to respond, he suddenly caught hold of her wrist and dragged her down the steps into the gardens, cursing her under his breath all the while when she attempted to wrest free of him.

"What do you think you're doing? Let me go! You're hurting me!"

"Not as much as you hurt me!" he shot back, his

voice a snarl as he yanked her into a secluded arbor. "Why did you do it, Arabella? Why did you marry him? You were promised to me—you *know* that—and I had made it clear that I intended to wed you!"

Gervase ranted on, enraged, not giving her a chance to explain, scaring her. He had no right to haul her into the gardens like this, to hold her here. Arabella could not believe his behavior. He had always been a perfect gentleman. She had never expected him to confront her like this.

"If you will not release me, I have nothing to say to you, Gervase."

"Well, I have a great deal to say to you—and you're going to listen, you stupid little fool! Do you know *why* he wanted you? Because you were mine, Arabella! He wanted revenge! I took his first wife, Verity, from him, you see. He's a monster, and she hated him; she was terrified of him. We were in love and had planned to run away together; but he found us out at the last minute, and he killed her, he *murdered* her! Yes, yes, he did! But that wasn't enough for him. No, he had to pay me back, and so he took you from me!"

"No!" Arabella cried, shocked, stricken. "No! You're lying! I don't believe you!"

"Don't—or won't? I saw how you looked at him in there in the ballroom. You're in love with him! Oh, he must have played you like a master, flattering you, gulling you into believing that he cared about you, that it was you alone he wanted—when, all the time, he was after revenge, and your fortune, too, of course. With that ridiculous tale of IOUs, you and he might have fooled poor Father into turning over your inheritance. But *I* know the truth, I tell you! Listen to me: I have no gambling debts, Arabella!''

''I think that you've said quite enough, Gervase! Now, take your hands off my wife!''

Lucien had stepped from the shadows. Arabella had never seen him look so angry, so . . . *murderous*. His eyes blazed like twin flames; a muscle throbbed in his set jaw; and the thin scar upon his cheek stood out whitely against his dark, grim face. When Gervase did not immediately release her, Lucien lunged forward, wrenching her free, then backfisting Gervase insultingly across the face, staggering him, splitting open his lips.

''By God, if you ever touch her again, I'll kill you!'' Lucien spat the words.

Although Gervase's eyes burned, too, as he gingerly wiped the blood from the corner of his mouth, he did not fight back, nor did he deign to reply to Lucien, but instead addressed Arabella.

''Remember what I told you,'' he growled. ''It was the truth!'' Then he pivoted on his heel and strode from the arbor, brushing roughly against the protruding branches of a lilac bush, scattering leaves upon the ground.

''Are you all right?'' Lucien inquired after a moment, breaking the strained silence that had fallen following Gervase's departure.

Rubbing her bruised wrists, Arabella nodded, her eyes wide.

''I take it that you did *not* come willingly with Gervase into the gardens?'' he remarked as he noticed her action, the fierce red marks that encircled her wrists, from where Gervase had gripped her so tightly.

"No, you must know I did not," she answered quietly.

"Yes, I knew I could trust you."

His words implied that he hoped she trusted him, as well; but Gervase's ugly accusations had planted a tiny, poisonous seed of doubt in Arabella's mind. What if Gervase had spoken truly? Lucien *had* been tried and convicted in England for the murder of his wife; he *had* been transported to the Colonies, sentenced to fourteen years hard labor. Certainly, he had wasted no time in compelling Uncle Philip to hand over her fortune—and could she really be sure that Lucien was not juggling her accounts? After all, loving him, trusting him, she had left the management of her funds and investments up to him. Since their marriage, she had been so certain of his innocence. Had she, like a blind fool, seen only what she had wanted to see, endowed him with qualities he had never possessed? Had she given her heart to a man, a murderer, who had wanted only revenge and money instead of her?

"How long . . . how long were you standing there listening, Lucien?" she asked.

"Long enough." His mouth tightened with ire.

"And was what Gervase said true? Did you . . . want me only for revenge?"

"Revenge? Is that what you would call this, Arabella?" he snarled as, without warning, he jerked her into his arms and crushed his mouth down on hers savagely, kissing her until the world spun away and she knew nothing but him.

Chapter Nineteen

Interlude at
The Rocks

He was a giant bat, winging his way through the night, in search of a special prey. The Rocks was his hunting ground, his personal playground. It might have been made for him, with its twisting cobblestone streets and dark, narrow alleys slithering like a nest of snakes between the close-packed rows of shabby dwellings and shoddy grog-shops, the gutters running with refuse, some of it human. Like a shroud, his black cape swirled around him in the salt-tinged wind that blew in from the harbor. As he walked, his malacca cane tapped upon the street, the sound like that of a hammer tapping nails into a coffin. Tap-tap-tap. It echoed through the mist that rolled in off the sea, twining sinuously along the streets and alleys, settling in the low-lying areas nearest the harbor. He loved the mist; it, too, was like a cerecloth, winding its way around the stinking, rotten corpse that was The Rocks, that crawled with human flies and maggots. They meant nothing to him; they were the dregs of society, beneath his lofty notice. It was the few he aspired to save—not the masses—the Veritys, and now the Arabellas, of the world.

Like a predatory animal, he prowled through the shadows, stalking his prey. Soon. She would come soon—and then the hunt would begin. His blood surged at the thought, sending a rush of adrenaline coursing through his powerful body. His muscles bunched and rippled beneath his black broadcloth suit as he moved; he trembled with excitement. His hunts were always successful: This one would prove no different. The Rocks was like a maze; but like a rat, he knew its every twist and turn, the streets that led into Sydney's business and fashionable districts, the blind alleys that ended in walls, trapping his target. Against him, his quarry would be as helpless as all the rest had been; she would not elude him. His cane tap-tapped; the coins in his pocket jingled, pennies with which to pay the ferryman for his victims' safe passage to the realm of the dead. He did not want them to suffer condemnation to eternal hellfire and brimstone; he never wanted that for them. They had fallen from grace, yes . . . but they had been pure once—as they were again, once he had saved them. As he would save her.

Salvation. Not from the river Jordan, as was commonly but mistakenly believed, but from rivers of blood. Hot, red, sweet-flowing, draining away, life to death, dust to dust, ashes to ashes. Blood in the streets, the gutters. Dust in the wind.

From the dingy buildings, soft yellow light spilled

into the streets along which he padded, glimmering upon the pools of slops that stood in the gutters. In the distance, lightning flashed, splitting the night sky, and thunder grumbled, a low growl like that of a dingo on the prowl. The drifting mist clung to everything in its path, clammy, carrying a sprinkling of rain, precursor of the storm that was brewing, blowing up in the east, over the sea. Already, the mass of roiling black clouds on the horizon had blotted out the moon and the stars, and now was moving westward, rolling and rumbling, like the wheels of a carriage clattering over cobblestones. No, it *was* a carriage.

She was coming!

Quickly, he stepped back into a dark doorway, watching, waiting, his heart pounding with exhilaration, the blood roaring in his ears. It was time. She was here. The carriage came to a stop; and after setting the brake, the coachman climbed down from the box and, like a cockroach, scuttled away, not looking back. Her white face appeared in the window, terrified. She called out. Then, after a moment, she slowly opened the door and stepped down from the carriage.

Arabella!

The hunt had begun.

Perhaps she needed glasses, Arabella thought as the figures in the columns on the pages of her account book blurred before her. At last, sighing heavily, giving up, resigning herself to not finishing tonight, she closed the book and leaned back in her desk chair, rubbing her eyes vigorously. There was nothing wrong with her sight, of course. She was just tired, had worked late too many evenings since Lucien had left town. He had business in Adelaide, he had claimed before his departure. But while he had had no reason to lie, she still had not been able to rid herself of the uneasy feeling that he had not told her all the truth. It bothered her. Arabella did not want to think ill of him. Yet she could not deny that, despite their lovemaking, there had been a strain between them ever since that night in the gardens at Howland House, when Gervase had made his monstrous accusations. She remembered Lucien's bronzed face when he had threatened to kill Gervase for touching her, and she shuddered, thinking that her husband was not a man to suffer a faithless wife lightly.

She had thought that with the purchase of the property for her house for convict women, they could, through their mutual concerns, reach an accord again. Lucien had dutifully played the role of host at the party they had given to celebrate the founding of Haven—as Arabella had named the house—but since then, he had had little to do with the project, insisting that it was all her idea and that she must therefore handle it as she thought best. Almost with a frenzy, she had thrown herself into the work of establishing Haven, of publicizing the house and its purpose. At first she had thought that she would fail, that no one would come, such was the skepticism with which the project was viewed by the very people she wished to help. Then, one day, a young ex-convict woman by the name of Penny Thatcher had appeared on the doorstep, begging for aid; and Haven had truly begun.

Now, seven young women were in residence, learning everything from speech to delicate embroidery, from table manners to polishing brass—in training as ladies' maids and parlor maids, cooks and scullions. When they had first come to her, Arabella had questioned each, seeking information about Chrissie, but to her disappointment, she had learned nothing. Still, she had taken the women in gladly, wishing that more of them would overcome their natural fear and doubt to seek out Haven. She now knew that, while it *was* true that many convicts received their tickets-of-leave straightaway upon their arrival in the Colonies, it was *not* true that most of the prisoners, even those on parole and living elsewhere than the prisons, were well treated. Instead, they suffered untold horrors, many of which, to her shock and outrage, were permitted under the laws of the Colonies; to the rest, the authorities more often than not turned a blind eye. Lucien's own story was just one of many.

Arabella rose from her desk, gathered up her cloak, and wrapped it about her, then slowly extinguished the oil lamps in her small office at Haven. After closing the door and locking it behind her, she stepped across the hall to where Tilly still sat, sewing, in the parlor.

"It's late, and I'm going home now, Tilly," she said, stifling a yawn.

"It's about time, Mrs. Sinclair. In fact, I was just about to look in on you, to suggest that you 'ead—I mean, *head*—for home. You work far too hard, and it's begun to drizzle outside. I'm afraid that a storm may be blowing up. I'll have your carriage brought around front at once." Tilly pronounced each word carefully, struggling to get her accent right.

Shortly after being hired by Lucien, Tilly and Declan

had married. Afterward, Arabella had moved them into Haven, so there would be someone at the house on a permanent basis, not only to oversee it in her absence, but also to provide a solid, stable anchor for the young women in residence. The more Tilly learned and grew as a person, the more Arabella recognized that her faith in her former maid had not been misplaced. It was Tilly and Declan most of all who had given the house such a warm and welcoming atmosphere. Their love for each other just seemed to spill out over everyone around them. But although Arabella was genuinely happy for the couple, seeing them together, she could not help but be reminded of how her and Lucien's own marriage, once filled with such hope and promise, now appeared, sadly, to have gone terribly awry. It was almost as though they had become strangers to each other, and when she thought of going home to Sinclair House, to its empty rooms, to her empty bed, it was all she could do to hold at bay the tears that brimmed suddenly in her eyes.

"Good night, Tilly."

"Good night, Mrs. Sinclair."

Outside, Arabella saw that her carriage already stood beneath the portico, its door open, and that it had indeed, as Tilly had observed, begun to drizzle. Quickly, Arabella climbed into the vehicle, settling herself against the squabs, closing her eyes wearily. She heard the click of the door shutting, the swaying of the coach as the driver clambered onto the box above. Then, with a crack of his whip and a lurch of the horses, the carriage rumbled forward into the night, its pace swifter than usual. The streets were fairly deserted at this late hour, and no doubt the driver hoped to have her home before the storm broke.

She must have dozed against the cushions, Arabella thought afterward, because she never remembered when she first became aware that the vehicle was traveling in the wrong direction, that instead of delivering her to Sinclair House, it was, in fact, taking her away from the business and fashionable districts of Sydney, into The Rocks. Once she realized, to her shock, where she was headed, she pounded upon the box and called out to the driver. But the coach did not stop its relentless progress; indeed, its speed only increased, so she could hardly lower the window to stick her head out. To her horror, she saw that the man upon the box was not her usual driver, Ned, but someone totally unknown to her, someone she could not recall ever seeing before at either Sinclair House or Jacaranda. Suddenly panicked, she shouted at him; but although she knew he must have heard her, he pretended that he did not, and never once looked around at her.

By now, the carriage was traveling so fast that Arabella did not dare to open the door to attempt to leap from the vehicle. Helpless, all she could do was hold tight to the strap inside to keep from being jostled from the seat and flung to the floor. The wheels of her mind churned as violently as those of the coach as it bounced and tilted precariously along the slick streets. A stranger had somehow taken the place of her driver, and now, she was plainly being abducted—but by whom, and why? Fear roiled in her belly and clawed its way up to her throat. She screamed until she was nearly hoarse, only to realize after a while that it was doubtful anyone could hear her over the clattering of the horses' hooves and the carriage wheels upon the cobblestones.

Then, at last, suddenly, with an eeriness that somehow frightened Arabella even more than her wild, horrendous ride through the town, more than the realization that she was being kidnapped, the vehicle slid to a jolting halt; and she heard the sounds of the driver scrambling down from the box. Her thudding heart lodged in her throat. But to her mingled terror and relief, he did not open the coach door, but instead ran away as fast as he was able, his booted feet pounding upon the damp sidewalk, his ragged coat flapping about him as she watched, pale-faced and horrified, from the window. She called out once, but he did not answer.

She was alone in The Rocks, cowering in a carriage, vulnerable to attack.

The door of the carriage could easily be kicked open; its plush velvet interior would no doubt be viewed as a good deal more luxurious and comfortable than one of the flea- or lice-ridden pallets that Lucien had told her served those who lived in The Rocks. Some strange, filthy man might force himself inside and upon her. Arabella's heart turned over in her breast. She had to get away!

Her pulse racing, she tentatively opened the door and, after glancing about warily, finally stepped outside. She had driven a team of horses before; and even if she had not, sheer desperation would have goaded her into making the attempt now. But after a single, futile try, it became clear to her that, dressed as she was, she could not climb up onto the box. Oh, God, why hadn't

she listened to Lucien and forsaken her hoops and crinolines, along with her corset? He thought women's current fashions ridiculous; more than once, he had advised
her to wear sensible gowns and petticoats instead of
giving in to what style dictated. But while Arabella had
been glad to do so in the privacy of her own home, she
had not been able to compel herself to flout convention
publicly. Herself the target of gossip, Haven considered
by many a scandal, Arabella had not dared to bend the
rules of society further, lest she be totally outcast and
ostracized. Well, the hoops and crinolines would just
have to come off, that was all.

She got back into the vehicle, her hands trembling
so badly that she could hardly divest herself of the
cumbersome undergarments that hindered her escape.
But at last, after what seemed like hours, she managed
and set about to climb to the box once more. She opened
the door again—and screamed.

"What are you doing here?" she cried, horrified.

But in her heart, Arabella knew—somehow knew
everything, of a sudden—and knowing, she began
wildly, blindly, to run.

His pale eyes glittered with excitement in the flashes
of lightning that erupted in the night sky, illuminating
The Rocks. It was as though the titanic tridents emanated from his own being, shot from his fingertips, just
as he had always imagined, and as though the echoing
thunder were a roar from his own throat, a shout at the
devil. He *was* a god! He could feel his great power
surging through him—bold, potent, throbbing. His nostrils flared; his mouth curved in a sardonic smile. It

seemed he had waited all his life for this moment; now, he was transfigured, exalted, the highest of the high, the ultimate hunter, pursuing the ultimate prey.

Yes, run, Verity, run, he called in his mind to her as he gave chase, his strong, corded legs closing the gap between himself and his quarry. *You shall not escape from me, even so. My hunts are always successful. Always, Verity. Remember that. . . .*

How often had he told her that, warned her of it? But she had never listened; and so he had to keep reminding her, over and over, because she was like a child who could not learn her lesson. But he *would* teach her.

He could smell her terror, taste it sweet upon his tongue—the tongue that had twined with hers, had tasted hers. Honey . . . ambrosia . . . nectar. Heady was the sting. He could hear her gasps for breath, knew that her mouth was open, as it had opened for him.

"Verity . . . sweet Verity . . ." he called aloud to her, his voice low, silky, hoarse.

Hearing him, Arabella glanced back over her shoulder, stricken. He was mad. Utterly, horribly mad. Everything he had told her had been a lie, a ghastly lie. How could she ever have thought otherwise? He was going to kill her, just as he had murdered Verity and all those other poor women, including Chrissie. Oh, God. Now, Arabella knew beyond a shadow of a doubt how Chrissie had felt that dreadful night, how she had run and run through the dark, serpentine streets and alleys of The Rocks—defenseless, lost, disbelieving, terrified. Knowing that her very life depended on it, Arabella raced on, cursing the mist that frequently blinded her and that sheened the cobblestones, making them so slick that it was difficult for her to gain any traction, to retain her footing. She was further hampered by her skirts and the stitch in her side that was making it hard for her to breathe. Now and then, she tripped on the garbage that littered the streets, the gutters. Once, she fell, scraping her palms and knees. But wincing, crying out, Arabella pushed herself to her feet and ran on.

Her skin was cold, clammy, not only from the drizzle, but also from her fear. She was going to die. She had seen not a single constable, and she did not expect that any aid would be forthcoming from any of the few, dingy, still-lit taverns she spied. In fact, she felt certain that, given the obvious quality of her clothing and jewelry, she would be in equal danger were she to enter one of the grog-shops and ask for help. Except for an infrequent and obviously drunken passerby, the streets were largely deserted. She tried to keep track of where she was going, hoping to circle back to the carriage, to escape. But The Rocks was like a labyrinth, and after the first few twists and turns of the narrow, mist-enshrouded streets and alleys, Arabella had no idea where she was or how far she had run. The rain still drizzled, growing steadier, dripping down her face. The scintillating lightning made the derelict buildings appear like the setting of a nightmare, and the man following her like the devil himself. Over the thunder's rumble, she could hear the click, click of his footsteps.

He was gaining on her, drawing ominously nearer and nearer. It seemed to her that she could feel his harsh, hot breath against her nape as she stumbled up a steep flight of steps, then rushed on down the street, turning in to another dark, dirty alley running with water and offal, rife with rubbish. She banged her hip painfully on a wooden trash barrel, but rushed on, only dimly aware of the dull ache, of the sound of a cane clattering upon the cobblestones, until she reached a dead end—a brick wall that rose up at the end of the alley, blocking her path, trapping her with her pursuer.

"Nooooo!" Arabella screamed as she was abruptly grabbed from behind, turned around, slammed up against the wall, and a silver-gleaming blade was pressed to her throat. "No!"

His dark, familiar visage leered evilly at her as he began yanking at her skirts; and she wanted to die, knew she would be glad to die, once he was finished profaning what she had once done in love. Then, without warning, the lightning cracked open the heavens again, thunder bellowed, a shot rang out, and there was blood everywhere, splattering all over her face, her bodice, her hands. She was screaming and crying hysterically, not realizing at first that it was not her blood, that the knife had fallen to the cobblestones, that the man before her was slowly crumpling to the ground, on his face a look of stunned incredulity at his own mortality. A sudden bright flare of torches flickered then, and men hurried forth from the shadows. A pair of arms enfolded Arabella so tightly that she could hardly breathe.

"Lucien! Oh, Lucien!" she sobbed wildly against his broad, comforting chest, not quite able even now to believe he was here, was real. "How did you get here? I thought—I thought that you were in Adelaide.

Oh, God! Can you ever . . . *ever* forgive me for even once thinking that the murderer was you? I never wanted it to be you. I didn't! I swear I didn't!'

"Shhhhh. I know. Don't you think I know that?"

"Forgive me. Please . . . forgive me."

"Yes, yes, I do. Hush, now. You're safe, Arabella. You're safe, do you understand? Do you really believe I'd ever let anything happen to you? I knew that the killer was Gervase. I've known it for years, but I've had no proof. He murdered Verity and Chrissie and the others. He would have killed you, too. But I've kept a close watch on you; you were never alone, not for a moment, my love. I never left town. I only let it be thought that I had, because I knew he'd come for you, thinking that I'd have real trouble documenting my whereabouts at every moment during my absence and be unable to prove that I hadn't slipped back to Sydney to murder you. He was quite mad, you know."

"Yes, but . . . *why*? Why did he kill Verity, Lucien?"

"Because she chose to elope with me rather than to marry him. Afterward, I suppose that Verity must have decided that she'd made a terrible mistake. I wasn't part of her world, you see, just some romantic fantasy, I think, that disappointed her in reality. She . . . liked pretty things, and parties; she missed them, missed having servants to wait upon her hand and foot. I didn't have any money then. I'd worked for her father, and of course, I lost my job when I married Verity. So I was poor, and she was unhappy and lonely, too, since I was scrambling just to make ends meet; and since she didn't know how Gervase despised and feared me, she permitted him to seduce her, after which he killed her.''

"But why does . . . did he hate you so, Lucien? I—I don't understand.''

"He was my cousin, Arabella. My mother was the colonel's sister; and all Gervase's life, the colonel has held me like a club over Gervase's head, reminding him that there was another legitimate male heir in the family who could inherit if he didn't toe the mark. Of course, the colonel had cut my mother off without a cent for running away with my father, so the last thing the colonel ever intended was to make me his heir. Even so, Gervase probably always viewed me as a very real threat; he lived in constant fear of not coming up to expectation, of being rejected. When Verity preferred me over him, he saw a chance to punish her and me both—ridding himself of me at the same time. He killed Verity and made it appear as though I had done the evil deed. Only the colonel's fear of the scandal I might cause by exposing the fact that I was his nephew prompted him to intervene to save my neck from the noose.''

"That's—that's horrible . . . that Gervase would commit murder, that he would deliberately incriminate you for the act! Did the colonel know that you were innocent?''

"I think he may have had his suspicions, especially when all the murders so similar to Verity's own began happening here in Sydney—''

"Oh, God . . . Chrissie! Her own brother killed her!''

"Yes, it must have seemed like history repeating itself to Gervase. My mother, Verity, Chrissie . . . all had run away, eloped with men not of their own class—"

"And me."

"Yes, and you. But that's why I had to compel you to marry me, Arabella. If you had attempted to enlist Gervase's aid in digging into Chrissie's murder, he would have grown afraid of what you might learn, and killed you. At least if you were my wife, I could protect you. It was he who burned the outbuildings that night at Jacaranda, too. He must have been counting on your fortune, as well as his own inheritance, to pay off his creditors. When you married me instead, he must have grown desperate, resented me even more for the riches I'd acquired, and struck out at me however he could."

Arabella shuddered as she glanced down at Gervase's bloody body, which the constables were even now loading onto a stretcher and into a wagon. Richard was there, as well, directing operations. Following his long discussion with Lucien at Jacaranda, Richard, while not wholly convinced of Lucien's innocence, had—since it would make it easier to keep a suspicious eye on Lucien—agreed to go along with his plan to expose Gervase as the killer. Dr. Munroe was present, too, and was now carefully examining Gervase's malacca cane. The knife Gervase had drawn from within it, the physician announced, was surely the murder weapon that had been used upon Sally Wheeler, "Rum Rosie" O'Doul, and Christine Wyndham, as well as other hapless victims. There was, also, as further proof of Gervase's guilt, the fact that he was dressed in a black cape and had two copper pennies in one pocket.

"Uncle Philip will not be able to hush up the scandal this time, Lucien, with Gervase dead and with so much evidence against him, so many witnesses to his attempt to kill me," Arabella observed as she struggled to regain her composure, to dash away her tears.

"No . . . but the witnesses were necessary to prove my innocence beyond a shadow of a doubt. I'm free now, free of suspicion, free of the stain of murder." He paused for a moment, lost in his memories of the past, she knew, dwelling on the years he had spent in prison for a crime he had never committed. Then he continued. "Come. There's nothing more for us here now. Let me take you home, Arabella."

The torches wavered in the heavy rain, but Arabella was not frightened of the storm. Just such a night had first delivered her into Lucien's strong and loving embrace. Now the downpour washed away the blood upon the cobblestones and, with it, his dark past forever. They were both free now, free to begin again, free to love passionately, without fear and doubt. As they walked from the alley together, clinging tightly to each other, Arabella knew that Lucien's thoughts mirrored her own; for like hers, his head was thrown back so the wind streamed wildly through his long mane of hair, and his handsome face shone with love and exhilaration, joyfully uplifted to the cleansing rain.

Epilogue

The Jacaranda Tree

Chapter Twenty

The Flowering

Jacaranda, New South Wales Colony, Australia, 1870

Sometimes when she came here to this tranquil grove of blue trees with its still, nearby pond, Arabella seemed to hear the sound of Chrissie's bright laughter on the wind, the tread of her light footstep in the whisper of the grass; and Arabella would remember that day of the Scarborough fair, when she and Chrissie had dared to venture into the pavilion of the old Gypsy woman who had told their fortunes. Then, Arabella had thought the crone horrible. But now, sometimes, she wondered if the old woman had been kinder than she, Arabella, had ever guessed, if the harridan had known far more than she had told them that day and, knowing, had spun a dream for Chrissie rather than telling her the truth about her unhappy fate. Arabella sighed. Whatever the real truth of that long-ago day, it did not matter now. Wherever she was now, Chrissie was at peace, Arabella thought, and she lived again in her namesake, Arabella's youngest child—blond-haired, blue-eyed Christine, now five years old.

"I look at my daughter, and it's like seeing you as a child again, Chrissie." Arabella spoke quietly to the grave she tended every week, dusting off her hands after she finished pulling a few stray weeds, then laying a fresh bouquet of flowers upon the grassy mound. "Sometimes, seeing her, it's as though I've grown older, while you've stayed the same, caught in time, somehow, even though I know that it's Christine and not you. You would love her, I know. Someday, when she's older, I'll tell her all about you, dear friend."

After a long moment, Arabella finally rose and, gathering her shears and empty basket, began to walk back to the serene white house that was still just as beautiful as it had been when she had first seen it so many years ago. At the fringe of the sweeping green lawn, she paused, smiling to herself as she saw Lucien, their three sons, and Chrissie laughing as they played what appeared to be a game of croquet that plainly lacked any rules, since the boys were busily moving hoops to accommodate obviously illegal shots.

"Arabella, my sweet!" Lucien called as he glanced up and spied her. "Why are you just standing there instead of coming to my assistance? You can see that I've been outnumbered and outflanked at every turn, can't you?"

"Yes, my love. Nevertheless, I have the utmost faith in your ability to prevail."

"Insolent woman!" he rebuked her, grinning.

"Arrogant man!" she retorted impudently, grinning back saucily. "When you get tired of the game, come and join me over there." She indicated the jacaranda tree that they had planted together at the heart of the lawn during the first year of their marriage and that had now grown tall and sturdy and beautiful with the passing of time, a living symbol of their love.

An old wooden swing whose stout ropes were twined with ribands of ivy hung from one of the tree's sturdy lower boughs. Arabella sat on the seat and started to swing gently, breathing in deeply the heady perfume of the purple blooms that drifted from the branches to strew the ground below her, reminding her sweetly of that night in the tropical woods when she had first lain with Lucien and surrendered not just her body, but also her heart to him for all time. Not for one moment did she regret that now; nor would she ever again. The sunlight kissed her upturned face; the wind streamed through her unbound hair, and her heart soared higher than the swing as, after a time, laughing with joy and delight, she confidently let go of the ropes, flying freely to Lucien's strong, enfolding arms that waited, as they always had and always would, lovingly outstretched, to catch her in midair.